MARY STEWART

Touch Not the Cat

FAWCETT CREST • NEW YORK

For my uncle George Rainbow

'And some win peace who spend
The skill of words to sweeten despair
Of finding consolation where
Life has but one dark end.

from "The Riddlers," by
Walter de la Mare

One

It is my soul that calls upon my name.
—SHAKESPEARE: *Romeo and Juliet*
(Act II, Sc. ii)

My lover came to me on the last night in April, with a message and a warning that sent me home to him.

Put like that, it sounds strange, though it is exactly what happened. When I try to explain it will no doubt sound stranger still. Let me put it all down in order.

I was working in Funchal, Madeira. Funchal is the main town of that lovely Atlantic island, and, in spite of its having been a port of call for almost every ship that has crossed the ocean since sometime in the fourteenth century, the town is still small and charming, its steep alleys tumbling down the lava slopes of the island's mountain spine, its streets full of flowers and trees, its very pavements made of patterned mosaic which glistens in the sun. I was working as receptionist and tourist guide at one of the new hotels east of the town. This sounds an easy job, but isn't; in tourist time, which in Madeira is almost the whole year, it is hard indeed; but what had led me to apply for the job was that very few qualifications seemed to be needed by a "Young lady of good appearance, willing to work long hours." Both these qualifications were mine; appearance was just about all I'd got, and I would have worked any hours to make some money. Whether I was the best for the job I don't know, but it happened that the people who owned the hotel had known my father, so I was hired. The old-boy network they call it. Well, it works, as often as not. You may not get the brightest and the best, but you do get someone who talks your own language, and who is usually someone you can get back at the way it will hurt, if they let you down.

It's barely a year since the things happened that I am writing about, but I find that I am already thinking of my father as if he were long gone, part of the past. As he is now; but on that warm April night in Madeira when my love told me to go and see him, Daddy was alive, just.

I didn't sleep in the hotel. The friends who owned it had a quinta, a country estate a few kilometers out of Funchal, where the pine woods slope down the mountains towards the sea. You reached the place by a lane which led off the Machico road, a steep grey ribbon of lava setts, bordered in summer with blue and white agapanthus standing cool against the pine woods, their stems vibrating in the draft of the running water in the levada at the road's edge. The house was big and rather ornate in the Portuguese style, standing in wide grounds full of flowers and carefully watered grass and every imaginable exotic shrub and flowering tree, dramatically set against the cool background of mountain pines. The owners lived there all winter, but at the beginning of April, most years, went back to England to their house in Herefordshire which lay just across the Malvern Hills from ours. They were in England now, and the quinta was shuttered, but I lived in what they called the garden house. This was a plain, single-story building at the foot of the garden. Its walls were pink-washed like those of the big house, and inside it was simple and bare—scrubbed floors and big echoing grey-walled rooms slatted all day against the sun, beautifully quiet and airy, and smelling of sunburned pines and lemon blossom. My bedroom window opened on one of the camellia avenues which led downhill towards the lily pools where frogs croaked and splashed all night. By the end of April the camellias are just about over, the browned blossoms swept away, almost as they drop, by the immaculate Portuguese gardeners; but the Judas trees are in flower, and the angel's-trumpets, and the wisteria, all fighting their way up through a dreamer's mixture of cloudy blossom where every season's flowers flourish (it seems) all year. And the roses are out. Not roses such as we have at home; roses need their cold winter's rest, and here, forced as they are into perpetual flower by the climate, they grow pale and slack-petalled, on thin, over-supple stems. There were roses on the wall of the garden house, moonbursts of some white, loose-globed flower which showered half across my bedroom window. The breeze that blew the rain clouds from time to time across the moonlight tossed the shadows of the roses over wall and ceiling again and again, each time the same and yet each time different, as the roses moved and the petals loosened to the breeze.

I was still awake when he came. He had not been to me for so long that at first I hardly recognized what was happening. It was just my name, softly, moving and fading through the empty room as the rose shadows moved and faded.

Bryony. Bryony. Bryony Ashley.

"Yes?" I found I had said it aloud, as if words were needed. Then I came fully awake, and knew where I was and who was talking to me. I turned over on my back, staring up at the high ceiling of that empty room where the moonlit shadows, in a still pause, hung motionless and insubstantial. As insubstantial as the lover who filled the nighttime room with his presence, and my mind with his voice.

Bryony. At last. Listen. . . . Are you listening?

This is not how it came through, of course. That is hard to describe, if not downright impossible. It comes through neither in words nor in pictures, but—I can't put it any better—in sudden blocks of intelligence that are thrust into one's mind and slotted and locked there, the way a printer locks the lines into place, and there is the page with all its meanings for you to read. With these thought-patterns the whole page comes through at once; I suppose it may be like block-reading, though I have never tried that. They say it comes with practice. Well, he and I had had all our lives to practice; I had known him all my twenty-two years, and he (this much I could tell about him) was not much older.

I suppose that when we were children we must both have stumbled and made mistakes, as normal children do with reading, but I cannot remember a time when we couldn't confront each other, mind to mind, with ease. To begin with it seemed like sharing dreams, or having (as I believe is common among children) an imaginary companion who shared everything with me, and who was more real even than the cousins who lived near us, or than my friends at school. But, unlike most children, I never spoke about him. I don't think this was through fear of ridicule or disbelief; the experience was something I took very much for granted; but somehow, imposed over those thought-patterns, there was a censor which wouldn't allow me to share him with anyone else, even my parents. And the same censor must have worked with him. Never by the smallest sign or faltering of the patterns did he let me know who he was, though, from the shared memories that we had, I knew he must be someone close to me, and it was a safe bet that he was one of my Ashley cousins, who had played with me at Ashley Court daily when I was a child, and who had later on shared almost every holiday. It's a gift that goes in families, and there were records that it ran in ours: ever since the Elizabeth Ashley who was burned at the stake in 1623, there had been a record, necessarily secret, of strange "seeings" and thought-transference between members of the family. By the same token my lover knew me, since I was the only Ashley girl, and for the last year or so had addressed me flatly as "Bryony." There again, I only use the name for convenience; you might almost say he called me "You," but in a manner which identified me fully. In return I called him "Ashley," in an attempt to make him identify himself. He never did, but accepted the name as he had accepted "Boy" and sometimes, in unwary moments, "Love," with the same guarded and gentle amusement with which he parried every attempt I had lately made to force him to identify himself. All I could get from him was the assurance that when the time was right we would know each other openly; but until that time we must be close only in thought.

I know I haven't explained this well, but then it is a thing I have known all my life, and that I gather very few people know at all. When I was old enough to see the gift as something unique and secret, I tried to read about it, but all that could be found under headings like "Telepathy" or "Thought-transference" never seemed quite to tally with this easy private line of communication that we owned. In the end I gave up trying to analyze the experience, and went back to accepting it as I had done when a child. Though I gathered from my reading that gifts like this could be uncomfortable, and had been in times past downright dangerous, it had never worried me to possess it. Indeed, I could hardly imagine life without it. I don't even know when he became a lover as well as a companion; a change in the thought-patterns, I suppose, as unmistakable as the changes in one's body. And if it seems absurd that one should need and offer love without knowing the body one offers it to, I suppose that unconsciously the body dictates a need which the mind supplies. With us the minds translated our need into vivid and holding patterns which were exchanged and accepted without question, and—since bodily responses were not involved—rather comfortably.

It was probable that when we met and knew one another physically it would be less simple, but at the moment there seemed to be no prospect of this. You can't, out of the blue, ask a second cousin who has given no hint of it: "Are you the Ashley who talks to me privately?" I did once try to probe. I asked Francis, the youngest of my three cousins, if he ever had dreams of people so vivid that he confused them with reality. He shook his head, apparently without interest, and changed the subject. So I summoned up my courage to ask the twins, who were my seniors by almost four years. When I spoke to James, the younger of the two, he gave me a strange look, but said no, and he must have told Emory, his twin, because Emory started probing at me in his turn. Full of questions he was, and rather excited, but somehow in the wrong way, the way the psychical research people were when Rob Granger, the farmer's son at home, said he'd seen a ghostly priest walking through the walls of Ashley church, and everyone thought it might be Cardinal Wolsey who was there as a young man; but it turned out to be the Vicar going down in his dressing gown to pick up the spectacles he'd left behind in the vestry.

My lover says—and he said it in clear only yesterday —that I have got so used to communicating in thought-blocks that I am not good with words any more. I never get to the point, he tells me, and if I did I couldn't stick there. But I shall have to try, if I am to write down the full story of the strange things that happened at Ashley Court a year ago. Write it I must, for reasons which will be made plain later, and to do that I suppose I ought to start by saying something about the family. What I have written so far makes us sound like something from a dubious old melodrama—which would not be far wrong, because the family is as old as Noah, and I suppose you could say it's as rotten as a waterlogged Ark. Not a bad simile, because Ashley Court, our home, is a moated manor that was built piecemeal by a series of owners from the Saxons on, none of whom had heard of damp courses; but it is very beautiful, and brings in something over two thousand a year, not counting outgoings, from the twenty-five-penny tourists, God bless them.

The family goes back further even than the oldest bits of the house. There was an Ashley—tradition says he was called Almeric of the Spears, which in Anglo-Saxon is pronounced something like "Asher"—who fled in front of the Danes when they came raiding up the Severn in the tenth century, and established his family in the densely forested land near the foot of the Malvern Hills. There had been settlers there before; it was said that when the British, earlier still, had fled in front of the Saxons, they had lived on like ghosts in the fragments of a Roman house built where a curve of the river let the sunlight in. Of this early settlement there was no trace except the remains of some tile kilns half a mile from the house. The Saxons dug a moat and led the river into it, and holed up safely until the Conquest. The Saxon Ashley was killed in the fighting, and the incoming Norman took his widow and the land, built a stone keep on the island and a draw-bridge to serve it, then took the name as well, and settled down to rear Ashley children who were all, probably to his fury, fair and pale-skinned and tall, and Saxon to the bone. The Ashleys have always had a talent for retaining just what they wanted to retain, while adapting immediately and without effort to the winning side. The Vicar of Bray must have been a close relation. We were Catholics right up to Henry VIII, then when the Great Whore got him we built a priest's hole and kept it tenanted until we saw which side the wafer was buttered, and then somehow there we were under Elizabeth, staunch Protestants and bricking up the priest's hole, and learning the Thirty-nine Articles off by heart, probably aloud. None of us got chopped, right through Bloody Mary, but that's the Ashleys for you. Opportunists. Rotten turncoats. We bend with the wind of change—and we stay at Ashley. Even in the nineteen-seventies, with no coat left to turn, and with everything loaded against us, we stayed. The only differ-ence was, we lived in the cottage instead of the Court.

Nothing is left now of the formal gardens, which had once been beautiful, but which I had never known as other than neglected, with the wild, tanglewood charm of a Sleeping Beauty backdrop. The lovely, crumbling old house on its moated island, and the wilderness sur-rounding, were all that was left of an estate which had once been half a county wide, but which by my father's time had shrunk to a strip of land along the river, the gardens themselves, the buildings of what had once been a prosperous home farm, and a churchyard. I think the church officially belonged as well, but Jonathan Ashley— my father—didn't insist on this. The church stood in its green graveyard just beside our main drive gates, and when I was a little girl I used to believe that the bells were ringing right in the tops of our lime trees. To this day the scent of lime blossom brings back to me the church bells ringing, and the sight of the rooks going up into the air like smuts blown from a bonfire.

This was all that was left of the grounds laid out by the Cavalier Ashley. He, incidentally, must have been the only Cavalier throughout England who did not melt the family silver down for Charles I. He wouldn't, of course. I suspect that the only reason his family didn't officially turn Roundhead was because of the clothes and the hair-cut. Anyway, they saved the Court twice over, because my father sent most of the silver to Christie's in 1950, and we lived on it, and kept the place up after a fashion until I was seven or eight years old. Then we moved into one wing of the house, and opened the rest up to the public. A few years later, after my mother died, Daddy and I moved out altogether, to live in the gardener's cottage, a pretty little place at the edge of the apple orchard, with a tiny garden fronting on the lake that drained the moat. Our wing of the Court was put in the hands of our lawyer to let if he could. We had been lucky in this, and our most recent lessee was an American businessman who, with his family, had been in residence for the past half year. We had not met the Underhills ourselves, because, eight months before the April night when my story starts, my father, who had a rheumatic heart, contracted a bad bronchitis, and after he recovered from this, his doctor urged him to go away for a spell in a drier climate. I was working in an antique shop in Ashbury at the time. We sold a bit more of the silver, shut the cottage up, and went to Bad Tölz, a little spa town in Bavaria, pleasantly situated on the River Isar. My father had often been there as a young man, visiting a friend of his, one Walther

Gothard, who now had a considerable reputation as a *Kur-Doktor,* and had turned his house into a sanatorium. Daddy went there simply to rest, and to be cared for by Herr Gothard, who, for old times' sake, took him cheaply. I stayed for a month, but he mended so rapidly in that air that it was impossible to worry any more, so, when the Madeira job was suggested, I was easily persuaded to go. Even my lover, when I asked him, said there was nothing to go home for. I only half liked this kind of reassurance, but it was true that none of my cousins was at Ashley, and the cottage in winter and the damps of early spring looked lonely and uninviting; so in the end I took the job, and went off happily enough to the sun and flowers of Funchal, with no idea in the world that I would never see my father alive again.

Bryony?

Yes. I'm awake. What is it? But the trouble was there already, in the room. It settled over me in a formless way, like fog; no colour, neither dark nor light, no smell, no sound; just a clenching tension of pain and the fear of death. The sweat sprang hot on my skin, and the sheet scraped under my nails. I sat up.

I've got it, I think. It's Daddy. . . . He must have been taken ill again.

Yes. There's something wrong. I can't tell more than that, but you ought to go.

I didn't stop then to wonder how he knew. There was only room for just the one thing, the distress and urgency, soon to be transmuted into action; the telephone, the air-field, the ghastly slow journey to be faced. . . . It only crossed my mind fleetingly then to wonder if my father himself had the Ashley gift; he had never given me a hint of it, but then neither had I told him about myself. Had he been "read" by my lover, or even been in touch with him . . . ? But there was denial stamped on the dark. With the denial came over a kind of uncertainty, puzzlement with an element of extra doubt running through it, like a thread of the wrong colour through a piece of weaving.

But it didn't matter how, and through whom, it had got to him. It had reached him, and now it had reached me.

Can you read me, Bryony? You're a long way off.

Yes. I can read you. I'll go . . . I'll go straight away, tomorrow—today? There was a flight at eight; they would surely take me. . . . Then urgently, projecting it with everything I had: *Love?*

It was fading. *Yes?*

Will you be there?

Again denial printed on the dark; denial, regret, fading . . .

Oh, God. I said soundlessly. *When?*

Something else came through then, strongly through the fading death cloud, shouldering it aside; comfort and love, as old-fashioned as potpourri and as sweet and sane and haunting. It was as if the rose shadows on the ceiling were showering their scent down into the empty room. Then there was nothing left but the shadows. I was alone.

I threw the sheet off and knotted a robe round me, and ran for the telephone.

As I put a hand on it, it began to ring.

Ashley, 1835

He stood at the window, looking out into the darkness. Would she come tonight? Perhaps, if she had heard the news, she would think he could not be here, waiting for her; and indeed, for very decency, he surely ought not to have come. . . .

He scowled, chewing his lip. What, after all, was a little more scandal? And this was their last time—the last time it would be like this. Tomorrow was for the world, the angry voices, the laughter, the cold wind. Tonight was still their own.

He glanced across in the direction of the Court. The upper stories showed, above the hedges, as a featureless bulk of shadow against a windy sky. No lights. No lights showing anywhere. His eye lingered on the south wing, where the old man lay behind a darkened window.

Something like a shudder shook him. He tugged at his neckcloth, and found his hand shaking. She must come. Dear God, she had to come. He could not face the night without her. His longing, stronger even than desire, possessed him. He could almost feel the call going out, to bring her to him through the dark.

Two

Find them out whose names are written here!
—*Romeo and Juliet*, I, ii

Madeira to Madrid, Madrid to Munich, from Munich the
express out to Bad Tölz in the Isar Valley; it was twenty-
seven hours after the telephone call came from Walther
Gothard before the taxi slid up to the sanatorium doors
and Herr Gothard himself came down the steps to meet
me.

Twenty-seven hours is a long time for a man to hold
on to life when he is rising sixty with a dicky heart and
has been knocked clean off the road by a passing car and
left there till the next passerby should find him. Which
had not happened for about four hours.

Jon Ashley had not held on for twenty-seven hours. He
was dead when I got to Bad Tölz. He had come round
long enough to speak to Walther, then he had slept; and
sleeping, died.

I knew, of course. It had happened while I was on the
plane between Funchal and Madrid. And then it was over,
and I blotted it out and watched the clouds without seeing
them, and waited in a curious kind of limbo of relaxation
while the Caravelle took me nearer and uselessly nearer
his dead body; and waited, too, for my lover to come
with what comfort he could offer. But he did not come.

Walther and his wife were divinely kind. They had done everything that had to be done. They had arranged for the cremation, and had telephoned the news to the family lawyers in Worcester. Mr. Emerson, the partner who dealt with the Ashley affairs, would by now have been in touch with Cousin Howard, the father of the twins and of Francis. And of course Walther and Elsa Gothard had been closeted, hour after hour, with the police.

The police were still asking questions, and with most of the questions as yet unanswered. The accident had taken place on the road up from the town, just at dusk. This was the way my taxi had brought me. The Wackersberger Strasse climbs out of the newish quarter of the town beyond the river bridge. Once past the last of the houses the road reverts abruptly to its country status and winds, narrow and in places fairly steep, through the climbing woods. My father, who had been so much better (said Walther) that he had been talking of going home for the summer, had gone down to the town to buy some things he needed, including a bottle of Walther's favourite brandy as a gift, and had apparently started to walk back. No doubt he would have taken the bus when it caught him up. But when the bus climbed that way there was no sign of him. A car, going fast, and clinging to the edge of a bend, had apparently struck him a hard, glancing blow which flung him clear off the road and down the slope into the edge of the wood. He hit his head on a tree trunk, and was knocked unconscious, hidden from the road by the bushes into which he had been flung. The car drove off, leaving him lying there, barely visible in the dusk, until some four hours later when a cyclist, pushing his machine uphill at the edge of the road, ran a tire over a jag of the broken brandy bottle. When he wheeled the crippled cycle to lean it against a tree trunk, he saw my father lying among the bushes. The man took him at first for a drunkard; the brandy still reeked in his clothes. But drunk or no, the wound on his head was black and crusty with blood, so the cyclist wobbled off down the road on his front rim until another car overtook him, and he stopped it.

It was Walther Gothard's. He, growing anxious after two buses had come and gone with no sign of his friend, had telephoned various places where he thought the latter might be, intending to drive down himself and bring him home. Finally, failing to locate him, he set out to look for him. He took the unconscious man straight up to the sanatorium, and telephoned the police, who, having examined the scene of the accident, confirmed the doctor's guess at what must have happened. But four hours' start is four hours' start, and the guilty driver had not been traced.

Herr Gothard told me about it, sitting in his big consulting room with the picture window framing the prospect of rolling pastures, smooth as brushed velvet, and looking as if they had been shaved out of the thick forests that hung like thatch eaves above them. A bowl of blue hyacinths on the desk filled the room with scent. Beside it lay the small pile of objects which had come from Daddy's pockets: keys, a notecase I had given him with the initials *J. A.* stamped in gilt; a silver ballpoint pen with the same initials; a penknife, nail clippers, a handkerchief newly laundered and folded; the letter I had written to him a week ago. I looked away from this at Herr Gothard, who sat quietly, watching me, the gold-rimmed bifocals winking on his broad pale face. No longer Daddy's friend, with a shoulder I could cry on if I needed it; now he was just a doctor, who had heard and seen it all before, and the room itself had held so much of pain and emotion and courage that it was coloured by none of them. I sat calmly, while he told me what had happened.

"He came round towards morning and talked a little, a very little. Not about the accident, though; we questioned him as much as we dared, but he seemed to have forgotten about it. He had other things on his mind."

"Yes?"

"You, mainly. I couldn't get it clear, I'm afraid. He said, *'Bryony, tell Bryony,'* once or twice, then seemed not to be able to put it into words, whatever it was. I thought at first he was anxious in case you had not been told about the accident, so I reassured him, and said I had talked to you on the telephone, and that you were on your way. But he still worried at it. We got a few snatches, no more, none of which made much sense, then in the end he got something more out. It was *'Bryony—my little Bryony—in danger.'* I asked what danger, and he could not answer me. He died at about ten o'clock."

I nodded. Between Funchal and Madrid; I knew the exact moment. Walther talked on, professionally smooth and calm; I think he was telling me about Daddy's stay in Wackersberg, and what they had done and talked of together. I have no recollection of anything he said, but to this day I can remember every petal on the blue hyacinths in the bowl on the desk between us.

"And that was all?"

"All?" Herr Gothard, interrupted in midsentence, changed direction without a tremor. "All that Jon said, you mean?"

"Yes. I'm sorry. I wasn't really taking in—"

"Please." He showed a hand, pale and smooth with scrubbing. "I did not imagine you were. You ask me what else Jon said at the end. I have it here."

He slid the hand into a drawer of the desk, and brought out a paper.

I don't know why I was so surprised. I just stared, without moving to take the paper. "You wrote it down?"

"The police left a man to sit by his bed," explained Walther gently, "in case he managed to say anything about the accident which might help them to trace the culprit. It always happens, you know."

"Yes, of course. I knew that. One never quite thinks of oneself in those contexts, I suppose."

"The officer spoke very good English, and he took down everything Jon said, whether it seemed to him to make sense or not. Do you read shorthand?"

"Yes."

"It's all here, every word that was intelligible. I was

with Jon myself most of the time. There was another emergency that morning, so I had to leave him for a while, but as soon as he showed signs of coming round they sent for me, and I stayed with him after that until he died. This is all that he said. I am sorry it does not make more sense, but perhaps it does, for you."

He handed me the paper. The pothooks straggled a little wildly across the page, as if written too hurriedly, on a pad balanced on someone's knee. Walther slid another sheet of paper across the desk towards me. "I made a transcript of it, just in case. You can compare them later, if you like."

The transcript was typed, with no attempt at making sense. Just a string of words and phrases, punctuated seemingly at random.

> Bryony. Tell Bryony. Tell her. Howard. James. Would have told. The paper, it's in William's brook. In the library. Emerson, the keys. The cat, it's the cat on the pavement. The map. The letter. In the brook.

It broke off there, and started again on a fresh line:

> Tell Bryony. My little Bryony be careful. Danger. This thing I can feel. Should have told you, but one must be sure. I did tell Bryony's [word indistinguishable]. Perhaps the boy knows. Tell the boy. Trust. Depend. Do what's right. Blessing.

I read it aloud slowly, then looked up at Walther. My face must have been blank. He nodded, answering the unspoken question.

"I'm sorry. That really is all, exactly as we heard him. You see where he found it too much for him, and stopped for a while. He was still conscious, and worrying at it, so we let him speak. The last word, I'm not sure about that. I thought it might have been 'bless him,' but the officer was sure it was 'blessing.' Does it make any sense to you at all?"

"No. Scraps here and there, but no. Nothing important enough to be so much on his mind then. I'd have thought —I mean, if he knew how ill he was, I'd have thought . . . you know, just messages."

"Yes, well, it may mean more later, when you have had time to study it."

"There's this about a letter. It might all be there. Did he leave a letter?" I knew the answer already. If there had been a letter for me, Walther would have given it to me straight away.

"I'm afraid not," he said, "and there was nothing mailed from here within the last day or so. I checked. But it is possible that he took something down with him to mail from Bad Tölz yesterday. In which case it will be on its way to Madeira. No doubt they will forward it straight away to your home."

The last sentence came with perceptible hesitation. There is something strange, I suppose, in the idea of a letter arriving from the dead. I didn't find it so. It was a break in the clouds of that dark day. Something of the sort must have shown in my face, because Walther added, gently: "It's only a guess, Bryony. The word itself was a guess. If there is anything, it may not even be for you."

"I'll find out once I get home."

I would of course have to go home to England now, and it had already been arranged that I would take my father's ashes back to the Court, as he had wished.

Walther nodded. "And after that? Do you intend to stay there?"

"I'll have to, I think, until things are settled."

"It may take a long time."

"It's sure to. It'll be beastly complicated, I gather, but Mr. Emerson will do all the fixing. I suppose Daddy told you that the estate doesn't go to me, but is entailed to the nearest male heir? That's my father's cousin, Howard Ashley, who lives in Spain."

Walther nodded. "Your lawyer said something about it when we spoke over the telephone. He had not been able to get in touch directly with Mr. Howard Ashley, he said. It seems that he is ill."

"Yes. Daddy told me so last time he wrote. It's a virus pneumonia, and I gather that Cousin Howard's been pretty bad. I don't suppose he'll be able to attend to any business for a long time. Emory and James will have to see to things."

"So I imagine. It seems that this was one of the things your father had on his mind. Emory—a strange name, surely?"

"I suppose it is. It's an old Saxon name that crops up in the family from time to time. I think it's the same as Almeric."

"Ah, then I have also heard it in Germany. They are twins, are they not, this James and Emory?"

"Yes, identical twins. When they were boys, no one could tell them apart, except the family—and sometimes, when they were trying it on deliberately, not even the family. It's not so hard now, but I still wouldn't bet on it if they really tried to fool you. They're twenty-seven. Emory's the elder, half an hour's difference, something like that."

"A big difference when it comes to inheriting an estate," said Walther drily.

I said, just as drily: "A crumbling old house that never quite got over the flood ten years back, and a few acres of garden gone wild, and a ruined farm? Some legacy."

"As bad as that? Jon loved it."

"So do I."

"And your cousins?"

"I don't know. I don't see why they should. They were brought up there, the same as me; Cousin Howard had a house less than a mile away. But whether they want a beautiful old millstone round their necks I've no idea. Beautiful old millstones take money."

"I understood they had plenty of that."

"I suppose they have." Whether they would want to spend it on Ashley was another matter which I didn't pursue. I did not know a great deal about the wine shipper's business which Howard Ashley had started some years back, except that it had always seemed to prosper. In the early days, when it was relatively small, it had been based in Bristol, and the family had lived near us in Worcestershire. Then when the twins were about thirteen, and Francis eleven, the boys' mother died, and after that the three of them seemed more or less to live with us at the Court. Certainly they spent their school holidays with us; their father was in Bristol during the week, and his housekeeping arrangements were so erratic that my mother finally intervened and took my three cousins in. There would have been ample room, in those days, for Howard as well, but, though there had never been anything approaching coolness between him and my parents, they could not have happily settled to share a house. The three boys were dispatched home to their father most weekends, until, some five years after his wife's death, Cousin Howard went off to Mexico City to negotiate a deal of some kind, and met a Spanish-Mexican girl and married her. Her family was wealthy, and also connected with the wine trade. Howard's deal had been with the girl's father, Miguel Pereira, who owned a share of a prosperous business in Jerez. Howard took his new wife off to Europe, and they eventually settled in Spain. Emory took over the Bristol offices, and James more or less commuted between the two.

"Would your cousin Howard want to come back to live at Ashley?" asked Walther.

"I've no idea. I don't honestly know him so very well. I was only fourteen when he left, and I was away at school most of the time. I doubt if his wife would want to live there, though. She's years younger than Cousin Howard, and she'd hardly want to settle in a remote little place like Ashley. But I suppose one of the boys might."

"The boys . . ." Walther said it half to himself, and I realized that he was thinking of the paper I still held in my hand. But he only said: "I understand the two elder ones are in their father's business. What about the youngest?"

"Francis? Oh, he is, too. Rather reluctantly, I think. He doesn't have his family's head for business—he's more like our side. But he's with his father now in Jerez. I think he went into it almost absentmindedly, while he marked time and thought out what he really wanted to do. He has to earn a living some way, and I suppose Spain is as pleasant a place as any. He's a poet."

"Oh." Walther smiled. "A good one?"

"How would I know? I never got much beyond Yeats and Walter de la Mare. Didn't want to, considering the sort of things that get printed now. I can't understand a word Francis writes, but I like Francis, so let's say he is a good one."

The sun twinkled on the gold-rimmed glasses. "He's not married, is he?"

"No." I met his eyes. "And nor are the twins, Dr. Gothard. At least, they weren't when I last saw them. We're not wildly good correspondents, my cousins and I." (Except for you, Ashley my lover. Emory? James? Francis?) I raised my brows at Walther. "You've been listening to Daddy, haven't you? That was his plan, too. Get me back to Ashley somehow. . . . But Francis would be no good, obviously. It would have to be the eldest, and that's Emory."

He smiled. "Something of the sort was in my mind, I confess. It is such an obvious solution. You stay at Ashley, and so do your children. I am sure your father had some sort of hope that it might happen. I think he saw you staying on there."

"He didn't say who with?" I was looking down at the paper in my hand. *"This thing I can feel. . . . Perhaps the boy knows."* And then, *"I did tell Bryony's"*— Bryony's what? Bryony's lover? I wondered sharply, but with a kind of certainty about it, whether my father had known, or guessed, enough about my secret love to bank, entail or no, on my lifelong connection with Ashley Court.

"No," said Walther. "He didn't." My thoughts had gone on from my own question with such speed that for a moment I couldn't make out what he was referring to.

He saw this; he was very quick, was Herr Doktor Gothard. He nodded to the paper in my hands. "You were studying that. Have you worked some of it out?"

"Not really. It sounds as if there's some paper, perhaps the letter he speaks of, where he's written something important to me, and perhaps to Cousin Howard."

"And James."

"Yes, I suppose so. But why James? I mean if Daddy *had* told Howard, then Howard could have told the boys, whatever it was. It sounds as if it was a family matter. So why just James?" (Like a treasure hunt, I was thinking, the mystification of papers and letters and maps. It wasn't like him. Jon Ashley was sane and direct. So what did it mean? And why James?) I added, aloud: "This paper or map or whatever, he says it's 'in William's brook.' Well, that simply does not make sense."

"I know. A brook's another word for a stream, is it not? I thought it was, and I looked it up to make sure. It cannot mean anything else. I thought you might know what he meant."

"No idea. You said you were sure the words were right."

"Those, yes. To begin with he was pretty clear. I thought there might be a stream at Ashley, something with a local name, perhaps."

"Not that I know of. There was a William Ashley, certainly, early last century. 'Scholar Ashley' they called him; he was a bit of a Shakespeare scholar, in a strictly private and amateur way. He was a poet, too. But the only brook in the place, apart from the river, is the overflow channel that helps to control the level of the moat. It's never been called anything but the Overflow." I stopped, struck by an idea. "It might have been made by William, I suppose. There's a maze at Ashley, and he built a pavilion in the middle, where he used to retire to write. The stream runs past the maze."

" 'The map'?" suggested Walther. "A map of the maze?"

"Perhaps. I don't see why it should matter. I've known

the way in all my life, and so have my cousins." I shrugged. "In any case, it's nonsense. How could a paper —a map, whatever you like—how could it be in a stream?"

"I agree. But the next bit is surely more sensible. This paper could be in the library, of which perhaps Mr. Emerson has the keys? Does he keep keys to the Court?"

"I suppose he must have a set. One complete set was handed over to the tenants. They live in the south wing, and normally all the rest of the house is locked up, except for cleaning, and when the place is open to the public, but the Underhills have to have the keys to the locked rooms, because of fire regulations."

He merely nodded, and I didn't elaborate. I assumed that Daddy had told him about our latest tenants. The Underhills were wealthy Americans with permanent homes in Los Angeles and New York, and temporary ones, one gathered, here and there all over the world. Jeffrey Underhill was President of Sacco International, a heavy construction firm which carried out government contracts in every part of the globe. The family had been living in Los Angeles while the daughter, Cathy, was at school there, but now they had come to England for a year's stay, to be near Mrs. Underhill's sister, whose husband was stationed at the USAF base near Bristol. As far as Mr. Underhill was concerned, it didn't seem to matter where he was based; I gathered he managed to struggle home most weekends, but spent his weeks shuttling between Paris, London, Mexico, and Teheran, where the company's current major operations were. He had told Mr. Emerson that it didn't make a bit of difference where he was actually domiciled as long as he got "back home" to Houston, Texas, for Board Meetings, and that his wife was keen to live for a while in a "real old English home," and that it would do Cathy a world of good to have a taste of country peace and quiet. Myself, I wondered about that; I had never been to Los Angeles, but one could imagine that Ashley, in contrast, might possibly not have much to offer to an eighteen-year-old girl with all the money in the world to burn. But they had stayed, and liked it, and I gathered that Cathy was still there with them.

"The bit about the cat," I said. "Do you think the car might have swerved to avoid a cat, or something, and was going too fast at the bend, and mounted the pavement and hit him?"

"It is possible. That's the way the police see it. There actually is no pavement on that section of the road, but there is a kind of footway worn in the verge of the wood, and, heaven knows, Jon might have been speaking loosely when he talks of a 'pavement.' That was where he had to stop talking and rest for a while."

"But this last bit, Dr. Gothard. He wasn't speaking loosely there. He says I have to be careful, and there's some danger."

"Indeed." His eyes were troubled. "When he speaks of 'this thing I can feel,' he seems to mean danger of some kind. It could hardly be pain; he was under sedation."

"He wouldn't mean that." I took a breath and met the kind pale eyes above the glinting half-moons of glass. "You're a doctor, so I don't expect you to believe me, but some of us—the Ashleys, I mean—have a sort of . . . I can only call it a kind of telepathy. Empathy, perhaps? Er, do you have that word?"

"Certainly. We say '*mit fühlen*.' The power of entering imaginatively into someone else's feelings or experience."

"Yes, except that in our case it's not just imaginative, it's real. I've only known it work between members of the family, and it's kind of spasmodic, but if someone you love is hurt, you know."

"Why should I not believe you?" he asked calmly. "It's reasonably common."

"I know, but you'd be surprised—or perhaps you wouldn't—what people don't believe, or don't want to believe. The Ashleys have had this thing in one degree or another as far back as about the sixteen hundreds when the Jacobean Ashley married a gorgeous girl called Bess Smith, who was half gipsy. She was burned for witchcraft

in the end. After that it seems to have cropped up every
so often, but we kept quiet about it. Anyway, it isn't the
kind of thing you tell people. Nobody likes being laughed
at."

"You really think this is what your father meant?"

"It might be. I've sometimes wondered. We never spoke
about it, but I'm pretty sure he had it to some extent.
I know once when I was at school and fell out of a tree
and broke my leg, he telephoned about ten minutes later
to ask if I was all right. And last night in Madeira . . .
Well, I felt something, and I think some of it came from
him. And on the way here in the plane this morning, at
ten o'clock, I knew."

He said nothing for a while. An early bee zoomed
in through the open window, circled droning in the sunlight, then homed in on the hyacinths and crawled up
them, its wings quiet. Walther stirred. "I see. But at the
end, as you see, he states that he 'told' someone, presumably meaning that he told him about this important paper,
and about this danger to you. If it is so very important,
no doubt 'he' will tell you. And if 'the boy knows,' then
perhaps 'the boy' may tell you, too?"

I watched the bee. I wasn't prepared to meet those
kind, clever eyes. I still had this one to think about, myself. *"I did tell Bryony's . . . Perhaps the boy knows."*
Bryony's lover? It would take a bit of adjustment to come
to terms with the fact that my father had known. And if
he had told my lover something that mattered urgently to
me, then my lover could tell me, and the mystery was no
mystery.

The bee, abandoning the hyacinths, shot straight for
the window like a bullet, achieved the open pane by a
beewing's breadth, and was gone.

Walther straightened in the big chair. "Well, we shall
leave it, I think. Yes? You must try to forget it for the
moment. When you have rested, and when the next few
days are over, then you may find your mind fresher, and
you will see. It is very possible that Mr. Emerson may

have the answers already, or whoever of your family comes over on Friday. One of them surely will, and will take you home? It may be 'Bryony's cousin,' the one who knows it all."

"So it may. Dr. Gothard, will you tell me something truly?"

"If I can."

I knew from his eyes that from a doctor that meant "If I may," but that was fair enough. I said: "If the driver of that car had brought Daddy straight up to you here, could you have saved him?"

I saw the wariness relax into relief. That meant he would tell me the truth. "No. If he had been brought straight in he might have lived a little longer, but I could not have saved him."

"Not even till I got here?"

"I think not. It was a matter of hours only."

I drew a breath. He looked at me curiously. I shook my head. "No, I wasn't thinking of anything as dramatic and useless as revenge. That's a kind of self-defeat, I always feel. But if you had said 'Yes' I'd never have slept until the police found the driver who did it. As it is, he ran away out of fear and stupidity, and maybe he's being punished enough already. If the police ever do find him—" I paused.

"Yes?" he prompted.

I said flatly: "I don't want to know. I mean, I don't want to be told who it is. I won't burden myself with a useless hate. Daddy's gone, and I'm here, with a life to live. Those are the facts."

I didn't add what I was thinking: that he might not be quite gone, not from me, not from such as me. I would go back to Ashley, and there, perhaps . . . But I wasn't sure where that path would lead, and anyway that was another secret that was not for daylight. Walther said something about its being a sensible attitude, and something more about my being very like my father, and then we talked about the arrangements for the cremation on

Friday, and for the day after that, when nothing more would remain for me but to take my father's ashes home.

Ashley, 1835

The wind moved in the boughs outside. Creepers shifted and tapped against the walls of the pavilion. Since the old man had been ill, the place had been neglected—mercifully, he thought, with a wryness that made the young mouth look soured and wary.

He strained his eyes against the darkness. Still no movement, no sign. He pushed the casement open a fraction, listened. Nothing, except the rush of the overflow conduit past the maze, and the wind in the beeches. Sudden gusts combed the crests of the yew hedges towards him, as if something were flying past, invisible. A soul on its way home, he thought, and the shudder took him again.

At least let us have some light. He shut the window, and the night sounds died. He pulled the shutters close, and fastened them, then drew the heavy curtains across.

A candle stood on the writing table. He found a lucifer and lit it. At once the room flowered with light; golden curtains, rose-wreathed carpet, the bed's rich covering, the glittering sconces on the walls.

If he ever came here again, he would light those, too.

Three

Good King of Cats, nothing but one of your nine
lives. . . .   —*Romeo and Juliet*, III, i

I didn't go straight home when I got to England. The
first priority was a visit to Mr. Emerson, our solicitor,
to find out if he had had a letter from my father, and if he
could throw any light on the jumble of words on Walther's
paper.

No one had come to the cremation. Emory had telephoned from England, not to me but to Walther, to say
that Cousin Howard was still very ill, and that since
Francis was away on leave, James was tied to the Jerez
office. Emory himself could not be free on Friday, but
would come to Ashley as soon as possible. He had no idea
where Francis was; walking somewhere, he thought, in
the Peak District. Presumably the news had not got to him
yet. No doubt he would call me as soon as he came back.
Meanwhile, said Emory, love to Bryony . . .

So much for Bryony's cousin who would tell me what
Daddy had meant, and take me home. And so much for
Bryony's lover, who said nothing, either by day or night.

When I arrived in London I took the train straight
to Worcester and booked in at a small hotel where no one
knew me. Next morning I telephoned Mr. Emerson, and
went to see him.

He was a youngish man, somewhere (I guessed) in his upper thirties, of medium height and running a bit to flesh, with a round, good-tempered face and hair cut fashionably long. He had a small shrewd mouth, and small shrewd brown eyes camouflaged behind modishly huge, tinted spectacles, like a television spy's. Otherwise he was correctly dressed and almost over-conventionally mannered; but I had seen him fishing the Wye in stained old tweeds and a snagged sweater, up to the crotch in the river and swearing in the far-from-legal sense of the word as he slipped and splashed over the boulders, trying to land a big salmon single-handed. I liked him, and Daddy, I knew, had trusted him completely.

It was almost a week now since my father's death, but Mr. Emerson did not make the mistake of being too kind. We got the first civilities over, then he cleared his throat, shifted a paper or two, and said: "Well now, Miss Ashley, you do know that you may call on me to help you in any way. . . . It will take a fair amount of time to sort out your father's affairs, as you know. None of that need trouble you, as long as you find yourself quite clear about the way the house and property are left."

I nodded. I had practically been brought up with the terms of the Ashley Trust, as it was called, which had been designed by an ancestor of mine, one James Christian Ashley, who had inherited the property in 1850. He was a farsighted man, who had seen, even in the spacious days of Victoria, that there might come a time when the incumbent of a place like Ashley might find it hard to protect what he, James Christian, thought of as a national treasure, and might even seek to disperse it. This, James Christian was determined to prevent. He created a trust whereby, though the Court itself must go outright to the nearest male heir, no part of the "said messuages" might be sold or disposed of unless with the consent in writing of all adult Ashley descendants existing at the time of the proposed disposal. My grandfather James Emory had managed, with the connivance of his brothers and one distant cousin, to sell a couple of outlying farms which edged the main road, and to make a tidy sum out of some meadowland earnestly desired by the Midland Railway, and the proceeds had kept the place in good heart until the cold winds sharpened to the killing frosts of the Second World War. Since then, apart from the family silver, which had been sold with his cousin's consent, all the articles my father had sold had been things bought since 1850 or brought in by marriage, and consequently uncontrolled by the trust. If my cousins had been in need of funds they would, I knew, have found themselves fairly well down to the scrapings.

Mr. Emerson was going on. "There's no immediate hurry over that. We can perhaps have another meeting when you are less, er, pressed." I knew that Walther had told him what my first business was at the Court. He shied delicately away from that, and went on: "Then there is your father's Will. He told me you have seen a copy, and know all about its contents. It covers everything not included in the entail, or embraced by the trust. The most important item is of course the cottage which is now your home. This, with the orchard and garden, and the strip of land running along the lake as far as the main road, was purchased after the creation of the trust, and comes, in consequence, outside its terms. It is left to you in its entirety. The Will is quite straightforward. There may be things that you wish to discuss at a later stage, but for the moment, would you like me just to take everything over for you? Settle what bills there are, and sort your father's correspondence? Or perhaps you would rather go through his letters yourself?"

"The personal ones, yes, I think so, please. I'd be glad if you'd deal with any business. Mr. Emerson—"

"Yes?"

"Has Daddy written to you recently? I mean, in the last few days?"

"No." He looked down at his fingernails for a moment, then back at me. "I was talking to Dr. Gothard on the telephone yesterday, as a matter of fact."

"Oh. Did he ask you about a letter, too?"

"Yes."

"And tell you about the paper?"

"Paper?"

"The notes he took about what Daddy said before he died."

"Ah, yes. Of course he did not tell me what had been said. This"—with a sudden, dry primness—"was on the telephone."

"I wanted to ask you about that, too. Most of it Herr Gothard and I couldn't make out at all, but there is one reference to you, which we thought you'd be able to clear up for us. I made a copy for you. Here."

He took the paper and read it swiftly, glanced briefly up at me, went through it again slowly, and then a third time. Finally he laid it on the desk. He leaned back in his chair, with his hands flat on the blotter.

"Well. Yes. I see."

"It's nonsense to you as well?"

"Pretty much, I'm afraid. But I think I can explain the reference to me. The tenants of the Court have a set of keys, but not a complete one. Certain keys were detached from that set, and are in my keeping. I have, for instance, the strong-room key, and the one to the old muniment chest in the Great Hall, and—yes, the small wall safe in the master bedroom, and also the key that opens the locked cases in the library."

"Have you?" Here, at last, was a fragment that might make sense, though I was still far from knowing what sort. The locked cases in the library at Ashley housed William Ashley's collection of Shakespeariana, and his own mercifully slim volume of verses, along with the distinctly curious (in the book-trade sense of the word) collection made by William's son, the scapegrace Nick Ashley. The grilles had been fixed after my father had found Emory and James, at the age of twelve, happily conning one of Nick's tomes called *Erotica Curiosa,* fortunately in Latin, but with illustrations. Within a few days it was behind bars, along with the rest of Nick's additions to the library, and those of William Ashley's Shakespeare

books that we imagined might be valuable, and a few
other odd volumes, mostly in Latin. I remember how
Emory worked at his Latin for a whole term, till he found
he would never get near the keys anyway, so he went back
to normal.

"The wall safe's empty, I know that," I said. "Do
you know what's in the strong-room nowadays?"

"There's very little. Only what's left of the eighteenth-
century silver, and one or two small things. I believe
there are some pieces of your mother's which are to be
yours."

"Those, yes, I know about them. Nothing else? No
papers, letters, maps?"

"Not that I recollect. No, I'm sure there aren't. All
the Ashley papers are lodged with us. That goes for the
muniment chest, too. There's nothing there now but spare
blankets and the old stable books and various other odd-
ments. Oh, and a dozen or so volumes of Emma Ashley's
diaries." He added, drily: "A voluble lady. She was James
Christian's mother, wasn't she?"

"She was. Is that where the diaries are? They used
to be in the locked section of the library, along with the
other family books, but heaven knows *they* never needed
to be locked away from anyone. She was a very good
woman, and a fearful bore. I think she spent her whole
life trying to expiate poor Wicked Nick's sins." I thought
for a moment. All the rest of the family books were presumably still in the locked cases, and by the terms of the
trust they would go with the house. Most of the valuable
books that did not come under those terms had already
been sold. Perhaps it would not be such a formidable job
after all. "Do I need Cousin Howard's permission to look
around in there?"

"No."

"Then—" I stopped and sat up. "I've just remembered something."

"What is it?"

I said slowly, thinking back, "I think Daddy was going
through the books in that section not long before we

went to Bavaria. I remember seeing a stack of leather-
bound books on one of the library tables. He'd been dressing the bindings. He'd done that with other valuable books
from time to time, so I thought nothing of it. He took one
or two of them home, too, to the cottage. Perhaps he
found something about the family, or even about the trust,
that he thought we ought to know."

"It sounds reasonable. It could be checked, but it'll
be a big job. Books always take the devil of a time to look
through. You can hardly tackle that library on your own."

"I could look, though, couldn't I? The shelves are
pretty empty now, apart from the family tomes, and they'll
all still be there." I smiled. "I might for decency's sake
have to hand some of Nick Ashley's lot over to my cousins
to go through. If they don't want to be bothered, I've a
friend who would help, Leslie Oker, who has the secondhand bookshop in Ashbury. I suppose that, in any case,
everything will have to be valued?"

"I'm afraid so. Well, I think you're right to take this
very seriously." He laid the paper down on the desk in
front of him. "Anything that was so much on your father's
mind at such a time . . ." He let it hang. His eyes went
to the paper again, and he read for a minute, frowning.
Then, with a quick movement like a dismissal, he opened
a drawer and slipped the paper into it. "You're going to
Ashley today?"

"Yes. This afternoon. Mr. Emerson, what's the position
about the Court? Am I still allowed access to everything?"

"Certainly. Nothing may be removed or sold, naturally,
but it is still your home until your father's Will is proved
and the estate is wound up. That will take quite some
time." His eyes twinkled. "The mills of God work like
lightning, compared with the law."

"So they say. What about the tycoons?"

"The what?"

"Sorry. It slipped out. It's what Daddy and I used to
call the Underhills."

He laughed. "It figures. They have a year's lease, which will be up in November. Mr. Underhill spoke to me on the telephone and offered to move out straight away if it would help you, but I told him that I imagined you and your cousins would wish him to stay put, at any rate for the time being. Things won't be settled for months, and at the least it means the Court will have a caretaker. Do you approve?"

"That's the kind of thing I leave to you. It sounds fine to me."

"Good. Your cousin Emory agreed, too. He was speaking for his father. You knew Mr. Howard Ashley was ill? Yes, of course . . ." He cleared his throat again. "Look, I know you want to go back to Ashley as soon as you can, but do you really want to stay there on your own? My wife and I would be delighted if you'd come to us for a few days. . . . And it was her suggestion that I should ask you, so I'm not putting my head on the domestic chopping block, I promise you."

"Well, thank you very much. It's terribly good of you both, but honestly, you don't have to worry. I'll be all right, really I will." I didn't add that I would not be quite alone. I never was. I thanked him again, moved by the kindness of these people who had known my father well, but me hardly at all.

He waved my thanks aside. "Still, I'll give you our number—not the office, which you have, but my home number. I think you're going to find the next few weeks very difficult ones, and I want to insist to you that though we—my firm—will be acting for Ashley as before, which will in future mean on Mr. Howard Ashley's behalf, we'll do all that we can to help you. I know it goes without saying, but still one says it."

"You're very kind."

"And have I made it clear I don't only mean legal help? For instance, how do you propose to get out to Ashley this afternoon? Have you a car?"

"No, I came up by train. I'll take the bus to Ashley

Village. There's a good one that stops at the road end beyond the church."

"And on your way back?"

"I've got a Lambretta. It's stabled at the farm."

"What about your luggage? If you're going to move back into your cottage tomorrow—"

"I haven't much; most of it's still in Madeira. But Rob Granger can come in for that. He has a car."

He nodded, and we talked for a while longer. He still seemed worried about my decision to stay alone in the cottage, and I spent some time in reassuring him. He also cast out feelers, very delicately, to find out what I proposed to do with my future, when Ashley was no longer mine. Would I, he asked, go back to Madeira when everything was, er, settled?

"I don't think so. They'll have replaced me by now, anyway; you just can't do without a receptionist for an indefinite period. In any case, I'd thought of that job as strictly temporary, just till Daddy was well enough to come home. I don't suppose my old job in Ashbury's still open, but I expect I'll find something."

"What's the money situation? I can advance you something, you know, out of what your father has left you."

"I'm all right for a bit, but thanks." I got to my feet. "You said you had a lunch appointment, and it's nearly half past twelve. I'd better go." I held out my hand. "And thank you for everything, Mr. Emerson. You've been terribly kind. Believe me, I'll come running to you the moment I need help of any kind."

"I hope you will."

We shook hands, and he moved to open the door for me. I paused in the doorway. "I almost forgot . . . I wonder, would it be all right for you to let me have the keys to the Court? I don't want to go to the house today, but I might go in tomorrow, and I'd rather not trouble the Underhills yet."

He looked surprised. "Of course. But surely, you can use your father's keys? The master set has them all."

"I haven't got them. I thought you must have. Do you mean you only have the ones you mentioned?"

"Yes, only the four. I gather they were detached from the ring Mr. Underhill has. The other set, the complete master set, was certainly in your father's possession. Didn't Dr. Gothard give you his things?"

"Yes. He did have keys on him, but only the ones for the cottage, and for the side door to the Court—the kitchen door, really, at the East Bridge." I hesitated, obscurely troubled. "If you haven't got them, who could he have left them with? One of my cousins?"

"I don't see why," said Mr. Emerson, slowly. "How very strange." He frowned over it for a few moments, then the professional mask was smoothly back in place. He went to a drawer, unlocked it, and took out a small ring of keys, which he gave me. "You must certainly have these. I'll get in touch with your cousin Emory and see if he knows anything about it. It may even be that both sets were left with the Underhills, or with someone else at Ashley. Whoever has them will probably give them to you as soon as it's known you're home. Otherwise, I'm afraid you will have to approach the Underhills."

"So it seems," I said. "But it is all right for me to go in?"

"Certainly."

"And if I get the keys, to keep them for the time being?"

"Yes, indeed." He opened the door for me. The brown eyes behind the trendy spectacles were anxious and kind. "Miss Ashley, let me insist to you that the Court is still yours until the Will is proved, and the estate duly handed over."

"Yes. Thank you."

"As for the keys, no doubt there will be some perfectly rational explanation," he said, as he showed me out. I got the impression that he was talking to reassure himself as well as me, and that in reality he disliked and distrusted mystery as much as I did myself.

"No doubt," I agreed, and went downstairs and out into the street.

Just outside the offices of Meyer, Meyer, and Hardy there is a pedestrian crossing. The light was at red, *Don't Walk*. Just under it, on the very edge of the pavement, a black cat was sitting, waiting apparently for the light to change to green. As I paused beside him he glanced up. I said to him, "Can't you reach? Allow me," and pressed the button. I have a theory that the button never has the least effect on the lights, which are totally unaffected by pedestrians' needs, but at that exact moment the light switched to green. *Walk*. The cat got straight up and walked across the zebra-striped way, tail in air. He was black as coal. "I may need you yet," I told him, and followed him onto the crossing.

There was a shriek of brakes. I jumped half out of my skin, and stepped back to the pavement. The cat bolted clear across and vanished into a shop doorway. A white E-type Jaguar clenched its big groundhog tires to the road, and stopped dead half a foot from the crossing. The girl who was driving glanced neither at me nor at the fleeing cat. She sat watching the red light with impatience, one hand tapping the wheel, the other pushing back the long, dark-blond hair. I had a glimpse of dark eyes shadowed under an inch or so of mink eyelash, a sallow, small-featured face, with that Pekinese look which is for some reason typically American, and a wide unpainted mouth. When I had gained the other pavement in the black cat's wake, the lights changed behind me, and the E-type snarled off into the traffic of the crowded street, cut competently between two buses, and vanished. Something made me glance back. On the other pavement Mr. Emerson had emerged from his office, complete with bowler and rolled umbrella, presumably on the way to his lunch date. He, too, had paused, and was watching the E-type out of sight. Then he noticed me, and mouthed something across the roaring flood of traffic pouring between us. I thought he said, "The cat," but he was pointing after the

vanished Jaguar. I nodded, waved, and smiled, and walked
back to my hotel.

Ashley, 1835

On the writing table, beside the candle, lay his
father's books and papers, held down by a glass
weight shaped like a peeled orange. The wax-
light glimmered in the curved segments, and
a dozen tiny images mocked him; the fair young
man, a silent figure in frilled shirt and panta-
loons, standing there, somehow incongruous and
lonely against the richly elegant background of
his mother's room.

He moved abruptly, striding over to the table,
scattering the papers that lay there. He pulled
open a drawer. From inside it, his mother's
picture smiled up at him. Always, when he had
used the pavilion, he had hidden her; or hidden
from her. Now he lifted the portrait, and stood
for a long time looking at it. Then, smiling, he
set it back in its place on the writing table,
facing the room.

Facing the bed.

His father's papers, those dry, exquisitely
penned little verses, lay unheeded on the floor.

Four

Come, he hath hid himself among these trees ...
Blind is his love, and best befits the dark.
                            —*Romeo and Juliet,* II, i

The big gates at Ashley Court stood, as always, open.
I went in, soft-footed on the mossed surface of the
avenue, and walked up under the lime trees towards the
bend from which one could see the house.

Evening, and the last of the rich, slanting sunlight
threw the lovely tracery of the gates long-drawn across the
uncut verges. Windflowers and pale blue speedwell sprin-
kled the grass, hazing the green as delicately as a breath
misting glass. Fetlock deep in wild flowers, the lime boles
shone bronze through their feathering of sorrel-coloured
buds. The young leaves overhead, just unfurling, showed
as transparent as stained glass against the light.

I reached the bend in the drive. From here one could
see the house, its walls of rosy Tudor brick reflected
richly in the still glass of the moat. No one was about; no
movement anywhere. I stood in the shadow, looking at
Howard Ashley's home.

For anything so old it was curiously serene. It stood
foursquare on its island, an oddly harmonious hotchpotch
of the centuries' building. The Norman keep still stood,
altered and added to when the main gate with its battle-

ments was built in the twelfth century. The original draw-
bridge had long ago been replaced by the single span of
stone, just wide enough for a car, which now leads into
the small, square courtyard. The Great Door lies opposite
the main gateway, and is Tudor, giving straight onto the
big hall with its vast fireplace and blackened beams. The
rooms to the right of the courtyard are Tudor, too; the
parlour with the priest's hole (reopened in 1880) and the
small dark Council Chamber with its coffered ceiling and
coats of arms. To the east of the main gate stands the
banqueting hall, a fourteenth-century structure with the
mediaeval timbering still intact. I had never known this
used, except to show; it had been damaged in 1962, when
money had been too tight for too long, and the big storm
of mid-September brought the river down in flood and
broke the High Sluice which controls the flow to the moat.
Before the lower sluice could be opened to relieve the
Overflow, and let the water safely into the lake, the cellars
and the low-lying floors of banqueting hall and kitchens
were flooded. My father repaired the High Sluice and
made good the kitchen premises, then dried out the banqueting hall and left it alone. The only good thing, he
had remarked, about the Court's precarious situation between river and lake was that fire insurance premiums
were almost nil. . . .

"Lake" was rather too grand a name for the sheet of
water which lay below the banked-up moat. I forget when
the artificial pool was first dug; to begin with it had been
a stewpond for keeping fish, then later it had been en-
larged and planted with lilies, with a willow or two and
a monstrous grove of gunneras. It was still called Mistress
Nancy's Pool, which sounded better than The Stew, as it
was labelled on the maps. Between moat and Pool was a
grassed bank which Rob, the gardener, kept cut after a
fashion with the Flymo, just as he kept the beech walk and
the main avenue clear and neat-looking. He kept some
sort of order, too, in the walled garden with its two remaining glasshouses. We sold most of the produce, and
this paid Rob's wage and that of the village boy who

helped him. Beyond that there was little that could be done. The rose garden with its mouldering statues was an impenetrable Sleeping Beauty affair, and the woods beyond the Pool had long since engulfed the orchards, with the exception of one stand of apple trees beside the water, where the cottage stood that was now my home.

It was dusk already. As I stood there the sun, imperceptibly, withdrew, and the light cooled to blue and then to shadow. Still nothing had stirred except the two swans, serene on the moat, and the whisper of a rising breeze in the branches. No light showed in the house. I went quickly up the drive for another fifty yards or so to where, on the right, between banks of rhododendrons, the Court's private pathway led to the churchyard.

This had originally been the only way to the church. The lych-gate stood there, and beyond it a tunnel of ancient yews. The lych-gate cast a thick blanket of shadow as I went through, and suddenly, it seemed, day had gone and the evening was here. From overhead came that twilight sound, the rooks settling on their nests, their muttering broken from time to time by the sudden flap of a wing, or a throaty yell as some bird flung upwards, startled, from its perch. Ahead of me the church showed only as a looming shadow against the furred and shifting shadows of the trees. The yews flowed upwards in the breeze like smoke.

I didn't mind the dark. I had trodden every centimeter of this path since I could remember. Someone had mowed the graveyard grass recently, and there was the smell of the sweet cuttings in the air; some of the swaths had fallen and dried on the pathway. I could not hear my own footsteps until I trod on the stone of the church porch and, shifting the crematorium's casket carefully into my left hand, groped for the big iron ring of the south door.

It opened readily. Ashley (it seemed) was still secure from the contagion of the world's slow stain; we had never locked our doors; and please heaven we might never need to. Inside the church it was almost dark. The smells, familiar as childhood, met me as I went in and shut the door behind me; old dusty hassocks, wood gently warping in the scent of the beeswax and turpentine still used by Miss Marget the church cleaner, like her mother and her mother's mother before her. The smell of leftover Easter lilies rather past their best. The smell of hymnbooks and dead candles.

I didn't touch the light switches. I walked slowly up the center aisle towards the faint glimmer of the east window.

I had come tonight with the casket, instead of in the morning when the Vicar expected me, because there was a kind of vigil I wanted to keep first. I would leave the casket overnight in the church where all the Ashleys had been baptized and married and buried, and where my father's memorial stone would stand with the rest; then in the morning—early, early, when there was no one to see—I would come and scatter his dust. So much I had decided for myself, and it seemed right.

But now that I was here, alone in the dark church, there was no more self-deception possible. I had not come just to keep vigil. I had come for something of my own. I wanted, with a queer uncomfortable mixture of longing and guilty hope, to try with all the strange power that I knew I had in me, to see if here, in the place where the Ashleys came from and returned to, I could open my mind to whatever message Jonathan Ashley's maimed brain had tried to send me. *"Tell Bryony. Tell her. . . . My little Bryony be careful. Danger."*

When I was halfway up the chancel, I paused. There were ways and ways of trying to talk with the souls of the dead, and here, I knew suddenly, darkness was wrong, smacking of things which a church should not be asked to house. I would light the sanctuary lights. Feeling somehow absolved of what I meant to do, I took the casket up to the altar steps and laid it there. Some faint residue of light from the east window showed the great jars of lilies, ghosts full of fading scent. These, I knew, would have come from the Court. Rob and the Vicar, between them, grew them each year for Easter. . . . Again, familiar as

the cot blanket of childhood, the place wrapped itself
about me. I stepped back, rehooked the cord across the
chancel rail, and went to the vestry where the switches
were.

This door, too, was unlocked. I pushed it open, fumbled on the wall beside it, found the switch and pressed.
Nothing. I flicked it again. Nothing. Tried the other three
on the board, and with each one, nothing.

All this took only a few seconds, but I suppose my
mind was preoccupied, so I took in, but failed to register,
that the vestry was as airy and as full of tree sounds and
rookery sounds as the churchyard itself. Also, that the
papers on the Vicar's table were lifting in the light breeze.
Even as I noticed them, one or two drifted to the floor.
Simultaneously another movement caught my eye, sending
the blood out of my heart with a contraction as painful as
a blow. The outer door of the vestry stood open, and
against the darkness beyond it, another darkness moved.
A tall figure, robed. Then the door shut with a click of
the Yale lock. The papers subsided with a rustle to the
floor. The only sound was the tick of old wood settling in
the night, and the chime of the clock in the church tower
telling the three-quarters. Only the papers on the floor,
barely seen in the dimness, affirmed the truth of what I
had seen. The open door, the vanishing figure, seemed
no more than the negative of some dream still printed on
the retina as one opens one's eyes from sleep.

I swallowed hard, and willed my heartbeats to slow
down again. A robed figure in a darkened church? Absurd. They had a word for the silly penny-dreadful, didn't
they? Gothic, that was it. Robed nuns and ancient houses
and secret passages, the paraphernalia of melodrama that
Jane Austen had laughed at in *Northanger Abbey,* and
that we had all laughed at when the psychical research people had investigated Rob Granger's specter in this very
church. My specter would, of course, be the same as his;
any robed figure leaving a church vestry and locking it
after him was reasonably likely to be the Vicar. And the
dead switchboard? No doubt Mr. Bryanston thought it

safer to turn off the mains at night. And probably, I thought, as I reached for the main switch bar, which was certainly up, he would come back when he saw the lights go on.

I had left all the switches on, vestry, chancel, altar floods, organ steps. When I pressed the bar down, the whole east end of the church leaped into light. I stood for a moment, listening, but could hear no sound of returning steps. I picked the papers up from the floor, and took a quick look round the vestry. No sign of any other disturbance. I laid the papers on the table, beside a neat pile of books that looked like parish registers, and weighted them with an ink bottle. They were accounts, I noticed; no doubt parish accounts left here for the next council meeting. I waited for a little longer, listening, but there was no sound. I switched out all the lights except the altar floods, then made my way back into the dimness at the west end of the nave, and sat down. The lights bloomed softly on blue carpet and bistered lilies and the gilded heads of the angels that held the hammer-beams. Slowly, the silence settled back like dust.

There are parts of one's life that are, and ought to remain, private. What passed then between me and whatever else was to be spoken with in the dark of All Hallows' Church is my affair. I believe I had had some idea that trying to open my mind's powers here would sanction the act, but the Hallows themselves apparently didn't see it like that. In the way I had known it before, in the way I wanted it now, nothing came; nothing but silence.

Till, just as I got to my feet and started for the vestry to put out the light, the vestry door opened and a robed figure entered the church.

The Vicar. As I had thought, the Vicar, a prosaic figure in his cassock, with his spectacles glinting in the light. It didn't stop me jumping half out of my skin before I registered who it was and went sheepishly to meet him.

"My dear child! It's you! I understood you were coming over in the morning. I saw the light just now when

I went into my study, and came across to see who it was. Did I frighten you?"

"You did give me a start. I'm sorry I dragged you out again, Mr. Bryanston. I hope you don't mind my coming here this evening? I'm coming back in the morning, as I told you, but I—I wanted to leave the casket here overnight. I was going to call and tell you, before I went back to Worcester. Do you mind?"

"Of course not. Come whenever you like, the church is never locked."

He took his spectacles off and began absently to polish them on his cassock sleeve. He was a man comfortably into his middle sixties, with curly grey hair thinning back from a high forehead, a rounded face with the fresh skin of a child, a long upper lip and a habit of looking over his spectacles down the arch of his nose. He had longsighted grey eyes distorted by the thick lenses of his goldrimmed glasses. He had been at Ashley as long as I could remember. He was a widower and, it was hinted, lived a good deal more peacefully since the departure to a better world of his ambitious and lively wife. Mrs. Bryanston had seen Ashley merely as a stepping-stone to preferment and a town living or a place in the Close, and thither, with the relentless efficiency of an earthmover, she would have transferred her gentle husband, who asked nothing better from life than what he found at Ashley and his other parishes of One Ash and Hangman's End. But fifteen years ago he had buried her in the churchyard, and now he would no doubt be a peaceful permanency, plodding happily from church to garden and back again, gently delivering Sunday after Sunday an address from notes on suspiciously yellowed pages, and keeping the whole parish supplied with seedlings grown in the Court gardens, of which he had the run. He and my father had got on very well together; they seldom discussed anything more spiritual than chess, but I had heard Daddy say that Mr. Bryanston's faith was the kind of rock on which any Church could be built. At any rate, the Vicar suited Ashley as well as Ashley suited him.

He was talking now to me, with an ease quite unlike Mr. Emerson's hesitant kindness, about my father's death. Comfort, you might say, was his profession, but he had a way of offering it, not as if it were his daily stock-in-trade, but as if he really cared, not only about my father, which I knew, but about me. To me—as indeed it had been to Daddy—churchgoing had always been so much a part of country life that it was something one never even thought about, as much a part of Sunday's order of the day as the ritual sherry before lunch (which also invariably included the Vicar); the Church's feast days and holy days were ways to chalk the year off on the calendar, so that Michaelmas was the time of bonfire smoke and purple flowers and getting one's woollies out again, and Easter was lilies and spring cleaning, and Lady Day was high time to prune the roses. But now, coming with trouble in my hands, I saw a little of what was behind the sober yearly ritual. There were things one grew away from and, I knew, would never again see one's way to believing, but I listened and felt the better for knowing that the Vicar believed as literally as might be in the resurrection of the dead.

"You said you were going back into Worcester for the night?" he asked finally.

"Yes, but I'll be here again in the morning. I'll come first thing, so that I won't get in anyone's way."

"You won't do that, my dear. Come as early as you wish; you'll want the world to yourself, I have no doubt." He fished a thin old half hunter out of a pocket and peered at it. "Dear me, you've just missed a bus. I shouldn't have kept you so long . . . the next one doesn't go for an hour and a half. Perhaps you'd like to come across to the Vicarage? I don't know what Mrs. Henderson has left for my supper, but no doubt we could stretch it a little."

"That's awfully good of you, but no, thank you, Vicar. I wasn't planning to catch the bus anyway; my Lambretta's at the farm, and I'm going across to get it now. They've got it stored for me in the barn there."

"Ah. Well, take care. The roads get busier every day, and it's dark already. Dear me, and it will soon be summer, will it not? If you see Rob will you tell him that I'll be down in the old orchard tomorrow, not in the greenhouse? I must finish the spraying before it's too late."

"Of course. Well, thank you for everything, Vicar. I'll go out by the south door. If you want to put the main switch off again, don't wait for me. I can see quite well."

"Main switch?" He looked about him vaguely, as if the thing should be to hand. "What do you mean? Why should I put it off?"

"I thought you had, just before I got here. You mean it wasn't you who was in the church when I arrived?"

"Certainly not. I haven't been over here since about three o'clock. When was this?"

"About an hour ago, I suppose. I came in the south door and went up to the vestry to put on the altar lights. The main switch was off, and there was someone just leaving. I didn't see who it was, but I thought it must be you."

He was looking puzzled. "No. It might have been one of the churchwardens, I suppose, but why should he turn the mains off? How very extraordinary. I suppose you're quite sure the main *was* off?"

"Certain. And there's another thing I'm sure of: if it wasn't you in the vestry, then whoever was there didn't want to be seen. I've a feeling he threw the switch when he heard me at the door, to give himself time to get out and away without being recognized. I thought it was you because you're the most likely person, and besides, I think he was wearing something long, like a cassock. You haven't suddenly acquired a curate, have you?"

"No, alas. I suppose it might have been one of the choir men, coming back to pick up something he'd forgotten after service yesterday. . . . But why should he be wearing his cassock, and why turn out the light? It would hardly have mattered if either you or I had seen him."

"I may have been wrong about the robe. It really was only an impression; it was pretty dark. Perhaps it was just one of the churchwardens. He was carrying something— I'm quite sure of that."

"What sort of thing?"

"It's hard to say. A box, perhaps, or it could have been a book, about the size of those registers on the table."

"I can't see any reason why one of the wardens should come for them. They're not the Ashley registers. I only brought them over from One Ash after Evensong yesterday. I promised to do a search for a Canadian who wrote to me about his forebears, but I have not had time to look at them yet. . . . And there again, the main switch, I really cannot see why . . . Dear me, it's beginning to look like a real mystery, isn't it?"

He was looking so worried that I tried quickly to reassure him. "I don't suppose it's anything at all, really. I may easily have been mistaken."

"Let us hope so, my dear, let us hope so. All the same"—turning decisively back to the vestry—"I'd better take a look to see if anything has been touched. The church safe . . . perhaps it could be a temptation. But surely, no one at Ashley . . ."

He paused in the doorway of the vestry and looked carefully about him.

"I had a look round when I put the light on." I spoke from behind him, looking over his shoulder. "It all looked tidy except for those papers, and some of them were on the floor. But that was the draft from the door. I put them back, but you'll probably find them out of order."

"No matter, no matter." He went to the table and glanced through them. "All here. And the registers, too . . . eleven, was it, or twelve? There were some from Hangman's End, as well. I shall have to check them. But really, there is nothing there of interest to anyone. And nothing else even disturbed. The cupboard . . . yes, that's all right. And there was nothing in this drawer but pencils and so on, and there is my spare cassock still hanging by the door, so that was not what you saw. . . ."

He turned finally, with reluctance, to look at the safe. "Well, let us hope not. . . ."

But when he stooped over the big clumsy metal cupboard the look of anxiety deepened. I saw him fingering some scratches near the lock. "These, would you say they look new? It's so hard to tell. Unless something happens like this to make you look closely, you don't notice the marks that your keys make every day. I'm afraid we had better look inside." He reached into his cassock pocket and pulled out a ring of keys.

"I suppose you keep the Communion plate in the safe," I said. "Anything else?"

"Nothing that anyone might want to steal. Only our own registers. And the Communion plate itself is of very little value—though value, as always, is relative. The plate we use now is quite modern, as you probably know; it was your father who suggested that we lodge the old plate in a safer place than this, when the prices went up so steeply, though I doubt if anyone else would have realized how very valuable the old church silver was. Did you know that the chalice and paten were Elizabethan, by John Pikenynge, and the alms dish even rarer? 1534, I believe, with the maker's mark of a basket. The ones we use now, though pleasant enough, are not—Ah," as the safe door swung open, "thank God."

He said it as if he meant it. I was looking over his shoulder. It certainly looked as if nothing had been touched. The back of the safe was stacked with registers, and some baize-wrapped shapes stood in line in front of these. "Exactly as I always put them," said the Vicar, counting. "Yes, yes, all present and correct. He didn't try the safe at all, or else he found the lock too much for him. I prefer to think—I do think—that his visit was an innocent one. Yes, indeed, that is almost certainly so. We live in sad times when one can entertain suspicions on such slender grounds." He shut the safe, locked it, and got to his feet. "However, this is a lesson to me. I cannot bring myself to lock the church, but perhaps I will—yes, I think I must—lock the vestry. And I shall do so straight away. There. Perhaps you'll come out this way after all. . . . Dear me, it's really quite dark now, isn't it? Can you see your way to the farm?"

"Yes, thank you. And don't worry about it, Vicar, I'm sure you'll find it was one of the wardens, or someone quite harmless like that. May I come and see you in the morning? If you're in the apple orchard, I'll see you anyway, when I go to the cottage. I'm moving in tomorrow. I'll give Rob your message."

"Thank you, my dear. God bless you. Good night."

Ashley, 1835

Seeming a long way off, the church clock chimed the three-quarters. He glanced at the gilt carriage clock on the bed table. It was fast. Five minutes.

He fidgeted about the room, fretting like a spurred horse. His foot struck one of his father's books, lying with the papers, where it had fallen. He stooped, and began mechanically to collect the scattered things together. The book, lying spine uppermost, showed the name *Juliet*, glinting in gold. He slapped it shut, and, straightening, stuffed book and papers together in the table drawer, and shut it.

The sound was sharp, final. The old man was dead. His father was dead. He was Ashley now, Nicholas Ashley, Esquire, of the Court. Now, he thought, it will soon be over and done with. If each of us, in our own ways, can find the courage.

But habit made him twitch the curtains closer over the shuttered windows, to hide even a glimpse of the candlelight.

Five

O Lord! I could have stay'd here all the night
To hear good counsel. . . .
—*Romeo and Juliet*, III, iii

The buildings of what had once been a fine home farm lay about a hundred and fifty yards beyond the churchyard. The quickest way to get there from the church was by the lych-gate, and through a corner of the Court gardens. I made my way carefully along the pitch-dark tunnel of the yew walk. I was conscious of my empty hands. The black yews smelled unbearably sad, sharp and smoky; frankincense and myrrh, memory and grief.

I would not think that way. I would not.

> The Yew alone burns lamps of peace
> For them that lie forlorn.

That was the way to think of them. Peace I had had offered to me, and loss was not yet. This was still my home, and it still held what I had come here to find.

I went slowly down the muffled path towards the gate. The shadows of home reached out for me, comforting me, closing me round.

So, at the same moment, in the same shadows, did

my lover. He was here. He was here in the cool night, stronger and closer than at any time since I had left Ashley. Every shade of feeling came, direct as if spoken, strong as the scent of the breeze sieving the yew trees. There was welcome, pleasure, and with it all a kind of apprehension. I paused to identify this, and unbelievingly registered it as guilt, or shame. . . .

I had just reached the lych-gate. The darkness here, cast by the roof, was palpable. I paused, groping before me for the latch of the gate. Guilt or shame? From him? From me he must have been getting a mixture almost as confusing: surprise, questioning, reassurance making it clear that whatever it was, I was with him, and part of it. . . .

My hand, groping in the dark, touched cloth. For one wild, heart-stopping moment I thought he was here, and that I had touched his sleeve. Then through the loose folds I felt the wood of the gate. Some garment or rug had been left there, draped over the top bar. My brain identified it even before my fingers had felt the ribbed silky surface, the weight of the cloth. A cassock. The robe I had seen him wearing, flung down here as he left the churchyard . . . Guilt and shame indeed. The kind of thing he might be feeling if he had recently been in the vestry, trying locks he should not have tried, carrying away things he did not want anyone to see?

What is it? Was it you in the church? I asked the question sharply, but got no reply. The patterns were fading. He was moving away.

At the same moment I heard, close at hand, steps going fast through the graveyard grass, away from me. He must have been standing all this while, motionless, on the other side of the wall of yew.

Lover? Lover!

He ignored me. The steps quickened. I heard the faint *ping* and thrill of the wire that crossed a gap in the broken wall between the churchyard and the Court gardens. Beyond the gap was the tangle of a neglected shrubbery, and a door into the old, high-walled garden where the glasshouses were. And now, faintly behind the black of the trees, I saw the light slacken into silver. The moon was rising. In a moment she would be above the trees, and there would be light enough to see.

Near me was a gap between the yews. I thrust through it, and ran across the grave-humped grass. I knew every tombstone, and its name, as well as I knew the books in the schoolroom shelves. The dead would not mind my step; we had known each other a long time. I reached the gap in the wall just as the moon showed enough to send a gleam along the wire. I laid a hand to it; it was humming still. I clambered through into the whippy undergrowth of the shrubbery. Elderberry and ash saplings, raspberry canes gone wild, ivy trailing snares along the ground, and somewhere the peppery sweetness of lad's-love. Nettles, too, knee high. I swore under my breath, and plunged forward onto the trodden twist of moss that was the path to the walled garden. The gate in the high wall stood ajar, and there was moonlight on the apple trees beyond. I ran through, and paused at the head of the shallow, slippery steps.

Across the center of the garden, from east gate to west, ran a wide avenue of apple trees, espaliered with stretched arms like stiff ranks holding hands. The moon, sailing as swiftly as a galleon with a fair breeze, cleared a beech tree to light the ranked blossoms, and between them the empty pathway hatched with their shadows. Nothing moved, except the boughs of the high trees beyond the wall, shifting in the light wind and sending dark and glitter flying across the glasshouse roofs.

Then I saw him, for the second time that night, still no more than a tall shadow melting into the other shadows. He, too, had paused. He was standing in the shelter of the far gate. Beyond him lay the old rose garden, and then the maze, and the apple orchard where my cottage stood, and the water meadows beyond the Pool, where the field path led to the village.

I hesitated. He must know who was pursuing him. If he wanted me, he had only to wait for me. In fact—I realized it now—he *had* waited for me. I had been a long time in the church. He could not have failed to catch my response to him, back there at the lych-gate, and now, standing as I was full in the moonlight, he must see me and know I had followed him.

He was looking, I was certain of it. I heard the creak of the gate opening in the far wall, and then the pause. I stood getting my breath and trying to open my mind to reach him again. But nothing came except that muddled mixture of exhilaration and amazement and guilt. I wondered again, but this time wholly without blame, what he had been doing in the church. Whatever it was, I was with him; I had to be. I sent him all I had of love, and need and longing, and got the answer, more clearly even than the wind across the trees. *Not yet. Trust me. Not yet.* There was another creak as the garden gate shut fast. The latch dropped. I was alone in the garden.

I trudged back the way I had come, and, regaining the churchyard, went by the normal route to the farm.

The darkness hid the dilapidation of the big farmyard. Barns and sheds lay on the left, and on the other side the chimney stacks of the farmhouse stood up into the moonlight. The house had been empty ever since the farmlands, which were not part of the trust, were sold. The farmer who had bought the land had not found it worth his while to repair the house, which had stood empty now for years; it was used as a storehouse and even, occasionally, to house young stock. The hens roosted there, and pigeons nested in the attics. Adjoining it, and in heartening contrast, were the two farm cottages, which still belonged to Ashley. These showed whitewashed walls reflecting the moonlight, and brightly lit windows with gay curtains.

In the cottage nearest to the farmhouse the Hendersons lived; Mr. Henderson, a man well into his sixties, was sexton and gravedigger to Ashley and One Ash; his wife "did for" the Vicar, and obliged at the Court when asked. She also cleaned and mended for Rob Granger, who lived in the other cottage. When I was a child the Grangers had lived at the big farmhouse, but a couple of years after Mr. Granger's death, when the farm was sold, Rob and his mother moved into the cottage. Mrs. Granger herself had died not long after, and now Rob lived alone.

As I crossed the yard the door of his cottage opened, and he peered out, silhouetted against the light.

"That you, Miss Bryony?"

"Oh, Rob, hullo! How nice to see you again. Yes, it's me. How did you guess?"

"Well, I reckoned you'd be coming across for the bike. I knew you were here. I saw you come out of the church. You went after him, did you?"

I stopped dead. "You were there? Do you mean to tell me you saw him?"

"I did. Quick as a hare out of the vestry door and behind the yew walk. He stood there the best part of an hour."

"You actually *watched* him?"

"Aye, I did."

"And you didn't ask him what he was doing?"

"I didn't rightly like to, seeing who it was."

There was a pause of seconds. At the moment when it would have been remarkable, I asked: "Well, who was it?"

He looked surprised. "You didn't talk to him, then? I made sure he was waiting for you."

"Apparently not. Who was it?"

Something, in spite of me, must have come through my voice. He said quickly: "You've no call to worry. It was only your cousin. One of them, that is. I couldn't tell for sure, not in that light, or lack of it. But an Ashley; I couldn't mistake that."

"Then why did you stay to watch him?"

"I don't rightly know." He showed no resentment at

the rather sharp question. "The way he came running out of the vestry . . . I didn't recognize him at first, so I went up, careful, under the bushes by the wall, where I could see. I saw the church lights go on then, for a minute, and I saw it was one of the Ashleys. I guessed that it might be you in the church. Then the main lights went off again, but you didn't come out."

"No," I said. "I—I wanted the dark."

"I guessed that. And I think he did, too. He stayed there, waiting for you."

I said nothing. I was fighting back disappointment so acute that I was afraid he would notice it. I stood looking down, uncertain what to say next. I had quite forgotten my errand to the farm.

"Won't you come in?" said Rob. "No sense in standing out in the yard. Come in now, do."

He stood back in the doorway to let me through. I went into the kitchen where, it was obvious, he had just been about to cook his supper. There was a place set for one at the table, and beside the stove were a pack of sausages and some tomatoes, with a packet of peas defrosting in the warmth.

I checked. "I'm afraid I've come at a bad time."

He went past me and threw a couple of billets of wood on the fire, then hooked a foot round the leg of a chair and hitched it forward.

"You haven't at all. I've got your bike here for you; it's not in the barn; I brought it into the scullery. And I got a can of petrol for it. It'll not take a minute to fill up and get it ready. But look, why don't you stay a bit first? I was just making a bite of supper, and you're welcome to have some. There's plenty. It's only sausages, dead easy if it suits you."

Since I had obviously interrupted his cooking, and just as obviously he wanted his meal before he started getting the bike ready for me, I accepted. "I'd love that. Look, I'll cook while you set for me, shall I?"

"O.K. Want some chips with it?"

"Yes, please."

Mrs. Henderson had left her apron hanging behind the door. I put it on, and busied myself at the stove. I got the grill going, and laid the sausages and tomatoes to cook while Rob took things from drawers and cupboards, and, neat-handed as a sailor for all his size, laid the extra place and sliced some bread and tipped another helping of frozen chips into the frying basket. There was no question of looking out the best china for Miss Bryony; I had been an intimate of the Granger household all my life, and had taken things just as they came. Fish and chips straight from the newspaper, and yellow shop cakes with marsh-mallow cream, had been the "tea at Mrs. Granger's" treat of my childhood. I watched Rob set the knife and fork and find an extra plate to heat, and I felt the blackness of the yew walk, the loss and disappointment, recede from sight. Here, with the bright fire and the tick of the cheap alarm clock, the hiss of frying chips and the smell of sausages, was yet another welcome that Ashley was hold-ing out to me. This, too, was home.

Rob glanced up and caught the tail end of the look, but gave no sign that he understood it. He was a tall young man, big-boned, with big hands and feet and the decep-tively slow movements of the countryman. He was very dark, brown as a gipsy, with black hair, and eyes so dark that it was hard to tell iris from pupil, and harder still to read the expression in them. His speech, too, was slow, but the soft country voice and his habit of silent pauses masked a fair intelligence which should have had a better chance to develop. His mother had been the village school-teacher, a gentle, lonely girl who had fallen for good looks and what she thought of as simple ways, and had married Matt Granger, a handsome lout who first of all neglected, and then frankly ill-used her and her child. I myself as a child had never realized why little Robbie, as he was called then, had sometimes stayed off school, or some-times come with bruises as if he had been fighting. But when Matt Granger tumbled drunk into the Overflow one night and was drowned, Rob took on his father's job of running the home farm with no emotion apparent other than deep satisfaction and relief; and though she said nothing at all, Mrs. Granger, quiet as ever, seemed happier. She died some two years later of a neglected cancer, soon after Rob, for all his struggles, had had to admit defeat over the farm, which his father had run into the ground and deep into debt. My father, having sold the land, invited Rob to stay on as caretaker and man-of-all-work around the Court. It was something of a surprise to everyone when Rob, who understandably enough had never been devoted to Ashley, and who might have done better for himself elsewhere, accepted and stayed.

He came to my elbow, watching as I turned the sausages under the grill. "Shall I do those now?"

"It's all right. Nearly done."

"I'm sorry about your dad."

"Thank you. I brought his ashes home, did you know? That's why I came tonight. I wanted to put them in the church. Did the Vicar tell you?"

"No."

"I'm coming back in the morning to—well, to scatter them."

He had lifted the pan of peas off the stove, and was busy draining them. He added a knob of margarine and shook them to dry in the hot pan. He said nothing.

"Rob—"

"Mm?"

"You're sure you couldn't even make a guess?"

He must after all have sensed my trouble, back there in the yard. He didn't ask me what I was referring to, nor did he lift his eyes from the peas. He shook the pan thoughtfully. "If I had to, I'd have said it was one of the twins, but you know yourself they're bad enough to tell apart in daylight, let alone a black evening like this."

"Could it have been Francis?"

"Might have been, I suppose. But I'd have thought he was a mite too tall for Francis."

"But it could have been?"

He did look up at that. "I suppose so. Why, were you expecting Francis?"

"No. But if it wasn't Francis, it would have to be Emory, and—"

I stopped. I had never taken it further, even to myself, and I certainly could not do so to Rob. It could not be Emory, the secret friend with whom I had shared my thoughts since childhood. It could not. If it had to be one of those two, it must surely be Francis . . . Francis, who was nearer my own age, and of whom—where one could touch that elusive and self-contained personality—I was unequivocally fond. Emory, the eldest of the three, was, as they say, something else again. I had never had any illusions about Emory. As a child, of course, I had adored my tall cousin, so easily dominating the rest of us, but generous about allowing a small girl to tag along where he led the Ashley gang. He had grown into a tough-minded man, determined, and quietly self-sufficient. James, his twin, had a touch of the same ruthlessness, but tempered with something less aggressive. Francis, as tough in his own way and very much quieter about it, had opted out of most of our ploys and gone doggedly on with his own affairs. A loner, my cousin Francis. But then, I supposed, that was what writers had to be. And surely, if it were he, I would have had a hint of it from him . . . ?

Francis or Emory . . . But, in spite of the knowledge, I found myself thinking about James as I had last seen him.

An Ashley to the fine bone; tall, with fair hair which had darkened slightly—to his relief—as he grew older. The long grey eyes of all the portraits, straight nose, hands and feet too small-boned but well shaped. Pleasant voice. A way of doing what he wanted, and doing it so charmingly that you overlooked the self-interest and thought he was doing you a favour. Clever, yes; shrewd, yes; not perhaps over-imaginative about other people's needs, but kind, and capable of great generosity. About his attitude to women, or his relationships with them, I knew nothing.

I had my mother to thank that I was able to be so objective about my father's family. She had been a highly intelligent, incisive woman, who had written a couple of novels that had dropped dead on the market, but that had contained a good deal of quiet but acid observation of the people around her. It was she who had taught me to stand back sometimes from life and look at it, even to stand back from those I loved.

Certainly from those I thought I might love. Which brought me back to my troubled thoughts, and the cottage kitchen, and Rob saying: "Why should it?"

"Why should it what?"

"Be Emory?"

I must have looked quite blank. He said patiently: "In the churchyard."

"Oh. Because James is in Spain, and Emory's over here. He rang up from England on Wednesday, when I was in Bavaria. Look, Rob, the chips are done, can you strain them?"

"Sure." He lifted the pan over to the draining board. "Well, then, say it was Emory. Seems funny he didn't want to see you."

"Maybe. Rob, you said you saw him coming out of the vestry. Did you see when he went in?"

"No. I was down shutting up the greenhouses, you see, and when I came back I heard the dogs barking, so I took a look around, and I saw the vestry door was standing open. I didn't think it could be the Vicar—for one thing the dogs wouldn't bark for him; then I saw whoever it was was using a flashlight, so I waited to see him. I thought it might be some of the village boys out for a lark. Then I saw you going into the porch." He grinned. "Say this for you, Bryony, you don't make more noise than a bitch fox. Remember when I used to take you poaching? I never heard you till you came right up to the church door."

"Then?"

"I'd half a mind to follow you in, in case there was something wrong, but then the flashlight went out and I saw this chap coming out of the vestry, sharpish, and bolting away across the graveyard. I'd have followed him, only I saw it was one of the Ashleys. And he didn't run far; stopped right by the yew trees, and waited. I reckoned he was waiting for you. He was out of sight of me there, but I'd have seen him if he'd moved. I hung around and watched, just in case. . . . Then the Vicar came down, and went into the vestry, but the chap didn't budge. Did he see you, do you suppose?"

"I think so. If not then, he must have seen me later in the kitchen garden. The moon was quite bright."

I spoke flatly, with my back to him, but I felt him pause. Then he said: "Well, when he bolted across the wire I came home. It was no business of mine, and he didn't mean you harm, that was obvious. What was he at in the vestry, do you think? It seems funny, bolting away like that when he must have known it was only you."

"Yes, doesn't it?"

"There's another queer thing, he had a long coat on or something. Does Emory wear a cloak? Someone told me they were all the fashion now in London."

"I don't think so." I hesitated. "Actually, Rob, he'd taken a cassock from the church. It must have been one of the choir men's—the Vicar's spare one was still there. He must have snatched it up when he heard me. Don't ask me why, I've no idea. He left it under the lych-gate."

"Funny thing to do."

"You're telling me. Did you see what he was carrying?"

"No," he said. "Look, those sausages are done."

"So they are. Can you eat four? Not too many chips for me, thanks. Oh, before I forget, the Vicar told me to tell you he won't be in the greenhouses tomorrow, he's going down to the old orchard. What are you doing down there?"

"Spraying the trees, and tidying up a bit. Things that

should have got done this winter past, but there wasn't time, with all Mr. Underhill wanted doing about the house. But now, with you coming back . . . are you coming to the cottage?"

"I think I might, for a bit anyway."

"Moving in tomorrow?"

"Yes. I thought I might see Mrs. Henderson and ask her to get things aired for me."

"You don't need to bother. It's done." He grinned at my look. "We thought you'd be back soon, and when the Vicar told us you were coming over tomorrow we got the cottage opened up. So you can settle straight in any-time you like."

For some absurd reason I felt the tears sting suddenly behind my eyes. He could not have seen, because I had my back turned to him still, but he said, just behind me: "You've given me too many sausages. Divide them properly. The kettle's boiling; will you have tea or coffee?"

"Coffee, please. I only want two sausages, honestly. Are they from Roper's? Their sausages were always the best."

"Aye." He spooned Nescafé from the jar and made two cups. "Remember the sausage rolls we used to get at Goode's stall on a Saturday?"

"Do I not! Here, then, let's start."

Over the meal we talked easily, he of the Court and the Underhills, and of his girl who belonged to Ashley and whom he meant to marry before the year was out; I of Madeira and Bavaria and then, irresistibly unloading it all, of the accident, and the puzzle of my father's final message.

"Rob, does the phrase 'William's brook' mean anything to you?"

"William's what?"

"I think it was 'William's brook.' "

He shook his head. "Uh-uh. Never heard of it that I can remember."

"Could it be the Overflow?"

"I never heard it called anything else but that, did you?"

"No. I only asked because I'd wondered if Daddy meant you when he said, 'Perhaps the boy knows.'" I sighed a little and pushed my plate away. "That was fine. Thanks very much, Rob."

"You're welcome." He got up and began stacking the plates. "Shall I fix your bike for you now?"

"If you would. I'll wash up while you do it."

"O.K." Then, easily: "Where are you putting your dad's ashes? In the enclosure?"

He might have been saying something about the washing up. I found it oddly comforting. Family talk; as familiar as with my own cousins, and without the constraints that I had, for obvious reasons, felt there sometimes.

"No, he didn't want that. Too much like putting fences round him, he said." The enclosure was the Ashley grave plot, where, within the iron railings, the family had lain since the Giles Ashley who had died in 1647. "He said he'd had enough of that when he was a prisoner of war; he wanted the open air. So I'll be coming back in the morning, very early, before there's anyone about."

"I'll be about, very likely, but I'll not disturb you. If you want breakfast when you've done, I'll be frying up at about seven o'clock. You can go down to the cottage after. I'll take your things along. Suit you?"

"Suits me."

He disappeared whistling towards the scullery, and I began to carry the dishes over to the sink.

Ashley, 1835

Surely she was not often as late as this?

The sane part of him insisted that she was. There had been nights when she had been prevented from coming at all, and he had waited all night long in this fret and torment, raw with longing, only to rant and curse at her when, the next night, braving who knew what rough perils from her family and the village see-alls, she came again.

He spared a thought for her, hurrying to him through the windy dark, wrapped in her old cloak, the maze key clutched in her hand. "The key to heaven," she had called it, and he had not laughed at her for the phrase as he might have done, my God, yes, even a month ago. He had had to bite his lips to stop himself saying, "The key to my heart."

That had been when he first knew for sure. She was the one. Of all of them, she was the one.

Six

With tears augmenting the fresh morning's dew. . . .

—*Romeo and Juliet,* I, i

Five o'clock in the morning. England in May. The time they always used to sing about. And well they might, I thought, buzzing along the country roads on the Lambretta with the early sun brilliant on the wet hedgerows, and the meadow grasses furred with dew as thick as hoarfrost. Heaven knew when last I had been out so early; I had forgotten the light, the sweetness of the air, the newly washed smell of everything, the fat lambs' calling, the thrushes going wild in the hawthorns. Forgotten the hawthorns themselves, frothing with maybloom along the road, with cowslips and cuckooflowers almost hiding the hedge bottoms. Forgotten the cuckoo, shouting in the echoing distance. Forgotten, even, the other preoccupation that went with me.

But here he was, crowding me. *Hullo,* I said, but gaily, without anxiety. *Shall I see you today? Shall I see you today?*

I wouldn't be surprised, said he, and the doors slowly closed between us like a cloud drawing over the sun.

There was no sign of life from the Court. Curtains hung close over the windows. On the moat the swans sailed

72

with their six grey young, and a blue heron fished busily for roach. The air was pure and very still.

I took an hour, alone in the great neglected gardens. The swans cruised unheeding, the heron fished on. The rabbits in the orchard sat bolt upright to watch me, their fur outlined with light and their pricked ears as transparent as shells. The beautiful old house dreamed above its reflection, rose-red brick and glittering windows mirrored in the still moat, and moving faintly in the wake of the swans. Not mine, I thought; never mine again. All that had vanished, blown away on the sweet morning air with Jon Ashley's dust. *Hic manet.* Here lies he where he longed to be. And where shall I lie? Shall I be brought back here one day, to become, however insubstantially, part of this garden and this glimmering air? And who will bring me?

I walked for an hour, but nothing spoke and no one came.

There were bacon and eggs for breakfast, and fresh bread baked by Mrs. Henderson. Sunshine poured into the cottage kitchen. Last night's fire had been cleaned out and relaid, and the room was neat as a ship's galley.

"You do yourself well," I told Rob Granger. "She'll be lucky. Do I know her, by the way?"

"I doubt it. She's a kind of cousin; used to live near Ashley Village, but her folks moved away. She'll be back soon, then we'll be making plans."

"Well," I said, "tell her from me that she's on to a good thing."

He grinned, and said, "Oh, she knows," and cut a couple of slices off the loaf. "Honey?"

"Thanks." And not just with the cooking, I thought, as I spread honey on the lovely, crusty bread. There was something solidly dependable about him, a kind of inbuilt strength; the sense that day-to-day frets would pass him by like the rain driving against a tree. Not a man to hurry; he looked, and was (as I remembered from childhood squabbles), as obstinate as a mule, and apparently as set

in his ways as a plough horse that knows no other job.
His ease of manner with me came from long acquaintance,
but it came also from a self-confidence that was part of
him; not the kind of confidence that was bred into my
elegant Ashley cousins, but something hacked out of a
hard life, as a fluid line of sculpture is in time hacked out
of hardstone. Yes, she would be lucky; it was to be hoped,
for my cousins' sake, that she would be content to stay at
Ashley, and not persuade Rob to leave.

I said something of the sort, but he merely made a
noncommittal sound through a mouthful of bread and
honey, then said, as soon as he could: "It'll be strange,
with Mr. Howard here. I can't imagine it, somehow. Will
you stay, yourself?"

"I don't know. I suppose I shall, for the time being.
I really haven't got round to deciding anything yet."

"Mm. I dare say there's no hurry. These things always
take a long time to settle, and the way the Court's tied
up, it could take years."

"Is that supposed to be comforting?"

"It comforts me," said Rob. "Give everyone time to
get used to the idea. It won't seem the same without Mr.
Ashley . . . and without you."

He spoke so simply that I took it straight, as a fact and
not a compliment. "It comforts me, too. I somehow can't
take it all in. Not quite yet."

"Well," he said, "don't try. There's plenty of time. And
maybe Mr. Howard won't want to come here at all." He
grinned. "Mind you, everyone in the village is wild to see
his wife. I don't know what they think a Mexican is like,
but I know Miss Marget was talking about totem poles,
and Mrs. Henderson told me that Mrs. Gray—you know,
the head of the Mothers' Union—made a speech last week
about race relations and the colour bar. Very broad-
minded, she was, I believe."

I laughed. "Actually, she's pure Spanish, and from her
photos, rather gorgeous. But I must admit I can't quite
see her—either of them—settling here."

"Then it'll be Emory's? Seems funny, doesn't it," said

Rob slowly, "that James loses all that by about twenty or thirty minutes? Must be queer to be a twin."

"Very, I should think. But I don't know if James counts it as 'losing.' There's no money here, Rob. The place is lovely, but very soon now there'll be a time when no one can keep it."

"So I reckon. But wouldn't you have thought the National Trust, or someone like that, would have taken it on? I mean, a place like this, that historians and such go wild about . . . ?"

"The National Trust won't take any property over unless it's endowed, and how would we manage that? I know Daddy tried everything and everybody. I think in the long run that someone—some body like the Pilgrim Trust, or even the Department of the Environment—would step in to preserve the house, but I doubt if they'd ever bother with the gardens and the land. That's bound to go, history or no history."

"Well," he said, "don't get me wrong, but it looks to me as if you'll be thankful yet that it's not your headache."

"I'm sure you're right. To start with, it'll be Mr. Emerson's, poor man. He'll have to sort out all the legal tangles —what he calls the dead man's hand."

"Dead man's hand?" Rob looked faintly shocked, and I paused in surprise, then realized that he must think the lawyer was referring to my father.

"I only meant the trust. . . . You seemed to know how the place was tied up? He meant my umpteenth great-grandfather, the one who created the trust, reaching from the grave to make things awkward for all of us."

"Oh, aye, I get it. Your dad did talk about it once. You all have to consent before you can sell anything, isn't that it?" He pondered it for a minute. "Could be awkward, yes, but he meant well, and it seems to me he's maybe made things a mite safer for you, the way it's turned out. I mean, they can't sell your cottage over your head, even if they want to."

"They couldn't anyway," I told him. "All the bit they call the 'cottage strip'—the old orchard, and the strip of land along the Pool as far as the One Ash road—none of that's included in the trust. It was all Daddy could leave me, but it's mine."

He was looking very thoughtful. "If they did want to break the trust, and sell the rest up, would you consent to it?"

"That would depend. We might have to sell the land, to endow the house. I know that Daddy had that on his mind. But I'm not quite sure what it would mean to you, for instance, and to the Hendersons. We didn't get as far as discussing that." I looked at him. "If the trust were broken, Rob, what would happen to you? Would you be able to buy this house for yourself?"

"I don't think so, but then I mightn't want to stay. You don't need to bother yourself about that. You've enough to think about for yourself." He straightened in his chair. "Anyway, this isn't just the morning to talk about the future. I shouldn't have asked you about your plans; I'm sorry. But, you know, once all this, your dad and everything—once it's gone a bit into the background, and once you've found out what he wanted you to find out, it'll all settle itself. It'll work out, believe me it will. Only, you've got to let it take its time."

I nodded, and finished my tea, soothed by his country common-sense. Time; there was always time in the country. Leave things to themselves, and they grew, and ripened, and were cut down, all in the right seasons. Now, it seemed, was the fallow time. "Well," I said, "we'll give it a chance to work out. I'm certainly in no fit state of mind to make decisions. I've got to get all the complicated legal stuff settled first, and by the time the mills of God have ground all the facts to a powder I'll have sorted myself out, too—or perhaps it'll be decided for me. But there is something I can do straight away. I can have a look for the paper my father spoke of, and try to find out what he meant; if there's something he wants me to do. I'll have to get into the Court to do that. I've got my own key to the east door, but I expect all the rooms are locked on the public side, aren't they? I don't want to explain myself to the Underhills yet. I suppose you've no idea who has the main house keys?"

"Yes," said Rob. "I have."

As easy as that. *"You* have?"

He nodded. "Your dad gave them to me before he went to Germany. Didn't you know? Mr. Underhill's got the other set, all the public rooms as well as their own; they have to have them because of fire, and because of the quarter-pounders"—this was our private name for the tourists who paid twenty-five pence each—"but your dad told me he'd given the private keys off that set to Mr. Emerson. He left his own lot with me."

"Well!" I said with relief. "There's an end to *that* mystery! You've no idea what mayhem Mr. Emerson and I were picturing! I've a feeling he suspected they'd been stolen from Daddy when he was knocked down. Apparently I'm allowed to keep them, officially, till all the legal business is settled."

"You'd better have them now." While I had been speaking he had pulled open a drawer in the dresser, and fished out from somewhere a bunch of keys which I recognized. "Here you are, then. Do you know which is which? They go in order, from here. That's the main door, then the Priest's Parlour, the Council Chamber . . ." He clicked the keys round on the massive ring, like beads on a rosary. "They're in order for the tour. Was there any room you wanted specially?"

"Yes, the library."

He selected a key. "That's it. No, leave those things. Mrs. Henderson will do them. Would you like me to go in with you this morning?"

"No, I don't think so, thanks. I've been thinking, Rob; there'll be quarter-pounders going round today, won't there? If I go in on my own, with keys, someone's sure to see me, and ask questions. I'll leave the keys with you for now, and I'll go round with the tour myself, and just take a look in general, then later on I'll introduce myself to the Underhills, and ask them if I can come and go in the house as I want. What time's the first tour?"

"Half past ten." He dropped the keys back in the drawer, and shut it. No question or comment. "Stay here till then if you like. Or do you want to go down to the cottage this morning?"

"Yes, I'll do that."

"That'll be Mrs. Henderson at the back door now. She'll want a word with you, I dare say. See you later." He smiled and went out.

Mrs. Henderson was small, brisk, and sixtyish, with greying hair "done" each week as unyieldingly and unvaryingly as a metal helmet by "our Eileen" who was the village hairdresser. She had vivid blue eyes and a high patch of colour on each cheek, and was as efficient, as quick, and about as silent as a computer in full schedule.

"Well, now, Miss Bryony, it's nice to see you back again, though I'm sorry about your poor dad, I was just saying to the Vicar last week, for all Mr. Ashley's had to go off to that hospital in Germany he didn't look all that ill to me and mark my words, I said, he'll be back here with us sooner than he thinks, but believe you me, Miss Bryony, I never thought my words would come to pass this way, nor that when I saw you back with us it would be just to pass on yourself. And when I say pass on, you know I don't mean what it might look as if I mean, I just mean that everyone knows now that the Court will have to go to Mr. Howard, though folk are wondering, and I know you'll not take it amiss, Miss Bryony, whether Mr. Howard's wife will take to it here, I mean, I'm the last person to have any prejudices at all, and nowadays you daren't even talk about nigger brown any more, dare you, but coloured is coloured, and she'll have been brought up different to us as like as not, not to mention religion, and that's another thing, coming from where she does she'll be a Catholic, I dare say, and whether Mr. Howard's turned or not, the children will, won't they, and what's the Vicar to do with the church and the living and all, and very funny it would look, wouldn't it, if the next Ashleys had to go all the way to the Catholic church at Hangman's End?"

While she was talking she had taken her apron down and put it on, helped me finish clearing the breakfast things, stacked them, run hot water into the sink, and started to wash up. I found the tea towel and wiped, letting the monologue run over me as I had let it run over me every time I met Mrs. Henderson, even after an absence of less than twenty-four hours. Sooner or later she ran down and stopped for breath, and then from long practice I was adept at picking out the one topic which I might want to pursue; or rather, at ignoring the dozen or so topics I wanted to avoid. I spared a thought for the Vicar and Rob Granger; how, each day, did they cope with this? Then I realized I had seen the answer: the Vicar went down to the greenhouses, and Rob, when she arrived, smiled sweetly and left by the other door.

"Mr. Howard's wife is not coloured," I said, "she's Spanish. And if you remember the portrait on the stairs, we've had a Spanish lady here before, and it seemed to work. I'm told Mrs. Howard's very beautiful, and she probably is an R.C., but I doubt very much if they'll come to Ashley. Have you seen my cousin Emory lately? Or Francis?"

But Mrs. Henderson was just as good as I was at fixing on the topics she wanted. "Now you come to mention it, of course I knew about the Spanish lady. There was that song about her, wasn't there? But that was in the days when everybody was Catholics, anyway, so it didn't matter. The Vicar told me. And now I come to think about it it wouldn't be her children that came to Ashley Court, it's Mr. Howard's own. And when I say 'own,' of course I mean—"

"Yes, of course. The twins and Francis. Have any of them been here recently?"

"And of course if Mr. Howard doesn't come back," said Mrs. Henderson, with obvious regret for a rich source of gossip slipping from her grasp, "then it'll be Mr. Emory and his wife, and a very nice girl she is, and everyone says the same, though a bit young for it—"

"What wife?"

"Not for marriage, I don't mean, because nowadays they're ready and willing for anything before they're turned fifteen, though I can't see myself that marriage and a family brings you much except a load of housework and cooking, but they will do it, and I suppose it's nature's way—"

"What wife?"

"What's that, Miss Bryony?"

"I said what wife? You said Mr. Emory and his wife. Is he married?"

She had certainly captured all my attention at last. She shot me a glance of triumph, turned on the hot tap, and held a jug under it to rinse, taking her time. "Well, not yet, but take it from me, it's only a matter of time. It's that Miss Underhill, Cathy her name is. Didn't Rob say?"

"No."

"If that isn't just like a man. They never take a blind bit of notice of anything that goes on under their noses, more interested in the football pools and the tomatoes down in those greenhouses than in what's happening right here in our village. Now, that's the dishes done. Don't you bother any more, I'll put them away. You don't know where they go."

"Of course I do. I'll do them. So my cousin Emory's been going out with the Underhill girl? Are they actually engaged?"

She wrung out her dishcloth and draped it over the edge of the draining board, then fished below the sink, brought up a red plastic bucket, and began to fill it with hot water. "I don't know about engaged, they don't call it that now, do they? They go with someone, or they have a steady, or they have a thing going, or they have it off with someone, if I've got that right—"

"I don't think you have, quite, but never mind, I know what you mean. How long has this been going on, and do you really think it's serious?"

"Knowing Mr. Emory, I'd say it was." She turned off the taps and for the first time stopped working and stood looking at me, the bright blue eyes shrewd and quite serious. "You know him, he was always one that knew his own mind and went straight for what he wanted, and pity help anything that stood in his way. Nice about it, oh, yes, of course, being an Ashley, but he gets what he wants."

The smiler with the knife under the cloak. Yes, we could do you down and smile at you with great charm while we did it. It was a useful talent, I supposed. At any rate it had got the Ashleys where they were, and kept them there for a few hundred years. I said: "Is she pretty? Tell me all about her."

She told me, but I wasn't listening. I would meet Cathy Underhill soon enough. I was thinking about my cousin Emory, that determined and clever man. Whatever he wanted to do, he would succeed in. Now, it appeared, he wanted the Underhill girl. If he had picked her and was serious about her, he must count her fortune just as a bonus; he had plenty himself, even though the business in Bristol (which had been very much Emory's pigeon for years) hardly put him in the Underhill bracket. "Never marry money, but go where money is." It was like Emory's hard good sense—the steel-hard Ashley wish for continuity—to marry an asset; and if he was fond of her it was the affection, and not the fortune, that was the bonus.

I was also thinking about my lover. Where did this leave us? And why, for heaven's sake why, could he not be as open with me as I was with him? I was rapidly, I thought, having more than enough of mystery.

Trust me. It came suddenly, clear and close.

Oh, you were reading me, were you? Well, you'll know what I think about you. Where are you?

Not far. It was fading. *Not far.*

Where, though? Here at Ashley?

The faintest quiver of amusement came through, mischief, but with a touch of comfort, like a pat on the shoulder which tells you to relax and it will be all right soon . . .

". . . Going down to the cottage this morning?" Mrs. Henderson was asking.

"Yes. Rob tells me you've opened it up for me already. It's marvellous of you, Mrs. Henderson. Do you mean I can move straight in?"

"Yes, indeed you can. It's all aired and clean, and if it's a matter of stores, groceries and such, I put what I thought you'd need for a start, and there's a list on the kitchen table, and you can pay me when you feel like it. And when I pop down to the village this morning, as I shall have to do, the Vicar being out of butter and self-raising, I'll call at the farm and tell the milk to come, and if I let Miss Marget at the Post Office know, then you'll be settled in in no time, and very nice it'll be. And the meat comes Tuesdays and Fridays, you'll remember that. I can take any orders you want up at the Vicarage, and pop them down to you—"

I left eventually, overwhelmed with kindness and offers of every sort of help under the sun, and made my way down to the cottage.

The Vicar was in the orchard, spraying the apple trees with fervour and a lavish hand. I could hear him talking busily, but then I saw Rob's dark head some distance off on the far side of a hedge, and realized that the latter could not hear a word. Nor was he meant to. The Vicar was talking to the apple trees. Rob's dog lay near him, head cocked and deeply interested, but when he saw me he got up and came over, tail waving. Neither the Vicar nor Rob seemed to notice me as I crossed the orchard and pushed open the wicket which gave on the cottage garden.

The first thing that struck me was the tidiness. If I had thought about it at all I would have expected the cottage garden to match the outlying parts of the Court gardens for enforced neglect, but this garden was a small marvel of neatness. The two plum trees were pruned and well shaped and budding fatly; the Fribourg rose around the window had been carefully trimmed, and the clematis was a cloud of blossom as high as the roof; the rows of rasp-berries were as regular as guardsmen, the strawberries were already strawed, and the plots to either side of the path were hoed and raked and planted within an inch of their lives. The path where I stood was clear of weeds, and thickly edged with chives and parsley. The brimming rain barrel below the gutter was painted the same new green as the door, and had a fresh metal ring. The step was clean, and the door open.

Inside was the same; Mrs. Henderson had put all to rights, and it was charming and neat, with a pot of pink geraniums in the window, and the fresh smell of polish everywhere. The box of groceries stood on the kitchen table. Upstairs, I knew, all would be ready for me. I had only to pay my bill at the Hog and Oak, get my things brought over here, and walk in.

Which was no reason why, leaning my elbows on the sill of the dormer window that looked from the bedroom eaves out over the apple trees, I should find myself, for the first time since my father's death, crying helplessly as if there was neither love nor hope left in the world.

Ashley, 1835

My God, he thought. I've forgotten the list. My father was right to rave at me for a vicious libertine. It had seemed amusing, once, to keep a list of them, like the stable books; physical marks, breeding, performance, staying power ...

And her name on it, too.

I'll burn the list. Not even read it again. I'll burn the books, too, all of them. No more light-o'-loves. She is the last, I promise it. Only let her come tonight.

But something in him, remembering, cast a lingering backward look at the time past, and he felt heavy and full of dread, as if he were signalling in vain across a waste of blowing darkness.

Seven

I'll go along, no such sight to be shown,
But to rejoice in splendour of mine own.
—*Romeo and Juliet,* I, ii

Two busloads of quarter-pounders were already lining up
when I got to the gate. There was a trestle table set up
the other side of the bridge, inside the gatehouse, and here
a young woman sat taking the money. I had never seen her
before, and she obviously did not recognize me. She
didn't even give me a glance as I took my ticket, declined
to buy a coloured brochure on Ashley Court, and wan-
dered out into the sunshine of the courtyard to join the
group waiting outside the main door.

The girl from the gatehouse escorted us round. She
had read what there was to read, and did her best to make
the place come to life.

"This is the Great Hall. It's from Henry the Eighth's
time, but there's no record that the King was ever here.
You see that little winding stair over there . . . ? It leads
to the gallery. When Cardinal Wolsey was a young priest
he lived here for a time; he was the family chaplain and
had to read aloud to them during meals. I suppose he got
his food afterwards. . . . Notice the carving on the gallery
rail. It's original. But the shield in the center with the crest
was added later, in the nineteenth century, when the

family took the motto 'Touch Not the Cat but a Glove'
from their Scottish connection. You can see the motto
again carved on the stone shield above the fireplace. It was
William Ashley the author who had the old Tudor
chimney-breast taken out and this Gothic one put in. It
was much admired. Thomas Lovell Beddoes mentions this
room in one of his poems. You'll find it quoted in the
brochure. This way, please."

We straggled along after her. It was a comprehensive
tour, good value for money. We saw it all. The Tudor
parlour where the priest's hole stood open to view, the
Council Chamber with the carved ceiling and the coats
of arms and the panelling polished like silk; the dining
room with the Queen Anne ceiling where the water-light
from the moat rocked and rippled as the swans floated by
below; the long drawing room with its terrace of narrow
lawn and rose-hung parapet edging the drop straight to
the moat. We saw the pantries and the stillroom, the cellars, the kitchens with the spits and the vast chimney (we
ourselves had done our cooking in one of the pantries);
then upstairs to the bedrooms and the gallery, and, at
last, the library.

This ran the full length of the north wing of the house.
It was a tall room with a heavily corniced ceiling, and
pillared Corinthian openings for doors and windows. The
walls were completely clothed with shelves, and at inter-
vals shelves stood out from the walls to create bays, each
bay a self-contained room in itself, with table and heavy
chairs of Spanish leather. Here and there stood glass-
topped display tables for more valuable volumes; and in
earlier days there had been, one to either side of the
fireplace, a pair of ancient celestial and terrestrial globes.
The fireplace was in keeping with the room, being a wide
affair with a carved marble mantelpiece, the top slab upheld by Atlas-like gentlemen with suffering expressions,
and the crosspiece decorated with carefree and rather
charming putti. The huge metal basket below, which had
been designed for logs, was empty, and in front of it,
inside the leather-seated high fender, stood the unlovely

device which was heater and humidifier all in one. The library had once been my favourite of all the rooms at Ashley; I could remember the firelight on the mellow leather of the books, and the warmth of the big rug before the blaze, and being allowed to turn one of the big globes while my father told me about the countries which passed by so quickly under my childish hands.

Now its only beauty was one of proportion; it was a sad ghost of a room, with the cool north light showing the empty shelves, or, sadder still, the shelves where two or three worthless and abandoned volumes took the space of twenty, and lay fallen in their places. Under the glass of the display tables the faded velvet showed darker patches where treasures had once lain. The globes had gone long since under the hammer. In the farthest bay were the locked sections, three sets of shelves behind gilded grilles. The section which had held valuable books was, like the display tables, empty of them; the other two were still filled with the books that Emory had striven in vain to be allowed to read—the private collections of Scholar William, and of Nicholas Ashley, his son.

The guide was saying something about Nick Ashley now, and people were smiling. One or two of them drifted over to look at the titles behind the grille, and I went with them.

The topmost shelves in William's section were filled with a miscellaneous assortment of volumes: a herbal, a few bird books, a county history or two, and a book of county maps, books on hunting and game preserving, a history of the Clan Chattan, and one or two thin reprints about local affairs. There were also a few stray volumes from the *Journal* of Emma Ashley. But on the more accessible shelves, Shakespeare predominated. The *Complete Works,* in a massive, illustrated edition, comprised ten of the volumes, and I could see at least three other editions, flanked by commentaries and essays, and a few separate copies of some of the plays. Notably, there were three different copies of *Romeo and Juliet,* and beside them the volume which explained this interest, a book entitled *A*

New Romeo to His Juliet, which contained, I knew, William Ashley's poems to his wife, Julia McCombie, whose badge he had scattered so lavishly through the house. It was a marvel, I thought, that he had not removed the Italian putti and put Julia's badge there instead: it appeared in every other room; it was scrolled over the front gate, carved in the panels of the staircase, even in two of the misericords of the church choir. It was also carved—a country job this—in the pavilion which stood at the center of the maze. Even looked at down the centuries, such devotion was a trifle overpowering; and to William's contemporaries, and possibly even to Julia herself, it must have been formidable, not to say stifling. After her death at twenty-six her widower, distracted with grief, had shut himself away with his books and his writing, and had had little, if anything, to do with the son who was too like the dead wife.

Our guide was telling the story now, under the portrait of Nicholas, aged eighteen, which hung over the chimney-piece.

". . . He was only seven when she died, and he was more or less left alone, one gathers, except for a series of tutors, none of whom lasted very long. He grew up wild, and he got wilder. I suppose it all sounds very corny and over-dramatic now, because it's been overdone as a story line, but of course this story's true, and it did have a really dramatic ending."

It was certainly dramatic, and it was probably most of it true. What we knew about Wicked Nick's life and death came mainly from the journal of his successor's wife, a lady almost as wordy as Queen Victoria, and every bit as virtuous. Poor Nicholas suffered a good deal in the telling, and the girl—the last of his girls—had been allowed to sink into oblivion. But the main facts were there in Emma Ashley's diaries, and were, indeed, the only interesting part of them.

Nicholas, who had adored his gentle mother, found himself, at her death, almost completely ignored by his father, and in turn bullied, deferred to, or encouraged in his growing wilfulness by a quickly changing series of tutors. What must have started as normal, healthy high spirits changed with this mishandling into wildness; and (one could read between Emma Ashley's disapproving lines) an affectionate nature, starved and repulsed, became sullen and intractable. Spoiled in the truest sense of the word, Nick Ashley had early succumbed to what his Aunt Emma called "corruption," though, from the veiled hints in the diaries, it was hard to gather whether this had been vice on the Gilles de Rais scale, or merely the sexual experimenting normal for a young gentleman of his time.

Nicholas' father fell ill when the young man was a few months short of twenty-two years old. William Ashley, who was sixty-one, was thought to be dying, but was sufficiently in command of his senses to worry about who should succeed him. A marriage contract was hastily drawn up between Nicholas and the Lady Helen Colwall, younger daughter of the family then living at Ledworth Castle. It is not known what the betrothed couple thought of one another, but the very drawing up of the contract must have been a miracle of diplomacy, because—*vide* the virtuous Emma Ashley—Nicholas, with his father safely bedridden, was indulging himself with nightly "orgies" of illicit love.

"There's a tradition," our guide was saying, "that he used to meet them in the pavilion in the center of the maze. How they found the way in I don't know; his valet is supposed to have led them in, like girls being brought to the Grand Turk. His father must have known something about it, and there are stories of terrible quarrels, because William kept the pavilion sacred to Julia's memory, and most of his poems were written there. Well, Nicholas took it over. There are engravings showing it made over as a love nest, with a huge bed, and a big mirror let into the ceiling above it, and lots of silk curtains and shaded lamps, but I should think that was just a myth; it doesn't seem likely that Nick could have had the

pavilion done up like that while William was still alive.
. . . Anyway, just a month before Nicholas was due to
be married to Lady Helen, William Ashley died. Nick had
been keeping company with a girl from a nearby village,
and this time he'd been a bit rash, because one of the girl's
brothers was the Court gamekeeper, and on this particular
night—the night after William died—the man was out
after a poacher, and his brother was with him for company, when they saw their sister coming out of the maze.
Well, they knew what that meant. They waited outside till
Nick Ashley came out. Nobody knows what happened,
whether they quarrelled with him, or just lay in wait and
shot him down, but Nick Ashley was shot dead. The
brothers weren't ever caught. They took a ship from Bristol, and got clear away. The Ashley estate went to Nick's
uncle—his father's brother. That was the Charles Ashley
whose wife wrote the diaries." She smiled. "And that's
the only story I've got for you. It's certainly the only
tragedy recorded at the Court. For a place as old as this,
it's got a strange reputation for peacefulness. There isn't
even the breath of a ghost."

"Not even at the pavilion?" asked someone.

"Not that we know of. But they say that no one except
the family—and of course gardeners and so on—has been
there since. So perhaps the sad ghost of Wicked Nick
haunts the maze to this day, but nobody meets him, and
the family keep him dark."

Did we? I never remembered feeling anything but
sympathy for poor Nick Ashley, bracketed, so to speak,
between the melancholy William, and the pharisaically
virtuous uncle and aunt who had inherited the place on
his death. The young face in the picture showed weakness,
rather than wickedness, and along with it a good deal of
charm. And already, at eighteen, the painter had caught,
in the expression of the long grey eyes, a look of settled
unhappiness. The story made the legends of the maze and
its "orgies," the tilted love mirror, and the collection of
pornography later locked in the Court library, appear in
an altogether kindlier light.

"The portrait is by Stevens," the guide was saying, "but it was sold, and that's a copy. Now, the clock underneath it . . ."

Nick Ashley was dismissed, and everyone looked obediently at the French ormolu clock which stood below the portrait, its gently swinging internal organs winking through the glass. I noticed in passing that it was still ten minutes or so lag of the truth, but then my attention fixed itself with a click about eighteen inches to the right of the clock. When I had last been in this room there had been a small T'ang horse there, which, though it was damaged, was worth five or six hundred pounds in any market.

But it was not going to market, not again. It was not there.

There was nowhere else for it to stand in the library, except perhaps in the safety of one of the display tables. I looked with a flicker of worry at the space where it had been. If the Underhills had taken a fancy to it and moved it across into one of the rooms they rented, it was their responsibility, and perhaps they had no idea of its value.

The party was beginning to leave the library. As I followed them, I lingered to look inside the display tables; it was just possible that some careful hand had removed the little horse to the safety of velvet and glass. But no. And, now that I looked with attention, there were fresh shapes showing in unfaded velvet among the remaining objects of virtu. Here, too, things were missing. A little oval—that had surely been a miniature? And that irregular bit of dark green had held a Chinese jade seal carved with a lion dog.

"Please?" said the guide. I looked up with a start. She was standing by the open door, waiting for me. All the others had gone. I could hear them making their way, chattering like a crowd let out of school, down the staircase. "I have to lock up," said the girl.

"I'm so sorry," I said, "keeping you waiting. I was interested . . . You do it very well, the place comes alive. I've enjoyed it such a lot. Er, did you say 'lock up'? You mean you lock the rooms behind you each time as you go?"

"Oh yes. It's such a big, rambling place, and there are still a lot of valuable things here. We have to be very careful. All the rooms are locked except the ones that are being lived in. We open and shut them as we go through."

"The keys you use; who keeps them as a rule?"

She looked faintly surprised, but answered me readily enough. "I have to give them back to the people who live here. They're tenants; the family's abroad just now."

"Oh. Well, thanks very much," I said, and went thoughtfully out in the wake of the others.

Ashley, 1835

She was here at last.

The light step on the verandah, the hand on the door, the slight figure in the shabby cloak slipping quickly into the room, then shutting the door carefully behind her so that no faint sliver showed. The cloak, thrown aside, falling across the writing table where, year after year, his father had sat alone, writing those sterile verses to his love.

"My love."

Her hair, loosened from the hood, fell like rain, straight and dark, but full of rainbow lights from the candle. Her dress slipped to her knees. She stepped from it, and her hands went to the laces at her breast.

Outside, as if at a signal, a nightingale began to sing.

His thoughts spiralled. The light, the night, the nightingale. *O, she doth teach the torches to burn bright!* Her breasts were bare now, her waist. Her petticoat followed her dress to the floor.

The room echoed with the nightingale's singing. That damned keeper, he remembered, had threatened to shoot the bird ... Damned keeper,

indeed. Her brother. My brother's keeper . . .
He was getting light-headed.

"What are you laughing at, then, love?"

"I'll tell you afterwards. Here, my sweetest
girl, come here to me."

Eight

... the wild-goose chase ...
    —*Romeo and Juliet*, II, iv

"Aren't you Miss Ashley?"

The voice, a woman's, and American, brought me out of my thoughts with a thump, and back to the sunlight of the courtyard, where I now saw a big American car parked in the shade on the other side of the yard. A man was just vanishing through the side door, carrying a suitcase; from his tailoring I guessed it was Mr. Underhill. I turned to greet the woman who had spoken. "Yes, I am. And you must be Mrs. Underhill?"

She was a woman in her middle forties, groomed to a high gloss with that combination American women have of know-how and sheer hard work and skilled use of materials. She was shortish, and without the hard work she might have been dumpy, but instead she was dainty, in a creaseless cream suit that might as well have borne its Fifth Avenue tag on the outside. A high-necked silk sweater hid her neck, and her face had the paled-off sunburn which afflicts Californians when they have been too long in sadder climates. Her skin was dry, with fine lines showing at eyes and mouth, and showed evidence of ceaseless care. The dark-brown lashes were a giveaway for the blond hair.

93

"I'm so glad to meet you." She put out a hand. "But Jeff and I feel awful that it had to be for this reason. It was terrible news about your father; I'm so sorry. We've both been so distressed for you. Everybody says what a very fine person he was."

She talked on for a little while about Daddy, asked where I was staying, and seemed pleased when I said I planned to live for a while in the cottage by the lake. She had a gentle voice and manner that went with her Dresden-china appearance, and seemed to feel a genuine regret about my father, and a real concern for me.

"How did you know me?" I asked her. "Did Mr. Emerson tell you I was coming?"

"No, he didn't. I knew you from the picture in our bedroom."

My parents' room, of course. I said: "Is it so like? It isn't a very good one, and it was painted years ago."

She laughed. "Well, I can see you're not seventeen any more, but you're not that much older, are you?"

"I feel it. I'm twenty-two."

"Look, what are we standing out here for? Come right in, Jeff's dying to meet you, I know. He's just flown in from Houston, and he'll be home for a few days. Isn't that marvellous? It seems kind of strange inviting you into your own home, but come right on in."

Like us, the Underhills used a side door. We went in together. I said: "I didn't actually come over just to call. I was planning to do that this afternoon. I've been down at the cottage seeing what was needed, and then I came up here, and—" I laughed rather apologetically. "Actually I went round with the guided tour. It seems silly, but I was rather curious to see how they did it."

"Did you really? Well, fancy!" Her eyes danced. "So I needn't feel so bad at inviting you into your own home, when you've had to pay twenty-five cents to go the rounds. . . . And I have to tell you, Cathy and I have been around a couple of times ourselves. It was a good way to learn all the history, and boy, have you had some history! Kind of uncomfortable, some of it, but very in-

teresting, and seeing everything right here in its own place
beats the schoolbooks hollow." She paused at a corner.
"We're in what they call the small drawing room; I don't
have to tell you the way. You'll stay to lunch with us,
won't you? Now"—as I made the ritual protest—"I won't
take no for an answer. We have a light lunch, salad and
such, and it couldn't be easier. In any case, we're having
a guest already, so it's easy to stretch it." She smiled like
someone with a secret that she knew would delight me.
"Guess who it is? Your own cousin."

Any delight I felt was certainly tempered with questions
and uneasy memories of last night in the churchyard, and,
too, with some speculation about the gossip Mrs. Henderson had passed on to me. I said: "You mean Emory?
How lovely!" with what was meant to sound like unmixed
pleasure, but as Mrs. Underhill opened the drawing-room
door and gestured me past her, I saw her eyeing me with
her own brand of speculation, a slightly wary look, which,
under the circumstances, was natural. One up to Mrs.
Henderson and the village gossip, I thought: it was just
such a look as might be given to the about-to-be-dispos-
sessed Miss Ashley, whose privilege ticket back to the
Court had been picked up by Miss Underhill.

"Yes," she said, "Emory."

"Well, isn't that nice!" I said cheerfully. "I haven't
seen him for ages. And of course I'd love to meet your
daughter. Thank you, I'd like to stay, very much."

The "small drawing room" opened from the longer
drawing room, from which it could be divided by a pair
of tall doors. These were shut now, making a room about
thirty feet by eighteen, with three long windows looking
out on the strip of lawn and rose beds which was the terrace above the moat. The water-light moved prettily on
the ceiling. They had hardly rearranged the room at all,
I saw, and there were bowls of tulips and bluebells, and
stands of cherry blossom which lighted the alcoves to
beauty, and which must have been arranged by Mrs. Underhill herself.

"Let's sit down, shall we?" she said.

There was a fire of logs in the hearth. She motioned me to a seat near it in the corner of the big chesterfield, and took the other corner herself.

"I gather," I said, "that you know my cousin quite well?"

"Yes. He and Cathy—Cathy's my daughter—met a while back, and after they got acquainted they found there was this connection, that she was staying at Ashley Court. A real coincidence, you might say. Well, of course she asked him over, and he's visited here a few times. He's a real charmer, don't you think?"

"I've always thought so," I agreed, "and so's his twin. You've met James? And Francis, the youngest brother? No, well, he's been abroad a lot in the last few months. They used to live here with us, most of the time, when we were children; I expect Emory will have told you all about that." I hesitated fractionally, then hit the ball into the open field. "You know, I suppose, that the Court will belong to Emory's family now?"

She looked embarrassed, and made quite a little business of picking up a cigarette box, offering me one, then taking one herself and lighting it. "He did tell us something about the way things were left, but of course it was all seemingly in the future then. Your father was still a young man, as things go, and nobody ever thought of a tragedy like this." She seemed to be going to say more, then let it go. "It seems you had some ancestor who tied everything up so that it had to be inherited by a man. I can think of some ladies I know who'd be hell-bent on doing something about that right now . . ." She smiled, leaned across to tap ash off her cigarette, then looked up at me frankly. "I must say, Miss Ashley, it seems kind of tough to me. Isn't there anything that can be done?"

She sounded as if she meant it. Some tension that I hardly knew I had been feeling slackened in me.

"I doubt it. Certainly there's nothing to be done about the 'heirs male' inheritance; that's been built in ever since the place started. The really awkward 'tying up' that the old man did was the trust that stops even the heir from

selling any of the unentailed property without the consent
of the whole family. Luckily, so far, we haven't fought
much over it." I smiled. "And I don't see why we should
start now. I expect Emory will do all right; he usually
does."

"You don't sound as if you minded one bit."

"I don't believe I do. People like the Ashleys had a
very good run for their money, after all."

She got up then to shift one of the logs in the fireplace, and I turned the subject with some compliment
about the flowers, and the talk went off at a comfortable
tangent to the garden, and the contrast between California
and the cool temperate climate that we in Britain use as a
daily basis for grumbling, but that produces the loveliest
gardens in the world. . . . I listened with only half an
ear; I was looking round the room, trying not to do it too
obviously, to see if the T'ang horse was there, or the seal,
or anything else which should have been in the locked part
of the house. I saw none of them, but I knew that soon,
and the sooner the better for her own sake as well as mine,
I would have to tell her about the missing objects. I wondered a little desperately how in the world one broached
such a subject. For a lunch guest, however much a part of
the furnishings, to ask her hostess suddenly where the
valuables were and who kept the keys to the rooms they
had been removed from was one of those things that even
Aunt Edna of the Problem Page would have found tricky.
Well, I thought, it wasn't something that would improve
with keeping. If you have to ask something, then ask.

"Mrs. Underhill, there's something I've been wondering about. Perhaps you can help me. The guide who
took the party round told me that the rooms on the public
side of the house—the ones you don't use—are always
locked, and that she gives the keys back to you and your
husband for safekeeping. What happens if you're out, or
away from home?"

"They're left with that nice Rob Granger. He has the
other set, and he always keeps an eye on things if we're
not here. He's hardly ever away, but if he is, he leaves

keys at the Vicarage. Why do you ask? Don't you have keys yourself?"

"It's not that; I can get Rob's if I need them. It's just . . . Mrs. Underhill, I noticed something this morning that worried me—maybe I should say puzzled me, because I'm quite sure there'll be a simple reason for it." I hesitated, then plunged. "One or two small things that used to be in the library aren't there any more. I wondered if you knew where they'd been moved to."

She looked startled, and her cigarette froze still, halfway up to her mouth. "Miss Ashley, there's nothing been moved that I know of. What sort of things?"

"Small things, ornaments. I wondered if perhaps they'd been put in the strong-room for safekeeping."

She shook her head. I noticed how sharply the lipstick outlined her mouth, standing out blue-red against the creamy colourless skin. "Do you mean really valuable things?"

"Well, there's a little Chinese horse, in unglazed earthenware, a sort of biscuit colour, with a mended leg. It doesn't look much, but—"

"A Chinese horse? Unglazed biscuit? For heaven's sake, not a T'ang horse?" She looked so horrified that I realized that, coming from America's West Coast, she probably knew far more about the value of Oriental ceramics than I did.

I said hastily: "Yes, but not a very good one; it was small, and it was damaged. Please don't look so worried! I just noticed that it had gone from the mantelpiece in the library, and there was a miniature gone from one of the showcases, just a little Victorian thing, and a piece of jade, a seal with a lion dog on it. You haven't seen them anywhere else, have you?"

"No, I have not. They're not in this part of the house, that's for sure. Miss Ashley, this is just awful!"

I saw with remorse that she had lost the remains of what colour she had. Her lips, under the paint, had puckered into fine, dry lines. I began to feel a bit like an executioner. "Look, please don't worry so, I only asked.

The odds are that Mr. Emerson's put them away in the strong-room. He may have decided they were too easily portable, with loads of people going through the rooms every day. I can ring him up and ask him. I should have done that before I bothered you. Please forgive me."

"Well, of course, but—oh, here's Jeff. He might know something about it . . . Jeff, this is Miss Ashley. She's coming back to stay for a piece, and she'll be living in the cottage by the lake. Isn't that wonderful? But right now she's staying to lunch with us. Miss Ashley, this is Jeff, my husband."

We said how do you do and shook hands, and, like her, he said the right things about my father with that enviable American warmth and ease of manner. He was a big man, broad in body, and of heavy build, with the same look as his wife of physical health worked for and maintained at concert pitch. He had dark hair greying, and a broad face with slightly flattened features, oddly familiar, though for the moment I could not place them. The cheek-bones were wide, with a slightly Slavic look, and the eyes were dark and very shrewd. The long mouth gave nothing away. He looked just what he was: a rich, clever man, a killer in business hours, and kindness itself in his time off.

Before I could stop her his wife had told him about the missing objects, and I was able to witness the Jekyll-into-Hyde transformation I had just guessed at. The pleasant smile vanished, the black brows snapped together, and hard dark eyes looked straight through my brain to scrape the back of my skull. Or that was what it felt like. "Tycoon" had not just been a joke word. In the business jungle of America, Jeffrey Underhill was one of the larger carnivores.

He didn't waste time on apologies or worry; he asked two or three questions, so smoothly that you hardly noticed they came barbed, and then said: "The first thing is to call the lawyer. I'll do that now. It seems to me very likely that he's taken some of the small things into safe-keeping." He glanced at the clock on the mantel. "Cathy went to pick Emory up, didn't she? They're not back yet?"

"No," said his wife. "He called up to say he had to get the later train."

He nodded, and made for the door, but paused there with his back to the room, his head bent, as if thinking. Then he turned back to me. He still had that gloss of calm which politicians and high-ranking businessmen affect, but the next question came out that little bit too abruptly. "You only noticed things missing from the library, that's right?"

"That's right. Though until I'd seen the T'ang horse was gone, I didn't really look. But, Mr. Underhill, please —I didn't mean to start a thing like this. This is making me feel terrible. There's probably a perfectly simple explanation, and—"

"Sure there is. But the sooner we have it the better. I'll call this lawyer right away, even if it does spoil his lunch hour for him. But the point I was going to make was, would you like to go look around again on your own, and make a check? You might find the things somewhere else, or you might find more things missing. Either way, the sooner we get them tagged the better. It's barely a quarter of twelve. I doubt if my daughter and your cousin will be here much before one o'clock. What do you say?"

"Yes, I'd like to. Thank you."

"Fine. Now, Stephanie says you went around with the guided tour; that means you've no keys of your own. Right?" He crossed to a bureau which stood between two of the windows, took a small key from his vest pocket and unlocked it, pulled open a drawer and took out the big bunch of house keys. No, I could acquit Mr. Underhill of carelessness. He handed me the keys, said, "Fix me a martini, for God's sake," to his wife, and went out. One got the impression that the dust began to settle as soon as the door shut behind him.

My search, which was fruitless, finished at length in the big schoolroom of the nursery wing.

I don't quite know why I went there; I certainly never expected to find any clue to the missing objects, and I have no recollection of climbing the noisy lino-covered stairs to the third floor. It may be that I was still a little breathless at the Underhills' swift reaction to my inquiries; possibly it was just Jeffrey Underhill's normal way, but I felt as if I had started a full-scale criminal investigation almost before I was sure that anything was really missing. Before I faced them again, I wanted time to think. I glanced at my watch. Still something short of twelve-thirty. I shut the schoolroom door behind me, crossed to the wide window seat, and sat down, looking down at the tops of the big beeches that edged the Pool.

The sun poured into the shabby room. Dust motes swarmed like a gauze filter, making a soft-focus dreamworld out of reality. The sun was bright as the suns one always remembers from childhood. The dusty, slightly stuffy smell of the unused schoolroom was the same as it had been ten, twelve, fourteen years ago. Beside me on the faded cushions of the window seat sat three old friends, grubby and grey with much loving: the Hippo family, Hippo, Pot, and Amos, whose names Francis had chosen, and which, as children, we had found excruciatingly funny. The old dappled rocking horse stood gathering dust; I had christened it Dawn, which my cousins thought sickeningly girlish, refusing to call it anything but Rocky. There were the desks, with their dried and crusted inkwells, where James and Emory, and later Francis and I, had sat learning to read and write and cipher before we went to school. A white-painted shelf still held the beloved storybooks, the Andrew Langs and the Arthur Ransomes and the C. S. Lewises, their battered covers containing each its bright autonomous world, those magical kingdoms one is made free of as a child, and thereafter owns all one's life.

Below the shelves was the cupboard to which, prompted by Leslie Oker, my bookseller friend from Ashbury, I had, before going abroad, transferred some of our nursery treasures from the open shelves. There was a steadily growing interest, he had told me, in the work of illustrators like Arthur Rackham and Edmund Dulac and

Kay Neilson; and I myself, looking through Christie's catalogues, had seen prices ranging into the hundreds for the scarcer volumes. So I had locked the books out of sight, and hidden the key. Small beer, perhaps, compared with T'ang horses and jade, but there was love to be reckoned with as well.

T'ang horses and jade. Valuable books? Not dreaming at all now, but right back on the spot with my problem, I crossed to the cupboard and tried the door. It was not locked. With a jerk of sudden apprehension, I pulled the door open.

The books were all there, just as I had left them.

As I relaxed, I realized how falsely keyed up I had been: to be as valuable as the ones I had seen in Christie's catalogue, they would have had to be the "deluxe" editions, signed by the artist and limited to a few hundred copies; not the nursery editions we had had, read and re-read until the pages showed the handling, and the covers were dented and soiled. These were not objects of value, but only of love.

I pulled out the nearest. It was *Grimm's Fairy Tales,* and the drawings were so familiar that my own imaginary concept of the stories was little more than an extension of these pictures. There was the Goosegirl with poor Falada, over whom I had wept as a child; Hansel and Grethel with the dreadful old witch; the Princess dreaming on the rock among the yesty waves, with the Dragon's long head on her lap . . .

"The Princess and the Dragon." I swung round as if that underhung jaw had bitten me, and stared up at the schoolroom wall, where, dark on the faded wallpaper, two empty oblongs showed. Two pictures had once hung there, original illustrations by Rackham, one from Lamb's *Tales,* and the other this very drawing from Grimm, "The Princess and the Dragon." A great-aunt of mine had bought them for a few pounds when they were first exhibited, and given them to me when I was a child. I had taken them down from the walls and locked them with the books, away from dust and damage. Now, both cupboard and wall were bare of them. And this time I had not miscalculated. They were the real thing, irreplaceable, and worth the kind of money that few people could afford to lose. Certainly not me.

I still remember the rush of anger I felt. I slammed the cupboard door shut, got to my feet, and went back to the window. I pushed it open and leaned out. As I did so I thought I heard a car turn into the driveway. That would be Emory and Cathy, I supposed, but I made no move to go downstairs. I needed a little longer to myself before I faced the company and heard what Mr. Underhill had to tell me. I knew as well as if he had already said it, that Mr. Emerson would know nothing about the missing treasures.

The sun was blazing full from the south. I shut my eyes. The scent of the garden came floating, sweet and calming as sunlight on water. I opened them again, and watched the water itself below me. The bullrushes were still, inseparable from their reflections; the willows trailed their hair in the water; the irises were budding. The pen swan slept on her nest, head under wing, the cygnets beside her. The cob floated near with all wing set, in full beauty.

Lover?

I'm here. What is it?

I hardly knew that I had called to him, until the response came, quickly and warmly, like a hand clasping another that reaches out blindly for comfort. Call and reply, as clear and easy as if they had been formulated in words—clearer, for words confuse as often as they explain. Between long-familiar lovers the language of the body needs no speech; with us, our minds had for so long dwelt familiarly the one with the other that the exchange of thought was as telling and as swift as a glance between intimates across a crowded room.

But to describe it, words must serve.

What is it?

Things have disappeared. The horse has gone from the library.

The what? For once it came with a catch of puzzlement. *I thought you said the horse had gone from the library.*

I did. I sent him as clear an image as I could, and felt him accept it.

Oh, that one. Yes. It's gone?

That, and other things as well. And now I've found some pictures gone from the schoolroom, valuable ones . . .

He had already picked it up, before I even knew I had formulated it. *And you think they were stolen. Is he phoning the lawyer?*

You knew that? How?

Oh, from you. You're as open as daylight when you're upset.

Am I? Then why didn't you come when I was in the cottage?

Because it was time you cried it all out, and that's a thing one wants to do by oneself. I left you alone. But you should have known I was there.

Yes. It was resigned, almost flat. *I should have known. But I'd have liked you closer.*

Bryony—

Yes?

Sweet Bryony. The patterns came through delicate and warm, like gentle hands touching my cheeks.

Oh, God. It went out with all the longing of loneliness. *I want you so.*

The touch changed, no less gentle, but now electric, thrilling as live wire. There was a quick burst of something as strong and deafening as static, which grew in intensity like pain growing, like sound increasing up to the very limit of tolerance.

Then it shut off abruptly, and the door opened, and my cousin stood on the threshold.

Ashley, 1835

"I was afraid you'd missed the way."

"Oh, no, it's easy, now I've got the key."

"I thought you might have said, 'I'd always find the way to you, my lover.'"

"So I would, so I would. I didn't have to use the key tonight. I remembered every turning, just as you drew it for me on the map."

"There you go again. Well, I shall say it for you. If you were hidden at the center of the darkest and most tangled forest in the world, I'd find you."

"Like the prince in the fairy tale?"

"Or like the lover in the play. 'There is my north, and thither my needle points.'"

"Eh, now you're laughing at me. That would be dirty meant, surely?"

"It would. Do you mind?"

"Why would I? There's neither dirty nor clean between thee and me, just what's true, and what could be wrong wi' that?"

"Nothing. Nothing ever was, and now, why, now . . ."

Nine

Why, how now, kinsman!
  —*Romeo and Juliet*, I, v

"Hullo, Bryony."

"Why, Emory, how lovely!" To my own surprise, my
voice sounded quite normal as I greeted him. "I could
hardly believe it when they said you were coming to lunch
today! And to meet you here, of all places, just like this,
out of the blue . . . Doesn't it seem ages?"

"If you knew how guilty we all feel about 'here,'" said
my cousin. He smiled at me. "You're looking wonderful.
I was talking to Bill Emerson, and he said you'd taken
it all marvellously. How are you really?"

"Oh, I'm fine. Everyone's been sweet to me, and it's
been easier than I ever thought it could be. You mustn't
any of you talk about 'guilt'! That's just silly. We've
known all along just what would happen, and—"

I broke off. He had come into the room and was
approaching me, threading his way along the row of
desks. They looked very small beside his height; his fingertips barely brushed them. It put time in remembrance.
He caught the look, and paused. "What is it?"

I said, uncertainly: "James? It *is* James, isn't it?"

I faltered to a stop, meeting the amusement in his
eyes. Thrown off guard by the recent exchange with my

lover, and by the mental dramatics preceding my cousin's entrance, I felt myself colour as I stared up at him, absurdly at a loss.

The only thing certain about this man was that he was one of my cousins. He was a tall man, fine-boned, with the pale skin that tanned (even in the Spanish sun) no more than sallow; fair straight hair, thin-bridged nose, grey eyes. His shirt and tie were in complementing shades of grey that, either by accident or design—and with him I knew it would be design—exactly matched his eyes. But any impression of the over-trendy or the effete was wiped out as soon as you looked into those eyes and saw the set of the mouth. His mouth was the only feature that was not Ashley; a close mouth, long-lipped, folded at the corners as if it liked to keep secrets, or keep control. It gave him a withdrawn and wary look, rather at variance with the Ashley part of him. I remembered his mother; a child's view of her was all I had had, but I could still vividly recall a clever domineering woman who kept her own counsel, and secured her ambitions in her own way. If she had passed that driving side of herself to her sons it might augur well for Ashley Court. There was more character, I thought, in this clever and wary man than there had been in my own gentle father. Maybe, by that token, these Ashleys would do better here than we had done.

His smile put time in remembrance, too. It held a very familiar sparkle of mischief. "Don't tell me you're slipping, Bryony darling! We never could put one over you. No, it's Emory. Aren't I the one you wanted?"

"Yes, of course, but—"

"Didn't they tell you I was coming over from Worcester with Cathy?"

"Yes, they told me, but . . . Oh, all right, so I'm slipping." I returned the smile. "Well, whichever you are, it's up to me to say welcome to Ashley Court. And of course I mean welcome. This 'guilt' thing is nonsense, and Daddy would have been the first to say so. Don't let's hear about it any more, please."

I uncurled from the window seat, got to my feet, and

held out both hands for his. He took a couple of quick steps forward, and his hands closed round mine. He drew me into his arms and kissed me, a cousin's kiss, on the cheek.

I pulled away sharply, an instinctive movement that he tried to stop, then he let me go. He was laughing. I drew breath to speak, but before I could say anything, he put his hands up in a gesture of surrender.

"All right, all right, don't say it. I admit it. I should have known we still couldn't fool you."

"Then why did you try?" For some reason I didn't stop to analyze, I was angry.

"For fun," he said lightly, and waited, as if challenging me to say more. I was silent. It was not just the moment to start explaining that, even had I found it easy to confuse James with Emory, I could not confuse a touch, much less a kiss. The moment he had taken my hands, I had known who it was. The hazy sunlight drifted between us, dazzling. Through it I saw his eyes, still smiling, and— I was sure—aware.

But he began to talk about my father. I listened, and thanked him, and made some sort of reply, as well as I could for the crowding thoughts that just then were overriding all else. I found suddenly that I couldn't meet his eyes, and turned away to sit down on the window seat again.

The cool, pleasant voice paused. When he spoke again it had changed, subtly. "Bryony. Try not to be too sad. We'll look after you." He hesitated, then added, as if he were answering something and dismissing it, as indeed I supposed he was: "It's not time to talk yet, but don't worry, we'll work something out."

The words were gently spoken, but to me they seemed to go ringing on and on. I said something, I'm not sure what, and then asked quickly: "How's Cousin Howard?"

He half sat down on one of the desks. He seemed completely relaxed. "He's a little better; at any rate, he's out of danger, they say, but he's still very ill. He'll have to retire, did you know? Things have been a bit difficult all round . . . I'm afraid there'll be no question of his coming over for a long time. When did you think of having the memorial service for Cousin Jon?"

"I haven't talked to the Vicar yet. It could wait, I imagine, till Cousin Howard's mobile. That would be better, wouldn't it?"

"I know he'd like to be there."

"I suppose Emory's over with him in Jerez," I asked, "since you're here?"

"He did go over a couple of times, to see Father, but he's been here most of the time—in Bristol, that is, or London. Father's retirement has been putting the pressure on a bit."

"And you? When did you come over?"

"The last week in April. Miguel coped for us in Jerez, so I could help out here with Twin. We felt pretty bad about not getting over for the cremation, but it simply couldn't be done. I'm sorry about that."

"It's all right, I understand. Have you heard from Francis yet?"

"Not a word," he said. "I gather you haven't, either? He must still be incommunicado in Derbyshire. Who's he with, do you know?"

"No idea. I thought, knowing Francis, that he'd be on his own."

He lifted a shoulder. "Probably. Well, no doubt he'll turn up soon."

"James—"

"Yes?"

"James, was that you in the vestry last night?"

He straightened, startled. I saw the pupils narrow in the wide grey irises, then his eyes went momentarily blank, as if he were making some lightning calculation. Then he said: "Vestry?" as blankly.

"Yes, vestry. It wasn't?"

"It was not. Why the hell should I have been in the vestry?"

"I've no idea. I went to the church late last night, and I saw someone in the vestry. He was leaving just as I went in. He went out across the churchyard wall and into the walled garden. He saw me, but he didn't stay to talk."

"Sounds crazy. Why should you have imagined I'd run away, from you of all people?"

"I don't know. Could it have been Emory?"

"Well, the same applies, I would have thought." He looked at me. "What makes you think it was one of us?"

"I got that impression. Only vaguely—but I thought it was one of you."

"Well, didn't you try speaking to whoever it was?"

He waited for my reply, his eyes wide now, and guileless. I knew that look. It was the "I was never even near the orchard" look, with the apples literally tumbling out of his trouser-pocket. I smiled to myself, and let him see the smile, and watched the flicker in his eyes, and was certain. I turned away towards the window, picked up Pot, and set him on my knee. "No. Oh, well, never mind. What would you be doing there anyway? I just thought it must be one of you, and I got the impression it was you. And talking of Emory, what's all this about him and Cathy Underhill? Have they really got a thing going?"

"Yes. They met, quite by chance, at some do in town, and when they got talking they found the connection with Ashley. Then one thing led to another, and—yes, you might say they had something going."

"Serious?"

"I'm not sure. That is, I'm not sure from Twin's side of it."

"Then you are sure from Cathy's?" I asked.

"As far as one can judge, yes again."

"You and Emory used not to have secrets from one another."

"We're big boys now."

"Not too big, apparently," I said, rather sharply, "to go in still for all that 'Twin' stuff that used to annoy everyone."

"It's convenient," he said, with a slant of the eyebrows that he didn't attempt to explain. Didn't have to. I knew just when it had been "convenient"; when he and Emory were standing in for one another, either for fun and confusion's sake, or even for pay. One twin, who had pressing business elsewhere, or who was avoiding trouble, would cajole, blackmail, or just plain pay the other to substitute for him. It was significant that as often as not James was the one who was blackmailed into ringing for Emory. The maddening way they had had of calling each other "Twin" had made it desperately hard to catch them out when they wanted to confuse the issue. It was also typical that the habit had been deliberately cultivated. Even as boys, my cousins were to be reckoned with.

"Do you mean," I said slowly, "that you haven't just come here today with Emory and Cathy? That you brought Cathy yourself, and that *she* thinks you are Emory?"

He gave me a sideways glance, half amused, half wary. "You sound very fierce."

"Well, damn it, it could matter. Why did you do it, James?"

"Oh, nothing deadly. Just that he'd had to stand her up once before, and didn't care to do it again. Besides, I wanted to see you."

"Surely you could have come anyway?" I asked. A pause. "Who told you I was here?"

The fair brows lifted a fraction. "Why, Emerson, of course. How else would I have known?"

I glanced up, but he was looking out of the window over my head. "Have you stood in for Emory before—with Cathy, that is?"

"Only once."

"And now here, today, in front of her parents. Do you really expect me to back you up?"

"You always did."

"This could be different. I haven't met her, but it sounds like the sort of situation one ought not to play about with. If she is serious about him, she might get hurt."

"Why should she get hurt if she doesn't know? She'd be hurt if she knew she'd been stood up again."

"Oh, all right," I said resignedly. "Damn you, James, you've no right to put me in this kind of position. We're not children any more. It's a bit late to tell the truth now, so I'll try not to give you away."

"That's my girl." There was nothing in his tone but the offhand approval that there had always been when I helped him. I smiled, and pulled Pot's ears, and thought how little he'd changed, and how much.

"Penny for them," said my cousin.

"I was just thinking that we might never have been parted at all."

"Meaning?"

I sidestepped the question. "Oh, only that it seems like yesterday, you and Emory playing your games. James, I meant what I said. Don't ask me to do it again, because I won't."

But he wasn't listening. He was looking out of the window over my head, and I saw his gaze sharpen.

"Did you know one of the beeches had gone?"

"Yes. Rob told me it had to come down after a storm in February. It's an awful pity, making a gap like that."

"Yes, but have you noticed what you can see through the gap?"

I turned. "No. What?"

He nodded downwards. "You can see the pavilion now, and almost all the layout of the maze. You could never see any of that from the house before—Bryony!"

"What is it? You made me jump."

"I've seen it for the first time. Why didn't we ever think of it? It's the coat of arms!"

"What is? What are you talking about?"

"Look," he said impatiently. "The design. The layout of the maze. I know it's overgrown and all blurred in places, but it's the pattern—you know that queer geometric pattern carved on the fireplaces, round the 'Touch Not the Cat' crest? That's it, surely?"

I stared down at the intersecting lines of the maze. Overgrown though it was, the sun picked out the pattern in shadows sufficiently clear to prove him right. "Good heavens, so it is! Well . . . after all, the maze was very much William Ashley's fine and private place, wasn't it? I always wondered why he put that odd square design behind Julia's badge. He even uses it for a bookplate in his own books, I remember that. And talking of books—" I looked up at him. "James, some things from the library seem to have disappeared."

He seemed hardly to be listening, still intent on the sunlit maze below. "Ah, yes." He said it absently. "The horse and the lion dog seal. Did you find anything else gone?"

I didn't answer. Not aloud, that is. *So you knew, did you, Ashley?*

He seemed to come to himself with a start, and turned. "It's very odd, that maze. It makes one wonder . . . I'm sorry, you were saying? Something about the T'ang horse and the jade seal going missing."

"I didn't mention them. That was you."

He nodded. "The Underhills told me. They said you were looking round to see if anything else was gone. Have you checked?"

"As well as I can, without an inventory. I haven't found the things from the library, but then Mr. Emerson may have put them away somewhere."

"No. Underhill had just telephoned Emerson when we got here. He knew nothing about the things. It's certainly very odd. Did you find anything else missing?"

"The pictures Great-Aunt Sophie gave me. The ones from there." I pointed to the wall.

He frowned. "Those? Damn it, who on earth would have wanted a couple of nursery pictures?"

"Those 'nursery pictures,' as you call them, are originals, and they're really pretty valuable now, though they'd be hard to sell. I mean, they couldn't very well be advertised; they're unique. James, what on earth can have happened to them?"

"God knows. Are you quite sure they're gone? They may have been put away somewhere. Take it from me, you'll find them in a cupboard or something."

"I put them away myself, in that cupboard, and it was locked. It's not locked now, and they've gone. It's the obvious conclusion that they've gone the same way as the T'ang horse and the seal."

The frown deepened. "You may be right." He hesitated. "Look, Bryony, I can see this is rather worrying, on top of everything else, but do try not to fret yourself over it. Can't you just leave it to Twin and me, and Emerson? We'll follow it up. There'll be some harmless explanation, I'm sure. Who'd take this sort of thing, anyway? The schoolroom isn't even on the public side."

"That's the point, isn't it?"

He stopped, arrested. His brows shot up. "You can't mean the Underhills?"

"No, of course I don't. I know nothing about them, except that I like them, and surely to goodness they were vetted when they took the house. But the point is, what earthly reason could people like that have for wanting to steal anything like this—or anything at all, for that matter?"

"Well, leave it, honey." He hesitated. "Don't take me up wrongly, but you really don't have to worry yourself about it. That's our job." He paused, then slanted a gentle look down at me. "Do you mind?"

"Give me time. I don't know." I began to uncurl from the window seat. "Did they send you to take me down to lunch? We'd better go, I suppose."

"Bryony." His arm fell lightly across my shoulders. I sat very still. "I've got to talk to you. When can we talk? They said something about your moving into the cottage. Is that true?"

"Yes. I was down there this morning. Rob and Mrs. Henderson have got it ready, so I think I'll move in today. I—I'd like to talk to you, James. There's a lot to say . . . after lunch, perhaps? Or would 'Emory' have to take Cathy somewhere?"

"No. But after lunch he's got to have a chat with Jeff Underhill about the lease of the Court. After that I might be able to come down. You're going to stay the night there?"

"Yes."

"Then I'll see you. Now I think we'd better go downstairs. It's all right, there's no hurry. Stephanie said to take our time; she knew we'd have a lot to say."

"What's been decided about the lease?"

"Officially speaking, they should be allowed to stay till it runs out. That'll be in November. Neither Emory nor I see any reason why they shouldn't. Do you?"

"Does that matter?" I asked.

The arm moved a little on my shoulders. "So you do mind."

"I tell you, I don't know." I got up abruptly from under the arm and moved to the door. "Let's go down."

"Taking your old bedmate down with you?"

"Taking my *what?*" Then I realized that I was still clutching Pot. I dumped him back on the window seat, said, "Damn you, James," but not aloud this time, and made once more for the door.

He followed me. "When you were in the library, did you notice if all the books in the locked sections were still there?"

"There again, I wouldn't know without the catalogue. I didn't notice any gaps."

We clattered down the schoolroom stairs. "Perhaps you'd better leave that job for us, anyway," he suggested.

"Like hell I will. I'm of age, and in any case probably all the worst ones have gone. Don't forget Emma Ashley burned a few of them."

"Grandmamma Savonarola. So she did. Pity," he said cheerfully. "Well, you're more than welcome to William Ashley's collection. All his dear little verses to his Julia, and his Roman studies, and his own personal editions of the simpler Shakespeare plays."

"Are any of them simple?"

"I would have thought that *Romeo and Juliet* and *Julius Caesar* posed fewer problems than, say, *Measure for Measure* or *Timon.*"

"Would you? You might be right." I said it absently.
I was wondering whether to tell him now about my
father's last words to me, and my interest in William
Ashley's books. But we were already halfway down the
great staircase. A portrait hung there, a dark girl, painted
rather stiffly, but with beauty showing even through the
stylized familiar features of the minor "society" portraits
of the time. She was standing beside the sundial in the
old rose garden, one arm resting on the pillar, the other
holding a basket of roses. She looked stiff and faintly ill
at ease in the grey satin and starched lace of the seven-
teenth century. Bess Ashley, the gipsy girl who had talked
to a lover no one could see, and who went to the stake
for it. Behind her, almost obscured in the yellowing can-
vas, was a black cat, familiar of witches.

I stopped. "James, do you ever have dreams?"

"Dreams? Of course I do. Everyone does. What sort
especially?"

"Oh, about the future. People you're going to meet,
and then you do meet them. That kind of thing."

"Precognition, you mean?"

I hesitated, then was deliberately vague. "I wouldn't
say—no, not really that. Just something that's a bit more
than coincidence . . . You dream about someone, and—
and talk to them, someone you don't really know, and
then you seem to see them or hear from them almost
straight away. Next day, even."

There was a little pause. He seemed all at once to
notice that we were standing in front of Bess Ashley's portrait. He shot me a look, hesitated, and opened his mouth
to reply, but at that moment Mrs. Underhill came out of
the drawing room to the foot of the stairs and spoke, and
the moment passed. I ran down with an apology forming,
but Stephanie Underhill brushed it aside and began to
say something in an undertone which sounded like, "Do
you mind, I wanted to ask you, don't say anything—"
Then she stopped short, with a smile which didn't do anything for the anxiety in her eyes, as a girl emerged from

a door at the other side of the hall and ran across to take James's hand in hers and say:

"Emory! You've been an age! Where were you both, for heaven's sake? In the middle of the maze?"

It was the girl from the E-type Jaguar. I recognized her straight away, the look of her father somehow translated into long, dark-blond hair and mink lashes, and the wide, unpainted mouth that had been sulky then, but now was full of laughter and charm. She was taller than her mother, but not by much, and slim to swooning point in a tight pair of blue jeans with big stitched pockets, and a loose sweater reaching like a tunic to the hips. The sweater should have been white, but wasn't, and I saw that the edge of one sleeve was beginning to unravel. But the cult disorder didn't seem to go deeper than the clothes; she was glowing with happiness and well-being, and the glow, it was very obvious, began and ended with my cousin. Her fingers twined in James's and clung, and the look she sent him would have melted bedrock.

"Cathy—" began her mother, but James was already disentangling his fingers from hers, and saying:

"You haven't met my cousin yet. This is Bryony. Bryony, Cat Underhill."

"Hi, Bryony. Nice to meet you. I'd have known you anywhere."

She held out a hand, and I took it. "That's what your mother said. That portrait must be better than we thought."

"Oh, it's not just that picture. When you've lived here for a bit you certainly get to know the Ashley face." She sent a glancing look up at James again, then added, seriously, to me: "I'm sorry. I guess I should have said right away, I'm really sorry about your father. It was awful."

"Thank you. Didn't I see you in Worcester yesterday? You stopped at a crossing to let me and a black cat over."

"Gosh, sure, I remember that. At least I remember the cat; I'm afraid I didn't notice you. He had his nerve, didn't he? I nearly ran him down. And a black cat, too, just when I can do with all the luck I can get."

"Oh? Why, specially?"

She took me by the arm as her mother began to shepherd us towards the drawing room. "Nothing special. Just that I always seem to need more luck than I can get. Who doesn't? Come along in and get a drink. Pop's still away telephoning somebody. What'll you have? Emory will pour it. Did you and the cat both get away all right?"

"He was even quicker than I was. And I solved a problem, meeting you like this."

She widened her eyes at me over her martini. They were dark like her father's. The mink eyelashes made them look enormous, Bambi-type. "A problem?"

"Yes. I'd just left the lawyer's office.. It's beside that crossing, you probably know that? I saw him watching you, too; he pointed you out to me, and I thought he said 'Cat,' and I couldn't think why. I mean, if he'd meant the black cat, I could see that myself. . . . Now I know. We'd been talking about the Court, and your family, and now I've just heard my cousin call you Cat. He must have been meaning you. Well, that's one of the mysteries on the way out."

" 'One of the mysteries'?" she asked. "Are there some more?"

"I certainly hope so," said Mrs. Underhill warmly. I glanced at her in surprise, but she hurried on: "All this time in a moated grange straight out of Tennyson, and not even the sniff of a ghost or a secret passage or any of the things you might expect! Miss Ashley, Cathy and I have been just longing for you to come and tell us the secrets about the Court that aren't in the books. The guides seem pretty strong on history, but they can't know all there is."

So she didn't want to talk about the missing objects in front of her daughter. Fair enough. I laughed. "I'm sorry if it hasn't come up to expectation. There isn't much, but there is a secret stair, as a matter of fact; it's a very tame affair, but it may have been useful in its day. In a way it's a sort of secret inside a secret—it goes down from the priest's hole into the wine cellars."

While I had been speaking, Mr. Underhill had come back into the room. He had his tycoon look again; he must have finished his call to Mr. Emerson before James came up to the schoolroom, so perhaps he had been telephoning to business associates all this time. But he shed it, and said, genially: "I knew all those stories about priests were true."

"Would you show us this stairway, Bryony?" Cathy sounded eager, genuinely so, I thought, in spite of the slightly over-anxious touch which meant either that she was nervous of the "real" Ashley who had owned all this once, or that she was trying to placate the girl she was hoping to supplant. "Right away after lunch?"

"Of course, if you want me to."

"Honey," her mother intervened, "maybe Miss Ashley doesn't feel like doing that just now."

"Oh, for goodness' sake, I'm *sorry* . . ." The contrition, like the eagerness, was a little too emphatic. "I guess I just forgot. What must you think of me?"

"It's all right," I said. "It's sweet of you, but don't worry about me. I'll be delighted to show you the stair after lunch."

"And talking of lunch," said Jeffrey Underhill, "where is it?"

So for the moment mysteries were shelved, and we went in.

Ashley, 1835

He lay on his back, staring up at the dark square of the ceiling mirror. Beside him she slept deeply, like a child.

They had made love first, as always, with the candle still alight. He remembered how at first she had protested, and he had insisted. She had given way, as she always gave way. Everything, everything that he wanted, he had to have.

Strange that this, which had been almost the

rule of these affairs, had come so differently, granted by her. Strange that this acquiescence, subservience, even, should have taught him, not, as with others, boredom and then disgust, but gratitude and, finally, love.

The candle had burned low. Soon, when it was not too strenuous a task to stretch his arm for the candlestick, he would blow it out. The room smelled of burning wax, and the lavender water she made each summer, and used to rinse her hair. He would open the window to let the dawn in, but not yet. Dawn always came too soon.

Ten

... If ye should lead her in a fool's paradise, as they say, it were a very gross kind of behaviour, as they say: for the gentlewoman is young, and therefore, if you should deal double with her, truly it were an ill thing. ...

—*Romeo and Juliet*, II, iv

Lunch was a very American affair, plates of salad with cold chicken, cheese, and fruit all served together, with crisp rolls, and coffee poured for a starter. Apart from the coffee, which I persist in wanting later, it was delicious, and perfect for the middle of a fine warm day. Also, the water was iced, a luxury for Ashley. Contemplating the amount of ice in the crystal jug, I wondered if, in the interests of American sanity, the Underhills had installed a freezer of their own. Our old refrigerator had never made more than twelve smallish cubes at a time in all its long, long life.

During lunch conversation was general, and I thought I could feel Mr. and Mrs. Underhill working to keep it so. But afterwards, back in the drawing room over more coffee, Cathy came straight back to the subject they obviously wanted to avoid.

"When you talked about mysteries, Bryony, what did

you mean? Not the old stair, I guess; that would never be a mystery to you."

Jeffrey Underhill's head turned, and his wife bit her lip, but I had had time to think. I said smoothly: "Why, no, it was something that my cousin and I found in the schoolroom."

Cathy looked at James, then, quickly, at me. "In the schoolroom?"

"Yes. Have you ever been in there?"

"No, I have not! The only parts of the house I've been in outside our own apartments are the rooms they keep for show. Why would I go in the schoolroom? What's up there?"

"A few reminders of time past, that's all," said James. "A family of hippopotami in grey velveteen, and four battered school desks, with empty inkwells. Highly symbolic, but—"

"I suppose so," said Cathy, impatiently. "But what's the mystery?"

"What hippopotamuses?" asked her mother. "What on earth are you all talking about?"

I laughed. "Nothing that's in the schoolroom, anyway. Something outside. We found a new view from the window, a view of the maze."

"Oh, the maze!" Cathy, her eyes bright, came forward, looking excited. "If you knew how I'd wondered about that maze! And the elegant little roof you can see . . . a sort of summerhouse, isn't it? I've walked all around the outside of those darned hedges to find the way in, and I even went in at two of the entrances, but I simply couldn't get through all that stuff, and anyway, I knew if I did, I'd never get out again. Gosh, I suppose you know the way in? Do you mean you can just walk right in as far as that summerhouse and out again, without getting lost?"

"Oh, yes. So can my cousin, unless he's forgotten. Have you, Twin?"

I caught the glint in James's eye. He knew quite well

that I found it impossible to address him directly as "Emory." I always had; so I had learned to use, when necessary, the irritating expedient the boys had invented.

"I don't know," he said. "I'd hate to try, without you there to guide me. But that's what you were going to tell them, wasn't it? We've got a map now."

"A map?" asked Cathy. The excitement she was showing, genuine or not, generated a sort of extra emphasis, so that the word "map" set up an echo in my mind. *The cat, it's the cat on the pavement. The map. The letter. In the brook.* I pushed it aside for the moment. James was explaining.

"Yes, a map. That was the mystery we solved just now in the schoolroom. When we were up there we noticed that one of the old trees on the edge of the lake had come down, and we could see clear through the gap to the maze. And from that height on the third story the layout can be seen almost completely. A bit blurred where it's overgrown, and not altogether easy to follow if you drew a plan from what you saw, but what it did tell us was that there are plans everywhere in the house."

He paused for effect. The two women looked amazed, but Jeffrey Underhill's brows came frowning together for no more than three seconds, then he said: "The coat of arms. I've wondered about that."

"Good God, you're quick," said my cousin admiringly. "Yes, it does seem an unlikely design, now one knows, doesn't it?" He nodded towards the carved fireplace. "There, Cat, you see it? That uninspiring pattern surrounding our enigmatic motto. That's a map of the maze."

"Well, for heaven's sake!" Cathy jumped out of her chair and ran to examine it more closely.

"Do you mean to tell me," demanded Mrs. Underhill, "that you didn't know this, either of you, till this very morning?"

"We'd no idea," I said. "There's never been anywhere from which you could see the maze from above, unless perhaps you'd climbed out on the pavilion roof, and that's not really been safe for years. And of course from the garden you can't see the pattern at all."

"An aerial photograph?" suggested Mr. Underhill. "That could be interesting, if half what I hear about the history of this district is true. Has it never been mapped?"

Though his voice sounded interested, I got the distinct impression that he spoke with only half his mind on what he was saying. He was absorbed, a long way away from us, in some frowning abstraction. So, I imagined, must the tycoon's reaction always be to small talk; smooth from long practice, and clever because he couldn't help it, but with the burning-glass of his full attention focussed a light-year or so away from this pretty room, and the trivialities we were talking about the maze.

"I suppose the Ordnance Survey must have taken pictures," James was saying. "They certainly mapped the district. We've got their maps, but they don't show the actual design of the maze, and I've never seen a photograph."

"In any case," I said, "it's all terribly overgrown now, with the hedges leaning together in places. From the air, I think it would just look like a huge thicket. What you really need is a plain geometric map like the one on the coat of arms, and then a machete. Mr. Underhill, there was something—"

He looked up from his coffee cup. I had been wrong. His attention, all of it, was right here in this room. It met me, palpably, and stopped me short.

"Yes, Miss Ashley?"

"There was something I wanted to ask you. Would I be in anyone's way if I spent a bit of time in the library? I want to go through the family books in the locked sections. They ought to be sorted out fairly soon . . . if that's all right?"

"Well, of course," said Jeffrey Underhill. "The house is yours, you know that. You don't need my permission to use your own part of it. Or this part, for that matter. Did Emory tell you that he and I are going to talk later on about the extent of our lease?"

"Yes."

"Well, meantime, please do your best to forget we're in the house at all. Go where you like. Now, what about keys? Do you want to keep my set?"

"No, thank you." I fished them out of my handbag. "I can get Rob's."

"Good. Then there'll be no difficulty about the tours." He took the keys from me, and laid them on the coffee table in front of him. "Stephanie, will you let the guide have these back this afternoon, please?"

"You leave that to me, dear," she promised, and began once more to tell me how welcome I was to anything and everything the Court could still offer me. She was interrupted by Cathy, who was over at the fireplace, busily tracing out the design of the maze in the stone.

" 'Touch Not the Cat . . .' It's a queer motto, isn't it? Emory said it was enigmatic. I say it's just plain arrogant. What does it mean? What is this cat they put in the middle of the maze? It looks more like a tiger!"

"It's getting on that way," said James. "It's a Scottish wildcat. There are lots of stories about them, but one thing's for sure, they can't be tamed, even if you take them from their mother while they're still blind and sucking. You'd not touch one of those lightly, glove or no glove."

"Goodness!" exclaimed Mrs. Underhill.

"A bit out of place here, perhaps?" commented her husband. "One gathers that the gloves they use in these parts have been velvet for rather a long time."

"Yes," said Cathy. "How does a Scotch wildcat get down here, right in the middle of England? And what does 'but a glove' mean?"

"Without a glove," I said. "It comes from an old word, 'butan.' The motto belonged—still does, I believe—to the Scottish Clan Chattan. One of the Ashleys married a girl called Julia McCombie who belonged to the Clan. She was a beautiful girl, and he was wild about her. He altered the whole place for her, did the house up specially, and built the pavilion in the maze. . . . The maze itself was here already; there's an engraving somewhere that shows it newly planted sometime in the eighteenth century, with a pretty little classical folly in the middle, a sort of imitation Roman temple. William Ashley pulled that down and built the pavilion that's there now. It must have been lovely when it was new. He built it as a sort of summerhouse for Julia; he raised it so that she could sit there and have a view right across the hedges of the maze."

"I suppose that's why he put the Scotch cat in the middle of the maze on the coat of arms," said Cathy.

"And he took her family motto as well?" said Mrs. Underhill. "How very romantic. But didn't the rest of the family mind? Surely they must have had a motto already?"

"Oh, they did. But the odd thing is that it was almost the same. It was 'Touch Me Who Dares,' and the crest was a creature like a leopard, so I suppose it seemed natural to poor William to use the coincidence, and put Julia's crest everywhere instead."

"Why 'poor William'?" asked Cathy. "What happened?"

"They didn't have much time," I said. "She died not long after he'd got the pavilion finished. He went peculiar then, used to shut himself up in the pavilion, and blocked some of the paths in the maze, and devoted himself to his writing and his studies. He wrote verses to her, too. There's a little book of them in the closed section of the library, called *A New Romeo to His Juliet*. He had her painted as Juliet. She's the one on the main landing, with a view of the maze behind her."

"Why, that's really romantic!" Mrs. Underhill said in her gentle voice. "And that's my favourite of the portraits, too. This will make it very interesting indeed to see that pavilion, if you're really sure you can find the way—"

"Oh, yes!" cried Cathy. "Do say you'll take us in, please, Bryony!"

"Of course. We'll go now if you like. But if we're going through that maze, Cathy, you ought to put on something you don't care about. Whatever you wear will probably end up in tatters."

She grinned. "You English really are the politest folks. As if I didn't know just what you think about this sweater. Don't pretend you don't know these are my very smartest rags. Patches special extras by Bonwit Teller."

"You will do us all a favour," said her father crisply, getting to his feet, "if you get that sweater torn to pieces, so that even Cathy refuses to wear it."

"I'll do my best," I said, and Cathy laughed, and turned to my cousin.

"Emory, you're coming, aren't you?"

"Some other time," said my cousin. "Your father and I have some talking to do."

"Okay. I'll just change my shoes, Bryony." She ran from the room.

Mrs. Underhill saw me eyeing her cream linen suit, and shook her head. "Some other time I'd love to. But not right now, if you don't mind. I've things to do."

"If the things to do include the washing up, then let me help you do it before we go."

"No, you certainly will not. What's the machine for? And look how many dishes there are. It will take one minute and a half, and not a second longer. Now you just go off with Cat, and forget about it. And don't leave without calling in again, will you? It's been a real pleasure. Get Cat to bring you in for tea."

She went, with James pushing the trolley for her. Jeffrey Underhill, with a word to me, went after them. I waited for Cathy to come back, watching the flicker of the log fire which looked pale in the sunlight, and thinking about the echo of Herr Gothard's voice, and the "William's brook" which might or might not be "William's book," and the cat which might or might not be Cathy Underhill.

To have a view now from the pavilion, it would have to be built on stilts like a water tower. The yew walls of the maze were eight feet high, and hadn't been clipped for some half-dozen years, so leaned over, top-heavy, to make the path in places into a black-green tunnel. Underfoot the weeds had seeded and reseeded into a long pale pash of sun-starved grass and groundsel, all too generously sown with nettles. In summer, what with the weeds underfoot and the dust harboured by the choked evergreens, the labyrinth would be impassable, but the main hazard now seemed to be the roosting birds. The hedges were full of them, and as we pushed our way past they exploded angrily in every direction. The smell of the yews as we disturbed them was as thick as smoke. Here and there a thin patch let a probe of sunlight through to gild the tiny green cones that clung along the feathery branches. Lamps of peace. Or was that the fruit? Must I wait for autumn and the lovely green-and-rosy acorns to glow along the dark boughs?

Lover? Lover, are you with me?

The only reply was Cathy, bravely treading behind me like Wenceslas' page. "Why did they ever make mazes? Just for fun?"

"When this one was planted it would be for fun. It was the fashion then to have follies, like mazes and grottoes and Grecian temples, in your garden. But the idea was ancient, wasn't it? There was the Labyrinth in Crete. I don't know if that was the first one. The legend said that Daedalus invented it for King Minos to hide the Minotaur in."

"Oh, yeah, I knew about that. I just read that fabulous book by Mary Renault . . . it was really a sort of storehouse, wasn't it? Do you suppose," asked the tycoon's daughter, "that it was a sort of primitive safe? You know, the treasure right in the middle, and even if thieves got in, they starved to death looking for a way out?"

I laughed. "It's an idea. But you were more likely to find a tomb in the middle than a treasure. I read somewhere that a maze was supposed to be the path the dead follow on the way to the world of spirits. Once at the heart of the maze, and nothing could touch you again; you'd reached a place outside the world, a place without bearings."

"In other words, you'd died?"

"Yes. Like the ships that went astray in the magic mists, and ended up at the Wondrous Isles. They say compasses won't work in a maze."

"For goodness' sake! Have you ever tried?"

"I can't say I have."

"And you really have been to the middle and out again?"

"Lots of times."

"Then I'll risk it," said Cathy buoyantly. "Oh, look, there's a gate. Where does that go?"

Here and there in the thick hedges was a tall, narrow gate, more than head high. I tried one; it was locked. A wren flew out of somewhere to perch on it, chattering angrily. "They were really put in to make it possible for the gardeners," I said, "but they've been used when people got stuck, and couldn't find the way out."

"Are they all locked?"

"Oh, yes, and the keys have been lost for years."

"Are you *sure* you remember the way?" she asked, a shade uncertainly.

I laughed at her. "Fairly sure. We could always climb on the pavilion roof and scream."

"If we ever get there."

"If we ever get there," I agreed. "No, here, it's this way."

"But we're heading right back for the house! I can see the chimneys!"

"I know, but it's right, it is really. You can trace it out tonight on the fireplace."

"If I ever see the fireplace again. Okay, I have to trust you, don't I? It's like something in *Alice,* you just turn your back on the pavilion and find yourself walking right up its front steps. . . . Oh!"

This as, just in front of us, under the last bending frame of black evergreens, a bright patch of sunlight struck green from flowery grass, and, rising from the flowers, were the elegant steps of William Ashley's pavilion.

The pavilion was as overgrown with weeds and lichens, and as dilapidated as the maze itself, but it was still charming. It was built of wood, with a steeply pitched roof of shingles gone silver with time. The roof-ridge was scalloped with carved shells, and at the corners curly dolphins waited to spit rain down into the gutters. The gutters themselves were warped and gaping, and held a remarkable selection of flowering weeds. A verandah, edged by a balustrade, and sheltered by the overhang of the roof, surrounded the pavilion on all four sides. The front door had carved panels and a charming knocker of a leopard's head with a ring in his mouth. To either side of the door stood tall windows with slatted louvers fastened over them. Honeysuckle and clematis and a host of other climbers had ramped up the wooden pillars and along the balustrading, and were reaching to seal doors and windows. We pushed them aside and mounted the steps.

"Touch not the cat," said Cathy, and reached past my shoulder for the ring of the knocker. She rapped sharply at the door.

There are few sounds so dead and hollow as the knocking on the door of an empty house. I felt a kind of goose-feather of superstition brushing my skin, and must have made an instinctive movement of protest. Cathy, unmoved, sent me a smile.

"Just to wake Wicked Ashley up," she said. "What's the matter?"

"Nothing. You made me jump. Anyway, one's always better not waking things up that are sleeping."

"I thought you said there weren't any ghosts."

"I've never met one," I said. "But if there are any at Ashley, this is where they'll be."

"Well, whether he's awake or not, he's not answering," said Cathy. "Anything against me trying the door?"

"Nothing at all, but you'll find it's locked."

"You're right. Oh, dear, can't we get in after all?"

"There's a way in through one of the side windows. Round here."

There was a way of opening the window shutters at the south side of the pavilion, and we were soon inside and pushing the creaking leaves open to let in the light and air.

The pavilion was larger than such places usually are. It had once, of course, been elegantly furnished, but now all the furnishings had gone except for some relatively recent garden stuff, a table and a daybed and a couple of cane chairs.

"Well, here you are," I said. "I'm afraid it's rather a dusty end to the romance."

"Is that the table where he wrote his poems?"

"I doubt it. That's late Victorian. I'm afraid all the original stuff has gone."

Cathy's eye fixed itself on the one impressive feature which remained. This was the ceiling, which was made of one huge looking glass framed in gilt and mounted within the elaborately moulded cornice. Its smeared and flyblown surface was slightly angled, its frame of dirty gilt scrollwork supported, apparently, by birds and ribbons and swags of roses. The glass caught the sunshine from the open window, and laid a rhomboid of gritty light across the foot of the daybed and along the floor.

"Surely that's part of the original building?" she asked. "What a pretty idea, to have a mirror ceiling. If those brackets in the walls held sconces, the place must have seemed just full of candlelight. Is this in any of the old pictures?"

"Yes, I'm afraid it is."

" 'Afraid'?"

"There's a set of rather randy engravings," I told her. "I'm afraid the mirror's not a bit romantic, really. Oh, yes, it's certainly old, but I think it was put in by your Wicked Ashley, William and Julia's son. It rather gives one ideas about all the wild parties he had, and the lady-loves he brought here, till the brother of the last one shot him. The engravings are rather imaginative about it, anyway, and the mirror certainly shows in those, right over where the bed was."

"Oh, for goodness' sake, is that what it was for? You know," said Cathy, pivoting on her heel and watching herself in the tilted mirror, "I cannot imagine it would be any fun at all watching oneself having sex. Can you?"

"Distinctly off-putting, I'd have thought."

She turned again, slowly, on her heel, and her look round the grubby, echoing room was sad. "It surely is a dusty answer," she said.

"I'm sorry."

"Oh, don't be. I don't know why the past is always sadder if there's something a bit beautiful about it. And this place must have been beautiful."

"Keats says that about melancholy." I quoted it for her:

"She dwells with Beauty—Beauty that must die;
And Joy, whose hand is ever at his lips
Bidding adieu. . . ."

"Yeah, I remember that. He was right, too." Cathy's look dwelt on me for a moment, with something in it that I couldn't understand. Then she looked past me. "Oh, look, there's a little bit of Julia left here, after all."

Above the daybed, on the wall against which presumably Nick Ashley's big bed had once stood, was a moulding in plaster, a sort of bedhead applied to the wall itself. At its apex was the familiar coat of arms, thickly grimed and grey, with its motto and its rampant wildcat. This looked as if it had been moulded from one of the carvings in the house; it showed the grainy texture of the stone, and even a chip or two. There were still traces of paint, but time had done badly by it; it was rubbed and flaking, and in places barely distinguishable.

Cathy leaned across the daybed to look at it. "Well," she said, "what do you know, here's the map again. Just to make sure you could get out of the place, even if you'd forgotten how you got in." She licked a finger and rubbed the grimy plaster. "Did you notice? I think someone's marked the way. Yes, there's the bit just before we got here, when we were heading straight back towards the house."

I followed her, kneeling on the daybed and peering up at the dirty moulding. "I believe you're right. I'd never noticed."

She rubbed harder. "They're not done like that in the house, because I was looking." She laughed. "I expect Nick Ashley drew it in so that his girl friends could slink off home to their husbands, and leave him still peacefully sleeping it off. Hey, this plaster's crumbling a bit, I'd better leave it alone." She straightened, rubbing her hand down the patched jeans. "This place really could do with a paint job, couldn't it? I only hope that mirror's safe. It certainly doesn't look it. You know, with a good cleanup and a rug and some furnishing, this could be quite a place, still, wouldn't you say? It would make a guest cottage if you put a bed back in, and a few other things."

"For people you didn't like? Show them the guest cottage and forget to tell them the way out?"

She laughed. "Well, it's an idea. Anyway, what would you want a guest cottage for, with a place the size of the Court? No, it's fascinating just as it is."

I wondered if the gaze she sent around the pavilion was more than just idle. My next question came straight out of the speculation, but it sounded casual enough. "How long have you known Emory?"

"Not long. We only met last month, but it seems longer. I mean, he's easy to know, wouldn't you say?"

"I can imagine. And James?"

"I met him soon after, but I've only seen him a couple of times. My, but they're alike, aren't they?"

"Tweedledum and Tweedledee," I agreed. "Could you ever get them mixed up, do you think?"

She laughed. "I hope not. Could you?"

"I don't think so. I never did as a little girl, but that's a long time ago, and we don't meet so often now. I admit that when I saw him today at the Court I wasn't quite sure which it was till he told me."

We had gone outside while we were talking, and I pulled the long windows shut and fastened the louvers across. We went down the steps. The honeysuckle let its arras down behind us, and the pavilion was shut in once more with its dust and its silence.

"I guess," said Cathy, ingenuously, "I could still get them mixed up if they tried to fool me, but they're too nice to do that. Besides, Emory—" She stopped. "Say, what's that perfume? I don't see any flowers except daisies and those yellow things."

"Lilies of the valley. They've gone wild there under the hedge in the shade. You can't see the flowers—those stiff green leaves, see? Let's pick some for your mother, shall we?" I stooped and pushed the leaves aside, hunting for the waxy bells. She knelt beside me, and did the same. I said: "You were saying. Emory?"

"Oh, nothing."

I let it wait for a minute. "Emory's special, isn't he?"

"Special? Why, of course! Bryony, I'm just crazy about him!" She laughed up at me, her eyes brilliant. She meant, it was obvious, every word; but it came a thought too easily, as if she had said it before, and would say it again. Paradoxically, I found the over-emphasis soothing; it gave her confession the flavour of powder-room gossip, the easy euphoria of the evening out. "Don't *you* think he's just fabulous? I'd do just *anything* for him!"

She stopped, seeming to catch some echo in her own voice that embarrassed her. She bit her lip, and coloured up, turning quickly away from me, her hands searching busily among the green spathes. The long hair swung down to hide her face.

"Bryony, about Emory. Do you mind?"

"Mind?" Taken by surprise, I sat back on my heels, regarding her averted head. Then I answered as she had spoken, directly and without guile. "No, I don't. Of course I don't. There's no reason why I should."

She, too, sat back at that, turning to face me once more. The flush had subsided; she gave me a clouded, smiling look, where some obscure hint of trouble showed still. She started to speak, broke off, considering something else, then rejected that, too. Kneeling there among the flowery grass, with the rhinoceros-folds of the enormous sweater dwarfing her body, and her hair falling anyhow over brow and shoulders, she looked far younger even than eighteen.

I said, easily: "I don't wonder you've fallen for him: when I was your age I was wild about him. But then, I was wild about the others, too." I smiled at her. "Tell me, where's the difference when it comes to being 'special'? Why not James?"

"Well, for one thing, I haven't seen all that much of him, and for another—"

"Yes?"

The fabulous mink lashes dropped suddenly to shadow her cheeks. She bent to the flowers again. "He has a girl already."

"How do you know that?"

I hadn't meant the question to come out quite so sharply, but she appeared to have noticed nothing. "Because he said so," she said simply.

"Oh." I bent to add another flower to the spray in my hand. "Have you met her? Did he say who it was?"

"No. There." She straightened. "Mom'll be wild about these. Shall we go back?"

"Sure. Let's go back by the path along the Overflow."

We came out of the maze into full sunlight, and crossed the little bridge. Primulas were out along the stream, nodding in the draft made by the running water.

"Why do you call it the Overflow?" she asked as we followed the mossy path along the edge.

"Because it's just that. It controls the level of the moat. There are the two sluices, the High Sluice, on the other side of the house, that lets the water from the river into the moat, and this one here that lets it out into the Pool. The Overflow wasn't much more, originally, than just a ditch to carry floodwater away, but a few years ago the High Sluice broke in a storm, and the lower sluice couldn't cope with the flooding, so parts of the house were damaged. They put a new High Sluice in, and dug this channel deeper as a safety precaution."

"Gee, I'd never thought that living with a moat around you could be dangerous."

"It's not really. And if the sluice had been kept properly it never would have been. Actually"—I laughed—"the moat is pretty useful. Its main use being that it reduces the fire insurance premiums."

"Well, and that's another dusty answer," said Cathy. "Here I was thinking that a moated grange was the most romantic thing ever— Oh!"

"What is it?" I asked.

She had stopped, and was pointing. I had been walking behind her. I came up to her shoulder and looked.

Between the moat and the lake below it, cutting down through a corner of the grassed bank, was one of the prettiest monuments in the Court gardens, a cascade with a fishing cat. At the head of the bank was the heavy sluice gate, which was normally kept shut, and to either side of this the normal outflow from the moat was channelled to lapse, fall by fall, towards the Pool. The water stair, a natural-looking cascade of rock, thickly set with ferns and trailing plants, led the fall into a corner of the Pool from which, through bigger rocks green with the moss of many years, the water ran down into the deeply cut channel of the Overflow. On one of these rocks, just where the water slid towards the first rush of the Overflow, was a stone cat, its outstretched paw reaching into the flow, gracefully curved as if to hook a fish.

Or rather, the cat had been there. Now there was nothing but the gate with the water cascading down the rocks beside it, and on the stone where the cat had been, the ugly iron staples stuck out, rotten with rust and twisted crooked with the fall of the statue. The cat itself was lying in the basin under the water, with the fish tranquilly shuttling to and fro across it, under the broken paw.

Ashley, 1835

A sound from the door dragged him from the shallows of sleep. Someone was there, on the verandah.

He was alert, instantly up on one elbow. Perhaps Fletcher had come: something was wrong? His uncle had arrived before he was expected? This little world of peace and love had been broken before its time; the too short night was over.

But all was silence. He relaxed again, to see her eyes, darkly shining, watching him.

"What is it, love?"

"Nothing. Something waked me. Look, the moon's almost down. A little while, and it will be getting light. No, don't go yet. I have something to tell you, but it will wait. It will wait a little longer."

Eleven

Nor what is mine shall never do thee good:
Trust to 't. . . .
—*Romeo and Juliet*, III, v

As I had promised, I went back to tea with Cathy and
her mother, then took myself off to my cottage, to see if
Rob had brought my baggage in from Worcester.

He had, and had even carried it upstairs for me and
dumped it on the tiny landing.

Before I unpacked I went to the telephone and dialled
the number of the secondhand bookshop in Ashbury.

"Is Mr. Oker there, please? Oh, Leslie, it's you. This is
Bryony, Bryony Ashley. Yes, I came back a couple of
days ago; I'm back at the cottage. . . . How are you?
Good. How's everything going . . . ?"

Talking to Leslie had about it something (I imagined)
of the ritual of Eastern bargaining; you had to go through
the routine of question and answer first, the answer being
the shorter exercise of the two. Mr. Oker loved talking,
and there was no hurrying him; one got to business
eventually, but by way of health, the weather, trade
prospects, the latest news, and any extra juicy items of
local gossip that were worth passing on. The routine, I
suppose, had originally been evolved as part of a
softening-up process, the patter before the hard dealing.

In sober fact, Leslie gave very little away, but the impression he fostered, of a genial and impulsive gossip, stood him in very good stead: strangers who were deceived by his effusive and rather camp manner into hoping for an easy bargain would come suddenly, and to their disadvantage, up against a very knowledgeable and wily operator. Leslie Oker was about as impulsive as a two-toed sloth, and rather less effeminate than a tomcat. The kindness, though, was real.

Thanks to it, the preliminaries today were short. After only three minutes, at least two of which were devoted to my welfare, and to praise of my father, Leslie paused, and then said, directly: "But you didn't ring me up just to tell me you were home, dear. What can I do for you?"

"Well, something's come up, and I wonder if you could help me, please. Just a quick query. You remember showing me that limited edition of *Rip Van Winkle* last year, the one illustrated by Arthur Rackham? I wondered what sort of price his work was fetching now? I don't mean the books, I mean the original illustrations?"

"Well, it's not exactly my line, as you know, but I'd say you'd be lucky if you came across one at all. Is this some particular drawing you want to buy?"

I laughed. "You know me better than that. I don't want to sell one, either. I just want to know the sort of value, if you wouldn't mind. Just an idea."

"The last one I saw listed in a catalogue," said Leslie, crisply, "was a watercolour drawing from *Comus,* and it was priced at eight hundred pounds."

"Oh. I see. Thank you. Leslie—"

"Yes?"

"If you should by any chance come across some mention of Rackham drawings for sale, would you not say anything about this, but just phone me straight away?"

"Of course. But how very intriguing." The light voice showed little but a gentle and sympathetic interest. "I gather one is not allowed to ask why?"

"For now, no. But I'll come in as soon as I can, and tell you all about it."

"This *is* exciting," said Leslie comfortably. "Of course, Bryony dear. Count on me. And perhaps I could give the grapevine just a teeny, teeny shake? But tell me soon, won't you, before I *die* with curiosity?"

"That'll be the day," I said, and he laughed, and rang off.

James came down after supper, just as I was finishing the washing up. He hoisted the empty cases into the roof space for me, accepted a cup of coffee, then followed me outside to the seat under the lilac tree facing the Pool. Dusk was falling, and the air was very still. The surface of the Pool lay quiet and shining, ringing into ripples here and there as fish rose for the evening hatch. There was a heron still fishing among the reeds at the far side. The rooks were settling for the night, and making a great to-do about it. Like clouds behind the cottage roof, the orchard trees showed pale and frothy with blossom, and tallest of all, the pear tree, like a central fountain in a water garden, held up its plumes of springtime snow. A thrush was singing in it, alone, as freshly and as passionately as if this was the first song in the world. From somewhere in the middle distance, towards the Court, came the sound of someone hammering.

"Rob puts in long hours," said my cousin.

"I wonder if he's mending the fishing cat."

"Fishing cat?"

"The one at the sluice where the Overflow leaves the moat. It's broken. I saw it this afternoon when Cathy and I were coming back from the maze."

"Oh? That's a pity. It was a pretty thing. Did you ask him to fix it?"

"No, I've not seen him this evening."

"Well," said James, "why should he trouble? More likely he's propping up one of the gates, or mending a roof, or even chopping some bushes down. Wasting his time, whatever he's doing. The whole place is falling to bits, and it would take more than Rob Granger to stop it."

He spoke without bitterness, and quite without intent

to hurt, but with some special seriousness in his voice that made me look searchingly at him. He met my look gravely, then took my empty cup from me and set it with his own on the flagstones under the seat. Then, as before in the schoolroom, his arm came gently round my shoulders, drawing me close. I could feel his heartbeat, perhaps a shade too fast.

"Bryony, love, it's time we had a talk, you and I."

I waited, feeling my own heartbeat quicken imperceptibly to match his. I was very conscious of the beauty of the evening, the scent of the lilac and the song of the thrush and the lovely long planes of light on the lake in front of us.

My cousin cleared his throat. "You may be angry, and as a matter of fact I think you're bound to be angry, but if you've any sense you'll hear me out, and in the end, I hope you'll help me." His fingers, cupping my shoulder, tightened a fraction. "You have to be on my side. You know that. You have to be. It's the way things are."

The thrush stopped singing, as suddenly as a turned-off tap. The heron, too, had decided to give up for the night. He must have done well, I thought; he was having trouble with his lift-off. I watched him in silence as he lumbered into the air, and flapped away.

"Bryony?"

"Yes, I'm listening. Go on."

There was a short pause, while I felt him looking at me. I heard him take breath. "I'll start at the beginning. And I may as well start by confessing the brutal truth. My father—we, the lot of us, are in a jam. A real jam. We're desperate for ready cash and we have to find it some way, and find it fast."

This was in no way what I had been expecting. I was startled, and showed it. "But surely? I thought Cousin Howard—your family's always seemed to be doing so well. I mean—compared with us . . . And I thought you were riding really high now, with the Jerez office doing so well, and with the Pereira backing. I know Daddy thought the same. What's happened?"

"The trouble is, everything's happened, and all at once."
He stirred. "My God, that's the truest proverb in the
language: 'troubles never come singly.' All the demands
that we could have met if they'd come separately, and at
the right time, well, they all seemed to come at once.
. . . I told you that my father will probably have to
retire. If he does, there's not much guarantee that Pereiras
will go on backing us. Why should they? And the Bristol
offices are hardly an asset; they're mortgaged. If we had
time— But the point is, we haven't. This illness of Father's
has put a gun to our heads."

And now, I was thinking, this has happened. Because
of my father's death, this huge liability, Ashley Court, has
fallen on them, too.

"But I thought Juanita had quite a lot of money of her
own. Wouldn't she help tide you over with a temporary
loan, and give you the time you need?"

"Ironically enough," and his voice held no irony, but
only a rather flat distaste at having to talk about the matter at all, "the main part of her money is tied up in a
trust, and can't be touched. These trusts," said James, and
left it at that.

I said nothing. The evening was silent and empty. The
light had gone from the lake. The lilac's scent had evapo-
rated with the cooling air.

"So," said my cousin, "my father applied to yours to
see if he could help us."

This time I really was startled. I sat up. "James, you
can't be serious! You must have known we were run into
the ground."

"Oh, yes, we knew that. But you had Ashley."

"*Ashley?* But what on earth use is Ashley, when it
comes to meeting a mortgage? It's the biggest liability
this side of the National Debt!"

"As it stands, yes. It just pays for its upkeep and
nothing to spare, we know that." His voice went flat.
"What I'm talking about is the Ashley Trust."

"I see. You mean that's what you 'applied' to Daddy
for? To break the trust?"

"Yes."

"When was this?"

"The first time was in November of last year," he said. "I never saw his answer to my father's letter, but it must have given room for maneuver, since Father still seemed to have hopes he would consent."

"The first time? He asked him more than once?"

He nodded. "He wrote again recently, and he had a couple of telephone talks with your father. This was when Cousin Jonathan was in Bad Tölz, of course. My father didn't want to press it, because he knew Cousin Jon ought to rest, but—well, things were getting desperate. The last time, though, Cousin Jon said he couldn't even consider it." He was silent for a moment, his head bent. "I've been thinking about the reason for his change of heart, and I can't really understand it. As you know, things have been sold in the past, and no one's ever argued much about it. I think he must have been feeling so much better that he was planning to come back here, so he decided that as long as he could keep the place in some sort of order, he'd do just that. After all, it was your home."

"And his. He loved it. You're not just talking about 'things' this time, James? I take it you're talking about the place itself. The land."

"Yes." He gave me a gentle look. "Didn't you know anything about this?"

"Nothing. Of course if there'd been any question of breaking the trust he'd have had to bring me in as well. I'd have to consent, too, you know that." I thought for a moment. "It didn't occur to anyone to try and break Juanita's trust rather than ours? After all, she's Cousin Howard's wife."

"Well, of course it did. But that trust can't be touched at any price. It goes to her children, or, if there aren't any, it can be broken when she's forty."

"Which is quite some time away."

"Too long by half. If it was only six months, it would still be too long for us."

"So," I said, "now Daddy's dead, you come to me, and ask me to break ours."

He was silent.

"That's what you've been leading up to, isn't it? Isn't that what you want?"

"That is what we want," he said.

A pause. I said abruptly: "Did Daddy give any reason for being so dead set against it?"

"No. He would hardly even discuss it. He really never mentioned it to you at all, even indirectly?"

Even as I shook my head, I realized, in a sudden moment of enlightenment, that he had. *"Trust. Depend. Do what's right."* This was one of the things that had been weighing on his mind. Until I knew the rest, I could take no action.

I took refuge in a half-truth. "I can't say that he did. He may have thought that your money troubles were your own affair, and shouldn't be broadcast, even to me. But of course he spoke about the trust generally, once or twice. I do remember his saying that Cousin Howard seemed to have put down roots in Spain, and didn't seem to have the kind of feeling for Ashley that might bring him back to look after it. He didn't say it as a criticism, why should he? He said it 'wasn't to be expected, but it was a pity.' That kind of thing. But I know he hoped that Emory or you might feel differently. You'd lived here, after all, with us. Do you?"

"Are you asking me to speak for Emory?"

"If you can. I know you said you couldn't speak for him when I asked if he was serious about Cathy Underhill, but you must know how he feels about Ashley." I gave him an inquiring look. "And I would have thought the two might almost be the same. I mean, if he was thinking along the lines of marrying Cathy—"

"He'd be able to afford to keep Ashley as it should be kept? I suppose so," said James, "but the plain fact is, he doesn't want to keep it at all."

From beyond the lime trees the church clock tolled the half hour. It sounded remote and serene. The distant hoot-

ing of an early owl spoke of mystery and the coming
night.

"And you?" I asked him. "No, James, it's all right. I
do understand. But I've got to know the truth. You said
I had to be on your side, and that's true. I am; you know
that. We're not talking about family now, or people, just
about bricks and mortar and trees, which might mean a
lot to one person, but don't have to to another. So tell me.
Do you want Ashley yourself, or even a part of it?"

He took his time. When he spoke at length his voice
was quiet, but I could feel the tension in the arm that en-
circled me. "I think you know the answer, don't you?
When we were talking awhile ago about the fishing cat,
I said the place was rotten, and that's true. You know it
is. It's been falling to pieces, bit by bit, for years. It's a
burden to the living, even if you count keeping it going as
homage to the dead. That's not the way to live now, when
the dead can no longer supply the living with the means to
keep their memorials going." He took a breath like a sigh.
"I'm sorry, love, this is the wrong time to talk to you like
this, but you asked me. I doubt if you've had the time to
think about it yet, since Cousin Jon died, but you can't
seriously expect either of us, Emory or me, to go on running this—this National Trust reject, even if we did have
the money to do it with? There are other things to do
with money, Bryony. For us, anyway."

"I suppose so."

"All right, so Cousin Jon might have thought we should
want to. But you're a different generation, you know the
score. These are the seventies, and the world's wider than
Ashley Park. If there aren't the means to save it, then
it'll have to go. We've got to face that."

"James, I'm facing it."

His arm tightened, and he held me close. His cheek
touched my hair, but he didn't attempt a caress. "Well,
I've said what I promised to say, and I'll leave it. But you
will think about it, won't you?"

"Of course I will. But Daddy only died a week ago,
remember, and until I know what he wanted, and why—"

"I know, love, I know. I'm sorry. This is a hell of a time to talk to you about breaking trusts and leaving Ashley, but when we started this we weren't to know what would happen to your father. And now my own father's ill, and worried half out of his mind, and things are pressing, and—well, hell, there it is."

Another of those silences. The hammering had stopped. I thought of the fishing cat lying broken under the water, and, for some reason, of the pavilion with its riot of honeysuckle and the sagging walls of yew and Cathy's voice asking: "Is that the table where he wrote his poems?"

"Francis," I said suddenly. "How does Francis feel about all this? I thought he loved Ashley."

"He does," said James. "He's a throwback, is Francis. Anyway, he wouldn't notice if the place fell to pieces round him, as long as he could sit in the maze like William Ashley, making verses. What on earth did I say? You jumped."

"Nothing, really. Only you were reading my thoughts. Do you often do that?"

A pause, as long as four quickened heartbeats. Then he said, easily: "Twin and I do it as a matter of course. Shades of Bess Ashley, the gipsy, didn't you know?"

"It must save a lot of telephone calls," I said lightly.

He laughed. "Oh, it does. But you were saying about Francis. I doubt if he would refuse to help break the trust. The point is, even if we did break it, we wouldn't have any designs on the house itself. That's unsaleable, so one might as well make a virtue of necessity, and leave it alone as a corner of ancient England on its own tight little island. It's the land that would have to go."

"For what?"

"For whatever would bring the most money."

"Building land brings the most."

He answered what I had not said. "Well, and why not? People have to have houses. And when they drive the new motorway across Penny's Flats, we'll be in Birmingham commuter country." He must have felt something in my silence, because he added, rather edgily: "Look, Bryony, you said you'd be realistic. Just because we played here as kids doesn't mean our kids will ever have the chance, or, my God, *want* the chance."

"I wasn't. I was thinking about the other people involved. That must be what was making Daddy think twice. There's the Vicar, for instance. What happens to the Vicarage? I suppose that would be safe enough, though I can hardly see Mr. Bryanston hemmed in with housing projects, and without the garden. But there are the Hendersons, and Rob Granger. Would you sell their houses?"

"Why not? They'd have first option to buy them themselves."

"The Hendersons might, but I'm sure Rob can't afford to."

"Then he ought to. He had the farm, after all. If he didn't manage to make a go of that, there's no reason why we should be responsible—"

"Be fair. His father drank every penny they ever made, and knocked Rob and his mother around on Saturdays for good measure. He left them in debt up to their necks, and if Rob hasn't managed to save the price of a house since the old brute died you can hardly blame him. What's more, if it weren't for Rob this place would have dropped to bits a darned sight sooner."

"O.K., O.K.," he said, half laughing. "What have I said? Sorry, I didn't mean it like that. I've always liked Rob, and I know what he's done for you and your father. And now I've made you angry when I want you to listen."

"I'm not angry. It's not that I'm not on your side, James. I am. And I was listening. You were talking about commuter country. Well, all right, all being equal, that's the way things might have to go. But had you thought? Ashley hasn't an outlet to Penny's Flats."

His head turned, sharply. He stared. His eyes, in the close dusk, looked dark, gipsy Ashley eyes. I felt a queer little tingling thrill at the base of the spine, and looked away. He said, sharply: "Of course it has. That's its whole value. This strip along the Pool runs right through the apple orchard to the road."

"Yes, but that's not Ashley Trust. It's mine."

"Oh, I see." He sounded amused. "Holding out, are you?"

"For the present, yes. I've got to have a home, and I'm planning to stay here till . . ."

"Till?"

"Well, for a bit," I said, evading it. "James, let's leave it for now, may we?"

"Of course, if you say so. But—"

"Yes? But?"

"There was something else. As a matter of fact," he said, rather abruptly, "I haven't even got to the hard bit yet. Look, would you like—shall I get some more coffee?"

"No, don't bother, for me. Go right on. What is the hard bit?"

"Well, I was saying. After your father had refused to consider the trust any further, my father asked Emory and me to do what we could, as quickly as possible. Emory and I talked it over, and we agreed to go to Bavaria and talk to your father. He must obviously have had reasons for his decision, which he didn't want to talk about by telephone, and which might be too complicated to write. But before that it seemed only sense to—well, to take a look at Ashley itself."

"So then?"

"I meant, take a look at it with the idea of a sale in mind." He cleared his throat. "Obviously, we wanted to get into the Court and find out, as a basis for discussion with your father, what there was in the way of quickly disposable assets. We didn't approach your father about this because . . . well, damn it, it was a little difficult under the circumstances. He was ill, and he'd have thought we were being a bit previous. A foot in his grave, as it were. I'm sorry."

I said nothing.

I could feel tension running through his arm. He said abruptly: "We didn't get in touch with the Underhills either, because there was no need. I told you about that.

By pure chance—it really was pure chance—Emory met Cathy at a party, and she asked him down."

"Convenient."

I felt his look. "You sound a bit abrasive. Don't you like her?"

"From what I've seen of her, I like her very much. I'm just not sure that I like her being used by Emory."

"Did I say he was using her?"

"Isn't he?"

"I wouldn't put it like that." But I thought he sounded uncomfortable.

"That had better be true, you know. Jeff Underhill is what they call a tough cookie, and at a guess he adores his daughter. If she's fallen for Emory, and I think she has, and hard, then Emory had better reckon it as serious."

"I imagine he does. I only said that he didn't plan to live at Ashley on her money." He sounded thoroughly edgy now. "Damn it, do you have to assume he's going to damage her in some way? If a girl like that falls for you, you've got to be a bloody plaster saint not to take a second look, at least."

"So you have."

Somehow, almost unnoticeably, his hand had lifted from my shoulder, and his arm now lay harmlessly along the back of the seat. "It's the James-Emory thing that gets you, isn't it? You'll have to take my word for it that nothing's happened that Cathy would mind remembering, even if she ever found out we'd played that game with her. Which she won't." He glanced at me again, but I made no comment. "Actually, I don't like it any more than you do. . . . There are things I'd rather be doing than escorting an eighteen-year-old who's in love with someone else. I don't think Emory ever would have started it, but in a way Cathy herself forced it on us."

"How on earth?"

"Oh, there was one date they had made, and Emory couldn't keep it. When he phoned, she was so mad that he thought she'd call the whole thing off, and this was just at the time when we very much wanted to get down to the Court, and if there had been a quarrel with Cathy we could hardly have come down, even through Emerson. So Emory soothed her down and got me to go instead. It never crossed her mind. It was a harmless sort of date—she and Twin hadn't known each other more than a few days, so I didn't have any soft lights and hot music to face. . . . And today it was a case of coming down to see Jeff Underhill, rather than of making love to Cat. Believe me, I've no idea how far Twin's pushed the boat out, nor do I want to. I wouldn't bet on not giving myself away to Cat, and God help us all if that happened." I caught the gleam of a sideways, smiling look, and one finger came away from the seat back and touched my shoulder blade, a feather touch. "If you like, love, I'll promise you here and now not to do it again."

"That's up to you." The words were indifferent, but I felt myself relaxing, and the arm came round me again. "Go on," I said, "did you check the 'disposable assets' between you after all? Great jumping beans!" I sat up again, my hand to my mouth, regarding him wide-eyed in the dusk. "The T'ang horse? The jade?"

"I'm afraid so." He was speaking quietly, straight to the almost invisible flagstones at his feet. "Bryony, they were ours. I promise you we only took them after your father's death. This last week. I promise you. We badly needed a bit of ready cash, and Emory knew of a market, so . . ."

I listened to the tone, rather than to the words. I knew it well. James, led into something by Emory, loyal to his twin but knowing all the time that whatever they had done was, to say the least of it, dubious. Emory, I knew, was more than capable of playing rough, and James, playing with him, had sometimes suffered for it. But Twin had always been right.

I was aware of silence. He had run out of words. I heard myself asking, in a hard voice quite unlike my own: "Did you have to take the pictures from the schoolroom? You might argue that the other things were going to belong to your family anyway, but the pictures were my own, and I loved them."

"I know. I'm sorry. I—it was a mistake. They were taken by mistake. They haven't been sold. As a matter of fact, we planned to put them back, but there hasn't been a chance today."

"Today?"

"Yes, today. They were only taken yesterday. As soon as I found out, I said they must go back, but by that time you were at the Court, and you'd seen the T'ang horse was missing, and you had started asking about keys. It . . . well, it was awkward."

"I suppose it was." I felt a little dazed. "Just a minute, James. You said, 'They were only taken yesterday.' Who took them, then? Emory wasn't here, was he?"

"No. Cat took them for us."

"*What?*" A whirling pause, while I tried to assess it. " 'For us'? You mean 'for Emory.' "

"If you like."

"I do like." My voice was sharp. "It makes a difference."

"Well, then, for Emory. Look, don't worry, you'll get them back. It was just—"

"I'm not worrying about jade or pictures or anything else. I'm thinking about Cathy Underhill. You got that girl to steal for you."

"That's a hard word."

"It's a hard fact."

"Aren't you making a bit too much of this? The things were ours."

"Perhaps I am. But not nearly as much as her parents would make of it, I'm sure of that. I thought at the time they seemed almost too upset for what had happened. It made me wonder."

"Her parents? For God's sake, you're not going to make a thing out of it, are you? Bryony—"

"Wait a minute, James. This takes some getting used to. Let me alone for a bit."

I got up abruptly and walked away from him, across

the newly cut strip of lawn to the lakeside. There was a
low wall there, a length of ancient stonework that had
been left to edge the garden; its fissures were planted with
wallflowers and toadflax and some trailing glaucous fern
that looked silver in the dusk. I stood there with my back
to my cousin, staring out over the dimming Pool, but without seeing that or anything. It was wrong, so wrong. . . .
Yet because it was James, I couldn't give way to my first
instinctive reaction; because it was James I must make
myself stop and think. . . . Be civilized, I told myself,
this sort of shocked recoil isn't even instinctive, it's a con-
ditioned reaction to what you've been taught to call theft.

Well, all right, think. *Was* it theft? As soon as the
legal formalities allowed, all these things would belong to
Howard, and by the same token to his sons. James had
said with perfect justice that the day was gone when the
dead could help the living to watch over the property they
had amassed and handed down in designs too vast for today to cope with. And it was my cousins who would have
to cope, not I. The fact that Jon Ashley was now one of
the dead ought to make no difference. My reaction was an
emotional one, nothing more. James knew that; he had
tried to spare me; but I had forced his hand by my actions
at the Court today, so he had had to tell me now, raw
though I still was from my father's death.

I thought again, briefly, about Rob and the fishing cat.
. . . Yes, James was right here, too: the place, and the
life it had represented, was falling to pieces. Even this
cottage, the idyllic little cottage with the view of the lake,
with its fruit trees, and the honeysuckle and the Fribourg
rose, had woodworm and rising damp which I could not
afford to combat. If I sold some of my mother's Worcester
porcelain to pay for it, that would be ethical. Why should
not my cousins, the owners of Ashley, sell the pieces that
were theirs? And why, if they were driven for time, should
they not have done it this way?

It came back to the one answer: Cathy. And here I
had even less right to judge. I had no idea of the strength
of Emory's feeling for her; nor had I stopped to question

the circumstances under which she had "stolen" the missing articles for my cousins. For Emory, that is. My father had long ago said that Howard would never take on Ashley or any part of its responsibility; it was squarely on Emory's shoulders, and if Emory had chosen to jump the legal gun . . . Yes, it was to be laid at Emory's door; I still did not believe that James was, in this, anything other than a follower, loyal as ever to whatever course his twin suggested.

I sat down on the wall, still facing the lake, forcing myself to calmness. I owed my cousins something better than this shocked recoil. I thought again of the quiet nights filled with my lover's presence, of his support and warmth and love, of the strength he had given me. I thought, too, of the recent strange hesitancy, the impression of guilt and insecurity which, now, I thought I could understand. It had only showed itself since I had come back to England; it had begun last night, when I had seen James in the church vestry. Doing what? That, too, I had begun to guess. The object he had been carrying was large and flat, like a book, or a portfolio. He must just have picked up the Rackham pictures from some hiding place; not the vestry itself—that would have been asking for discovery. But, except on church-cleaning days, there were a hundred places—under the seats in the side aisles, under the pulpit, behind the stacked hassocks near the font—any of these places would have made a cache, safe and dry, where Cathy could have hidden the objects she had abstracted from the Court.

So James had snatched a cassock from the choir men's pegs, had fled up the nave in front of me, switched off the mains, and, while I was approaching up the church, fumbled with and opened the catch of the vestry door. Whoever came into the church would only see the vanishing cassocked figure, and would come to the same conclusion as I had done. . . .

Well, now I knew. And I understood my lover's refusal to come into the open. It was because the affairs of daylight must be settled first. Before anything could be

complete between us, we had to settle with the realities of
a difficult situation, the hard economics of how and where
to live, of Ashley Court and Daddy's Will and the theft
of the jade and pictures. What I had called to myself the
facts of the daylight world. And the other world, the starlight one, where love was easy because it ran like poetry
from mind to mind, that would have to wait. I knew now
what he meant by his repeated *Not yet, not yet;* I had to
come to terms with what he really was; the outer man, not
just that other half of me whom I knew as well as I knew
myself. We had reversed the norm, he and I. It had always
seemed to me that the love we had, being fuller, must be
easier than most; now I saw that it was harder. Nor was
the outcome certain. It would depend on my handling of
this uneasy and tangled affair, on my finding out what my
father had meant and what he had wanted. I must do my
job as Jon Ashley's deputy, and then, when Ashley was
accounted for, my lover and I could come to terms. This
was what he had seen already. He knew me, and he knew
that there were things about him which I might find it
hard to accept. He could not be sure of me until I had
seen the whole truth about him, and accepted it with love
and understanding.

I do not think that at that moment I had any doubts
about his identity. I stared at the water and opened my
mind to him, the query forming in the dimming air. *This
is why we have to wait?*

He came in. *This is why.*

*But I understand now, and I accept it all. Won't that
do? You know I love you, you know that. I have to. That's
the point, isn't it? Whatever you may have done. Whoever you are.*

A flurry of love, as real as petals falling, and the little
catch of amusement that I knew so well. *I'll hold you
to that.*

There really were petals falling. A spray of clematis,
caught in the breeze of evening, shed its fading petals
on the dim grass. I looked at my cousin at last, across the
dusk-filled space. He was watching me steadily, saying

nothing, just watching, patient and intent. Then he smiled, and something twisted inside me, like a cord stretched between us that had felt a sudden tug. Blood thicker than water, whatever that might mean; or creatures inhabiting the same pool, over whom the same wave breaks. There seemed no need to speak. There were the Ashley eyes, shadowed in the growing dusk, the fair hair, the casual pose that masked tension. The picture of the real man was blurring, almost as if the imagined picture of my lover was beginning to superimpose itself over the reality of the cousin who sat under the lilac tree and watched me. The outlines wouldn't quite fit. Not yet. Not, I suppose, until I had accepted him whole, starlight and dreams and the harsh light of tomorrow.

A shadow moved along the lakeside. Something flew up from the reeds with a squawk and a splashing of water. Rob's collie, hunting along the water's edge, had disturbed a moorhen from her nest. As if it had broken a spell, I spoke aloud.

"It's all right, James. Please don't worry about this any more. You've a perfect right to do what you think best about the stuff in the house. . . . It's yours, after all, and if you need it now instead of later, well, that's your affair, too. I suppose we'll have to think what to say to the Underhills, but let's leave it for tonight, shall we?"

"I wasn't worrying," he said, "not really. Blood's thicker than water, whatever that may mean."

I heard the smile in his voice. His easy assumption of my complicity (why did that hard word occur to me?) took me off balance again. I said nothing.

The flash of the smile then, and he got to his feet. He must after all have misinterpreted my silence. Almost before I knew he had moved, he had crossed the grass as silently as a cat, and putting out his hands, pulled me to my feet and into his arms. His mouth found mine, gently at first, then with quickly growing excitement.

"Bryony. Bryony. It's been so long."

A thrush broke out of the lilac boughs and went skimming across the orchard wall with a cry of alarm. I put my hands against my cousin's breast and held myself away from him. "James. But I thought—"

He kissed me again, stifling what I was trying to say. He said, against my mouth: "You've always known it was me, haven't you?"

"I—yes. I wasn't sure. It used to seem so easy once, but—no, wait, please."

"Why?" He pulled me close again, and when I moved my head away he began to kiss my hair, my cheekbones, my throat.

"No, please, don't make it any harder. I've just begun to understand. We've got to get all this business over first."

He persisted for a little while, but, meeting with no response, finally let me go, and laid a gentle hand to my cheek. "All right, all right. This isn't the time. But don't let's be too long about it. I'm so afraid you'll get away from me again."

"I won't do that. Let's go in, shall we, James? Do you mind bringing the cups?" He stooped and picked them up, then followed me back into the cottage. "Are you staying at the Court tonight?" I asked him.

"No. I'll go back to Bristol." That heart-twisting smile again. "I may as well, since you're turning me down."

"For heaven's sake!" I tried for a light tone, but it came out edged. "Did you really expect me to ask you to stay here?"

"Well, perhaps that would have been pushing it a bit. I'm a patient man." No overtone to suggest that there had been any other sort of conversation between us. "I'll telephone Herr Gothard tonight, I think, to see if there's any news. Have you got his number handy?"

"Yes. I'll write it down for you, shall I?"

I went to the bureau, and switched the lamp on. I found a pen and a used envelope, scribbled down the number, and handed it to him.

He glanced at it, and pocketed it. "Thanks. Oh, where did you find my pen? I dropped it somewhere, and I've been looking for it all over the place."

"Yours? Are you sure?"

"Sure I'm sure. It's mine all right. Look at the initials. Where on earth did you find it?"

"In—in the churchyard. Beside the path."

I thought he must have noticed my hesitation, but apparently he did not. "Oh. Yes. Well, thank you." He pocketed it, kissed me again, and went. I stood for a long time beside the lamp, thinking of nothing, my mind closed, a gate slammed shut in sudden panic to keep him out.

Because I knew something, now, that I dared not let him guess at. He and Emory had done more than know my father was ill when they had come to Ashley to check the "disposable assets." They had known he was dead.

The pen I had picked up, from among the small clutter of objects in the bureau, was the silver ballpoint pen with the initials *J. A.* It had been lying there, along with my father's other effects that Herr Gothard had handed to me. I had not recognized it as Daddy's, but there had seemed no doubt that it was his. It had been found, Herr Gothard had told me, beside his body, on that lonely country road in Bavaria.

I don't know how long I stood there, staring, but without seeing it, at the lamp and the big grey moth which had blundered in through the open door behind me and was crazily beating itself to death against the light. My mind, like the moth, beat and fluttered against a truth so alien and so destructive that I could not, would not, believe it on the evidence of the facts.

Heaven knew I did not want to draw the conclusions that followed from it, but they had to be drawn. The first, which seemed now hardly to matter, and which followed from his easy acceptance of my lie about finding the pen in the churchyard, was that James had in fact been the prowler in the vestry. The second was one that mattered very much indeed. James must have been there, beside my father's body. And he had neither helped the injured man, nor made his presence known.

I could see only one further conclusion to come to.

James had driven the hit-and-run car that had knocked Daddy down. James had killed my father.

That night, lying wakeful in the quiet little bedroom, I watched the moonlight moving slowly across the floor and, with every ounce of effort I could summon, kept the doors slammed against my lover. So strongly insistent was his presence at times that, as on that night in Madeira, I could have sworn I saw his very shadow move across the floor. In my grief and loneliness I must have faltered, because I caught it, as clear as a whisper; just my name, insistent and appealing. Then I turned away and shut him out again, and listened, for the rest of the night, to the church clock chiming in the tower.

Ashley, 1835

The candle guttered in a pool of wax. Beside him she stirred, and murmured something, then sank back into sleep. Light, cast by the mirror, slid over her bare shoulder and the curve of a breast. Light o' love, he thought. It's a beautiful phrase. She is my light of love.

He reached a hand and doused the small, fluttering flame.

Twelve

. . . a divine, a ghostly confessor,
A sin-absolver, and my friend profess'd. . . .
—Romeo and Juliet, III, iii

Next morning, as soon as I could, I went to see the Vicar.

He was on his knees in the biggest of the ruinous green-houses, contentedly rummaging about among the young tomato plants. The hothouse stood against the twelve-foot wall of the old kitchen garden, and many of its panes were broken, and had been replaced by odd pieces of ply-wood or polythene sheeting. The heating system, of course, had long been out of use. The original staging, too, had long since rotted; Rob Granger had dragged it out and burned it, and rigged benches from old trestles and some planks from one of the derelict farm buildings. The sun was pouring in, reflecting warmly back from the white-washed wall, and the place smelled pleasantly of newly watered soil steaming in the warmth, and the musky scent of tomato leaves.

"Hullo, my dear. Were you comfortable in the cottage last night?"

"Very, thank you. What are you doing?"

"Tying up the tomatoes. Rob strung all these canes last week, and now the plants are big enough to train. Excellent young plants, aren't they? I don't know what's so fascinating about tomatoes, but they really are delightful to work with. So easy, and such a big return for such a small investment."

I laughed. "That's too worldly by half, Vicar. You should be drawing morals about it; tall oaks from little acorns grow, and something something fountains flow."

"So I should, so I should. Well, there's a moral in it somewhere, I'm sure. . . . Dear me, now I sound like the Duchess in *Alice in Wonderland*. Did you want me for anything special?"

"I wondered if I might talk to you," I said. "Sometime when it's convenient. There's no rush."

His hands, holding the furred leaves gently, paused. His eyes, distorted so grotesquely behind the thick glasses, searched my face. "It's always convenient." He let go the plant, and began to get to his feet. "Here and now, or shall we go up to the Vicarage and make a cup of coffee?"

"Here and now, if that's all right. No, don't leave the tomatoes. Can't I help you with them? I know how to do it."

He made no demur, knowing, I suppose, how much easier it is to talk when one's hands are occupied. He started work again, and I moved to the other side of the row from him, and followed suit. Above us the robin, who was always on the watch for whoever was gardening, flew in through a broken pane, saw there was nothing doing, scolded for a moment, then flew away. Silence, except for the rustling of the tomato leaves, the snip of scissors cutting twine, and the drip of a tap into the tank.

"Mr. Bryanston, do you believe in telepathy?"

" 'Believe in'? I don't query its existence; I don't think one reasonably can. There have been too many instances of it, thoroughly documented; and now I think it is being seriously researched. Can you be more specific? I take it you mean thought-transference, but this takes a variety of forms."

"I think I mean it in its most straightforward sense, communication between mind and mind, straight across without even any bodily presence."

"Yes, I see. Well, my answer stands. One can't query the existence of such a phenomenon. I think I may say that I am bound by the history of my own Church to accept that such things have happened. Elisha, for instance, was telepathic—or else an uncommonly good guesser."

"Perhaps he was just a pretty good judge of human nature?" I suggested. "Gehazi had cheated him before, hadn't he? I suppose you are talking about the time Gehazi took pay from Naaman, then hid the cash and told Elisha he'd never been near him?"

The Vicar's eyes twinkled. "That was a very good education you had in Sunday school, my dear."

"Yes, wasn't it? Was that what you were thinking about? Elisha knew all about it all the time, didn't he?"

"He did. 'Went not mine heart with thee, when the man turned again from his chariot to meet thee?' A bad moment for the liar Gehazi. Perhaps, as you say, Elisha just knew his man; but the text does not preclude knowledge of what had happened at a distance, and out of sight."

We worked for a few moments in silence. Then I said: "When I said, 'believe in,' I think I meant have you had any experience of it?"

"Experience at first hand, no. At second hand, I am told so. Like everyone else, I had an aunt who had premonitions, at least thirty percent of which were correct. And we have all met people who claim to have foreseen things, some of them probably truthfully. No, I'm not joking; I can see that this matters to you. In any event, such cases as I have come across myself have mainly concerned the kind of instinctive prevision which used to be called divination, and was legislated against as far back as, dear me, Deuteronomy. Along with witches and familiar spirits it was an abomination unto the Lord." The fine eyes were gently merry behind the distorting lenses. "And that, I am certain, you are not, my dear child, and could never be. Am I to take it that you yourself have had firsthand experience of this 'communication between mind and mind'?"

"Yes, I have. Not just premonitions, either. Messages, conversations even, coming clearly from another mind straight into mine. What I would call telepathy."

"Well," said the Vicar, "you are an Ashley, are you not?"

My hands checked, the fingertips tightening on a shoot so that it broke. "Sorry," I said mechanically, then looked up at him. "You *knew?*"

"I know the history of your house. And I have read all the family papers that were kept in the library, including some of the otherwise lamentable stuff in the locked shelves. There are records of the kind of thing you talk about, and some of them have an authentic ring. And I know that in your family there's a history—a record, I should say, since some of it is undoubtedly spurious—of unusual mental powers which appear from time to time in members of the family. Elizabeth Ashley, the 'witch,' seems to have done little to deserve that title except to be heard talking to someone who couldn't be seen, and on two occasions conveying information which she claimed had come from her 'secret friend,' and which knowledge could not otherwise be accounted for. If she had escaped burning, her husband would almost certainly have repudiated her. Apart from the fear of witchcraft, he suspected her of taking lovers. But you know all this."

"Yes."

The kind eyes regarded me for a moment, before returning to the work in hand. "It's never easy to be different. But I gather you know that only too well? You too have a secret friend?"

"Yes."

He was silent, not looking at me this time. I said, and heard pleading in my voice: "Vicar, please believe me."

"My dear, I do believe you. I am afraid for you."

"My mind is *not* abnormal, not in any other way, that is. But as far back as I can remember, I've been able to talk to this—this person."

"Only one person?"

"Yes."

"A real person?"

His voice was mild and inquiring, but the question shocked me. I straightened, staring. This had never occurred to me. "Well, of course. It—it never entered my head . . . Do you mean it might be someone . . . Oh, no, Vicar, he *is* real. It's one of my cousins."

"I see." His look of trouble deepened. "Yes, I see."

"But what are you suggesting?" I demanded. "That it could be some fantasy thing I made up as a child, and now can't get rid of? I mean, I know that children do invent imaginary friends, but for heaven's sake, they grow out of that, and it isn't that, or anything like it! It's a real relationship, Vicar, I promise you!"

"I have conceded that already." His voice was sharp, for him. "My dear child, what have I said to put you in such a state? If this is true at all, and I have said that I believe you, then I prefer to believe that you are in touch with another real and living mind. I gather that you don't know yet just who it is?"

"No, not yet. But it must be another Ashley, and he's here somewhere, and we can talk—communicate—about what's going on. We can stay in touch at quite a distance, too. When I was in Madeira he told me about Daddy's accident."

And I thought I knew, now, how he had known. James had been in Bavaria. The message, made faint and difficult by sheer distance, must have come straight to me from the scene of the accident.

Something the Vicar was saying got through to me. "You're sure the news didn't come to you from your father himself?"

"It couldn't have. We didn't have that sort of communication, just a—well, a feeling for trouble. I knew he was ill, or hurt, but he himself could hardly have—" I stopped, swallowed, stared. "You mean you *knew* about this? You knew all along? And that my father had it, too?"

"To some extent."

I was silent, thinking again about the message that Herr Gothard had written down for me: *"My little Bryony be careful. Danger. This thing I can feel. . . ."*

"Did he know about my 'secret friend'?" I was grateful that the Vicar had given me this name for my lover. "Lover" was not a title I was prepared yet to use aloud.

"He never mentioned it, nor, indeed, did he give any hint that he knew you possessed this gift. His own was, I gathered, much slighter; he occasionally had moments of premonition, or perhaps extra clear-sightedness. They were all, as far as I know, connected with you. He seemed to be sure, rather beyond guesswork, when you were in trouble, or needing help."

"Yes," I said, "I knew that."

The Vicar carefully snipped off several lengths of twine, threaded them through a buttonhole, then shifted his kneeling pad, and addressed himself to the next row of plants. "You said your friend was an Ashley. That must surely narrow the field considerably?"

"Yes." Even to myself the syllable sounded harassed and dejected, hardly the tone used by a friend or a lover. Another of the shoots bent in my hands, almost breaking. I apologized, and, abandoning the tomatoes, went to perch on a rickety stool beside the water tank. The Vicar never paused in his work, but moved on steadily down the row, half turned from me. I leaned back against the warm wall. The robin flew in again, scolding, and I saw that he had a nest high in the roof, in the tangle of passionflower which flourished in a corner. He swayed on a bending stem, cocked his head to regard us with bright eyes, stopped scolding abruptly, and vanished into the leaves. The peace, the sunlight, the warmth, the steady rhythm of the work with the plants, slid down like calm over troubled waters. Without any conscious decision I found myself telling the Vicar all about my lover. Not about James; nothing about last evening; only the long communication between mind and mind until last night's slamming of the doors.

When I had finished there was another of those pauses.

Then he said, with his gentle, unsurprised calm: "Well, thank you for telling me. You make it very clear. Now, I take it, something has happened which has worried you and driven you away from him, to me?"

"Yes. I came because I think I know who he is, and I think he's done something very wrong indeed, and I want to know what to do. Normally speaking, I think I'd be able to tell right from wrong myself, but this is different. It's knowing him the way I do—being sure, after all these years, that we are more to one another even than normal lovers, that we are part of one another whether we like it or not. . . . Do you see? Betraying him, even if he's very wrong, would be like betraying myself, or even somehow worse."

He straightened up from his task, but did not look at me. He knelt there for so long, looking down at the tomato plants, that I thought he had forgotten my presence and my question. Finally he sighed. "My dear, I'm no help to you. Perhaps if I took time to think . . . Yes, I must do that. And pray, too . . . This is quite outside my experience, and outside my book of rules. There was a time when I would have said that right was right and wrong was wrong however one found out about it, but time changes one's mind about that. In a way one might say that an intimacy of the kind you've described is like the intimacy of husband and wife; and the law recognizes that; it would be intolerable if the one were allowed to betray the other. I think—yes, I think that if you do indeed hold the key to someone's inner thoughts, you must not betray them."

"I see," I said. "Yes, that's what I thought. At least, I didn't think, I felt it. Thank you."

"If he has done something so very wrong, then it will surely come to light without you. But I think that if you see him about to hurt others, or to do more harm, then you must use this unique relationship that you have, to dissuade him. In fact, if this bond between you does make you two sides of the same medal, then the decision for right in you could counteract his drive towards wrongdoing. Yes, perhaps this is the answer. Since you have this, er, privileged communication, you must pay for it in this way. In other words," said the Vicar, kneeling there in his old patched jacket, with the scissors in his hand, and looking like the law and the prophets rolled into one, "in other words it is your duty to act as the voice of his conscience, if he has not a sufficiently powerful one of his own."

" 'Stern Daughter of the Voice of God,' " I said, a little dismally.

"Exactly. Not an attractive lady, Duty. One of Wordsworth's more inspired descriptions, I feel. Does this sound so very daunting, child?"

"A bit. But just at the moment it does seem to be about the only thing I can do—if I dared communicate with him at all. I can't betray him out loud. Not to anyone else, I mean."

He had finished the row of plants while he was speaking, and now, getting stiffly to his feet, he crossed to a potting bench for a new ball of twine. Looking away from me, he spoke again. "Bryony."

"Yes?"

"This is not a safe road that you are treading."

"I've realized that. That's one of the reasons why I had to talk to you. Up till now, you see, it's been marvellous, and so familiar . . . I've known it so long . . . being able to talk to him about everything, exchange everything, just as if he was part of me and I of him. There was nothing but happiness, I was never alone, always someone I could turn to. . . . And it seemed to me that there was nothing but joy in the future, that when we actually, physically, found one another, it would just be a continuing of what's been going on all our lives. It was so serene." I looked down at my hands. "After Daddy died I thought all I had to do was to come home to Ashley, and I would be able to find him, my 'secret friend.' But he said no, it wasn't time yet, we must wait. And now I think this was because he didn't dare let me near him, knowing what he had done. I felt so much alone. . . . Then, just as I thought I'd found him, I discovered that he'd done something terrible, really terrible, so bad that all this time he's managed to keep it secret, even from me. I only found out by accident. That's why I came to you, to ask what to do."

"You found out 'by accident'? You mean that you read a thought he didn't want you to read?"

"No. You can't do that. I told you, you can close your mind. For instance, he can't know what I'm telling you now. No, this was a—a daylight thing. I saw something he didn't realize would give him away."

"Then you are not betraying your secret life if you do something about that. There's part of your answer, I believe." He looked at me, then gave a nod. "But that's not the whole answer, is it? You cannot think of betraying him, whatever he does, yet you cannot live with what he is doing?"

"Yes. Yes, that's it exactly."

"Then, my dear," he said gravely, "you must live without it."

It was the answer I had come to myself, but still it came like a knell. Like a full stop. Like the gate slamming.

"Without *him?*" I said.

"Yes. Without this private life that you have come to depend on. You cannot keep as part of you something that is alien to what you believe, something you know to be wrong. The ancients used to call it 'possession.' It was a good word, for ownership by something alien; the turning aside of oneself from one's own straight track."

"I know. I know. I've already cut him off. I knew I had to, and not only because I was afraid of his finding out what I knew about him. This is what made me wonder if the whole thing, this 'gift,' as I used to think of it, is evil? I can't believe it is. I've lived with it all my life, since I was tiny. It was comfortable and happy and good, and later, when it became more serious, it still seemed to be good. Believe me, Vicar, I know it was. I know he was, too." My hands had gripped together in my lap. "And the awful thing is that I can't bear to be without him. I feel worse than being alone, I feel mutilated, like losing half oneself, or not being able to breathe properly, or something like that. If it was so wrong, why is it worse without him?"

"That I can't tell you. I can only say that it is a grave mistake to commit oneself to anyone or anything that may get beyond one's control. I don't for a moment suggest that this gift of yours is fantasy, but it might be said, perhaps, to share the same qualities and defects. There's the same danger that, as reality approaches, there will be a falling off."

I had thought about this, too. "You mean like those people who spend all their time reading stories about ideal lovers and ideal relationships, so that a real ordinary man or woman never can measure up?"

"Something like that. Any imaginary world has its dangers. The edges between light and half-light are indistinct, and tend to blur more and more the longer one looks at them. You know, Bryony, you've given me almost too much to think about. Will you give me a little more time, and come and talk to me again? I'd like to clear my mind. I'm sorry I haven't been more help."

"Oh, you have, you have. You believed me, and that's almost enough in itself. Thank you for that."

"My dear child," he said, then, smiling: "You've relieved my mind, too. I said you were treading a dangerous road; I doubt if I need have worried about you. You have a clear head, for so young a woman, and you are not afraid to think things through. That's not as easy as it sounds, and not common at all. Was there anything else you wanted to talk about? I see Rob Granger on the other side of the garden, and he seems to be coming this way."

I turned to look out through the glass. Rob was standing between the rows of vegetables, pointing something out to the boy, Jim Makepeace, who helped him sometimes. Jim nodded and picked up his spade, and Rob headed towards the greenhouse. I turned back to the Vicar, and asked quickly: "Did you ever find out what the prowler was doing in the vestry?"

"Yes, indeed. What a very strange thing that was! I am glad to say that I was right in thinking that no one from these parishes would have attempted to open the safe. It had not been touched."

"No? Do you mean that nothing was missing after all?"

"Nothing of value—that is, none of the 'valuables,' but something worth much more in its own way, and quite irreplaceable. One of the registers."

"One of the *registers*? A parish register?" The ones at Ashley, I knew, went back without a break to the sixteenth century. It was a serious loss, but for the moment I could not get far beyond a sort of blank amazement and reassessment of what I knew. What in the world could James have wanted with one of the parish registers? Anything less like a "disposable asset" I couldn't imagine. "But I thought you said no one had opened the safe?"

"Oh, not one of the Ashley registers. One of those which were on the vestry table, from One Ash. Unhappily, it is one of the earlier ones which is missing, the second volume, 1780 to 1837. . . . The latter, as no doubt you know, was the date on which the full procedure of registration was instituted as we know it today. Before that it was a question of signatures, or indeed marks, from the parties concerned. In the registers before 1754, when the Hardwick Act was passed, there is merely an entry of the fact of marriage; nothing else was required. . . ."

"But surely—" I was thinking hard. If James had laid the pictures down on the vestry table in the dark, while he fumbled for the main switch, he might just possibly have picked the register up in error, and carried it away. It seemed unlikely, but I made a mental note to telephone him as soon as I could. It was obvious that the Vicar was very worried; the thing must be put back without delay. "But surely, it won't have been stolen, Vicar. Who would want it? It'll turn up soon, you'll see."

"Quite, quite. I comfort myself with the thought. I am not seriously worried," said the Vicar, looking very worried indeed. "It seems clear that someone must have wanted to consult it, and seeing it here, has simply borrowed it. It will be returned in time, surely. The fault is mine, and only mine. When I left the volumes in the vestry, it never entered my head that anyone besides my-self would be interested enough to abstract one of them. Ineded, I still may be mistaken; I shall be going to One Ash tomorrow afternoon, and will make sure. . . . Ah, Rob, good morning. Were you looking for me?"

"Good morning, Vicar. Mrs. Henderson said to tell you that a young couple called from Hangman's End about a license."

"Oh, dear," said the Vicar, "and I did want to get the plants finished this morning."

"I'll do them," I said. "That is, if you'll trust me after breaking that shoot."

"Of course, but you must have plenty to do."

"I'd like to finish them," I said. "Good morning, Rob."

"Good morning."

"Are the Underhills at home today?" I asked him.

"They're going out later. But Mrs. Underhill said if I saw you to say you were welcome at the house anytime. She tried to phone you this morning, but you'd gone out."

"Oh, thanks. I'm going to take a look in the library, Vicar. I thought I'd look through the family section."

"Oh, yes. Well, anytime you want me, you know where to find me. Rob, what have you done to your hand?"

"Nothing. Hit it with a hammer, that's all."

"Was that you mending the fishing cat last night?" I asked him.

"Fishing cat?"

"The cat statue at the Overflow. It's broken off. Had you seen it?"

"Oh, that, yes. The metal's rotten. I left it be. It's not much use wasting time on that kind of thing." It was an echo of what my cousin had said last night, but without the bitterness; Rob spoke with an indifference verging on the surly. He was already making for the door. "I was wedging the sluice gates shut, that's what you heard. Looked as if they'd been tampered with, but then the whole thing's rotten anyway."

"Is it safe?"

"Safe enough. The High Sluice can take care of anything the river likes to send down, and the Overflow's there to keep the moat level steady."

He was at the door, opening it. I got quickly to my feet. "I'm going over to the Court again. May I have your keys now, please, Rob?"

"You know where they're kept. Help yourself." The greenhouse door shut behind him.

"His hand must be hurting him more than he'll admit," said the Vicar. "He's not usually rude. I hope it's nothing serious. Well, I must go, I suppose. If you really will finish the tomatoes for me—?"

"Of course I will."

Alone in the greenhouse I went back to the plants. The silence of the glasshouse, the stillness of the air, and the monotony of the task were somehow soothing. God knows I had plenty to think about, but I thought about none of it, not then. I shut myself off from it as the glass shut me from the air outside, content to let my mind stay closed and blank, and to work automatically along the rows of plants.

What slipped it into my mind I do not know, but it was suddenly there, clear as if spoken . . . no, not as if spoken; as clear as if it were written up between me and the garden, scrawled on the steamed glass.

William Ashley, 1774–1835.

It might be pure chance that a parish record of William Ashley's time had vanished, but also it might not. And anything to do with William Ashley was of interest to me, at least until I had managed to interpret my father's cryptic words.

I was on the last row of tomato plants. I finished the job as quickly as I could, then let myself out into the air, and hurried towards the Court.

Ashley, 1835

"You have the key safely?"

"Aye. See? But I'll not need it."

"Never be too sure. You know what they say about a maze?"

"No. What, then?"

"That a compass won't work there. While we're here, we're in a world without bearings and directions. Even if you could see the weather-vane, it would be no help. We're outside the world."

"Sounds like we're dead, surely?"

"Hush, oh, hush. It just means that once we're here, at the center, no one can touch us."

"Till we go out again."

"Even then. Nothing can touch us now."

Thirteen

And what obscured in this fair volume lies
Find written . . .
                              —*Romeo and Juliet*, I, iii

No ghost had ever walked in the Ashley library, but now,
as I let myself quietly into the still, spacious room, it
seemed haunted, probably only by the frail parchment
ghosts of the books that had vanished from the shelves. It
was so empty that it echoed. Somehow, I thought, a library
looked worse than an ordinary room that had been
stripped of its furniture. The books had been the brain
of the room, its soul, its *raison d'être*. I shut the door
quietly behind me, as if afraid of disturbing those pale
ghosts, then, ashamed of the impulse even as I gave way
to it, turned the key. Quietly as a ghost myself, I walked
the length of the room to the locked cases which housed
William Ashley's books, and Nicholas' sad little collection,
pushed the library ladder up close, then climbed up and
unlocked the grille.

"*William's book* . . ."? I might as well start with
Scholar Ashley's own verses. I took out *A New Romeo to
His Juliet,* sat down on the top step of the ladder, and
opened the book.

There was the bookplate with the maze and the rampant
wildcat with its grim motto—how touchable had Julia

Ashley been? I wondered briefly—and opposite this the dedicatory letter with its extravagances which, for once, and how pathetically, sounded no more than true.

"To the peerless and beautiful Mistress Julia Ashley, my wife . . ."

I read it through. It was much the usual letter, fulsome to our ears and circumlocutory, but through it came very clearly the idolatry he had felt for her. The touch at the end was pure pathos.

> May we never reach that end, but if we do, let it be together, that we may never from our palace of dim night depart again.
>
> Your
Romeo.

I turned the pages slowly. The work was privately printed and very prettily produced; it was doubtful if William Ashley could ever have found more than a local immortality, but to me, another Ashley, the book was fascinating. A great many of the verses were about the Court. One or two of the shorter ones I knew already; they had been printed elsewhere, and we had been set to learn them as children. Each poem had, as head- and tailpiece, some small and rather pretty engraving, and these I found enthralling. There was a picture of the main bridge, more or less exactly as it was today; a distant view of the Court minus the Victorian gables and a chimney or two; a view of the orchard beautifully kept and improbably heavy with fruit; one of the maze, trim and neat and little more than shoulder high, with a detailed drawing of a pavilion perched for the artist's convenience on a high platform that had certainly never been there.

The poem below this picture was called "The Maze":

> In this fantastickal and Cretan maze
> No Theseus to find the centre strays;
> This gentler Monster lurked within these Groves
> What time the Romans trod their secret ways.

No Cretan Bull guards the abode of love,
But where the gentle waters, straying, move,
See! Dionysus' creature here enskied
To greet our 'raptured gaze . . .

And so on. It was bad verse; so bad and so meaningless that, conversely, I thought there must be meaning
there. William Ashley's poems were usually transparent as
glass, his conceits more than simple, only lamely imitating
the stately periods he admired. "Secret ways," I thought.
It was surely only the usual conceit about a maze, the
Greek myth of Theseus and the clue. Then why "Romans"? Well, it probably hardly mattered. But the maze
was William Ashley's private refuge, and the pavilion was
built for his Juliet. And past the maze went the Overflow.
I read on.

Time passed slowly. Somehow the silence of the library,
which should have helped me to concentrate, oppressed
and distracted me. The clear north light showing up the
half-empty shelves, the stuffy smell of a locked room, the
waiting echo of emptiness, seemed to symbolize the
vacuum inside my mind, the shut gate, the lack of
presence. . . . Try as I would, the parable of the swept and
garnished house kept coming back to me. "Possession,"
in any context, was a forceful, not to say frightening, word.

The thought came between me and the book, so per-
sistently that I knew I could not go on reading here. I
decided to take the books back to the cottage, make myself some lunch, then telephone Herr Gothard and find
what James had said to him last night. After that I would
settle down once more to my reading. I carried the *New
Romeo* down the steps and laid it on a table, then climbed
back to lock the grille.

A title in one of the Shakespeare shelves caught my
eye, and the name *Juliet* in gilt on tooled tan leather. The
real thing. Any comparison with Scholar Ashley's trans-
ports would be unfair in the extreme, but some impulse,
sparked off perhaps by the thought of the star-crossed

lovers and my own divided house, made me take the small volume out. Then I locked the grille, let myself out of the library, and locked that, too, behind me.

There was very little delay on the line.

Herr Gothard was at home. Yes, Herr Gothard would speak with me. . . .

"Bryony? How are you?"

"I'm fine, thank you, Herr Gothard. Can you hear me all right?"

"Perfectly. Now, how can I help you?"

"I'm awfully sorry to trouble you again," I said, "but there were one or two things I wanted to ask you. I, er, I understand that my cousin James was to telephone you last night?"

"That is so. He did telephone me. He has not been in touch with you about this?"

"I've been out all day. I wondered what news you had had for him."

"Ah." He sounded faintly surprised that I should have telephoned Germany rather than Bristol, but he went on with his usual calm courtesy. "I'm afraid there has not been much progress here. There is no sign as yet of the car which did the damage, but the police are still making inquiries."

"Yes, I see. Thank you. Did he—did my cousin ask you anything else?"

"No, only questions about the accident—had they found the car, were there any more clues to who had done it, all the same questions. I am sorry I have nothing more to tell you. And yourself? You are well?"

"Oh, yes, perfectly, thanks. There was one thing I wanted to ask you, though. Do you remember, among Daddy's things that you gave me, a silver ballpoint pen?"

"Ye-es . . . ach, yes, of course I do! It had his initials on it, yes?"

"That's the one. Where was it found, do you know?"

"Beside him on the road."

"That's definite, is it? It wasn't found in his pocket?"

"No. I remember that. It was found later, when the police went back to search the place."

"Herr Gothard," I asked, "do you ever remember seeing him use it?"

There was a pause while he thought. "No. I cannot say that I do. Why? Is it important?"

"I'm not sure," I said. "Look, Herr Gothard, something has turned up here. . . . If I send you a photograph, would you please show it to the police and ask if anyone in Wackensberg or Bad Tölz remembers seeing such a man? And surely they could find out if he hired a car, and all that sort of thing?"

"Certainly." I heard the sudden interest, and perhaps even enlightenment, quicken his voice. He had guessed, had Walther, why I had rung him in Germany rather than James in Bristol. "Why is this, Bryony? Does this mean that you have found some evidence yourself which points to someone? How definite is it?"

"I don't know. Something happened yesterday, and it made me wonder. . . . I can't say any more now. But, Herr Gothard—"

"Yes?"

"Please don't say anything about this to anybody but the police, will you? I mean, if anyone else should telephone from England—"

"I understand." And now I was sure that he did. His voice across the wire sounded troubled, even grim. "You can trust me. I shall say nothing until it is time."

"Thank you. I'll send the photograph straight away."

"Please do. I shall do all I can."

"Thank you," I said. "Good-bye."

I cradled the receiver, then came round sharply in my chair at the sound of a step on the flagged path outside.

"Hi, Bryony," said my cousin Emory.

I felt myself go white. He stopped short, and said contritely: "I'm sorry. Did I frighten you? I thought you must have heard me coming."

"Not a sound." I forced a smile. "Well, hullo. It's lovely to see you."

"Is it? You looked as if you were seeing a ghost, one of the nastier sort."

"Oh, dear, did I?" I got to my feet with a gesture of welcome. "Come in, Emory, do."

He bent his head under the lintel and came into the little room, and took my hands and kissed me, just as James had done in the schoolroom at the Court.

"You know, it is a bit like seeing a ghost." I said it apologetically. "I guess I must have stopped being used to you and James. And for heaven's sake, he was wearing that same shirt and tie when he was ringing for you yesterday, I'll swear he was. Don't tell me you wear the same clothes now? That really is taking it a bit far!"

I was talking perhaps a shade too fast, all the time casting back in my mind for what I had been saying on the telephone as he approached the cottage door. How much could he have heard? What might he have made of it? Certainly he seemed quite easy and natural, the old charming Emory I remembered, and none the worse for what the romantic novelists would have called a hint of steel under it all, but which I, who had known him too well since boyhood, had occasionally described as "bloody overweening Twinmanship."

He laughed. "Yes, and you had him taped in two seconds flat, I gather. Not that he was trying to ring the changes with you; it never worked, and neither Twin nor I have ever wasted time on things that don't work. . . . Well, it's lovely to see you again. I wish it could have been a happier homecoming for you."

I ushered him into one of the chairs by the hearth, and sat down myself where I had been before, beside the round table where William Ashley's books were lying. Emory leaned back in the armchair, took out cigarettes and offered them. I shook my head. He lit one for himself, and blew out a cloud of smoke.

"James rang Herr Gothard last night."

"Yes, he said he would." I made it sound as noncommittal as I could. He had of course seen me telephoning as he approached the cottage door. I knew I had used Walther's name towards the end of the conversation. How near had Emory been then? And when I referred to the photograph? If he had heard me, he would think it strange that I didn't tell him straight away that I had called Walther myself. Stalling for time, I asked him: "Would you like some coffee? Or tea, perhaps?"

"No, thanks." His voice gave nothing away, either of surprise or suspicion. "He would have told you about it himself, but the call came through rather late, so he didn't try to get you till morning. You must have been out?"

"Yes, I had to go out fairly early." I tried a safe tack. "Had Herr Gothard anything special to tell him?"

"Nothing, I'm afraid," said Emory. "That is, he said there hadn't been any progress, and followed it up with all the usual bromides—the police are still on the job, and so on."

"Yes, well, I would think that a hit-and-run accident is about the most difficult thing there is to trace, wouldn't you? And in a tourist area, in the tourist season, just about impossible."

He nodded. A pause, while he drew on his cigarette, inhaling deeply. I found myself beginning to relax. I was sure that he had heard nothing. He looked perfectly normal, calm, and unbent, with just the right hint of trouble showing in his face. My cousin Emory, the *alter ego* of my secret friend, who, whatever James had done, must know all about it, too.

He was saying gently: "You do realize, Bryony, that we may never know?"

My gaze met his, with, I hoped, exactly the same gentle concern and lack of guile. It felt strange to be deceiving my cousin, even though only by omission. What made it strange was, I knew, that he was so like James. . . . "Of course. To tell you the truth, I can't find it in me to agonize much about that." I turned, abruptly, to the real truth. "All that matters is that my father's dead, and, since I can't imagine that anyone would have wanted to kill him deliberately, I don't see that it helps much to run yapping after the fool who caused an accident." I looked straight at him. "Do *you* think it could have been anything but an accident?"

"I? No, of course it couldn't."

"Then you'd agree with me?"

"What about?"

"I mean, do you feel you can't relax or try to forget it until the police in Bavaria find out every last detail of what happened?"

He blew a smoke ring, and leaned his head back to watch it rise. With this new dreadful suspicion sharpening its rat's-teeth on the edges of my mind, I wondered if he couldn't meet my eye. He spoke to the ceiling. "It may sound an awful thing to say, but if it's going to take a long time, and cost a lot of money, no." He met my eyes then. "That may not sound pretty, but I'm paying you the compliment of the truth."

That it was indeed the truth, no more and no less, I knew very well. I waited, saying nothing, keeping a calm steady gaze on him; the old interviewer's trick by which you hope to stampede the victim into saying rather more than he meant. But Emory was not easy to stampede. He smiled at me as he leaned forward to tap ash from his cigarette. "That goes for the inquiry, too. What has happened to us as a family can't be changed by apportioning whatever guilt there is. That's a matter for the police, and they're the ones it will satisfy. It can't do anything for us, except keep a wound open. Both James and I feel that it's better forgotten."

"I'm sure you do." I said it flatly and pleasantly, but I saw his gaze flick towards me. I looked away, and began to arrange William Ashley's books neatly side by side on the table in front of me. "Well, I suppose the police will go on probing away until they do find something, or else have to close the case. There's no point in our doing anything more. When I'm next in touch with Herr Gothard, or with Mr. Emerson, I'll tell them so."

There was no telling whether Emory was relieved or not. He merely nodded, and drew on his cigarette. I looked away, afraid that my gaze was too intent and too inquiring. It was shocking how quickly I had been able to adapt myself to suspicion. Only two short days ago it would have been unthinkable. And now . . . It was shocking, too, how easily I had adapted to deception. I smiled, and peeled off smoothly into talk about my homecoming, and Madeira and Bad Tölz, and Emory followed my lead with the same smooth ease. I wondered if there were still things he wanted to know. For me it was simple; I stayed off the doubtful ground and waited to see if he would tread on it.

He did, but not straight away. He spoke of the Underhills, and I found myself hoping that he would keep off the subject of his relationship with Cathy; I had had enough of that for the moment, and there were things I was more concerned with. I need not have worried. James would certainly have told Emory of my reactions to the "theft" of the Court treasures, and for the present Emory preferred to let that lie. He did, when he was talking about the Underhills, make a sidelong and innocuous reference to Cathy as "a sweet girl and very easy to be fond of," but when I declined the bait he went on to talk about Jeff Underhill's business, and the family's eventual departure from the Court.

"And what are you going to do, Bryony? James seemed to think you wouldn't stay here—in the cottage, that is."

"How could he?" I said, more sharply than I meant to. "As far as I remember, I didn't tell him what I intended to do."

"And here am I," said Emory, with a smile that was as disarming in him as in his brother, "hammering at you within twenty-four hours about your future. And you know why, don't you? Cousin Bryony, dear sweet Cousin Bryony, have you had time yet to think any further about breaking that thrice-damned trust and letting your poor and dishonest relations have a pound or two to fiddle with before they're due to it?"

I had to laugh. "Well, if you put it like that—"

"I do put it like that. Cards on the table, cousin dear. An Ashley could always be relied on to look after his Ashley self with the greatest possible devotion."

"Which," I said smoothly, "is exactly what I'm doing."

The faintest line between his brows. "And what exactly does that mean?"

"It means no. I will not break the trust."

He flung his cigarette into the hearth. "For God's sweet sake, Bryony—"

"Not even for that. No. Not yet."

"But have you thought—" he began.

"Give me time."

I'm not sure what showed in my voice and face, but he bit back what he was going to say, and sat back in his chair. He gave me a long look. It was a shrewd look, and one I didn't relish under the circumstances. I said, rather quickly: "Emory, will you and James please do me a favour?"

"Such as?" He sounded understandably wary.

"Don't take me up wrong, but would you both just not hound me for a day or two? Just, in fact, keep away from Ashley till I've had time to get my bearings? I'm not saying that I refuse utterly and for ever to break the trust. I don't see that you should have the Court, just as it stands now, tied round your neck like a millstone for ever, but surely there can't be all that urgency about it? Good heavens, you haven't even let me talk to Mr. Emerson! I've got to, surely you can see that? Another week—only a week would give me time to think it all out . . ." I paused, and finished drily: "And surely you can live for a week on what you got for the T'ang horse and the jade Fo-dog seal?"

He looked startled, then he burst out laughing. "No police, Cousin Bryony?"

"No police. But leave it alone, Cousin Emory, or I might surprise you yet. And leave Cathy Underhill out of it, or I *will* surprise you, and that's a promise." I got up.

"Now I'm going to make some tea. Will you stay and have some?"

I half expected him to refuse, but I had underestimated him. He leaned back in his chair, still smiling. "I'd love some. Thank you." He was obviously enjoying the situation. Yes, I thought, as I went through to the kitchen, that was my cousin Emory; not the shadow of regret or guilt for anything he might do. That was the Ashley self-sufficiency—and just where, one might ask, did it part company with the criminal mentality? A look back through the family records might make one wonder; and these were days as wild and violent in many ways as the days of the Norman marauders with their rule of strength, or the days of their "civilized" counterparts the elegant duellists and the Mohocks of the eighteenth century. It threw the memory of James and his guilt-ridden contrition into very sharp relief. I had been right, I thought, I had been right. Whatever wrong had been done to Cathy, or even more to my father, it must have been Emory who had acted. It would not, could not, be James. Surely, the most that James had done had been to hear of it afterwards, and feel himself bound to stand by his twin's actions.

And the silver pen with the initials *J. A.*? There must be an answer even for that. Emory might have borrowed his brother's pen, and left it on the Wackersberg road. It was even possible that James had not missed it, and genuinely thought he might have dropped it in the churchyard.

When I went back into the sitting room with the tray, my cousin was standing by the table, with one of William Ashley's books in his hand.

"What's this?"

"I've been checking through the locked section," I said. "No, not the porn, so you can put it back. It's only Shakespeare. I thought it might be interesting to read *Romeo and Juliet* again, alongside William Ashley's attempt to play Romeo."

"Heavens, why?"

"Just a thought. Do you still take three sugars?"

"Yes, please." He turned the volume over and looked at the spine. *"The Tragicall History of Romeus and Juliet.* Hm. It's a poem, not a play. I thought you said it was Shakespeare? Listen to this:

"This barefoot friar girt with cord his grayish weed,
For he of Francis' order was, a friar, as I rede.
Not as the most was he, a gross unlearned fool,
But doctor of divinity proceeded he in school.
The secrets eke he knew in Nature's work that lurk;
By magic's art most men supposed that he could wonders
  work.

My God," said Emory, "they made their money easily in those days, didn't they? I could do better myself."

"What on earth? Let me see."

He ignored me. "It can't be a prologue or something, can it? No, I thought as much. It isn't the play at all. . . . Wait a minute, it isn't even 'Romeo.' It's 'Romeus.' *Romeus and Juliet,* and not Shakespeare at all. It's by a chap called Brooke."

"Brooke?"

It came out in a kind of yelp. He looked up, surprised. "Yes. Why? Do you know it?"

But I had myself in hand. "No. Sorry, I spilled some hot water on myself. It's nothing. Have a biscuit. You were saying?"

"This isn't the Shakespeare play. It's a poem called *Romeus and Juliet,* by Arthur Brooke, and it seems to be —hey, it's dated 1562!" He sounded excited. "I say, I wonder if this could possibly be Shakespeare's source for his play, or something like that. I don't know the dates, but surely 1562—hell, yes, that's long before he was writing, isn't it? When did Elizabeth come to the throne?"

That was the kind of thing we knew at Ashley. "1558," I said, reluctantly. "It might be, I suppose, but I can't see . . . Look, Emory, leave the books, will you? I haven't had a chance to look at them yet, and I really think we should go through them pretty carefully, and get someone who's an expert. They might be valuable. Wait till I've checked them; we don't want to risk marking them—"

" 'Might be valuable,' indeed! Anything first printed in 1562 stands a damned good chance of being valuable, I'd say."

"Well, don't start counting chickens till we know a bit more about it. I'll tell you what, Emory, I'll write, first thing in the morning. I think someone at Hatchards, or even perhaps the British Museum—"

"Why don't you just telephone someone now, this minute? This is your line of country. Isn't there someone local who might at least have a rough idea? What about what's-his-name, Leslie Oker, over at Ashbury? He'd have some idea, surely?"

"I don't really think—" I began, unwillingly, but he ignored me.

"At least he'd have some way of looking it up. Do you know his number?"

He already had the directory in his hand, so there was not much point in stalling further. I gave him the number. He pulled the telephone towards him and began to dial. His movements were quick, incisive, excited. At least, I thought, as I sat across from him sipping my tea, I would be able to read the thing before I had to send it away. Emory could hardly insist on taking it from me. From the length of the poem, and the apparent tedium of the verses, it wasn't a task I particularly looked forward to, but I would do it, even if I had to stay up all night. For that this, at last, was "William's Brooke," I was quite sure.

Emory was talking rapidly into the telephone. "Yes, Arthur Brooke, *'The Tragicall History of Romeus and Juliet*, written first in Italian by Bandello and nowe in Englishe by Arthur Brooke.' It's dated 1562. There's a piece at the bottom of the title page which says, *'In aedibus Richardi Tottelli Cum Privilegio.'* Yes. Yes, quite small . . . about four by eight . . . tan leather with a brown edge to the paper. No, no inscription, except the owner's bookplate, and that's reasonably historic, too. Put in by William Ashley, his own bookplate. He died in, let me see—?"

He raised a brow at me, and I supplied it. "1835."

"1835," said Emory into the telephone. "Yes, well, I don't know about such things, but I'd say it was in pretty good shape. No, no crest or anything on the cover. Oh, the title page is a bit yellow, with some of that brown spotting."

"Foxed," I said, behind him.

"My cousin says you call it foxed. Not badly, no, but I've only just glanced at it. . . . Yes?"

Silence from Emory, while the telephone talked. It was a loud telephone, and, even with the receiver held tightly to my cousin's ear, I could catch something of what Leslie was saying. But even without that, I could have caught the gist of it from my cousin's face, where growing excitement fought with worry and slight apprehension. Eventually, after a few more brief queries, and expressions of thanks, he rang off, and turned back to me.

"He knows the book." He spoke very quietly, with a calm belied by the gleam in his eyes. "That is, he knows of it; he's never seen a copy in his life. And for a very good reason. There are only three copies of this particular edition known. One of them isn't perfect; it's at Cambridge. A second is at Oxford, in Duke Humphrey, and I'm not sure about the third. If this is a fourth . . ." A short laugh, which betrayed his excitement. "He says he has no idea how valuable it might be, but there's only one thing certain, that it is very valuable indeed. There's a snag, of course, there'd have to be. It may have been re-bound. He couldn't tell, from my description. If it has, of course, its value will be diminished—but it would still fetch a lot of money . . . enough, anyway, to see us through. What's the matter, Bryony? You look as if you hardly cared."

I could not tell him that I was conscious of only one overmastering wish, to have him go and leave me alone with the book and let me read it. I picked it up and began to turn the pages. "Why, of course I'm pleased! It's marvellous, Emory! And I see no reason at all why you shouldn't sell it. The only thing we mustn't do is rush it, and even if we do send it to Christie's to sell, you know they might take ages. They wait for the right book sale, and that mightn't be for months."

"Yes, I understand that. But they could give us some idea, surely, of what it might bring? One can borrow on expectation, you know."

"Fair enough," I said. "I think the best thing to do is to send the book up to an expert, and let him have a look at it. No, Emory, please—" This as his hand reached for it again. "You'll have to leave this to me. I promise you I'll see about it tomorrow, but I want to ask Mr. Bryanston about it first."

"Mr. Bryanston? What does he know about it?"

"Quite a bit, you'd be surprised. And then I'm going to ring up Mr. Emerson, and see just where we stand."

His brows drew down quickly. "He can't have any objection, surely?"

"I didn't mean about this. I meant about the trust."

It was blackmail of a kind, and it worked. He hesitated, then smiled and nodded, and to my great relief, at last got to his feet and took his leave. He was going back to Bristol this evening, he told me, and yes, he would keep his promise and stop badgering me about the trust.

"But for heaven's sake, you will see about this book straight away, won't you? And if you can get into the Court and look at what else is there—?"

"Yes. As soon as I can."

"And let me know "

"Of course," I said. "Or James?"

"Of course." The echo held an inflection of surprise, as if it went without saying. As, I reflected, it did. I had been right. And that left me—and my lover—where?

"Emory?"

He was in the doorway. He turned. "Yes?"

"Where's Francis? Have you any idea?"

"Not the least. I dare say he'll turn up when he feels

like it. It's obvious he can't have heard the news yet. Why, do you need him for something?"

"It would be nice," I said carefully, "if he were here, don't you think?"

"Well, of course," said his brother, then kissed me again and went away.

I watched him right out of sight past the orchard and beyond the maze and the Overflow, then I went upstairs and began to hunt for a photograph which Walther could show to the police in Bad Tölz.

Ashley, 1835

He turned his head on the pillow, searching with his cheek for the hollow where her head had lain. The linen was cold now, but still smelled faintly of lavender.

"Eh—" he said it aloud, in her phrase—"eh, but I love thee."

The moon had set, but faint shadows moved with the breeze, as the creepers fretted at the walls. The shutter masking the south window moved, creaking, as if some ghostly hand had pushed it. For a half-dreaming moment he thought he saw her again, kilting her skirts to climb the low sill, then standing tiptoe, laughing, watching herself in the glass.

"What is it?"

Then the shutter went back with a slam, jarring him full awake. The room was empty.

Fourteen

... Comfort me, counsel me.
          —*Romeo and Juliet*, III, v

It was a good photograph, taken the last time the twins had been at Ashley Court together, showing them both with Rob Granger on the banks of the Pool. They had been fishing for eels, and the picture showed Rob just tipping the bucketful of wriggling creatures out on the grass, while the twins stood over him. James was laughing, while Emory, looking away into the middle distance, was sober. Both were good likenesses, even though the photograph was four years old. If either of the two had been seen at Bad Tölz, there would be very little difficulty in identifying him.

I wrapped the picture up and found an envelope to fit it. A very commonplace action, but it felt like burning a whole fleet of boats, and crossing a delta of Rubicons. Then I sat down and resolutely addressed the envelope to Walther. I had only the haziest idea as to how much it should cost air mail to Bad Tölz, but finished by putting enough stamps on to carry it well east of Suez. That done, I locked William's books away in a drawer, and, without giving myself time for further thought, set straight out to post the letter.

The pillar-box was nearly half a mile away, where the

side road from One Ash, winding past the church, met the main road. I took the shortcut across the farmyard.

In the old days of the farm's prosperity this had been the stackyard, with the row of stacks spaced beyond the big Dutch barn crammed full to the roof with straw. The cool caverns of the old cart sheds had housed the farm machinery, and whole families of cheerful hens that perched, crooning, on mudguards and shafts, and laid enormous clutches of eggs in various secret places which took, Mrs. Granger used to say, an expert egg-diviner to discover. Now the afternoon sun beat down through the gaps in the perished roof of the barn, striking a rusty harrow left there to rot, and the raw green paint of Rob's cultivator, a stack of oil drums and a pile of chain. An old wagon with a broken shaft stood like an exhibit from some badly kept museum. Two of the sheds had been fenced across with hurdles, and pigs slept there in the slatted sunshine. In another stood Rob's battered fifth-hand Ford Cortina, and the fourth opening was filled with a stack of firewood. The hens remained, diminished in numbers but not in stately cheer; they clucked and strutted and raked among the fallen straw, ignoring Rob's collie which lay curled asleep on the mat outside his cottage door. As I crossed the yard the collie woke and smiled with lolling tongue and tail beating the ground, but he didn't move. I caught a glimpse of Mrs. Henderson at Rob's window, then the door opened and she appeared in the doorway, wiping her hands on her apron.

"Miss Bryony! Won't you come along in and take a cup of tea? The kettle's just on the boil for Rob, and I've made a batch of scones."

My first impulse, with the package for Walther weighing heavily in my hand, was to make some excuse and go on my way, but something made me hesitate. The smell of the freshly baked scones came meltingly out on the air, along with the scent of woodsmoke and polish and the smell of ironing. I could see the laundered clothes hanging on the kitchen pulley. Details hardly noticed, but adding together to something deep out of the past that answered, like an echo to a bell, the distress in me that I had hardly recognized as yet, and had barely yet begun to suffer: James and my dead father, and the evidence of the silver pen; my rejection of my secret friend, and now, in this envelope in my hand, something that might be his betrayal. Before I even knew I had spoken, I said, "Thank you, I'd love to," and headed for the door.

"Come along in then, dearie," said Mrs. Henderson, "and I'll make the tea. Rob's just got in."

She vanished into the doorway. I followed her.

Rob was there at the sink, in his shirt sleeves, washing his hands. I saw he had taken the bandage off his left hand, and had been carefully cleaning the injured thumb. He greeted me rather shortly, as he had done that morning, then his eyes fixed on my face and he straightened, speaking in quite a changed voice.

"Is something wrong, then?"

I opened my mouth automatically to deny that anything could be wrong, but somehow no words came. Instead of the brittle, conventional denial of "Nothing at all. What should be wrong?" I found myself saying with all the force of unhappiness, "Oh, Rob, it's all so awful," and I put a hand to my eyes.

His hand, still damp, took me very gently by the elbow and steered me to a place at the table. "What you need's a cup of tea. It's making now. So come your ways and sit down."

I don't remember that I ate anything, but I drank the strong, scalding tea, and watched Rob and Mrs. Henderson eating scones and bramble jelly, and listened to the two of them talking over the commonplaces of the day—the shirt she would take home to mend, the pie she had made for him to heat at suppertime, the mousehole that she had found when she swept the back bedroom. The two of them addressed remarks in my direction from time to time, but never anything I had to answer; the talk went around and over me with the instinctive tact of long-standing affection. They were hedging me about with kindness, and I knew why the sunlight in the stackyard, the cottage smells, the sound of Rob's warm country voice, had suddenly and unaccountably broken me down. I had been here before. As a little girl I had come often to the Grangers' house, sometimes for comfort and refuge from the boys' games, sometimes just for a "visit" with Mrs. Granger on the days when Rob's father was safely distant at market or down at the Bull. It had been the farm kitchen then, not the cottage, but it was the same: the faded rug, the old dresser with the green and blue plates, the brown teapot, the smells of baking and freshly ironed clothes, and the warmth and welcome that all these things added up to. I had loved these visits, tea with "bought cakes" (which as a child I had thought so much better than anything we had at home) and sardines on toast and tinned fruit and condensed milk, while Mrs. Granger listened to Rob and me boasting about what we had done and dared that day at school in the village. I had never understood her faded edginess and her air of always listening for an unwelcome footstep; nor did I guess why, if Mr. Granger came back while I was still there, I was expected to get up and go straight home. Nor had Rob's sullenness meant anything except "Robbie's sulks." What happened when Matt Granger came home at night was a well-kept secret, and had never touched little Miss Bryony. Well, that was over now, and the familiar warmth lapped me round, and from somewhere came comfort and calmness.

When tea was done. I helped Mrs. Henderson clear and wash the dishes, while Rob pushed the cloth back from his end of the table, and spread his account book and papers out and got on with his figuring. He was surprisingly quick and neat. The sums. looked complicated, but long before I had dried and stacked the dishes he had shut the book and put the papers aside and picked up a sheaf of what looked like highly coloured catalogues or holiday brochures. He read them intently, paying no attention to the two women moving around him. He might have been alone in the room. It was curiously soothing.

Mrs. Henderson took her apron off and hung it behind

the door. "Well, that's it for today. I'll let you have the shirt by the weekend, Rob. Shall I feed the hens for you?"

"Thanks, yes, I'd be obliged."

She took her leave of me then, and I thanked her for the tea. She had obviously assumed my distress to be caused by my father's death, and by the loneliness of my first night back at Ashley. She had too much natural delicacy to say anything directly, but she came as near to it as she could. "Are you all right at the cottage, Miss Bryony? Is there anything else you want?"

"Nothing at all, thank you, Mrs. Henderson. Everything's fine. You got it lovely." She went then, leaving me with Rob.

He laid the papers down and pushed them aside. "Now what's to do? Can't you tell me? Seems like it might be bad trouble, to upset you like that."

"It might." I sat down at the other side of the table from him. He watched me, saying nothing.

It was very different from the recent tête-à-tête with Emory; no tensions, no careful reticences, no attempts to see past an apparent meaning to a real one. And different, too, from talking with my cousin James; there, as well, had been the sprung overtones of emotion, of a difficult affection, of a personal distress. And in both interviews I had felt the impact, doubled because united, of a strong personality and a calculated desire to drive me into action over the Court and the trust.

Here there was none of that. The dark eyes that watched me steadily were not Ashley eyes, those wary, clever eyes with their cool self-sufficiency and their self-absorption. Rob could have no axe to grind, nothing to gain, nothing he wanted from me. He was not even, like the Vicar, bound by a set of rules which could force me to an alien action like the betrayal I was contemplating. He was just an old friend, someone belonging to the Court, who had known it and me and Jon Ashley all his life; a real person, kind, uncomplicated, who would listen without judgment unless I asked for it, and would answer me then with plain and disinterested common-sense. I supposed he loved the Court; I didn't know; but he knew it, and he knew me. Neither fear nor favour . . . He had never feared anything, Rob Granger, except perhaps, when he was a child, his brutal father. And he had no reason to show favour, now that my father was gone, to any of us above the others; only to Ashley itself. Or so I thought.

"Rob," I said, "it's something awful, and I oughtn't to tell you, but I've got to tell someone, and there's no one else."

Vaguely to my surprise he didn't say, "What about your family?" or even, "What about the Vicar?" He merely gave a little nod, as if that was reasonable, and waited again.

I swallowed. "I think it was James who knocked Daddy down. I think he was there, in Bad Tölz. They picked up a silver pen with the initials *J. A.* just where the accident happened. When they gave me his things I assumed the pen had been his, though I'd never seen it before. And yesterday—yesterday James saw me using it, and said it was his own. He didn't know where he'd dropped it, he said, but it was his . . ."

He had listened without moving. Now he stirred, and asked, sharply for him: "Did you tell him where it came from?"

"No. Oh, no. I told him I'd found it in the churchyard the night before last."

"Did he accept that?"

"Yes. He didn't even seem surprised."

"Meaning that it was him in the vestry—or at any rate in the churchyard—that night."

"You could say so," I said. "Oh, he denied it when I asked him before, but I know James, and I was sure then that he was lying, and he knew I thought so. He took it as a joke. Last night he didn't even trouble to go on pretending. I know what he was doing there, too—though I don't really understand all about it. It doesn't matter anyway, not compared with this."

"What does matter," said Rob bluntly, "is that he

shouldn't know you've any call to suspect him of being in Bad Tölz."

"I'm sure he doesn't. It was all quite casual. He just pocketed the pen and went out."

"Wait a minute." Rob was frowning. "What was the date your dad was knocked down? The thirtieth of April, wasn't it? Well, James was here then, or thenabouts."

I sat up abruptly. "Are you sure?"

"Sure enough. I saw him. He called here to pick up the Underhill girl."

"Rob, are you sure it wasn't Emory?"

"Well, no, I suppose it might have been. I didn't speak to him—I was busy working along the drive when he drove out with the girl. But the Underhills said afterwards that it was James. I remember that, because of course I thought it was Emory with her; you'll know they're sweet on each other, of course?"

"Yes." I added, thoughtfully: "So he wasn't ringing for his twin that day? I wonder why?"

I had spoken softly, to myself, but Rob had not only heard, he had got there with almost electronic speed. "So they've been doing that, have they? Can I take it that that wasn't Emory here yesterday, then?"

"No, it was James. It was Emory today, though." I looked at him across the table. "Rob, don't you see? It probably was Emory here that day with Cathy. Which means it was James in Bad Tölz."

"Would it matter which of them it was in Bad Tölz," said Rob forcefully, "if he was driving that car?"

I didn't answer. I was looking down at my hands, which were pressed flat on the table in front of me, covering the letter as if to hide it. Then I looked up at him. I knew that all the strain and uncertainty, yes, and the longing, too, must be there, naked to view, in my face and eyes. I didn't care. I saw him take it all in in one swift, summing look, then he said, in a voice carefully empty of sympathy: "Yes, I can see it would. But it doesn't help to take on about it, not till you know a bit more."

It braced me, as it was meant to. I sat back in my

chair, and let my hands fall into my lap. "I'm sorry. Throwing it all at you like this. It's your own fault, you know, for being so easy to talk to."

"Maybe because I'm just part of the fittings. I belong in the garden, sort of, along with the trees." There was no edge to the words. He was smiling. "It's all right, you know. You can tell me anything—it's likely enough I'd know it anyway, with my ear to the ground most days."

"Like telling the bees?"

"I reckon," he said, comfortably. He stretched, then got to his feet and leaned his shoulders back against the mantelpiece. His look was solemn again, a little heavy. "Well, you've told me. Never mind why, but you don't want it to be James. But you can't leave it at that, you know. You'll have to find out. Whichever of them it was, even if you don't want to know the answer, you've got to go on and find out. That's true, isn't it?"

"I suppose so. But—"

"And there's something else you'll have to face." He hesitated, then finished abruptly. "As far back as I remember, Bryony, whatever one of them was in, the other was in just as deep."

"Not James." It was meaningless and purely defensive, but he answered the implication rather than the words.

"Maybe not. But he was always there after the fact, as they say. Anyway, we have to find out, don't we? Are you up to facing that?"

Somehow I wasn't up to facing him. I looked down at my hands. "I have to, haven't I? You just said so."

"Yes." It was abrupt and uncompromising. As unswerving a judgment, I thought with vague surprise, as the Vicar's. I still couldn't look at him, but I turned my head to the window, where the curtains swelled and swayed in a sudden breeze. There was a pot of pink geraniums on the sill, the twin of the one at my cottage. The breeze brushed a fading head of flowers, and a scatter of petals floated down into the room. One of them, drifting to the floor beside me, stirred a memory; the petals floating from the clematis last night. Last night; before I had

known what I knew now. When all I had had to worry
me was the "theft" of a few things from the Court. It
seemed a lifetime ago.

Bryony. Bryony, love.

I must have jumped in my chair. I felt my nerves
tighten like a net pulled in by a fisherman. Somehow, in
that unguarded moment of memory, he had managed to
reach me. It came with the breeze, sweet as the summer
air; it was round me like the falling petals; comfort, love,
longing as strong as anguish. So strong that for one awful,
choking moment I thought he would be able to see
through my mind into the contents of the envelope that
lay beside me on the table.

*Get out! Do you hear me? Leave me alone. You
know why.*

Yes, I know why. Bryony . . .

All right. Did you do it?

No reply. Just that longing and love, hopeless and
receding.

Did you do it? Were you there when he died?

No answer. He was gone. Above me Rob's voice was
saying, with that careful lack of warmth: "You don't have
to look like that, Bryony. Whoever was driving that car,
you surely can't think it was anything but an accident,
so—"

"Well, of course it was an accident! But why keep
it quiet? Why not stay and—and help him? He wasn't
dead."

"Would it have saved his life if they had?"

"No. No, Herr Gothard said not. But it might have
prolonged it. He might have lived till I got there . . ."
I choked on that one, and then managed to add, more
steadily: "That's not true, no. Herr Gothard said it made
no difference. But one can't help feeling—"

"No, you can't," said Rob, "but you can think as well,
and that'll help. Come on, think about it. Say it was one
of your cousins knocked your dad down. O.K. What was
he doing in Bad Tölz in the first place?"

"I—I suppose he must have gone there to see Daddy."

"Right. Must have. Well then, what about?"

There was only one answer to that, too. "About the Court, breaking the trust. They need money. James says they need it very badly."

"Who doesn't?" said Rob drily. "I suppose the difference is, what do you do to get hold of it? Yes, I know, but there's no need to look like that, love"—the country endearment came out as "luv," as natural and meaningless as when the local shopkeepers or bus conductors used it—"because we're taking it as an accident, aren't we? All right, go on thinking. Your cousin—we'll call him Emory if it makes you feel better; and he could easily have had a loan of his brother's pen, and never missed it when he dropped it—Emory goes to see your dad to talk him into something; it doesn't matter what, but it was urgent, or he wouldn't have gone to that trouble. Now, since your doctor pal never saw him, Emory must have been on his way up to the hospital when he overtook your dad on the road. Didn't recognize him in the dark, we'll say—"

"Of course he didn't recognize him! You couldn't ever think—"

"Hey, calm down, I said we were taking it as accident. Well, he knocked him down in the dark. And after that he panicked and drove off and never said a word. It happens. It's human. It's the reason for all the hit-and-run jobs there are."

"I'd like to accept that. But it doesn't fit, does it? He must have recognized him *after* the accident. Don't forget that whichever of them ran Daddy down must have got out of the car to look at him, and if Ja—Emory leaned over him long enough to let that pen drop from his pocket, he must have recognized who it was. The car's lights would be on, too."

Rob nodded. "He ran away *because* he recognized who it was. Don't you see? Your cousin went there to talk your dad into something. He went because he was desperate for money, and his own hadn't managed to get yours to part with anything, or agree to break this trust. Then by accident he knocks your dad down on the road

and hurts him badly; he must have known how badly.
Anyway, he knew about his heart. . . . Well, put yourself
in his place. How's it going to look if he, of all people, is
involved in an accident like that, and then your dad dies?
The people who stand to gain are him and his family.
They're the only people in the world who might want your
dad dead. No—" quickly, to forestall me. "I'm not saying
they did. I'm saying that's what the police would have
said once they ferreted the story out."

"Yes. Yes, I see. But even if they didn't dare pick him
up and get help for him, surely they—Emory—could
have telephoned from somewhere and *told* someone where
he was, and to go and help him?"

"What sort of German do they speak?"

"Oh, yes, that would have given them away. Of course.
But, Rob, just to leave him lying like that—"

"I know, it takes a bit of swallowing. But I've known
your cousins as long as you have, remember, and I'd say
they were realists. You told me yourself it wouldn't have
helped your dad if they'd stayed by him." He left the
fireplace and sat down where he had been before, resting
his folded arms on the table and leaning forward on them.
"That's it, you see. I dare say you'll find that they were
only planning to look after their own interests. But it went
wrong, and now you've found out, and the very thing's
happened that they'd have given their eyeteeth to avoid;
you've been set against them."

I said nothing. It fitted, all too well. Whichever twin
had been beside my father and dropped the pen, the other
would no doubt have been ready to create an alibi by
confusion, either in Bristol or in Spain. This was why
neither man had come to the cremation, or showed up at
Bad Tölz to see me home. I would have recognized him,
and if there had been questions later, this might have
destroyed whatever alibi they had concocted between
them. It could have been either of them telephoning from
England; Walther was not familiar with their voices, and
it was perhaps significant that the caller had not asked
to speak to me. I began to wonder, but with the dullness

of emotional exhaustion, if Cousin Howard was involved as well. If neither twin had been in Spain at the time of the accident, would their father say so? Was he, even, well enough to know? But, with England, Spain, and Bavaria only hours apart by air, heaven knew it would have been easy enough for the twins to create their own kind of alibi.

And Francis . . . The thought came suddenly, unbidden and unwelcome. He could not be mistaken for his brothers by anyone who knew them, but at a frontier, with a passport belonging to one of the twins . . .

I slammed the door on that one. I would not even think it. I sat slumped in my chair, staring at the envelope, while my thoughts trailed off into weary confusion.

"How long have you been sweet on him?"

My eyes came up to Rob's with a jerk, but somehow, I wasn't startled. It seemed natural to be asked. The strange thing was that now I found myself hesitating. The old, direct country phrase didn't fit what I was feeling; the half-guilt; the two-way pull of the affection I felt for my cousin, contrasted with the total abandonment to the possession of my secret friend. "I— It's hard to say. Of the three of them, I suppose it was always James. But in the last few years . . . And now, since I got back home . . . In love with him? I just don't know."

No one could have claimed this for a coherent answer, but he nodded, his rather somber look lightening as he smiled. "Well, you've got yourself into a rare muddle and no mistake, love; and I doubt it hardly helps to have the pair of them taking turns to sit on your doorstep and pressure you to do things you don't want to do." The smile deepened at my look. "I told you I was just part of the landscape. You'd be surprised the things I know. It was obvious, anyway. It'll take months to prove your dad's Will and get everything sorted out, but if you'd agree to break the trust now and let the land go, they could borrow on that promise straight away." A pause of silence, broken by the uneven ticking of the clock. "Bryony, how much do you really care about this place? Would you want to stay on here?"

I said, rather wearily: "Everyone keeps asking me that, and I keep saying I don't know yet. How do I know what I want to do with the rest of my life? And how do I know— I mean, are you talking about James?"

"No, I wasn't. We've gone through all that. Whether you're sweet on him or not, you'll have to find out what really happened, or you'll never be able to get along with either of them, will you? No, I was talking about your cottage. What the Vicar calls Naboth's Vineyard."

"Calls it *what?*"

"Naboth's Vineyard. I asked him what he meant, and he said something about the Polish Corridor. Talks very sideways, sometimes, Mr. Bryanston."

"I know what he meant, I think," I said. "The cottage and the orchard are the only outlet from the Court to Penny's Flats. The gardens wouldn't be much use to a building contractor without access to the main road."

"Aye, that's it." It was apparent that Rob, too, knew exactly what Mr. Bryanston had meant. "So you see how much it matters to them to keep on the sweet side of you. And you see why it matters not to let them make a guess at where you really found that silver pen."

I must have been staring. I suppose I knew quite well what he was saying, but something in me could not accept it.

"All right," he said, with a return to the old, uncompromising manner, "I'll spell it out. You won't like it, mind, but I've got to say it. I've had it on my mind ever since you told me what your dad said. You've got to give a thought to its maybe not being an accident at all."

"But it must have been! You can't honestly think that James—or even Emory—"

"I'm thinking nothing. I'm telling you that you've got to be ready to believe anything of anybody. Your dad talked of danger, didn't he, and told you to be careful? There's no magic about an Ashley that says they couldn't kill a man, is there?"

"No. My God, plenty of them have. . . . But nowadays, one of my cousins kill my father for gain? No."

"Well, I agree with you. I'm only saying it could happen. We none of us know what a chap's capable of, or even what we might be capable of ourselves. I'd have thought the last few years would have taught anyone that." He reached a hand across the table and touched mine, gently. "All I'm asking is that you do what your dad said, and be careful. Keep it in mind that even your cousins might get nasty, even with you. There's a lot here we don't understand, and till we do . . ."

He let it hang.

In the silence that followed, without looking at him, I turned the envelope over and showed him the address.

"I see." His voice held satisfaction, and something else I couldn't put a name to. "You mean I've been wasting my breath? You've made your own decision all along?"

"In a way. But you haven't wasted your breath, Rob. I'm not quite sure if I ever would have mailed it, but I will now."

"What's in it?"

"A photograph. Do you remember the one of the twins and you that day you caught all those eels? When you tipped them out beside the lake?"

"Aye, and the half of them went straight back in." He laughed. "And Emory called me a—Emory was pretty mad."

"There's no need to be coy. I remember quite well what Emory called you. He had a right to be mad. They'd spent hours catching them, and they needed the money."

They always needed the money. Neither of us said it aloud, but amusement died abruptly. He put out a hand.

"Will you let me take that to the post for you?"

"Thanks very much, but don't bother. I was going anyway."

"I'd rather you let me take it."

"Don't you trust me to post it?"

"Don't be daft," said Rob. He got to his feet and stretched, then gave me that disarming smile of his again.

"Well, maybe you'll let me walk you along to the corner, and we can watch each other post it? Come on."

The collie got up to follow him, and so did I.

Ashley, 1835

Memories stung him, banishing sleep.

"Nick?"

"My love?"

"He won't speak? You're sure he won't tell on us?"

"Certain. He knows where his duty lies, or, better still, where his meat and drink come from."

"But your father? Oh, Nick—"

"My father be damned."

He had meant it, too. He shut his eyes.

Fifteen

This night I hold an old accustom'd feast,
Whereto I have invited many a guest,
Such as I love; and you among the store,
One more, most welcome, makes my number more.
—*Romeo and Juliet*, I, ii

When I got back to the cottage there was someone sitting on the seat in the shadow of the lilac tree. My heart jerked painfully, once, then settled back to its even beat as Jeffrey Underhill got to his feet and came out into the mellow sunshine of the lawn.

We greeted one another. The tycoon manner was as much in evidence as before, but somehow scaled down by the setting of lake and sky and the huge trees beyond the orchard. Perhaps a man like Jeffrey Underhill needed rooms and company, the setting of his own kind of jungle. Then I saw that I was wrong. This was still the same high-octane personality, but the mask of power was being held, as it were, deliberately in front of a very ordinary, anxious father. His manner was as smooth, as pleasant, as incisive as before, and with never a hint of worry showing, but the Ashley seventh sense, prompted by what I knew, saw it as the manner of the Chairman of Directors preparing to present an adverse report to his Board. *Cathy*, I thought, with my heart accelerating ever so slightly, *he wants to talk to me about Cathy*. I found myself looking away from him, as if it was I who had been at fault rather than my cousins and this man's daughter. As I led Mr. Underhill into the cottage I reflected, with a twist of wry amusement, that this Chairman of Directors had a very good technique indeed. In this case it had even been unconscious; I thought I could acquit him of using it deliberately on me.

He settled himself in one of the armchairs as if he had all the time—and the quietest mind—in the world, refused the offer of tea, waved aside my apologies for not having any gin, and opened the meeting without delay.

"I had to come and talk to you, Miss Ashley. Something my daughter Cathy has told me has disturbed me very much."

I made some kind of assenting sound, and waited, with what was meant to look like mild inquiry, but the clever dark eyes probed mine for a millisecond, then the brows twitched down, as Mr. Underhill registered that I already knew what he was about to tell me.

He told me, all the same. It was Cathy's version of the story I had heard from James. Emory—and James passing for Emory—had persuaded the girl that the contents of the Court were legally theirs, and that "Cousin Bryony," when she knew, would not mind a few small objects being abstracted and used straight away, rather than wait for the long processes of law. Cathy had obviously had no idea that the estate must by law be left intact for valuation; and the twins had told her that I, Bryony, was, if not firmly engaged to James, at any rate his for the asking, and therefore an interested party. So she had taken the T'ang horse and the other small objects from the library, and then—this time on her own initiative —the Rackham pictures from the schoolroom. The church, always left unlocked, had been used as a cache and a pickup point.

Mr. Underhill told me the whole story, straight and without excuse, just as he would have put a report across. Facts and only facts. The rest I could supply for myself. He still obviously had no idea that the twins had been playing tricks with identity; he referred all the time to "Emory," with no apparent suspicion that sometimes the man had been James. I looked away from him, kept my thoughts to myself, and worked it out as he talked.

He had got to my own return from Bavaria. The night when I had inadvertently seen "Emory" in the church, said Jeff Underhill, he had been picking up the pictures which Cathy had taken. They had been hidden in the old ambry which was now blocked from casual sight by the choir men's wardrobe. Next day had come my discovery of the theft, and my questions.

"My wife and I guessed right away that Cathy might have something to do with it, but naturally we had to talk to Cathy first, before we could say anything to you."

"Of course." I must have looked surprised. "But why should you have guessed that? Had she said anything?"

He was leaning back in his chair, his eyes on the prospect of leaves and sky beyond the cottage window. He might have been studying the weather, to judge the fishing prospects for the morrow. But then he turned his head, and the eyes that met mine were those of a deeply troubled man.

"I have to be honest with you, Miss Ashley. We guessed it might be our daughter because we have had this kind of problem before."

I felt my eyes widen. Though something in me— perhaps that Ashley seventh sense again—had almost seen it coming, I couldn't think what to say. But he did not wait. If it had to be said, he would say it and have done.

"It started when she was in high school. We lived in California then, just outside Los Angeles, and—well, it's not perhaps the easiest city for a young boy or girl to grow up in, and Cathy soon got problems. She is—" a pause, so brief that one hardly registered the effort it hid "—a very loving and warmhearted girl, and she follows her impulses without always seeing where they will take her, or what they will cost. She takes," added Jeffrey Underhill, quite unnecessarily, "more after her dear mother than after me."

I said something that was meant to sound both soothing and noncommittal, and was rewarded by the flash of sudden humour in his face, as he said, with a return to his old manner: "I am neither generous nor impulsive, Miss Ashley. Nor am I easily guided. But my wife and daughter are altogether better folks than I can ever be. So when my little Cat got into bad company, the next thing we knew she was right there in the middle of a full-scale classic teen-age problem, and believe me, she could have finished anywhere. She was in with a real wild bunch. They used to steal things—things that didn't matter, but it was stealing for all that—and wreck things, and drive cars away—having fun, they called it, getting kicks. There was this boy she was crazy about, and while that lasted . . . Well, I'll spare you the rest. She got herself out of it in the end. It took a long time, but, being basically sweet and good like most of these silly kids if they get the chance, she got herself out of it, with God's help and with ours."

He spoke with devastating simplicity. Once again, I could think of nothing to say. But he didn't seem to expect an answer. He was going on.

"That was one of the reasons we decided to live away from home for a few years. You'll understand, it doesn't much matter to me where I'm domiciled, as long as I'm within commuting distance of Houston, Texas, and of New York." The gleam of a smile again. "Well, I can't rightly say that Ashley Court is commuter country for New York and my other current ports of call, but as you know, the girls—my wife and Cathy—took a real fancy to it, and things seemed to be working out just fine. Then, as you know, this happened. When you told us there were valuable things missing, we were terribly afraid it was beginning again. When Cat and her set had stolen things before it was a kind of wild thing, not a real sickness; but now we were afraid she was really sick. This kleptomania is a mental thing, you know that, not just a teen-age problem that can be gotten through. So Stephanie and I talked it over most of last night, and again this morning, and then we asked Cathy about it. She told us everything. She'd had it on her mind ever since you came here, and she—I think she was glad to tell us."

My mind was twisting and turning like some trapped thing trying to find the light. It was worse, far worse than I had thought. Even this minor affair of the "disposable assets" had in it the possible springs of tragedy. Yet one more thing for Twin to answer for . . . I hardly noticed that this time I hadn't specified which twin.

"But, Mr. Underhill, this is awful!"

He misunderstood me. "Miss Ashley, I know that it's as bad as it can be, and it might look a real hanging matter from where you're sitting right this minute, but I have to tell you that when Cathy went into all this legal routine about trusts and disposable assets that Emory really owned, and all that stuff, we were so relieved that our daughter must almost have gotten the impression that what she'd done was quite O.K. Which," he added, with uncompromising dryness, "it was not."

"Mr. Underhill—"

He lifted a hand about an inch from the arm of the chair, and I stopped. "No, let me say it first. I'm not often stuck for words, but I find this very, very hard. We owe you an apology, that goes without saying, and Miss Ashley, you have it. I must say this as well: if there is anything we can do to put this thing right for you, you have only to ask. That is the least I can say. I'll get those items back, and into their places, just as if this had never happened, if it takes all I've got."

Coming from someone like Jeffrey Underhill, it was quite an offer, but somehow it didn't seem in the least absurd. And he meant every word of it. As for the apology, there was no point in my disclaiming, since for once my honest opinion was probably the exact one that it would comfort him to hear. But before I could speak he said, with another of those probing looks that seemed to get right past the eyes and into the mind: "You don't seem very surprised by what I have been telling you. You knew how the things were taken."

"Yes. My cousin told me last night."

"And it troubles you a whole lot, I can see that."

"Not really. Other things trouble me, but not that. Honestly. I'll tell you exactly how I feel about it, Mr. Underhill. When my cousin told me, I was shocked. It was wrong, though perhaps it wasn't quite as dishonest as it seemed. But what I was really angry about was the fact that they'd used Cathy. I don't have to go into the reasons for you—and I certainly didn't know what you've just told me about her trouble, or I'd have been angrier still—but it seemed to me a terrible thing to do, and I said as much. My cousin would pass that on to his brother. As for the horse and the other things, please forget them. No, I mean it. Officially they will belong in the end to Emory's family, and if we start looking for them now to buy them back, all this might have to come to light, and that wouldn't help anybody. It might even put us on the wrong side of the law." I remembered something. "Mr. Underhill, did Cathy say anything about a church register?"

"A what?" He sounded blank.

"One of the parish registers they keep in the church. It's gone missing."

"She certainly said nothing about that. I'll ask her. But why should anyone want to take a thing like that? Is it valuable?"

"Not intrinsically. It is very old, and I suppose it's interesting, but only to local people, one would think."

"Maybe someone borrowed it for research, and forgot to bring it back."

"Probably. I only asked because when I saw—er, my cousin that night in the church, I thought he was carrying something like a big book, but it was probably the Rackham pictures."

"Yes, now, those pictures. They're a different matter from the other stuff, surely? Aren't they your own?"

I nodded. "And they're unique, and recognizable, I'm afraid. If you could get those back for me, Mr. Underhill, I'd be terribly grateful. There won't be any trouble, either,

I promise you; I'll say I sent them for sale myself, but I thought better of it. That should put us all in the clear."

"You're very generous."

Here I did disclaim, but he insisted on thanking me, and then, as I had half expected, went on to tell me that he and his wife had decided to cut short their tenancy of Ashley Court. They had, he assured me, been considering going well before November, because of my father's death and the legal business which would ensue. Now they had decided to move immediately to London, staying there for just as long as it took Mr. Underhill's agents to find him a house to rent in Paris. They were going, he said, with a quick look at me, tomorrow. He had talked with Mr. Emerson, and all was settled. The rent of the Court was paid till the full term . . . and so on and so forth. Everything but the real reason for the sudden departure.

He finished. Then, because this was Jeffrey Underhill, and because I respected him, I came straight out into the open with what, in delicacy, he had not said.

"You're taking Cathy away from Emory."

This time a pause that could be felt. Then he said, flatly: "Yes, I am. I think it best. I'm sorry."

"You needn't be." I said it equally flatly. "I respect your reasons, and what's more, I think you're perfectly right. But what will Cathy say?"

"That I can't tell." He spoke a trifle heavily. "She's been in and out of love, the way these kids understand it now, ever since she was fourteen years old, so we'll hope this is no more serious. Right at this moment the only thought she seems to have in her head is that we're going to live in Paris, France. I told you that it makes no difference to me where we live, and it will certainly be more convenient to live in Paris than in the village of Ashley. I've given that as the reason, and I'm just hoping that Nature will do the rest."

I laughed. "You're a clever man, Mr. Underhill, and she's a lucky girl. I doubt if even Emory can compete for long with Paris, France."

He got to his feet, and I followed suit. He stood there

on the hearthrug, seeming to dwarf the little room. He looked down at me. "I find it a great pity that we should leave the Court just when you come home, Miss Ashley. You are a very lovely girl, and I'm proud to have met you. I reckon you know how hard this has been, and it's good of you to understand. May I hope that you will come and visit with us in Paris? I know the girls would appreciate that very much."

I didn't point out that I wasn't quite in the bracket that makes weekend visits to Paris. I just thanked him, and saw him to the door, and down the flagged path towards the wicket gate.

"Shall I be able to say good-bye to Mrs. Underhill? I expect she'll be far too busy packing and so on, but perhaps I could telephone her in the morning?"

"She's certainly hoping to see you soon. I'm not sure how she's fixed tomorrow, but she'd like to have you call her, I know. She had some plan that she wanted to put to you, and I was hoping that Cathy—" He paused with a hand to the gate, and turned his head. His face changed subtly, and he cleared his throat. "Why, here's Cathy coming now. I kind of thought she would."

Cathy was coming down through the orchard. She had a frock on this time, of some pale summery stuff that gave a floating movement to her walk as she came slowly through the dusk of the old grey trees. The effect was romantic and ethereal, like those soft-focus films they use for television advertisements, but when she saw us at the cottage gate and waved, the halfhearted quality of the gesture gave her away. She was taking her time, and being self-conscious about it, because she was nervous. In other words, she was coming down to apologize.

As I waved back and called out a cheerful greeting, I realized that Jeffrey Underhill had left me. He had melted from my side as quietly as a real jungle cat, and was standing over by the ruined wall, looking out at the sunset light on the water, and making quite a ceremony of lighting a cigar. He was just nicely out of earshot. Yes, a smooth performer, Mr. Underhill. I liked him very much.

. . . "Had to come to tell you I was sorry." Cathy hurried it out in a small, breathless voice, like a child who wants to get it over, and is not sure of her reception.

She had stopped on the other side of the wicket gate, and was gripping the top with both hands. I dropped mine over them. I was almost four years older than Cathy, and just at that moment felt about four hundred. "It's all right," I said quickly. "You don't have to say any more. Your father's been talking to me about it, but I knew already. I know you only did it because you were fond of Emory, and it's his fault and not yours. I mean it, really. I'm not just saying it to comfort you. . . . How could you be expected to know what's right or wrong in English law? And besides"—I smiled—"I know my cousins rather well. If I started to tell you now about the things they'd pressured me into doing that I knew I never should have done, we'd be here till midnight. So forget it, please."

"Oh gosh, I wish I could! You're just sweet, but honestly, you don't fully understand." The pretty Pekinese face was intently earnest. She hadn't put on the mink eyelashes, and her eyes looked oddly unprotected. I thought there were tears there. "Honestly, Bryony," she repeated, "I wouldn't have done such a thing to *you,* but I thought it was all on the level, and it was just a case of getting a few things out for the boys to use, to save all the fuss with those people who fix the tours. And then I found those pictures upstairs, in the cupboard along with the books, and when I found they were valuable, too, why, I just took them as well. . . ." She swallowed. "And then you came and started asking about the things, and I began to think it wasn't O.K. after all, and then I found the pictures were really yours, your very own, all along. . . . And honest, Bryony, I just feel so awful I could die. Will you ever forgive me?"

"I did, just as soon as they told me about it. Hey, Cathy, don't cry." I slid my hands up to her wrists and gave her a little shake. "I told you I never thought it was your fault. It's all over and done with, and there's no harm done, and your father's going to get the pictures back for me, so let's forget it, shall we?"

I talked on for some time, reassuring her, being careful not to throw too much of the blame on Emory, for fear of putting her on the defensive for him, though I thought that she was a little less than starry-eyed about him herself; in fact, I got the distinct impression that she would rather not have talked about him. So far, so good. The very fact that she had come to talk to me like this, when it would have been so easy for her to go tomorrow and never see me again, showed that Cathy Underhill must have a grain of her father's toughness in her after all. I didn't share her father's fear that she might revert to her teen-age "problem," but it was no thanks to Emory that she had not done so. I found myself feeling a little better about mailing that photograph to Bad Tölz. About James, I refused to think at all.

Cathy, however, had him on her mind. "You know, James didn't have anything to do with it. Truly he didn't. And I know that when he saw those pictures he would have wanted to come straight and make me put them back. James is very, very fond of you, and he wouldn't do a thing that would hurt you."

"I know."

One freak shaft of sunlight, molten red, shot through the horizon clouds and touched the highest tip of the pear tree. The thrush was there, sitting preening his breast feathers, ready for a song.

I looked back at Cathy, watching me with those vulnerable, anxious eyes. "And now," I said, smiling, "what's all this about Paris?"

Jeffrey Underhill's cigar was about half smoked through before Cathy, talking now about Paris, and her mother's plans, came gradually back to her sparkling norm.

"And we're going tomorrow, and there's this fabulous

party, and we want you to come! Please say you will, Bryony! Mom particularly told me to ask you."

"Well," I was beginning doubtfully, when Mr. Underhill, catching the new tone of his daughter's voice, turned away from his scrutiny of the Pool, and came back to us across the grass.

"Cathy means to London, Miss Ashley. I left her to invite you herself, but I don't think she's explained. We're giving a party tomorrow night. It's been planned for quite a while; it's our anniversary, so we're having a few friends along to celebrate, and we'd be honoured if you would join us. As I told you, we're settling down in London for a few days before we go on to Paris, so we thought we'd make this a good-bye party at the same time. Stephanie's been on the telephone all afternoon, and she's wild for you to be there, too. Say you will come."

"Please say you will!" urged Cathy.

"It's terribly kind of you, and thank you very much. I'd love to, of course, but—" I hesitated.

Cathy immediately looked anxious. "Bryony, we wouldn't want to pressure you into doing anything you didn't want. Maybe it's too soon after losing your father?"

"No, it's not that." I was thinking that if the party had been arranged some time back, then no doubt Emory and James would both be there. Unless, of course, Jeffrey Underhill had let Emory know that he would no longer be welcome? I thought him quite capable of it.

"Then please do come," urged Cathy. "It'll make me really feel as if you forgive me for the awful thing I did. When I *think* about it—"

Jeffrey Underhill, at my shoulder, intervened. "Perhaps Miss Ashley has too much to do here, Cat. Remember, she has only just got home." Then to me: "It would be wonderful if you could spare us the time, Miss Ashley, but you mustn't let Cathy pressure you. I know she and Stephanie would feel very honoured if you could come, but please don't trouble to decide now. If you'd like to call us in the morning, when you've had time to think it over—?"

"Look," I said warmly, "I'd love to come; I really would. I can get the late afternoon train."

At this they both joined in, with such enthusiasm that you would have thought the party was being given solely for me. They would drive me there themselves in the morning; they would put me up—"hire a suite for you" was Jeffrey Underhill's way of putting it—at the Dorchester; they would bring me down again next day, or whenever it suited me. They would do anything, if only (they seemed to be saying) I would grace their party by being there. I could hardly tell them what was in my mind: that if my two cousins had indeed been invited earlier, and if Emory, who could be as impervious to snubs as he wished to be, took the trouble to come, and to lay on the charm . . . It was for Cathy's sake as much as anything else that, in the end, I accepted, thinking grimly that, even if I had to use blackmail again, I would see that my eldest cousin kept his distance from her, and gave her breathing space. Then, glancing at Jeff Underhill, I saw that he had read my thoughts. He gave a half nod, threw his cigar away towards the water, and said: "Don't you worry; I can take care of that."

"Take care of what?" demanded Cathy.

"I'm sure you can," I said.

She looked from one to the other of us. "What are you two talking about?"

Her father let himself out through the wicket, put an arm round her, and scooped her up towards his side. "Nothing to do with you. Now say good night, and we'll leave Miss Ashley in peace."

"Good night," I said.

They went together through the dusking apple trees, arms round one another, his head bent to listen, hers raised in excited talk. A child who had been let off punishment, and a man who could take care of anything. So that, I thought, was that. And now, back to my own problems.

The thrush, unnoticed, had been singing for some time. Soon the owls would be out, and after them the stars.

Rather drearily, I latched the wicket and went back

into the cottage, fished William's Brooke out from its hiding place, and turned on the reading lamp.

Ashley, 1835

He threw back the coverlet and, still naked as he was, trod lightly across the carpet to the window. Beyond the open shutter the daylight showed an oblong of grey. He pushed the glass wide and leaned out. The hedges of the maze loomed dark, but with a faint shine on them of dew.

It was later than he had thought. Already a thin plume of smoke was rising from the kitchen chimney stack. No matter, though. No lights showed yet, and no one would be there to see him as he let himself in through the side door.

And she—she would be home by now, and they were safe.

Sixteen

My dreams presage some joyful news at hand . . .
　　　　　　　　　　—Romeo and Juliet, V, i

I had had supper, and read for an hour, and I had still only reached line 357.

"What hap have I," quoth she, "to love my father's foe?
What, am I weary of my weal? What, do I wish my woe?"

So Arthur Brooke's Juliet . . . Sighing, I lowered the book and sat back, pushing my hand through my hair as if I would clear a quicker way through the shuffling press of words. It would have been dull reading anyway, but I found it hardly possible to take in any meaning, with my brain running ahead looking for something, no matter what, that might be the tenuous clue to this other Ashley maze. But look I must—even, if I had to, as far as line 3020 . . . I tried again.

But when she should have slept, as wont she was, in bed,
Not half a wink of quiet sleep could harbour in her head,
For lo, an hugy heap of divers thoughts arise,
That rest have banished from her heart, and slumber from her eyes.
And now from side to side she tosseth and she turns,

And now for fear she shivereth, and now for love she
    burns.

I soldiered on for perhaps twenty minutes more, then
shut the book with a snap. It could surely wait. It was
impossible to get right through it tonight, and if I was
going to London tomorrow, I would take the book with
me and hand it over to someone at Christie's who would
know how to value it. It would have been civil to let Leslie
Oker look at it first, but he would surely understand.

I put it to one side and picked up William Ashley's
New Romeo. Here again, from the center of the maze on
the bookplate, the wildcat snarled and clawed. "The map?"
Certainly the map. But why? I turned a page and ran my
finger down the list of contents.

> The Catamountain.
> The Maze.
> Corydon's Farewell.
> The Minotaur's Lament.
> What Palace Then Was This?
> The Lover Leaves His Mistress.
> The Lover Returns.

And so on. Well, the poems could not be worse than
Arthur Brooke's, and at least they had the merit of being
short. I turned to the first one, "The Catamountain."

> What hunter is there who could think to meet
> In these low lands the leopard from the sun?
> Long hath he lain here, silent 'neath the feet
> Indifferent, which all unknowing tread
> Across the spotted catamountain's head.
> See! By his side the wine-god Bacchus runs,
> His basket brimming o'er with lusty grapes
> And in his train the lesser godlings go . . .

The Romans again, it seemed. Probably, I thought, only

the usual classical conceit. But no, here was the cat I was looking for . . .

> And now in this late age he comes anew
> From Scotia's heights, the catamountain wild,
> Brought here by thee, my gentle lady mild.
> As Venus led him locked in flowery chain,
> So thou, my Julia, bring'st thy wildcat tame.

A shadow fell over the page. I looked up with a start, but it was only Rob, pausing outside the casement. The thrush hadn't even faltered in its song.

"I thought you were going to be careful. Sitting here with the window open, and so deep in a book that you never even heard me coming."

"Well, but it's early still. I never thought . . . that is, I thought you meant tonight."

"I did, mainly. I just came down to see you were all right, and properly locked up."

I shut the book and put it with the others, making rather a play of it, to hide a touch of embarrassed shame for my cousins' sake. "You're taking this very seriously, aren't you?"

"Aren't you?"

There was no answer to that one. I got up. "All right, I'll shut the window now. Are you coming in?"

"For a minute, then."

I shut the casement and drew the curtains. I heard his voice speaking to the collie, then a vigorous scrubbing of shoes on the doormat, and he came in rather gingerly.

"Sorry about the shoes, but I think they're dry now. I came across the orchard after I'd shut up the greenhouses."

"Would you like a cup of Nescafé?"

"I wouldn't mind." As I went into the little kitchen he picked up *Romeus and Juliet*. "What's this?"

"I forgot to tell you. That's what Daddy must have meant by '*William's brook*.' See it? William Ashley's copy of something by a chap called Brooke. It's awfully rare, apparently. Daddy must have found out how valuable it was."

"Hm." He turned the small volume over, weighing it in his hand as if that would somehow give a clue to its worth. "Maybe so, but I wouldn't have thought he'd be troubling himself about that; not then. What else was it he said? Something about a paper or letter in it?"

"There's nothing. I looked. I was reading it to see if there was something in the text that would give me a clue, but it's next to unreadable."

"Looks it." He put it down, and picked up the *New Romeo.* "Is this valuable, too?"

"Oh, no. That's just William Ashley's own poems. They're not much better than poor Brooke, but I like the pictures."

" 'What palace then was this?' " read Rob, and puzzled his way through a few more lines. Somehow, I thought, the artificially stilted verses sounded even worse in Rob's voice with the soft country vowels. Worse than hothouse, somehow; distorted, wrong.

He put the book down and followed me into the kitchen. He leaned against the jamb and settled down companionably to help me watch the kettle boil. "Is that stuff supposed to be good? It sounded terrible to me, but then I'm no judge."

"I'm not, either. I don't think it's anything great."

"What was all that about, anyway?"

"Heaven knows," I said. "I haven't read that one yet. I got bogged down over Ariadne's clue in 'The Maze.' "

"Harry Who's clue?"

I laughed. It was the first real laugh since I had come home. "Oh, Rob! A girl called Ariadne. She gave Theseus the clue to follow into the maze. Greek myths, you know. William's writing about the maze, and getting a bit precious with his Greeks and Romans."

"How should I know? We can't all do Greek and Roman at school, can we?" said Rob, unworried.

The kettle boiled and I made the Nescafé. "Don't come the ignorant peasant over me, Rob Granger. You did Greek myths at Ashley School along with me. I remember it perfectly well. Here."

He took his mug from me and followed me back into the sitting room. "Don't be daft. I never did Greek in my life."

"Well, heavens, neither did I. I meant we did the stories in English. Don't you remember that book with the pictures? Icarus with those gorgeous big wings, and the Gorgons with snakes in their hair, and the Minotaur? That was the monster who lived in the middle of a maze, and Ariadne got this ball of wool or whatever, and gave it to Theseus, and he went in and fought him."

"Yes, I remember that." He sat down in the armchair, stretched his long legs in front of him, and stirred his coffee. It was the chair Jeffrey Underhill had sat in, and I could not help a flash of comparison. Rob did not, as the American had done, dominate the room, but somehow his quality of relaxation, of looking at home wherever he happened to be, made itself quite as strongly felt as the other man's powerful composure. "He had a bull's head. A black Dexter, by the look of him. Tricky-tempered beasts."

"Don't you remember, we used to play it here in the maze? I had the ball of wool, and you were the Minotaur, and I had to show Theseus the way in."

"And got lost," he said, grinning. "I remember sitting there in the middle and hearing you hollering for help, and wondering if I'd ever get out myself. Then James came in and killed me."

"I told you you knew the story."

"Aye, I remember it now. I never was much of a hand at stories, was I, but I was good at sums. I had the better of you there, every time. You used to copy from my book."

"I did not!"

"You did. And who was it told the teacher that a polygon was a dead parrot?"

"Isn't it? Oh, Rob, you've made me feel better! Another cup?"

"No, thanks."

He set his empty mug down on the hearth beside him. "Did I see Mr. Underhill going up through the orchard with Cathy? Had they been here? I suppose they came to tell you they'd be leaving tomorrow?"

"You knew?"

"Well, yes. I'm the caretaker, remember? She told me when I went up to the house. Must have been while he was here with you."

"That wasn't all he came for," I said. I gave him the gist of what had passed, and he thought it over for a few moments, then looked up.

"Are you really going to this party?"

"I think so. Cathy was very upset, and I think she'd feel that everything was all right if I did go. Besides, I'd like a chance to put things straight with Mrs. Underhill."

"Will your cousins be there?"

"I didn't like to ask, but the party was arranged some time ago, so I imagine they will be, unless Mr. Underhill tells them they're not welcome any more. I wouldn't put it past him."

"Then I'll take you to the train."

"Well, thank you, but I can use the Lambretta, and leave it in the station yard."

"And carry your party frock?"

"I've done it before." I smiled at him. "But it was nice of you to think about it."

"I wasn't," said Rob uncompromisingly. "I was thinking that I didn't want James or Emory to drive you."

I was silent for a moment. "Rob, you can't, you really can't think that this 'danger' thing could involve Emory or James deliberately harming me."

"I don't know." He made a restless little movement, rather unlike him. "We've had all this. Which of us knows what he'd do when pushed? And they are being pushed. Let's not leave it to chance."

"That's pure melodrama."

"Maybe." The stubborn line was very pronounced round his mouth. "But to see that they don't is pure common sense." A glimmer. "We peasants have a lot of that."

"But they don't know about the silver pen and the photograph."

"No, but they know you're no fool, and they want something badly enough to make them do what they've already done."

"Yes, I see. Once we admit that the thing's been done at all, it doesn't matter about the motives. I'll be careful. Well, all right, thanks. And the Underhills asked me to stay the night, so you don't have to meet the milk train . . . Rob?"

He looked an inquiry.

I asked: "Have you heard anything yet about Francis?"

"Not a thing, but then you know Francis. He never did write letters, or listen to the radio, or behave like anyone else. I remember him saying once that he had his own means of communication, and that was good enough for him."

I looked up. "Did he? What do you suppose he meant?"

He moved an indifferent shoulder. "His poetry, I suppose. Is it any better than that stuff there?"

"What? Oh, yes—that is, I don't know. I don't understand a word of it." I picked up my own empty mug, and crossed to pick up Rob's from the hearth. "I wish he'd show up, that's all. I just get a queer feeling that it might solve a thing or two."

He got to his feet. "Well, I'd better be going. Thanks for the coffee."

"You're welcome. At least you won't worry about me tonight if the twins are both away in Bristol."

"No. But I'll still take a look, if I may, to see if the door has a decent bolt. That's something I never checked. Would you like me to leave Bran with you?"

"Oh, no. He'd whine all night. I promise I'll lock the doors and windows, and I've got a telephone."

And time was, I thought, as Rob went to look at the back door, that I'd have had a private line if I needed it. But not any more. Not one I can use . . .

He finished his inspection and came in. "Seems O.K. You should be safe. Well, I'll go now. Good night, Bryony."

"Good night. And Rob—"

"Yes?"

"Thanks for everything."

He smiled. "For nothing. 'Night."

When he had gone, with Bran like a shadow as usual at his heels, I locked and bolted the door behind him, feeling a fool as I did so. For all that had happened, for all he had said, this was still my old familiar place, and the men we had been talking about were my own cousins. One of them, in spite of all seeming, might still be my own dear friend.

But I bolted the back door and checked the window catches for myself, and when I went up the narrow stair, I took the Brooke with me, and went to sleep with it under my pillow.

I woke with the feeling that I had just come out of a lovely and familiar dream. There had been a beach, a long, long shore of golden sand which stretched as far as the eye could reach. Farther. Ninety miles . . . Why did I think it was ninety miles long? There were dunes behind it, pale sand with long reeds blowing in the wind. The ocean poured and poured eternally in from the west. Tall grasses with feathered tops nodded and blew. The sky was huge and clean and the sand felt hot and the wind full of the sea's salt. Lonely, beautiful, quiet and safe.

Safe, safe, safe . . . The word went on echoing in Rob's voice round the dim walls of my bedroom. I remembered it all, then, the book under my pillow, the locked doors and windows, my cousins away in Bristol, the telephone by my bed if I should need reassurance.

The moon was bright. I slipped out of bed and went to the window. The striped print curtains hardly kept the moonlight out. The lattice was open. Feeling half silly for doing so, I kept carefully behind one of the curtains and looked out.

The window faced on the orchard. The moon was full on the blossoming trees. At the near corner, tallest of them all, the old pear tree lifted its graceful boughs, etched as black and symmetrical as the leads across a white window where moonlight poured. The bloom was like a cloud, piled shapes of light, and shadow that wasn't shadow, but just a dimmer moonwhite. It was a tree in a dream.

A shadow moved under it, intercepting the moon. Someone was standing there.

No, I was wrong. The pear tree's clouded shade was still again, and empty. It had been a trick of the moonlight, nothing more, something conjured up by moon and blossom, and a silence that should surely have been filled with nightingales. Lovers' time; Juliet at her window; Romeo under the orchard trees in the moonlight:

> Lady, by yonder blessed moon I swear,
> That tips with silver all these fruit-tree tops . . .

But it was not. It was an ordinary, empty night, where I dared not even summon what I had been used to of comfort. No lover to lure back like a bird on a silken thread. If I were to play Juliet at all, it would be Brooke's Juliet, with her hugy heap of very prosaic fears and her hithering-thithering torments of indecisive love.

I went back to bed. But not to sleep. The hugy heap was as oppressive as a heavy quilt. I lay and watched the ceiling and thought about James, and all the uneasy tangled skein of what had happened.

I could not believe, even with the evidence, that he was guilty. But Rob had said—and it was true—that we none of us know what we are capable of. . . . And if he was guilty, what then? Was I to deny this powerful tie between us? Was I to believe it was only an accident of blood, of family, rather than a natural—God-given?—

indication that we were sides of the same complete human being, that we had to be mates? Was it both arrogant and foolish to pretend that I was any better than, or indeed any different from, him? We are all capable, Rob had said. Not of killing my father, no, that I would never believe. But if it had been an accident, and the rest the result of natural panic afterwards . . . I had said that I would forgive. And if I could extend that charity to strangers, how much more to my cousin?

I sat up, hugging my knees. I put my forehead down on them, pressing it hard against them as if that would clear my thoughts. Was I, like so many of my generation, so afraid to condemn, so fearful of "priggishness," that I was in danger of letting the good things slide, and accepting the far-from-best, till it became the norm, and excellence was forgotten? Society kept him and protected him. Was it priggish in me to want him to obey its laws?

I lifted my head again. No, it was simpler than that. Panic after an accident was forgivable; to use it for profit was not.

But there was nothing I could do until the answer came back from Herr Gothard. I was still on my own. And I must stay that way until the mystery, such as it was, was solved.

It sounded easier than it was. I lay down again in my quiet airy bedroom, and watched the moonflung shadow of the pear tree move imperceptibly across the ceiling, and so strong was his insistence at that darkened door that I could have sworn that I saw his very shadow move with it, more substantial than the image of the blossoming boughs.

For one weak second I took my hand from the bars, and felt him close beside me, so close that . . .

Close beside me. I sat up like a pulled puppet. It had been so near, so insistent, so powerful and instinct with protection, that I knew he was here in the flesh as well. And I knew where. In the same moment's flash my opened mind had received another pattern: the pear tree's blossoming boughs, between my eyes and the moon.

He was in the orchard, under the pear tree. And whatever he had done, whoever he was, he meant me no harm.

I flung back the bedclothes and reached a coat down from behind the door. It was a soft light fur fabric, with a high collar and a tie belt. I fastened it round me, then, barefooted as I was, ran lightly down the stairs and out into the orchard.

The collie met me before I had gone two steps past the gate. I stopped dead.

Rob came out from under the pear tree into the moonlight.

I managed to speak, but it came out like a croaking whisper. "What are you doing here? It must be two o'clock."

I thought he hesitated, but his voice sounded quite normal. "I said I'd keep an eye on you, remember? Are you all right?"

"Yes, thank you. But—do you mean to stay here all night? I'm sure there's no need."

"It's a nice night. I was thinking."

"What—what about?"

"As a matter of fact I was thinking about New Zealand."

"New Zealand?" It was so improbable that I found my voice. "Oh, I remember—those brochures in the cottage kitchen."

"Aye." He hadn't moved. He seemed to be waiting. The collie was jumping up at me. I fended it off absently, and went slowly towards him over the wet grass.

"What about New Zealand, Rob?"

"I was thinking that's where I'd like to go when I leave here. Up to the North. I was thinking about the Ninety Mile Beach."

I said shakily: "So was I."

I took another step towards him. He moved as fast as the collie had, and took hold of me, pulling me tightly against him. As he began to kiss me, the hugy heap of trouble melted like snow, and above us in the pear tree a nightingale began to sing.

If the laden arches of pear blossom had suddenly sprung to life like a fountain, tossing a plume of bright water as far as the moon, it would hardly have seemed surprising, so great was the release, the flood of joy that swept through me. Through him, too. I felt light and happiness pouring through his mind into mine, and back again, like a tide race meeting the outflow of a river, clashing and doubling and throwing up drowning waves of pleasure. We were both perhaps a little mad. We clung and kissed and clung again, wordless. I doubt if either of us could have spoken. Everything had already been said, everything shared. This was the end of the courtship, and not the beginning. Even my body seemed already to know his. This was how I had thought it would be, this complete knowing, this spontaneous melting and meeting. This was why, when James had made love to me, and I had found myself shrinking from him, I had been puzzled and afraid, no longer trusting the bond between myself and my secret friend.

Now it was I who held fast, and murmured: "It's been so long, so long. No, don't let me go."

"I'll never do that. Not ever, not now." His voice was muffled and husky, the country accent sounding stronger than usual. I was shaken yet again by a wave of love so powerful that it seemed to tear me apart to take him in.

"Rob, oh, Rob." I ran my fingers into his hair, tilting his head back so that the moonlight, intercepted faintly by the blossoming boughs, lit his face. "How on earth I didn't guess it was you . . . All the time, all the time I'd been thinking it had to be James or Francis, and yet it never seemed right. And all the time it's been you: it was you I ran to when I wanted help or comfort; it was your house that was home. And then this last few days, it was always you. . . ."

"Bryony." It came out on a long breath, fierce with relief and the pent frustration of years. "Bryony . . ."

It wasn't returning sanity, but the chill of the soaking grass on my bare feet, that made me draw away eventually and say: "Rob, let's go in now."

"Go in?" He repeated it as if he had hardly heard me, then shook his head like someone surfacing from deep water, and said it again, understanding. "Go in?"

"Yes. The grass is wet, and my feet are like ice."

"The more fool you for not putting your shoes on." His hold on me was relaxed now, affectionate. His voice was his own again, and he was smiling. "All right, you'd better go in. High time you did, if you ask me. Come along." He picked me up as easily as if I were a sack of meal, and began to carry me back across the grass to the cottage.

"Actually," I said, "I meant both of us. Won't you stay?"

There was a pause of seconds, then he shook his head. "No. I've waited all my life for you, and I reckon I can wait a bit longer. We'll leave all that for its right place."

"Which is?"

"After we're married." Then, as I took a breath: "Tomorrow night."

"Oh, Rob, be your age. You need a license, and a special costs twenty-five pounds, and where do you think we can raise that? And if *you* start on at me about breaking the damned trust for a bit of ready money—"

Rob said something rather rustic about the trust, and stopped to kiss me again.

I pulled my mouth away. "It can't be tomorrow night. It can't be for ages."

"Why not?"

"Well, even if you could get a license tomorrow, the Vicar probably wouldn't consent to marry us on the spur of the moment."

"Spur of the moment nothing. I told you I've waited all my life, and so have you. Anyway, I've talked to the Vicar. He thinks it's a good thing."

"*Does* he? But he didn't know that I—"

"Oh, yes, he did. He's known for a long time how I felt about you, and then after you'd talked to him yesterday I reckon he saw the whole thing. He never told me anything you'd said to him, but he did let on to me that your dad had said he'd sooner see you wedded to me than to anyone else he knew."

"*Daddy* did?"

"So the Vicar told me. Better ask him yourself. But I don't think he'll worry much if we ask him to marry us straight away."

"N-no. Perhaps not. I did tell him about—well, about what we had together. And if Daddy really said that, and if the Vicar knew all the time that it was you—"

"Seems so," said Rob. "Well, I'll see him first thing, shall I? All he can do is refuse, but I think he'll consent."

"But the license!"

"I've had a license burning a hole in my pocket for two weeks now. It cost six pounds," said my lover. "Far-sighted and thrifty, us peasants. Do you think I'd spend twenty-five quid on getting a woman when I can get one for six?"

"You could have one for nothing right now."

"Marriage or naught," said Rob austerely, and set me down laughing on the cottage step.

Ashley, 1835

It was cold. Shivering, he dragged his clothes on, and flung the fur-lined cloak round himself. His hands were shaking again. Defiance ebbed. He tried to recall his earlier mood of courage, but the cold hour before daylight was not the time for bravery. This was the hour when men were executed; the hour when they were least resistant, cared less. He supposed there was some mercy in it; but for the condemned, as for lovers, dawn always came too soon.

Seventeen

Believe me, love, it was the nightingale.
—*Romeo and Juliet*, III, **v**

Next morning I was up early, so early that the dew was still thick on the fruit blossom, and the orchard grass shone and glittered as if newly hosed down.

I sang as I got my breakfast ready. When I opened the back door I found a milk bottle standing on the step, and propped against it a package wrapped in brown paper. I knew the neat, slightly over-careful writing. And I guessed what I would find in the package; the books about New Zealand. I carried them into the kitchen and propped them against the milk jug and read them with my breakfast.

It already seemed as if the idea of New Zealand had been in my mind for a very long time; I wondered if, all unknowing, I had been sharing Rob's thoughts about it. Certainly, as I turned the pages, I found here and there pictures which seemed familiar, and names which came like echoes of something already spoken. Already I had accepted the idea of going there; of leaving Ashley, perhaps not exactly without a backward look, but without any of the heart-tearing that until yesterday I would have thought inevitable. I suppose that I was so much a part and product of this old, old place that I had never really envisaged life outside it, but now it seemed as if this had always been a foregone conclusion. My feeling was one of release rather than of loss. If this escape from old ties was what my lover had in mind, then by definition so did I. . . . A shared mind—and how well I knew this—was a shared desire.

I could see clearly, now that I knew him, the reasons for his doubts and hesitations, and for his long-drawn-out refusal to reveal himself. Perhaps he would not, even now, have nerved himself to come into the open, had it not been for my father's death. That had left me homeless and alone; it had also left me, perhaps no worse off than I had been before, but without Ashley itself at my back. It had, so to speak, brought me into Rob's orbit.

So much became clear, and with it the whole pattern of my lover's actions. The night I had come home to Ashley church, it had been Rob, waiting and watching for me, whose thoughts had come to meet me; and the mixture of exhilaration and nervousness, which I had misconstrued as guilt, was now explained. Later, the curtness which I had ascribed to his hurt hand could well have been because he had been held a helpless witness to my scene with James. Rob could never have doubted "what we had together," but I could see that he might well have doubted the outcome. And what he had feared most of all—I could see it now—had been my first reaction to the discovery that my beloved secret friend was only Rob, the boy from the home farm.

But now it was done, and here we were, and this bright morning with its dew and day-song could not dispel one stranded cobweb of last night's spell. "Tomorrow," he had said, and now tomorrow was "today," and it did not feel a day too soon.

Rob, where are you?

The signals were perceptibly fainter, like batteries beginning to fade. I stepped the query up and got the answer. He was in the greenhouses.

As I approached I saw him through the glass. He was up on a tall stepladder, mending the hinge of one of the ventilators. He saw me coming, gave me a smile and a sideways lift of the head, and went unhurriedly on with the job. He looked just the same as ever, his movements as he fitted the screwdriver to the thread and began to turn it, quite deliberate and relaxed. If I had not been receiving from him a current of excitement something akin to a burst of a thousand volts or so, I would have thought him unmoved. Nor did I have to ask him what the Vicar had said; I had known, roughly since breakfast time, that this was really and truly my wedding day.

I sat down on the stool beside the water tank and watched him in silence. In silence? The air was fizzing like champagne. The sun-motes sifting down through the tangle of white jasmine stung like sparks along the skin. Rob hadn't even looked at me again. He laid the screwdriver down and reached in a pocket for a fresh screw. Then, still with those steady, unhurried movements, he tackled the other hinge. He might have been alone.

I thought it was time to calm things down into words. "Thank you for the picture books."

"Don't mention it. Like them?"

"Love them."

"So when do we start?"

"Any time you like. For our honeymoon, perhaps?"

He gave the screw a last twist. "I reckon our honeymoon will take care of itself."

"I reckon it will. Rob, how long have you had this New Zealand dream?"

"Years now. There was something on the telly a long time ago—colour it was; I saw it down at the Bull. It got at me, I don't know why. It seemed right for me, somehow. Ever since then I've read about it, off and on. Happen you never knew, but some folks of mine went out there, years back, and they've done well farming up in the North Island. Jerseys, mainly. Mum used to keep up with them, writing at Christmas, you know how it is. Then after she died I wrote to New Zealand House in London, and asked about emigrating. It seems there's no problem for a farm worker. I wouldn't need a sponsor, either; the

Makepeaces—my folks out there—laid a welcome on the mat for me."

"But you didn't go."

"How could I? I was waiting for you." He said it quite simply, moving the creaking hinge experimentally as he talked. "It's true, you know that. After Mum died there wasn't anything much to keep me here. I liked your dad, but if it hadn't been for you I'd have gone, all that time back."

"I wondered why you stayed here. There didn't seem much future for you. Rob—"

"Mm?"

"Would you have asked me, if my father had still been alive?"

The mended hinge seemed to satisfy him. He picked an oilcan up off the top step of the ladder and began to trickle a few drops through into the rusty joint. "I don't know. I've asked myself that. Maybe I'd have talked to him first. I don't know."

"If you had, he might have told you what he told the Vicar."

"He might," said Rob. "I still don't really understand that."

"Don't you?" I smiled to myself. He didn't look down, but he caught it, and a little current of affection ran between us, as settled and placid as if we had been married for years. The champagne sparkle had subsided slowly from the air; the place was a deep, still well of contentment. I laced my fingers round an upraised knee and tilted my head to him. "So you see you needn't have worried, after all."

"Maybe not. But I wasn't to know that. The way I saw it, it'd have been a queer enough thing anyway, a man like me and a girl like you, let alone having this link between us as well. . . . That would have taken some explaining, wouldn't it?"

"He'd have understood."

He gave a slow nod. "I think so, too. I used to tell myself that. It didn't help much. There was always the moment when I was going to have to say, 'Mr. Ashley, sir, I want to marry Miss Bryony.' "

"I meant I think he'd have understood because he had something of the same gift." He looked, not surprised, but inquiring. I nodded. "He never said so, but I think he did."

"How d'you make that out?"

"Oh, one or two things that happened. There was a time once when I was hurt at school, and he knew without being told. That kind of thing. And I think that when he was dying he tried to get to me, and couldn't, but he had enough of a link with Ashley to get here. And you were here, and you got the signal and sent it on to me."

"A sort of Telstar?"

"Sort of, I suppose. Yes. It worked, anyway. The news came from you, not from him."

"It was a bad night, that." He propped the ventilator open, pocketed his tools, then leaned his elbows on the top step of the ladder, chin on fist, looking away from me to the creepers that festooned the rafters. "I'd been asleep, and I came awake, all very sudden, as if someone had kicked me in the head. It ached like that, too, I remember. First of all I thought I must be sickening for something, then after a bit I got there. And I didn't like what I got. Then somehow, like I always did, I began to think of you, and I knew what I was telling you. I suppose if boiling water or something flows through a pipe, the pipe gets scalded. That's what it felt like."

"Poor Rob. But you helped. Oh, my God, you did. If he hadn't been able to get to you . . . And that's another thing. This—this gift we share. I'm sure now that neither Emory nor James has it. James did tell me once that they could 'read each other's thoughts,' but I'm certain that— if it was true—he was just talking about the sort of link a lot of twins have with each other, a kind of sixth sense —intuition, really. Not what we have."

"And ours is the seventh, maybe?"

"Well, isn't it?" I tilted my head to smile at him. "That's how I think of it, anyway. Special and magic . . . I'm certain the twins don't have anything of the same sort. If they had, this last few days would have been even more difficult than they have. It was so awful having to shut you out."

He reached out a hand and began absently to guide the jasmine tendrils to their curled grip on the wires. "I once saw a picture," he said reminiscently, "called 'Love Locked Out.' It struck me at the time he shouldn't have been drooping there propped against the doorpost. He should have been hammering the bloody door down."

"You didn't. Not quite, anyway."

"Not for lack of wanting to."

"I suppose it was just as hard for you as it was for me. Harder, really." A spray of jasmine, too sharply jerked, loosed a tiny flight of fading flowers. They drifted past me, some of them to float on the water of the tank. I reached an idle finger to rescue the nearest. "Rob, there's something I still can't understand. It's what's been setting me wrong all this time about you, even though I know I must really have *wanted* it to be you. I thought it had to be an Ashley. So I never looked beyond my cousins, though heaven knows, since I grew up, I've never really felt anything about them at all. Not this way. It's really had me coming and going. But in that case, where do you fit in?"

He smiled. "Didn't you know? Straight down the wrong side of the blanket ever since donkey's years back. Makepeace, she was called, Ellen Makepeace. That ought to tell you that my stock's just as bad as yours, Miss Bryony Ashley."

"Ellen Makepeace? That was the girl Nick Ashley was shot for, surely. Her brothers shot him."

"That's the one. And they got on the next ship to Australia, and ended up in New Zealand." He started down the ladder. "And as for Ellen, a nice decent village lad called Granger married her, and they had a baby nearly nine months later. She said it was a Granger baby, and so did he, and everyone took it that way, it being easier. Our family certainly took it so. But now you and I know better, don't we? It must have been Nick's baby, and the Ashley thing—this mind-talking—came down with it, right to me." He stood over me, smiling. "What is it? Why are you staring? Can't stomach the idea of me being part Ashley, too?"

"I was wondering why I hadn't seen that, either. You've even got the looks. Oh, not what they call the Ashley looks, but you've got Bess Ashley's hair and eyes."

"The gipsy look. Aye." He laughed. "I could see it myself, once I knew where to look."

"Well, but if you know, then all the Grangers must have known. . . . Your father and mother—"

"No, why should they? It's only this mind-talking that made me even begin to guess at it. Oh, everyone knew the story about Nick Ashley, of course they did, but I never heard it told any other way except that the Granger boy made an honest woman of Ellen, and it was his own baby. It's a long time ago; why should anyone bother? But then this started, this between you and me. When I was a kid I thought nothing about it, but since I've got older, and thought a bit more, that's the only explanation I can see. I'm the only one who guessed it, because no one else knew the way you and I can talk."

"Did you find it harder this morning?"

"Yes. And I reckon this might be why. . . ." His arms went around me, and we closed again, mouth to mouth, body to body. Two creatures becoming one, lost and oblivious, glassed in from the world in our own quiet well of content. "As good as last night?" he asked at length.

"Better, except there's no nightingale."

"What do you mean?"

"The nightingale last night, singing in the pear tree. Didn't you hear it?"

"There was nothing in the pear tree."

"There was a bird singing. It must have been a nightingale. Heavens, Rob—"

"You were imagining it. If that's what kissing me does for you—"

"I was not imagining it, and if kissing *me* stops up all your faculties—"

"Not all. Some it starts going."

"About the wedding, Rob——"

"Yes?"

"The license was all right? It really is today?"

"Eleven this morning. It's all arranged."

"It is?" I got my breath. "Look, isn't that perhaps rushing it just a bit——?"

"Who was rushing it last night?"

"I didn't mean that way. I meant it's after half past nine now, and——"

"Great jumping beans, so it is, and I haven't fed the hens yet!" said the man who hadn't heard the nightingale. He kissed me hurriedly again, for good measure, then let me go and picked up the stepladder. On the way to the greenhouse door he hesitated, and turned. I got it again, the love and the longing and the uncertainty which, now, I understood. "Bryony, honey, am I rushing it? I thought when you said last night——I thought you wanted——"

"You thought right." I went to him, and put the palm of my hand gently against his still rough cheek. "Oddly enough, my darling Rob, you read my very thoughts. . . . And now go and feed your hens, while I find something to wear for my wedding. See you in church."

Mr. and Mrs. Henderson were the witnesses, and Mr. Bryanston, gently beaming, took the service. Rob even produced a ring, which fitted. The church was full of the smell of lilac, and the flowers massed by the chancel steps still had the dew on them. He must have picked them at first light. The church door stood open, and the churchyard scents came in, elder-flowers and dewy grasses and the violets that grew by the porch, along with a faint smoky spice from the avenue where the yew burned its lamps of peace. For me no longer. I would lie forlorn no more.

The Vicar flattened a hand on the pages of the register, and Rob signed it. Not "farmer" or "gardener," but "man of all work." I liked that. It sounded proud, somehow, coming from him. When he put the pen in my hand I signed against my own name, "unemployed." I saw him watching over my shoulder, and the corners of his mouth deepened in a smile that did something severely clinical to the base of my spine.

"By the way," said the Vicar, "I almost forgot to tell you. The missing register is back, and I think quite unharmed."

"Which goes without saying"—this, unexpectedly, from Mrs. Henderson—"seeing as where I found it."

"*You* brought it back?" asked the Vicar in surprise.

"I did. I'm sorry you've been worrying yourself, Vicar, because there was no call. It's been in my house since Sunday, safe and sound, and to tell you the truth I clean forgot about it."

"Well, I must say, I'm very glad to have it back." There was some restraint apparent in the Vicar's voice. "Though, my dear Mrs. Henderson, I wish you had told me. If you wanted to consult it—"

"Me consult it? Why, Vicar, what would I want with those old books?"

"Well, then—" began the Vicar, but I had seen Mrs. Henderson's sidelong look at me.

"Where did you find it, Mrs. H.?" I asked her.

"In your cottage, Miss Bryony. I found it when I tidied up ready for you to come home, and I took it home with me, meaning to take it straight to the Vicar, but then Martha Gray came up, wanting a bite of tea, and we got talking, and I clean forgot. I won't pretend I'm not at fault, because I am. When your dad left he asked me most particular to take it back for him, him having been too ill to see to everything, and there, if I didn't forget it again till this very morning!"

"Talking about our wedding she was, and it put her in mind." Mr. Henderson made his first and last contribution to the conversation. It was hard to tell whether the dry sound of his voice was the result of long disuse, or of some disillusion provoked by the memory of that earlier wedding.

As ever, he was ignored. The Vicar, indeed, began

to say something, but Mrs. Henderson was still looking at
me, and I raised my brows at her. "I'd no idea it was
there. Just whereabouts did you find it?"

"In your dad's room, it was. I wouldn't be likely to
have mentioned it to *you*, Miss Bryony, not wanting to
remind you of things, and I thought nothing of it, seeing
as I expected Mr. Ashley would have told the Vicar he
had the book. If," said Mrs. Henderson, showing signs of
taking umbrage, "the Vicar had seen fit to mention to
Henderson or me that it was missing—"

"I should have, I should have. The fault was mine.
Indeed, now I come to think of it, I believe Mr. Ashley
did mention his interest. . . . Now, why did I not think
of that? Of course no one blames you, Mrs. Henderson;
indeed, we are most grateful to you for bringing the book
back. And now perhaps, this morning, on this very happy
occasion . . ."

As the Vicar, soothing with long practice, trotted
competently into the breach, Rob moved quietly past me
to the table, and began to leaf through the pages of *One
Ash: 1780–1837* which lay there.

I looked over his shoulder. The pages were all numbered, in beautiful copperplate, and they were all there.
But Rob turned each one, looking, I knew, for some other
paper which might have been hidden between the leaves.
The paper. The letter. My father must have been studying
this register, along with the family books, just before he
had succumbed to the last attack that had banished him
to Bad Tölz.

"Nothing there," I said in an undertone.

"Seems not," said Rob. "It looks as if some of them
signed it after the wedding breakfast instead of before,
doesn't it? But then maybe their hands were shaking as
much as mine was. Weddings," said my husband, his left
arm sliding round my shoulders, "are strictly for the
birds." He added, softly: "So far."

"You took a lot of care that this bird should have a
pretty wedding, all the same. The flowers are lovely."

"Well," said the Vicar cheerfully, appearing at Rob's

other side, "we must be very thankful that all has ended so well. I confess I was worried about our little mystery. But now all is clear, and no blame attaches to anyone. I am quite certain now that the fault was mine, and mine alone. I am sure that Jon must have told me he wanted to look at the old registers, and I have simply forgotten. Dear me. I shall lock it away now, with the others. Were you looking for something in particular, Rob?"

"Not really, Vicar. But look, here's something. A funny sort of coincidence, wouldn't you say?"

His finger pointed to an entry, the third from the top on page 17. It was dated May 12, 1835. The signatories were Robert Granger, Labourer, of Ashley Parish, and Ellen Makepeace, Spinster, of One Ash. "Signatories" is not quite the correct word, for whereas Ellen had signed her name in a writing that was tremulous but correct, against the name of Robert Granger, Labourer, of Ashley Parish, was his mark, a large *X*.

"See?" said Rob to me. "It's happened before. I'd better put the kiss in, too." He did so, while the Vicar, beaming, and tut-tutting over the coincidence, carried the register over to the safe to lock it away. Mrs. Henderson bustled forward to follow up Rob's kiss and take one for herself, and Mr. Henderson, seizing my hand, pumped it up and down silently, as if conceding that this wedding, at least, was a matter for congratulation.

"And now," said Mr. Bryanston, "you'll all come over to the Vicarage for a glass of sherry, I hope? Rob didn't give us very much notice, so I'm not at all sure what we can manage in the way of a wedding breakfast, but I imagine—?" This with a justifiably nervous glance at Mrs. Henderson, but that lady remained miraculously unperturbed, while Rob shook his head.

"No, thanks very much, Vicar. We'd like to come over for the sherry, but don't trouble yourself further than that. We've got an errand to do in Worcester, and then we'll find some lunch for ourselves."

"Ah, yes, excellent." The Vicar straightened from shutting the safe. "Well, that's that. Now I still have one

duty to do, and it's one I never forget: to kiss the bride.
Bryony, my dear . . ."

And then, the formalities completed, the wedding party
trooped across the churchyard between the somber beautiful yews, to sherry at the Vicarage.

Since there was now no question of my going to London
for Cathy's party, we had decided to take the copy of
Romeus and Juliet straight to Leslie Oker for a first opinion. Leslie himself was not there when we called, so we
left the package with his assistant, and then made our
courtesy visit to the offices of Meyer, Meyer, and Hardy
to tell Mr. Emerson what had happened. The interview
with a surprised and—though he hid it well—slightly
shocked Emerson was brief and to the point. Rob left the
first part of it to me. Once the lawyer had got over his
surprise he seemed to assess the marriage and find it good.
At any rate it was a solution to my future, which had worried him. He said so, diplomatically, and added his wishes
for our happiness. He knew Rob well, of course, and
obviously liked him; but there were adjustments to make
in considering him now as my husband. Mr. Emerson did
it well, and with great tact. I saw the tiny smile at the
corners of Rob's mouth again, and thought suddenly, "My
God, I've married him. Rob Granger, the garden-boy."
The mixture of strangeness, tenderness, and sheer sexual
excitement took away the power of coherent thought and
struck me silent. I saw from the flicker of his lashes that
Rob had taken it in, then he, as smoothly as any prac-
ticed politician, took over the interview. He told Mr.
Emerson about his plans for emigration, discussed some
of the details, touched on the trust and the future of the
Court, arranged another appointment in a few days' time,
and got himself and me out of the office and back into the
sunny street with a minimum of fuss.

He slid a hand under my arm. "And now we eat?"

"We certainly do. I'm starving."

"It takes me that way, too. Would you have liked

to go to the Star, or the Olde Talbot, or some place like that?"

"Not unless you've thought better of that picnic basket I saw on the back seat of the car." I laughed. "So that's why Mrs. Henderson didn't fuss when the Vicar asked about lunch. Did she get it ready for us?"

"She did. Do you mind?"

"I do not. Lovely. I don't want other people yet, just you and me. Where are you taking me?"

"Mystery tour," said Rob, opening the car door. Then he got in beside me, and the car threaded its way out into the traffic, through the crowded sunny streets, then turned over the river bridge and headed for the open country.

He took me to a place I had never visited before. A narrow lane crept downhill between high hedges, and there at the foot, where a humped bridge crossed the river, was a patch of grass verge just wide enough to park a car. "And not a square foot for anyone else," said Rob with satisfaction, as he set the brake and killed the engine, and the sound of running water took over the peaceful afternoon.

Beyond the bridge was a steep wooded bank, through which the lane curled up again and out of sight. On the nearer side, cut in a wide green hollow, was a flat pasture as smooth as a lake, through which the river wound, deep and slow, between clay banks alive with nesting martins. Behind us the pasture rose in a steep green bank seamed with flowering hawthorn, and honeycombed by rabbit warrens. A few sheep moved slowly along the hillside. Rooks cawed by their nests in the trees along the river, and a woodpecker worked somewhere out of sight. In the distance the sound of a tractor emphasized, rather than disturbed, the peace.

Rob spread a rug in the sun on the river's bank. The big trees shifted and rustled overhead, casting towards us a light-leaved net of shadows. The breezes shifted and ran, cuckooflower and marsh orchis and cowslip faintly moving, with the grasses shining and darkening between them. The sheep watched us incuriously, and their lambs watched us not at all, being more than busy over some intricate game halfway up the rabbit-pitted hillside. No other creature was in sight except the birds that went past on the May breezes.

"The Garden of Eden," I said, surveying it with pleasure.

Rob dumped the basket beside the rug. "And not an apple tree in sight. Now, which comes first, love or food?"

"Rob, you've got to be joking! If anyone came down the lane——"

"I was joking. If you knew how hungry I was . . . I was up all night, remember? I think I got some breakfast, but it doesn't seem to have had much effect. What's she given us? Cold duck, is it? That'll do for starters, anyway. Come on, love, let's get this lot unpacked before I fall apart."

I started on the basket, while he unearthed the beer and put it in the edge of the river to cool, then we both got going enthusiastically on the food Mrs. Henderson had provided.

I suppose it was a very strange wedding breakfast. I can't remember now all that we talked about. It may even be that we didn't talk to begin with, but that our thoughts moved out and mingled as they had done before. We knew each other so well already that all the important things had been said. If we talked at all it was about the food, the day, the reactions of people to what Rob persisted in calling, with amusement, our "mixed marriage."

"It's plain old-fashioned you are, Rob Granger," I told him.

"Maybe. But it's only your sort that keep saying that class doesn't exist or doesn't matter. Let them go down on the wrong side of the blanket like me, and see how much it doesn't matter."

"You mean Ellen Makepeace's slipup with Nick Ashley? That's a long time ago."

"No, I didn't. I meant the cottage and castle thing."

"Oh, is that all? Well, my cottage is a good bit smaller than yours now."

"So it is."

"And we're sharing the same blanket."

"So we are." He handed me his plate, then stretched his length contentedly along the rug, leaning up on one elbow. He reached for a stalk of grass and began absently to chew it. A lock of dark hair had fallen forward, half hiding his face; the sun, splashing light through the moving leaves, sent sparks of colour through the black. His shirt was open, and I could see the glint of a gold chain against the hairs of his chest, and the pulse beating strongly in the hollow of his throat. There was a faint moist shine on his skin, from the heat, or from the beer. I shut my mind to him before he read me, and stolidly began to pack the debris back into the basket. Once again, irresistibly, I was remembering the patterns of his love that had come to me in the past, the love mixed with doubt, and with something that at times had been hopeless longing. That lover was gone for ever. I could forget the starlight, where love had been easy because it was in the mind, like poetry. This was the real, the daylight man. This was the man I would lie with tonight, and live with for the rest of my life.

"If you chew grass you get liver flukes," I said.

"Then I'll be crawling with 'em by this time," he said equably, but he threw the chewed stalk away. He pushed the hair back from his face. "Anyway, what you were saying about class, that wasn't the point."

"I know. And I don't say it doesn't exist, but I think it's nothing to do with money or family, or the old-fashioned things that went to make it up. I think it's habits of mind and ways of thinking."

"Well, yes, but that takes you right back to family, doesn't it? You're always more comfortable with people who were brought up the same way as yourself."

"Till something else overrides it."

He smiled. "Like now? Aye, but if ways of thinking count, then you and I aren't far apart."

"That's what I keep trying to tell you. Anyway, as long as neither of us minds, it doesn't matter."

"Why should I mind? I'm getting the best end of the bargain. And you're useful around the garden, which will be something when we're trying to scrape a living for ourselves out of the bush."

"And you're pretty good about the house, which ditto."

"So," he said, picking another grass stalk and beginning to chew that, "if we both make out in bed—"

"Well, for heaven's sake, don't you know how you make out in bed? I thought country boys spent all their time smooching in haystacks."

"Haystacks are overrated," said Rob. His voice had an odd expression, and looking up I saw the faintest of tinges under the brown of his cheeks. I thought at first, not really believing it, that he was embarrassed; then, with a stab of surprise that was curiously poignant and even nervous: Great heavens, I do believe he doesn't know any more than I do. . . .

His eyes came up to mine, and I knew he had read me. I went scarlet in my turn, and then suddenly we were both laughing, and in each other's arms.

"Oh, Rob, I just thought you were conventional."

"What's conventional mean except right? I didn't want it last night because if it was worth waiting for, it was worth waiting till now; and I don't want it now because I don't want it out here in a field with thistles. I want it at home, in bed, and for keeps, on a dark night with no one interrupting. And now you know why."

"Oh, Rob. Darling Rob . . . I suppose we'll manage somehow. People have."

"Well, there's evidence. At least between you and me there'll be no questions to ask."

"At any rate you can't pretend you've never kissed a girl before."

"I didn't tell you that, did I?"

"No. No . . . In fact, I'd say at a guess that you've had rather a lot of practice."

"Practice was what it was, then. Come to think of it, why should I go into haystacks—old-fashioned you are, aren't you, it's the back seat of a car these days—with girls, when I've had my own girl lined up since I was knee high to a grasshopper? I don't deny I've let a bit of steam off now and again, but I reckoned the real thing'd keep for you."

"Rob, love, you're out of the Ark."

"And a proper old sex-ship that was, come to think of it. Well, all right, you tell me: would you have gone with anyone else?"

"No."

"Because you were waiting for me."

It was a statement, not a question, but I answered it. "Of course. Rob, if you had been with another girl, do you suppose I'd have known?"

"Probably not, if I'd taken care to keep you out. But you'd have found out afterwards, I guess." He gave me a look that was only half amused. "I knew when you were kissing James the other night. I was about ready to strangle the pair of you, except that I knew the muddle you were in."

"So you were. And there was I thinking I'd found him—you—at last, and wondering why I didn't even like it."

"I didn't get it all that clearly." He lay back on the rug, thinking. "Somehow, this one thing, sex, I mean—it's the only thing you and I don't seem to know about each other, right down to the last thought." He rolled over on his back, put his hands behind his head, and narrowed his eyes against the sky. "Maybe because it's something we've got to share physically. The one seems to switch the other off, somehow. I don't know. . . . Anyway, somehow, I don't think it'll be all that difficult." He was silent for a little, relaxing in the sun. "What would you like to do now?"

"Do?"

"What I mean is, how are we going to put the rest of the day in till it's decent time to go to bed?"

"Oh. Well, there's always television."

"Aye." The syllable sounded sleepy, and it occurred to me suddenly that the "man of all work" who had watched outside my cottage most of the night had probably been up again at five o'clock, going about his jobs.

I touched his hair. "Why don't we just stay here till we feel like going home, and get a cup of tea somewhere on the way?"

"Fine, if that's what you'd like. I think this day'll hold up till then. But we'll get storm before night."

"Oh, no! Are you sure?"

"Pretty sure. There's been rain in the hills, and I think it's coming this way. But not yet, don't worry. . . ." The dark lashes shut. Time passed. He lay so quietly that I thought he slept, but then he said, without stirring: "Day's beginning to drag a bit, wouldn't you say?"

" 'Gallop apace, you fiery-footed steeds.' "

"What's that?"

"Something Juliet said when she was waiting for Romeo."

"Them again."

"Yes." I did not say what I was thinking, that it had occurred to me, thinking about the play yesterday, that in some ways our secret love was much like theirs, a starlit descant to the family feuding and matchmaking of daylight. As long as the lovers could hold their private world inviolate, all was well, but when the warring factions crowded in . . .

"Forget it," said my lover. His eyes were open, and he was watching my face. "Whatever it is, we'll work it out together. And right this moment, today's our own, and after we've got your cousins' affair sorted out, so's the rest of our lives. Forget it. This is us."

He stretched an arm across and I slid onto it, with my head in the curve of his shoulder. The sun was hot. Overhead, the lacing of boughs slid a light and moving shadow over us, tempering the sun. A heron flapped ponderously upriver. The lambs slept on the warm hillside. Even the rooks were quiet.

I think we talked awhile longer. Our thoughts moved and mingled, but without the same clarity and force as before. No need now, I thought sleepily, with our bodies touching; with his hand cupped warm and gentle under my breast, and my hair under his cheek. No need. Here is my rest. We slept.

Ashley, 1835

At the door he paused, and looked back at the room. The faint light showed it clearly enough to his sharpened senses, but he could have shut his eyes and traced, accurately, every flower on the carpet, every line of the plaster maze on the wall, every fern on the frame that held the ceiling glass.

Fletcher would come later and straighten the bed, and put all to rights.

Never again, he thought. It would never be the same again. They had had their time outside the world, at the still center, in the Wondrous Isles. Now they must submit to the drag of the polar world outside. That they might change one happiness for another did not occur to him. Happiness was not the air he breathed.

He shut the door gently behind him, and trod down the slippery steps into the maze.

Eighteen

How cam'st thou hither, tell me, and wherefore?
—*Romeo and Juliet*, II, ii

We had arranged to go back to my cottage rather than to
Rob's, because the latter, so near to the Hendersons', gave
less privacy. When we got there we found that Mrs.
Henderson, though respecting our desire to be alone, had
nevertheless contrived that we should be welcomed. On
the sitting-room table was a note which wished us well
in the most substantial way possible. "Supper in oven," it
said, and we found an excellent casserole gently bubbling
there, with jacket potatoes hot and soft beside it on the
shelf. The table was laid, and held, besides, an apple pie,
a bowl of cream, and a generous wedge of cheese. We had
brought a bottle of champagne in with us, and we drank
this with supper, then washed the dishes together, while
the dusk drew slowly over the shining lake outside, and
the thrush sang its heart out in the pear tree.

"Make the most of it, mate," said Rob. "It's going to be
a rough night." He caught my look, and grinned. "I was
talking to the thrush. I warned you we'd get a storm,
didn't I?"

"You did. Is it really going to rain? It's been such a
lovely day."

He cocked his head to one side as he picked up the last dish and started to dry it. "Listen."

I listened. I heard it then, behind the thrush's song. Volleys of wind sifting the orchard trees; blowing and ebbing, then blowing again in gusts suddenly strong enough to keen in the telephone wires. The lake water darkened and gleamed under the racing cat's-paws.

"This'll fetch down a deal of the apple-blow," said Rob. "Here, I don't know where it goes." He handed me the dish, and I saw him glance at the clock, but I was wrong about the reason. He was reaching for his jacket, which he had hung over the back of a chair. "Bryony . . ." His apologetic look, which in someone I didn't love I'd have called hangdog, spoke for itself.

"I know," I said, "don't say it. You've got to go and feed the hens."

I found I had been watching for just that smile. Eleven short hours, and already a half-glance from him, amused and tender, could do this to me. We forge our own chains.

"They'll be in bed long since. Mrs. H. did them for me. But I'm afraid I will have to go up to the Court and take a look around. I always do a night-watchman round on the public side, and tonight, with the family gone up to London—"

I clapped a hand to my mouth. "Oh, Rob, I quite forgot! I never rang Cathy up to say I couldn't go to the party! I did try this morning, but no one answered, and I meant to try again from Worcester, but I forgot all about it. How awful!"

"Couldn't you ring up now? It's barely ten. Happen they'll forgive you when you tell them what made you forget. Will you tell them?"

"Will I not! They'll be delighted, I know. They think the world of you. But I can't telephone them now, I don't even know where the party was to be held. I was to go to their flat and have dinner with them, and then go with them to the party. They'll have gone by now. . . . Oh, how awful of me."

"I shouldn't worry. They'll think you missed the train or something. They may ring up here to find out what happened."

"I hope so. I could try the flat again, I suppose."

He still hesitated. "Do you mind my leaving you? I'll be about an hour, I expect. If you like, I'll wait till you've phoned, and you can come with me?"

I shook my head. "No, go ahead. And don't hurry yourself; after I've done the phoning I'm going to have a bath, and I've got a lot of tidying up to do. Heavens, what on earth will I say to them . . . ? It'll sound a bit funny as an explanation, coming out of the blue. Would you call yourself an accident, or an act of God, or what, Rob?"

He grinned. "I'll leave that to you. Maybe you'll be clearer about it, come the morning." He had been checking doors and windows as we talked. He came back to me. "Now, as your husband, Bryony Granger, do I rate a latchkey?"

I went to the bureau where my father's things still lay in a little pile, and took his key. I held it out on the palm of my hand.

Yours now, Ashley. The familiar name-pattern slid through.

Mine now.

Our eyes met and the signals faded abruptly. He took the key delicately, as if he dared not touch me, hesitated briefly, then smiled and went. The door latched shut behind him, and seconds later the garden wicket swung and clashed. I heard a pause in the thrush's song, then it began again.

As I dialled the Underhills' flat, and then sat listening to the vain threshing of the bell, I reflected that I could very well do with the hour on my own. It was a little disconcerting to have to stage-manage one's own honeymoon at such short notice.

No reply. I put the receiver back, then ran upstairs to find that Mrs. Henderson, bless her, had been there, too. She had put fresh sheets on the double bed and turned it down ready. There were clean towels in the bathroom; she had even brought Rob's things across for him, and laid out the razor, with pajamas and dressing gown and a clean shirt for the morning. The room had been newly cleaned, and smelled of polish and the sweet scent of cowslips jam-packed tight in a bowl on the windowsill.

After all, there was plenty of time. I had a bath, hunted out a pretty nightdress I had bought in Funchal, then sat down to brush my hair. It was barely half an hour since Rob had gone, but already it was full dark, and without, tonight, even the light of moon and stars. Clouds had come piling up, seemingly from nowhere, into a black sky, and the fitful wind drove a loose bough of the Fribourg rose knocking against the glass. Even as I paused to listen, hairbrush in hand, the force of the spasmodic gusts increased. I could hear the growing fret and rush of wind in the orchard branches, and the slapping of water on the shingle at the Pool's edge. Rob had been weatherwise; it would be a rough night.

On the thought, I heard him come in, the soft click of the spring lock almost drowned by a sudden rattle of rain flung against the casement. A current of fresh damp air came with him.

I half turned towards the door, but he did not approach the stairs. He trod lightly into the sitting room, and paused.

No further sound. He seemed to be standing still, listening. I could picture him, head aslant, wondering, perhaps, what his cue would be to come upstairs.

My bedroom door opened straight on the small landing, from which an open stairway descended into the sitting room. I pulled on my housecoat, went to the head of the stairs, and leaned over the banister. The room below was in the shadows. I could see him standing near the door, with a hand up to the light switch.

"Rob? You've been quick. D'you know, Mrs. H. even got the bedroom ready and laid your things out—?" I stopped dead. He had turned quickly at the sound of my voice, and looked up. It was not Rob. It was my cousin James.

We stood staring at one another for a few stretched seconds of silence. Juliet with a difference, I thought, with a wry flicker that had nothing to do with amusement. Then, forcibly, damn and damn and damn. We were to have had tonight, at least, before the world broke in.

Perhaps after all I could save it. It would be twenty minutes or so before he got back from the Court; if I could get this over, explain what had happened, and get rid of James before Rob had to come back and face him . . .

"James—" I began, and started down the stairway.

Stopped again. The cottage door opened a second time, and Emory came in. He took out the bunch of keys which James had left in the lock, dropped it into his pocket, and shut the door carefully behind him. As he turned, he saw me. I couldn't see his face, but he stopped still as if he had been struck.

"Bryony! I thought you were in London!"

"Well, as you can see, I'm not." I said it slowly, looking from one to the other. "I forgot the party. Silly of me, wasn't it? But here I am. What do you want?"

"You forgot the party?" James's voice sounded strange, quite unlike his usual assured manner. "What do you mean?"

"What I say. You seem to have forgotten it, too."

"Well, not exactly." Emory's ease of manner was a little too good to be true. "Our invitations were cancelled. I suppose we have you to thank for that."

"It's possible. So what brings you here?"

Dark as it was, I saw the glance that went between them, vivid as an electric spark. "I saw your light go on," said James, as if that explained everything.

"So?" I said coldly. "That still doesn't explain why you let yourself into my house like this, and how you happen to have a key. Or why you came here, thinking—hoping?—I'd be away. Well?"

"The fact is—" began James, but Emory cut across him.

"We thought you'd be in town, so we borrowed Mrs. Henderson's key."

The word "borrowed" held no touch of irony, but I knew that, had they spoken with Mrs. Henderson, she would be bound to have told them about Rob's and my marriage, and that we would be home tonight. I could translate well enough. She kept the cottage keys hanging on a nail inside her back door, which, like most doors in the country, was rarely locked. My cousins must have watched their chance to abstract the keys from their nail, then come down here.

Emory flashed me a smile, which, however, did not colour his voice; this was the voice of a man thinking quickly; of a man in a hurry. "It's a diabolical liberty, I know, but time pressed. Since you're here, that makes it easier."

"Makes what easier?"

"There was something we wanted rather urgently."

"I see." And I thought I did. I pulled the housecoat closer round me, belted it, and began slowly to descend the stairs. I was remembering, with a quick slam of the blood in my heart, the mysteries that had yet to be solved. And I remembered, as clearly as if it were my lover telling me again, that these two could be dangerous if they were driven to it. Perhaps, I thought suddenly, they had put two and two together about the silver pen, and that was why they had come here. . . . But no, they had thought I was in London; this visit had nothing to do with that mystery.

Resolutely I put the thought aside. I concentrated on the present, and on keeping my mind shut to Rob: if he had received the sudden jagged pattern of fear which had zigzagged across my brain a moment ago, he would come straight here at the run, and an awkward—surely no more than awkward?—scene could easily become nasty. There was still time enough, I thought, to grasp the nettle and tell them what had happened, and then get rid of them.

I reached the foot of the stairs. The light from the bedroom door, spilling out on the landing above, showed me James's face. It looked tense, and rather pale, and his eyes burned on mine with what looked like anger. I said, as easily as I could:

"It's late, and as you can see, I'm on my way to bed. What did you come to get? I suppose it was the books? Well, I'm sorry, but they'll have to wait till morning." I crossed to the window and began to draw the curtains. "Put the light on, Emory. That's better. The Brooke isn't here, anyway. I told you I was taking it to be valued. And I'd like to keep the other one for a couple of days longer, please. After that, you'll be welcome. And if you've anything more to discuss, that will have to wait, too. So, since there aren't any other objects of virtu to interest you, then I suggest—"

"Not even you, seemingly," said James.

"What?" I had been straightening the curtains. I swung round and looked at him. I saw Emory turn, too. A tiny chill stroked the skin along my bare arms, like a cat's fur brushing up.

"You were expecting Rob Granger," said James. Then, across me to his brother: "She thought I was Granger. She called down to tell him the bedroom was ready, and then came out. Like that."

"Rob Granger?" said Emory, then, drawling a little: "Well, well, well." Silence for two blood-beats, while the eyes of both cousins took me in from head to foot. Hair loose to my shoulders, the hairbrush still in my hand; slippers, the scent of the bath; my housecoat wrapping me to the ankles, but parting to show the nightdress underneath.

I crossed to the fireplace, sat down in one of the armchairs, and regarded them both calmly.

"Yes, Rob Granger. So now, if you don't mind, I'd

rather you went. He'll be coming soon, and it would be embarrassing for everyone if you were still here."

James came slowly forward. He was looking sick. It came to me with surprise that perhaps he had really cared; the scene in the garden the other night had not just been part of the twins' play for the breaking of the trust.

"I'm sorry, James." I said it gently. "What can I say? Only that it took me as much by surprise as anyone. And it's for real. I know now that nothing else was. . . . You know how I felt about you when we were in our teens; well, it just didn't work out. I don't know why. It's the way things go. It turns out it was Rob, all along, but I hardly realized it till today. You might say it was just one of those things; you don't see them coming, but then they come out of nowhere like the Severn Bore, and everything gets swept away in the flood."

A sound from Emory, a muffled exclamation that sounded almost like a laugh. Then he said, impatiently: "Look, Bryony, what the hell's it matter if you're sleeping with Rob Granger? Leave it, Twin. Can't you see it makes it a whole lot easier?"

"Makes what easier?" I demanded. "And I'm not sleeping with Rob Granger, not in the sense you mean. I married him this morning. Now do you see why I forgot Cathy's party, and why I want to get rid of you both?"

It was a bombshell, of course, and I hadn't meant to drop it quite like this. But even so, it didn't explode in quite the way I had expected. Emory moved forward, and the two of them stood, one to either side of my chair, staring down at me. Though I was used to the resemblance, had played with them both since childhood, it was somehow uncanny, the two faces, so very alike, looking at me with the same still, rigid expressions.

But there were differences. James was as white as paper now, with that curiously sick look, as if something in his mind was cringing from reality. Emory wore a look I was unfamiliar with: a pale, hard expression, the grey eyes narrowed, with the lower lids lifted and the eyes themselves quite expressionless.

I said, steadily: "Yes, we're married. It really did happen just out of the blue. I'll tell you about it some other time, but we just found out quite suddenly how much we meant to one another. So there it is. . . . And here we are." I turned a palm upwards in my lap. It was a sort of gesture of relegation; an "over to you."

The pause seemed to last for ever, then they both spoke at once. As Emory began, quickly: "So he'll be over here soon? How soon?" James found his voice. He seemed to speak with difficulty. "So you're going to stay at Ashley? Here?"

"This is a much nicer cottage," said Emory, "than the one he has in the farmyard."

I suppose I must have gaped up at the pair of them. The conversation seemed to be taking a turn towards sheer irrelevance. Or so one might have thought, if it had not been for those cool Ashley eyes meeting on me like searchlights concentrated on a target, and the impression I got of those quick Ashley brains reappraising some situation I hadn't yet grasped.

"No," I said, rather sharply, "not here. I've some other news for you. I'd have told you tomorrow, in any case. We plan to emigrate. Rob's been thinking of it for ages, and we spoke to Mr. Emerson today about it. I want to go, too. It's the best thing, you must see that." I looked at James, and tried a smile. "I told you before that all I wanted was time to let the future show itself, and now it has. So surely that's your problem solved, too?"

James didn't answer. Above my head the concentration had shifted. I looked up at Emory. They were consulting one another in silence across me, as if I wasn't there. It is always irritating to be ignored; this was more, it was curiously disturbing. So was Emory's next remark.

"You can stop worryng, then, Twin."

I raised my brows. "Doesn't it concern both of you? I

meant that I am now prepared to break the trust. I told Mr. Emerson so today."

No answer. My over-sensitive mental antennae picked up some powerful and urgent message that couldn't be spoken. James's eyes were still fast on his brother. Emory nodded to him, then smiled down at me.

"You must forgive us for seeming so eager to lose you, but you know the situation. Of course that's wonderful news about the trust. So, since it's working out so well for everyone, it seems we can offer you our congratulations. And the bridegroom, too, of course."

Plain, ordinary words, kindly, even; but there was no kindness in his voice, only briskness, with a burnish of flippancy, that left nothing to respond to.

James saved me the need. He was pursuing something of his own, still with that disturbing urgency. "Then you'll sell the cottage strip?"

"Well, yes," I said slowly. "I hadn't thought about it yet, but why not? This is one bet I don't feel like hedging. We shan't come back."

James's face went slack with relief, and I saw colour come creeping back. I had some reappraisal to do there, myself, it seemed. Not only did he urgently want the property; he was eager to see me go. Emory pegged it home, saying, swiftly, and with an easiness that seemed worked for: "What splendid news. It really is reprieve, Twin."

"Reprieve?" I queried.

Emory moved away from me, to perch on the edge of the table. He seemed relaxed now, and totally at ease. "I think you should be told, cousin dear, that it really was becoming more than ever urgent that we should be able to sell the Court, and sell it quickly. We've got a big speculator interested now, but he won't look at the property without access to Penny's Flats. And we are being hurried. Our dear stepmother's father finds himself suddenly in need of funds, so he proposes to transfer back to Spain some of the capital he put into the Bristol business. Something to do with marriage trusts for the two other daughters; dowries, they call it still. Quaint, don't you think?"

"I see. And it's tied up, is that it?"

"You could put it that way if you like." Emory sounded amused. "It so happens that it's in use elsewhere. We've been repaying the interest so far in installments, but now they want the principal back. . . . And I'm afraid it isn't there."

The reappraisal was easy after all. "You mean you stole it," I said.

"You have such a way of putting things," said Emory.

Another silence. Then I got to my feet. "Well, there doesn't seem to be much more to say, does there? My husband and I"—the phrase was like a shield—"will see Mr. Emerson again as soon as we can, and let him get on with breaking the trust and transferring the cottage strip to you." I took a breath, trying to control my voice, but it came out edged. "I hope he'll be able to get its worth out of you, and in cash, because Rob and I are going to need it. But for the present the cottage is still ours, and I should like the keys back, please, and then I'd like you both to go."

Without a word Emory drew the keys from his pocket and dropped them on the table. They fell with a little jingle. He slid lazily from the table's edge and straightened up, still smiling. James cleared his throat again, but said nothing. I suppose we must have stood there for only a few seconds, but it seemed to stretch out like a year; three strangers, parting, in a cold room.

I felt curiously numb, I suppose with shock, though I should have been prepared, after the Bad Tölz affair, for the realization that Rob had been only too right about my Ashley cousins; they were more than just self-willed and ruthless men; they were criminals. There was no need, now, to hear from Walther about the photograph. I knew for certain, as if my father himself had told me, that it had been Emory there on the Wackersberg road, and Emory who had gone (in the person of James) straight to Jerez, while James had doubled for him here at home. As before, I crushed the thought aside, in case Rob should catch its echo and react to it. All I wanted now was to be rid of the twins and their dealing, and for ever. I was conscious of a dull kind of hope that, once the arrangements were made with Mr. Emerson, I need never see my cousins again.

But even so, when the keys fell from Emory's hand to the cottage table, the sound they made was a tiny knell to the past. Yet another knell. Ashley was gone from me, and with it, how much more.

I shook it off, and, turning abruptly, went to the door and opened it. The wind was higher than ever, tempestuous. The beech trees beyond the orchard roared and swayed against a fast-moving sky where the clouds, massing and countermassing, piling and breaking and streaming off in spindrift, left blinks and glimpses of the moonlit immensity beyond. The orchard, with its pale tents of blossom, reeled in and out of light and shadow, its torn flowers snowing down the gusts of wind. The rain had stopped.

To my relief the flying moonlight showed me the path still empty, and away beyond the roaring boughs a light still in the Court. But it showed me something else. The lawn in front of the cottage was under water as far as the lilac tree. The level of the Pool must have risen half a meter. And while I watched, a gust of the driving wind sent the water slapping across the flags almost to the doorstep.

"It's all right," said Emory, just behind me. "That's what we meant by 'reprieve.' We'll go across now and shut the High Sluice. So, dear cousin, lie easy in your marriage bed."

"Shut the High Sluice?" I whirled on him. I felt myself go as white as a sheet. "What do you mean?"

He took me by the shoulders. Behind me the door, caught in a gust of wind, slammed shut again. He shook me, quite gently. "I told you it's a reprieve. We haven't been quite honest with you, my dear. We didn't come all this way just to get the books. You were going to give those to us anyway, weren't you? We came to—well, to hasten your decision to sell the cottage strip."

No misunderstanding this time. I got the whole picture straight away. "You wanted to flood the place again? You mean you opened the High Sluice deliberately, and on a night like this?"

"We could hardly choose our night. We had to take the chance, with you and the Underhills away. The weather was just a bonus. It quickened things up a bit for James—he was the one at the Sluice. I was otherwise engaged."

"And you needn't tell me how. You made the alibis. It was your turn, wasn't it?"

The grey eyes narrowed. "What do you mean?"

I caught at my flying thoughts. I had been thinking about the Bad Tölz alibis, but I knew better now than to push my luck, not under those Ashley eyes. I said hoarsely: "I was thinking about Cathy."

"Oh, that. Yes, that was work wasted, but I've always been one to write off my losses. I don't bear you any grudge over that, Bryony, my dear; not the way things seem to be turning out now." A brief laugh as Cathy was dismissed. "Well, now you know the lot. We reckoned another bad flood would put paid to the cottage, and force your hand. Brutal of us, wasn't it, but needs must, they say, and the devil's certainly been driving for the last six months or more. . . . Believe me," said Emory, sounding sincere and very charming with it, "we'd have been sorry about the cottage, if you really liked it, but you should have more sense than to get sentimental about a gold mine."

The words set up an echo of some kind: James speaking with regret and genuine bitterness about the Court and the dereliction everywhere. And somewhere in the distance the sound of hammering.

"Luck all the way," said Emory. "Luck for you, too.

Your being here tonight might have bitched the whole thing up, quite apart from the fact that Rob Granger usually goes home as soon as he's done his rounds at seven, or else away down to the Bull. As it is, I suppose he'll be coming along this way at any minute, and he'll be bound to notice the water level. Tell him there's no need to trouble; we'll go straight to the High Sluice now."

"But—" I began, then shut my teeth on it. I wasn't going to tell them that Rob was doing his rounds now, and would certainly, darkness or no darkness, have seen the level of the water. His reaction, I knew, would be to check straight away on the sluices. He must not run into my cousins tonight on the same errand. If I could get rid of them now, I could call him in my own way, and warn him off.

"You'd better hurry, then," I said quickly. "The way the Pool's risen it looks as if the Overflow can't carry it all away. It must be coming over the bank already. For pity's sake, Emory—"

"Calm down, calm down. We can get the Low Sluice open."

"You certainly can't! It's been wedged shut again. You should never have touched it, it's been unsafe for years! Just get the High Sluice closed before there's some real damage done. . . . You'd better get going."

But as I turned to open the door for them again, the telephone rang.

Ashley, 1835

A cock crowed from the direction of the farm-yard. Night's singer was silent, and day's first chorus had died to desultory pipings. A rustle from somewhere near the edge of the maze made him pause and listen, head aslant. A badger on its way home, perhaps. Or a roe. If deer had been in the garden again he must tell the keeper to take the gun out after them today.

Today . . . Today was not just another day.

Today he would have to face them. His father was dead, and he was Ashley. From somewhere he must find the courage to face them with what he had done. Then, afterwards, she would be with him.

Something showed pale on the grass near the mouth of the maze. Stooping to peer, he recognized the kerchief he had given her: it was of silk, and, for fear it should be seen, she wore it always in her bosom. Wondering how she had come to drop it there, he picked it up, and, smiling, held it to his face. The gentle fragrance of lavender brought her near again, and with her the sweet days of summer.

Still smiling, he walked out of the maze.

Nineteen

The letter was not nice, but full of charge
Of dear import, and the neglecting it
May do much danger.
                    —*Romeo and Juliet*, V, ii

The three of us stood as if struck still, while the harsh threshing of the bell drowned out even the wild sounds of the night. Then I made a move. Emory's hand shot out and gripped my wrist.

"We're not here, remember? And neither are you. Leave it."

"It might be Cathy."

"And if it is? She doesn't know you're back here. Leave it."

I was angry now. "It's my phone, Emory. I shan't tell anyone you're here, if you're afraid. But what is there to be afraid of now? Your crime's been called off, hasn't it?"

"There's a light in the Court." James spoke quickly, from the window. "Rob must have gone over. If he's seen the water level he may be telephoning here before he goes over to the High Sluice. She'd better answer, or he might think something's up."

"Could be," said Emory. Then, to me, swiftly: "Is he likely to call help in if he's seen the level?"

"I doubt it. He's quite capable of dealing with it himself. He's kept the Court going for long enough."

I did not trouble to keep the bite out of my voice, but Emory didn't seem to notice. "Well . . ." he said, and stood back.

Only as I picked up the telephone did the other possibility present itself. As late as this, the call must be urgent. It would certainly not be Rob, but it might well be Herr Gothard. He would not have received the photographs yet, but he might speak of my promise to send them; or he might even be ringing to tell me of some other progress made towards identification of the guilty driver. I had the receiver half back to its rest, but a voice was already talking quickly, and very audibly, through it. Not Herr Gothard; it was Leslie Oker, not even waiting for me to respond, but in full and joyous spate with his news.

"Bryony? My dear, I simply had to ring you. I know it's a dreadful hour of night, and I'm sorry if you were asleep, but I've been trying to get you off and on all day, and when you hear what I have to tell you I'm sure you'll think it was worth it. My dear, the book . . ."

It was a loud telephone, Leslie's obvious excitement carrying through almost as if he were in the room. Beside me, Emory made a sharp movement of interest. I started to speak, but Leslie wasn't listening. He swept on.

"I just had to tell you—I'm as certain as can be that the book's genuine. It's been re-bound, and that will take something off its value, but it's still very valuable indeed. I wouldn't like to guess at a figure, until I've found out a little more about it. . . . In any case, when you come to the real rarities, you can't put a figure on them until they go into the sale room. But it could be very valuable, very valuable indeed . . . museum stuff . . . provenance . . ."

He talked on about the book, half technical jargon that I hardly took in. I put a hand tightly over the mouthpiece, looked up at Emory, and spoke under my breath. "Well, there's your answer. Ready cash, or at any rate something to borrow on—collateral, do they call it? Now

I hope you'll leave my home to me for as long as I need it?"

I doubt if Emory even heard the bitter little gibe. His eyes were gleaming, and he mouthed something; I thought it was "How much?" I shook my head as the telephone quacked what was obviously a question, and took my hand off the mouthpiece again.

"Sorry, Leslie, I didn't catch that. What did you say?"

"I said, when I lifted it, I found something that might be in its own way even more interesting. It's a bit long, but do you want to hear it now?"

"Hear what? Lifted what?" I asked unguardedly.

"The bookplate. That curious rectangular design with the crest in the middle and that weird motto of yours, 'Touch Not the Cat.' "

Something jarred me right back to the alert. "Oh yes, that," I said quickly. "Well, look, Leslie, I should have told you sooner, the book isn't officially mine any longer. Since Daddy's death all the family things belong to my cousin Emory. I'll tell him to get in touch with you, and—"

He didn't hear the rest, and for a very good reason. Emory's hand had come between my mouth and the telephone, covering the mouthpiece again. His other hand closed on the receiver, over mine, and lifted it away from me. Held in midair in front of me, the metallic voice quacked on, all too clear.

". . . Sorry to hear that, dear, because really, such a *find* . . . Of course, moving it won't militate against the value of the book at all, since the bookplate was put on so much later. After the rebinding, too, did I make that clear? In fact, it looked to me as if it had been lifted before, and pasted down again; reecntly, I'd say . . . so I felt quite justified in lifting it again, and indeed, I was right, because the original flyleaf was there. It puts the whole thing beyond the bounds of doubt. But this paper I was telling you about, that I found under the bookplate, well, that's of real family interest, I would think, because there's a note from one of your family, and the whole thing, love, looks like a *mystery* to me, too Gothic, really, but what fun. Listen."

We listened, all three of us. Whatever Leslie had found, I did not see now how I could stop Emory from finding out about it. All he had to do was ring Leslie back himself. It was his book, after all.

Leslie was explaining. "It looks like a page from a church register. It's numbered seventeen, and there are only three entries. They may all be interesting, I don't know, but the third one will just fascinate you. It's dated April fifteenth, 1835, and it records the marriage of Nicholas Ashley, Esquire, of Ashley Court, to an Ellen Makepeace, of One Ash."

Not for worlds would I have put the receiver back now. My mind meshed into gear like a racing engine. The consequences could wait; I had to know. *"The paper, it's in William's Brooke. In the library . . . The map. The letter. In the Brooke."*

"Yes," I said, "go on."

"Further down the page someone has written a note. It's signed 'Charles Ashley.' Do you know who he was?"

"He was Nick Ashley's uncle, William Ashley's brother. He succeeded to the Court after Nick Ashley was shot."

"Oh. Well, a note from him. It says—it's rather long, so I'll paraphrase the first bit—he says he bribed the clerk to recopy the page omitting the Ashley entry, and something about the incumbent—is that the Vicar, dear?— being a dependent. Does that make sense?"

"I think so. One Ash was one of the Ashley benefices. If there was a younger son or a poor relation they were given the benefice. I suppose Charles Ashley could put pressure on him to keep quiet about the wedding. Is that what he says?"

"Could be. He says—shall I read the rest to you?"

"Yes, please."

" 'It is said that the girl goes with child, and should she bear it before the nine months' term is up since my

nephew's death, there will be those who, for their own
base ends, will rumour it abroad that the child was already
begotten on her by my nephew, before she married her
husband. But it is neither right nor fitting that the fruit—
if it be so—of so hasty and base a connexion should take
the property from the hands of my own fair family who
are sprung from alliance with the highest in the County,
and who are of a fair age and disposition to administer
the Estate. Moreover, and it is this which has driven me
to act as I have done, the brothers of the said Ellen
Makepeace did kill and murder my nephew Nicholas, so
to my mind it were better that the child were born dead,
than usurp this place with blood upon his head. So, God
be my witness, it is not upon my conscience to do what I
have done. The girl bears herself lowly, and has avowed
publicly that the child is that of her own husband.'" A
pause, during which I could even hear the rustle of the
paper in Leslie's hands. He gave his little laugh. "She
would, of course, poor creature. The dear Squire would
probably have had the baby quietly put down otherwise.
Well, well, poor things. Past history is always a good deal
better in the past, isn't it, Bryony dear? Does all this mean
anything to you?"

Emory lowered the receiver to me again. I didn't look
at him. I cleared my throat, but even so my voice came
out rather unfamiliar, borrowing, falsely, a little of Leslie's
own over-exuberance:

"I think so. Yes, I think so. Leslie, I'm terribly grateful
to you. It's all so exciting, isn't it, and I'm awfully glad
you rang. May I come over tomorrow, perhaps, and hear
all about the book, and look at this paper? We'll have
time to talk about it then."

"Well, of course. This awful hour . . . But I knew
you'd like to know straight away. Look, there's a chap in
London who'd know more about the *Romeus* than I do.
I'll give him a buzz in the morning, shall I, before you
come?"

"Please do. Thank you, Leslie. But Leslie—"

"Yes?"

"This friend of yours—ask him about the book's value by all means, but would you please not tell him anything about the letter; not till we've had a look at it, and worked out what it means?"

"Well, of course not. It's safe with me, dear." No emphasis, but I knew it was. "Good night."

"Good night. Thank you for ringing."

The telephone went dead. Emory's hands relaxed, and he stood back from me. I put the receiver down half blindly, so that it fell with a clatter. James picked it up and replaced it, and I sat down rather heavily in the chair beside the table.

"That was sensible," said Emory. "Well, how many more surprises do you suppose this night will hold? This Ellen Makepeace . . . if she actually had that baby—"

I hadn't looked at either of them, but James, prompted perhaps by something in my expression, or by some stray instinct of the Ashley gift, or, what was more likely than either, by some residuum of jealousy, got there with frightening speed.

"She did. You can bet your bloody life she did. Makepeaces . . . One Ash is full of them, and the Grangers are connected." Then, savagely, to me: "That's it, isn't it? Rob Granger—that's who it is! You can bet your life he goes straight back to this stupid, so-called marriage. That's why you did it, isn't it? Why you married him? Because you knew he was an Ashley, and legit., at that. Why else would you marry a lout like that?"

"Shut up, Twin." This, sharply, from Emory. "That sort of thing gets us nowhere. Bryony, did you know about this?"

They would only have to look in the parish register, or even, country memories being what they were, ask any adult in One Ash, to find that Ellen was indeed Rob's ancestress "straight back." I nodded. "I knew he was an Ashley, but I didn't know about the marriage. Neither does he. He told me he was descended from Nick Ashley, but on the wrong side of the blanket. That was all."

"Oh, he knows that much? Then I suppose all his family know, too."

"Only the same story we've been hearing all our lives, that the brothers shot Nick for debauching Ellen, and that she married the Granger lad and had a baby son, but swore on the Bible it was her husband's, so people accepted it."

"And all the time," said Emory, with a twist to his voice, "she was telling the exact truth. Poor Charles. He must have fairly sweated it out until he saw she was going to be sensible."

I said nothing. I was thinking about Ellen Ashley. I felt consumed with pity for that girl, bereft and helpless, swearing on the Scriptures to protect her lover's child, and hugging to herself the comfort that all time it was the truth. Poor Ellen. I wondered how Robert Granger had been with her, and how much he had known or guessed of the things she kept in her heart.

"Are you trying to pretend," demanded James, "that Rob never guessed?"

"That he was legitimate? Of course not, why should he? If there had ever been a hint, even that he was an Ashley by-blow, our family would have known, but I told you, it was accepted that the baby was Robert Granger's. His family may have talked about it among themselves, but nothing more than that. Have you ever even heard a rumour? I haven't."

"But you said he'd told you that himself."

"Yes. He knew because"—I looked from one to the other—"because he has the Ashley gift. You know about that. Well, so have I. That's why our marriage happened as it did, so suddenly. I'd meant to tell you about that, anyway; I felt I owed you that."

It seemed very strange that I should ever have felt I owed James anything. Now, if I owed an explanation to anyone, I owed it to Rob. So I told my cousins quickly, the merest sketch, and they listened, not arguing or even very surprised; they were Ashleys after all. They knew the history of the "gift," and had themselves claimed some kind of intuitive link.

"You'll tell him all about it now, I suppose?" asked James, when I had finished.

"Can you think of any reason why not?"

"Well, my God"—" began my cousin, but Emory stopped him.

"Let her talk. Go on, Bryony."

"Well, why not? Do you think I can stay married to him all my life and not tell him something that might matter to him like this? He ought to know he's a true Ashley, and that his great-great-grandfather wasn't just a brat fathered on a light-minded girl. He ought to know that Nick Ashley loved Ellen enough to marry her."

"Or that he was scared silly of her brothers." That was James.

"That's stupid!" I spoke hotly, as if I were defending Rob himself. I knew, as well as if they had told me, why Nick and Ellen, just for those fatal few days, had kept their marriage secret. They were trying, like Rob and me, to keep something to themselves for a while before the world broke in. And with even less success.

I straightened wearily in my chair. "Look," I said, "why don't we call it a night and talk about it tomorrow? With Rob, if you like. As I see it, what we've found out will make no difference, one way or another, to what happens here at Ashley. But if you two don't get on your way now, and do something about the High Sluice—"

"To hell with the High Sluice." It was odd how James seemed to have taken over the scene. "Are you seriously trying to tell us that if you tell Granger all this—this old-time Gothic trash, do you seriously tell us that he won't be tempted to make it public? Claim the Court and everything that goes with it? Stay here with you and play lord of the manor? Someone like that couldn't resist it."

"Rob knows even better than you do what it would mean to have this place unloaded on him," I said hotly. "I know he doesn't want to stay here, and neither do I.

Do I have to keep telling you? This won't make any difference to us at all."

"Except that you'd have some money to emigrate with," said James. "Rather more than the cottage strip will net for you."

"If we claimed it, and if the claim was upheld."

"Are you trying to say that he wouldn't even try to claim it?"

"How many more times do I have to say it?" I regarded him with weary dislike. "Even if we wanted the Court—or wanted the money the sale would bring—can you see a claim like this standing up in a court of law? It wouldn't even be worth trying."

"Your father must have thought it would," said James obstinately. "This is why he refused to break the trust the second time we asked him. He must just have found out about Rob Granger."

"Yes." I spoke with sudden, complete illumination. (*"I did tell Bryanston that she and Rob should marry. Perhaps the boy knows already that he's an Ashley. Tell the boy who he is. This trust; it's his concern now. You can depend on him to do what's right. You have—both of you— my blessing."*) I sat up straight, speaking earnestly. "And he was going to do the right thing, as I am, and tell Rob all the truth, and leave it to him. He has to know. That's all, James. Further than that it's up to him, and I've told you what I think he'll do: cut his losses, as I'm doing, and go."

Emory stirred. "Leslie Oker saw the paper, and you can't tell me he'd keep quiet about a juicy item like that."

"He will if I ask him to. In any case," I said impatiently, "what does it matter who knows about it, if we don't press anything? Mr. Emerson will do as Rob asks him—and, for pity's sake, can you *imagine* a claim like that being made today, in the nineteen-seventies? Gothic trash isn't in it. Can you imagine a courtful of lawyers arguing over an 1837 parish register, and whether or not Bess Ashley really did hand telepathy down the family?"

"All right," said Emory, "so imagine it. Whether you want it or not, let Oker once start talking, and there'll be questions asked about our claim to the place and our right to sell it. And there simply is not time to let the lawyers make a meal of it, and spend ten happy years arguing the pros and cons of the Ashley gift, while in the meantime Pereira sues us for twenty thousand pounds in no time at all."

"We could destroy the paper, and square Leslie Oker." This from James. They were at it again, talking across me. I believe I said something more, but they ignored me.

"Even if he can be squared," said Emory, "he's probably talked already."

"Well, but without proof—"

"Any inquiry would mean the kind of delay we can't afford."

"That's true," said James.

"Too bad, isn't it?" said Emory.

"Well, what are you going to do?"

"It shouldn't be too difficult," said Emory, "to fix things."

I saw it then, through the weariness and worry, and I knew, against all belief, that Rob had been right. Cousins or no, these men were dangerous, even to me and mine. Quick thinking, violent men, who knew how to profit from accidents . . .

I don't think I moved, but James, still on that odd telepathic wavelength, took a swift step and got between me and the telephone. I had made no move to touch it. I shut my eyes and reached for Rob.

But across the first groping signal I heard James say, urgently: "It's true, you know, Twin, she can talk to him. Look at her." Then, in sudden, unbelieving revulsion: "Emory! No!"

Something hit me hard behind the ear, and I went out like a smashed lamp.

Ashley, 1835

His limbs were stiff, and heavy as if bound

with iron. The pain in his chest exploded through his whole body, then died to a slow, unmerciful aching. He moaned, but could hear no sound.

He was lying on cold, soaking grass. He must, he thought dimly, have fainted. He remembered—surely he remembered?—going out of the maze; the drenched grasses, and the yew trees glimmering, heavy with shining, under the faint morning stars. There had been shadows moving at the mouth of the maze, a rough whisper, a hand grabbing at him, then the skin-prickling sound of a cocked fowling piece . . .

The memory faded, and with it, slowing into a drowsy warmth, the pain died. His head felt light and empty, and he had the strangest fancy that he was floating above his own body, drawn upward from its chilling weight as if the air sucked him away, leaf-light. Then it, too, faded.

Twenty

And the place death, considering who thou art,
If any of my kinsmen find thee here.
—*Romeo and Juliet*, II, ii

I had a headache, and it was dark. At first I thought the noises were in my head, but, as I slowly swam up into the headache and the chilly air, I realized that the creakings and the splashes, and the keening gusts of wind, were realities, as was the slam of wood on wood that had finally wakened me.

It took me a little time to come fully to myself, and discover where I was. At first, groping for my bearings through painfully returning consciousness, I thought I must be somewhere out in the open; I was lying on what seemed to be hard ground strewn with twigs and dead leaves and broken shards, with the smells of wet earth and growing things and rotting wood blown round me strongly on the gusty drafts. But then, slowly, walls and a kind of roof built themselves out of the near-darkness round me, and I saw that I was in an enclosed space perhaps the size of the cottage sitting room, but with a ceiling so low—a meter or so above me—that I could hardly sit up without striking my head. I could only see this much because the walls, though surely solid enough, showed here and there a crack or a knothole through which filtered a grey and fitful light.

I dragged myself shakily to hands and knees, and crawled to one of these to peer through.

I saw a thick, ragged hedge, blocking a square of windy sky; grasses whipping in the wind; nearer at hand the dim tangles of some thick creeper swinging and beating like waves against the balustrade of a rustic stairway which cut diagonally across my vision. Everywhere was the sound of trees and water, and the reeling grey light of a moon behind wind-driven cloud.

I had it then. This was the pavilion, at the center of the maze. The slamming noise was the broken shutter which had worked loose and was swinging to and fro in the wind, and the stairs beside me were those leading up to the verandah and the pavilion's door.

They led upwards, past me. I was under the pavilion, in the space below the floor, with the access door beneath the verandah slammed shut and—as I groped dazedly to discover—securely jammed from outside.

A gust of wind, carrying a scatter of small debris, struck the pavilion, and a draft whipped through the crack where I crouched, blowing my hair stinging into my eyes. I came fully awake then, with all that had happened vividly back in mind, slotted neatly into place like items on a computerized account; and with it, all that was due to happen, which I suppose I had seen in that one brief flash of illumination, so brutally cut off by Emory's blow.

Some dim memory I still retained, of quick incisive instructions from Emory to James, and of protests overruled. I must have surfaced into consciousness from time to time, enough to catch snatches of the argument that ensued. I knew now why James had looked so strained and sick; he had after all cared enough—or been frightened enough—not to want to see me harmed.

"I tell you, Twin, she'll be perfectly safe." That was Emory, impatience held hard on the curb. "I'll put her in the pavilion and lock her in. She'll be above water level

there, and she'll be out of action long enough. . . . No one
to hear if she shouts, and by that time we can be on the
other side of the country."

"But she's seen us here, and for God's sake, Emory, if
anything happens to Rob Granger, you can't expect her
to sit mute. Our alibis are blown before we start."

"Very well, then." Quick and smooth. "She goes. You
agree?"

"No! Are you crazy? Look, we've got to think of something else——"

"Such as? You can't have it both ways."

A pause, then from James, slowly: "I think we can.
I'm willing to bet she'd say nothing, whatever she might
think she knows about an accident to Rob. . . . Yes, all
right, so she's married him; all that crap she gave us about
it, if you can believe it . . . never last out the honeymoon,
even, a lout like that . . . Look, Twin, I mean it. She's
never said a word about her father's death, has she? About
its being one of us . . . And she knows. She cottoned on
to that pen of mine that you dropped, I'm certain she
did; but she's never said a word, and it's my bet she
never will, just as she held her tongue about that stuff
Cathy stole."

"Well, but Cousin Jon's death was an accident. She'll
know this won't be."

"All the same . . ."

So much came back to me, more or less clearly. The
outcome, however arrived at, was clearer still. Whether
James had, in the end, agreed with Emory's plan to dis-
pose of me, or whether he had simply turned a blind eye
to whatever his twin might do, I did not know. But I
would have taken any bet that it was Emory who had
carried me into the maze, and Emory whose hand had
shut the trap on me.

Even so, I was far from acquitting James. So far he was
clean of anything other than minor villainy, but the very
fact that I was here proved that, as always, he would go
along with whatever Emory suggested. It was easy to guess

what that was. They would use the almost aborted plan
for flooding the cottage strip, and improvise with it an
"accident" that would take care of Rob. As for me, I
could not escape, nor, however hard I shouted, could I be
heard, even without the torrent of noise outside in the
stormy night. The twins would leave the High Sluice open,
letting the swollen river pour into the moat, and soon,
when the moat brimmed its banks and finally burst them,
and the Pool flooded clear down through orchard and
maze, I would certainly drown. No doubt the access door
of my trap was cleverly wedged to look as if some floating
spars or boughs had been jammed there by the flood's
force after my body had been washed under the pavilion.
And Rob? They would lie in wait for him and kill him,
and in the morning his body, battered by the flood, would
be found where apparently he had run to rescue me. The
two of us, star-crossed lovers, drowned on our wedding
night as the flood swept through the cottage; and all the
while the twins, securely alibied, miles away . . .

There was no flood yet. Straining my ears I could hear
the ripple and rush of the Overflow as it skirted the maze;
full, but not yet too full. I might still be in time. Emory
must have meant to hit me harder, and keep me out for
as long as was needed. Perhaps James had interfered as
his brother struck me; or perhaps Emory had not reckoned
on the streams of chill, reviving air that poured through
the trap where he had lodged me. By the time he had carried me here and wedged the door, then struggled back
again through the dark maze, the gap in my consciousness
might not have been too long.

Rob. Rob.

I put the call out with all the strength I could muster.
It was more difficult than it had ever been. I could sense
how faint the patterns were, reaching out through the
blowing dark. Without quite realizing I had done it, I
switched the signal, using the old pattern that I had been
used to—and which now, ironically enough, was real.

Ashley, Ashley, Ashley . . .

Yes? It was faint, the faintest of responses, but the wave of relief, that melted me back against the wall like wet paper collapsing, showed me the strength of the fear I had had for Rob. He was still alive, and, from the serenity of his response, unsuspecting and unmolested.

Bryony? Serene no longer. He had got the fear pattern. *What is it? What's happened?*

I lay back against the wooden wall, staring inwards, away from the garden, at the descending weight of darkness that was the pavilion's floor, so close above my head.

Danger for you. It was all I could do to send the warning patterns, without giving him some inkling of my own imminent peril. Some of my fear must have got through in spite of me, because his response was violent, a blast of static that rocked and splintered the thought-waves, and sent me back to simple messages of reassurance that took every ounce of control I had: *No. No. I'm all right. I'm safe. Wait . . .*

I found I was shaking and sweating, in spite of the cold. I made my mind blank, and rested for as many seconds as I dared. At least he was warned. I shut my mind momentarily, straining to shut out the image of the dark cage that trapped me, and to conjure up instead a picture of the pavilion above, with the moonlight wheeling and backing through the swinging shutter, sending light and shadow shimmering across the mirror overhead. Whatever happened he must have no whisper of the danger in which I lay, or he might do just as my cousins wished, and come running back towards me, past wherever they lay in wait for him. Forewarned might be forearmed, but there were two of them, and they had surprise and darkness on their side.

I opened to him again, and began painfully to send those patterns out. My cousins opening the High Sluice; the river racing through to fill the moat; the Overflow still taking it, but not quite, and somewhere the banks of the moat crumbling to let the great weight of water down into the brimming Pool. The slow flood lipping the cottage garden, reaching through the apple orchard for the low-lying floor of the maze . . .

The image of the lower sluice slid across the pictures, like a quick shiver of alarm. He knew, even better than I, what would happen if too great a weight of water piled against those rotten gates; or worse, what would happen if anyone tried to move them. He came back at me then, light-edged with relief: *The pavilion: that's where you are?*

I had got it to him, then: he thought I had taken refuge there, and was safe, perched above the encroaching water. *Yes.* I sent it urgently. *Yes, I'm safe. But you, Ashley, danger for you. Take care, love, take care.*

I knew he must have got from me the image of the two dark figures lurking in wait somewhere, watching for him. There was a brief flash of a reply, which came slightly distorted, zigzag, as if with interference, or as words would come if one was breathless: *I've got it. I'm on my way. Stay where you are . . .*

It was fading. If he had got my fear at all he must have thought it was only for him. As I believe it was. If he was to save himself, and perhaps me, too, he must not be weighed down by fear for me.

My little Bryony be careful. It sprang out of the night and faded, blown down the wind. A pattern coming strangely, not with the smooth familiarity of Rob's patterns, but as if straight out of the night, and as if spoken.

Then a sound, sharp and distinct, like a shot. From somewhere near the Overflow, at the entrance to the maze.

I hurled myself back at the wall of my prison, my hands straining flat against the wood as if nailed there, my face to that windy crack. *Rob? Rob?*

They could not have shot him, they could not. It was to have been an accident. Surely I could not have guessed wrongly about that?

A sound came, breaking through the very thought, shattering it. A cracking, creaking noise, like a big door strained to breaking point. The noise was drowned by a lashing gust of wind, then in the lull behind the wind it came again.

Ashley? He had gone, as completely as if a line had fused. I think I was still calling him, on a silent, jagged pattern of terror, when, drowning out all the other storm sounds of the night, the lower sluice smashed under the weight of wind and water, and the flood came.

It came in a tidal wave, that smashed through the ancient walls of the maze and broke, filthy and swirling with the weight of the whole moat behind it, against the pavilion. The old structure seemed to shake and groan as if it would tear from its moorings in the grass, and buck away down the flood like a ship dragging her anchor. Then the water found its way in. There was a choking, fighting eternity, in which every second seemed like an hour, when the water pounded the gaping walls, spurting through with terrifying power. The jets shot in from every side, splashing and swirling together to join in a whirlpool which started, as rapidly as a sink filling under the taps, to rise from ankle to crouching thigh, to waist, to breasts. . . . And with it rose the debris of years, whirling and battering its way round the trap, so that even the imminence of drowning seemed less fearful than the blows from floating spars and fragments of planking with rusty nails still in them, and the weedlike nets of twigs loaded with the slime of mud and clods and trailing grass. I thrust myself upwards against the ceiling as hard as I could, holding both arms bent in front of my face to protect mouth and nostrils from the swirling filth. If the pavilion floor were only as solid as it had seemed, it might trap even an inch of air for me to breathe, until the flood poured past, as it surely would in minutes, then spread through maze and orchard and cottage garden, and went down . . .

The pavilion floor was not solid. As I pressed up hard against it, it lifted slightly, like magic, into clear air. There was a crash as a section of planking upended itself, and fell aside. I straightened up, breast-high in the pouring floodwater, then pulled myself clear, and up on to the pavilion floor.

Almost before I was clear, the flood was at the brim of the trap. I slammed the square of planking back again, grabbed the end of the daybed, and yanked it across the floor till a leg stood squarely on the trap, then jumped on the bed and craned to look out through the broken window shutter.

What I saw was a worldful of moonlight, with neither bound nor horizon, just a glimmering, shadow-tossing expanse of water and sky merged into one, with clouds, and the shadows of clouds, driving and melting across the moon and the image of the moon. Trees billowed black against the sky, or flung down nets of branches to trap their own wild reflections. There was no maze, no orchard, no avenue of beeches between me and the Court; only this shining otherworld of moonlight, of trees like shadows, and shadows like clouds.

Something went past on the flood; an arm, a stiff hand clutching at air, a black shape slowly turning. Even as the terror took breath in me to cry out, I saw it for what it was, a dead branch borne along to lodge against the pavilion steps.

I shut my eyes, squeezing them tightly together, but inside the lids, against the fizzing darkness, there were still those images of death. I opened them again, straining through the chaos of emptiness and dying wind, to find my love.

There, as before, was the waste of moonlit water, broken with black shapes of trees and bushes, and, visible from moment to moment as ripples and wind swayed the intervening boughs aside, the smashed remains of the lower sluice where the loosened water of the moat plunged down to swell the flooded garden. No light glimmered now, where I knew the black bulk of the Court to be.

I stretched higher, straining to see. And I saw Rob.

He was bent half double, seemingly oblivious of danger, wrestling with the wheel of the sluice. For a numbed and speechless moment I looked to see my cousins jump out of the darkness at him, but nothing happened, and then I saw that where he stood the ground was dry, and willows grew there, and the monstrous shapes of gunneras, and I recognized, with no flicker of disbelief, or even surprise, the High Sluice, a full third of a mile away from me, and on the far side of the Court.

Whether I really did see anything, or whether—as happens with childhood memories—I have added his story to the shadowy and nightmare impressions that I, on the edge of the tragedy, received, I do not know. But it seems to me now as if, across the nearer scene, the other, now clear, now disliming and fading like an image stamped on gauze, or an old film twice exposed, came and went, as real and vivid to me as the window frame under my hands. It was something that had never happened before, nor has it again. I can only explain it by suggesting that in that time of near-death we were so close that there was more than communication between us, there was identity. I saw with his eyes, but at the same time I saw with my own.

The twins, intending to go back to the High Sluice, had left the wheel still in place. Rob wrenched at it, and it turned, smoothly in its oil, and the heavy gates surged slowly shut till, with a final suck and swish of water, their flanges met and gripped, held by the weight of the incoming river. He made sure of them, then tugged the wheel off its hub, picked up the flashlight which he had propped on the gate to light the job, and ran back the way he had come.

The path was still sodden along the moatside, but the level was dropping fast, as the bulk of the water poured through the broken sluice gate and the gaps it had torn in the bank of the moat. He sloshed and slithered past the end of the East Bridge, then paused to pitch the sluice wheel down among the roots of the nearest lime tree. Then he switched off the flashlight, and, more cautiously, began to make his way down the path that led to the Overflow.

The water was still coming over here, pouring through the lip of the moat where it had torn its way. In places it rushed down with frightening power, carrying a dangerous freight of branches and stones and pieces of timber. The moon spun out from a bank of driving cloud to show the swans, wings set like sails and the six cygnets safely aboard, paddling past on the flood with ruffled dignity. The rooks were up in the high night, complaining. The farm dog barked, but no light showed there, nor any through the Vicarage trees.

He floundered down towards the maze. Under the beeches it was black dark and he went cautiously, straining his eyes for any movement that might be a man. Beyond the beech trunks, and the islanded bushes of the shrubbery, the maze showed only as a moving flood laced with driftwood and the tracery of hedge tops. But the pavilion stood foursquare, with water no higher than the doorsill.

He paused, getting his breath, backing in against a beech bole in deep shadow. He held the heavy flashlight clubbed ready in his hand.

Safe, love? he asked me.

Safe.

At that moment, clearly audible above the noise of wind and flood, came another crack like an echo of the first, and with the crack a cry. It came from the lower sluice.

Rob ran forward. The water was almost to his waist. He struggled through the bushes, slipping and stumbling on mud, till he could see the sluice gate. Here, through the smashed gate, the water still poured in a white torrent, but the banks immediately to either side of the sluice were heavily reinforced with stone, and had held undamaged. Over them, where the double water stair had fed the Overflow, loud slopes of smooth water slid to swell the flood below.

Then he saw James. The latter was kneeling by the

sluice, half in the rushing water, one arm hooked for support across what remained of the smashed gate. In his
other hand was an axe.

Ashley!

The warning burst in my head, and I saw Rob check
momentarily. They were both clear to me now: James,
the wet leather of his jacket gleaming like an otter's, the
axe poised and ready; Rob armed only with the flashlight,
fighting for a foothold on the slimy stones as he scrambled
up through the sliding slab of the cascade. But my cousin
made no move to attack him; he seemed, indeed, not to
have noticed Rob's approach. He was stooping low over
the smashed rubble of timber wedged below the sluice.
Still holding with his left hand, he bent forward and
began to hack with what force he could at a spar which,
wedged clear across the channel, held down a mass of
wreckage.

Then Rob shouted something, thrust the flashlight into
his pocket, ran forward to the edge of the channel, and
dropped to his knees.

He had seen what lay below the spar, and so had I.

Emory was alive. His head and arms were clear of the
rushing water, his hands gripping painfully at the rough
stones of the wall, but his shoulders were pinned down
by the wedged spar, and his body held submerged by the
tangled mat of weeds and branches, invisible in the pouring flood.

Rob threw himself flat, and reached downward to grip
one of Emory's wrists.

James, with his back to him, had apparently neither
seen him nor heard him shout. As Rob leaned down,
reaching for Emory, my other cousin looked sharply
round. He abandoned the spar he was attacking, turned
quickly and got to his feet, axe in hand.

Neither Rob nor I was ever quite clear about what
James had meant to do. He was yelling something, and
the axe swung high. Then his foot shot from under him
on the slimy wood. He lost his footing, and fell hard across

he spar. The axe flew from his grip. He scrabbled there
for a moment, his body down across his brother's, then
the water swept him away and down, out of sight past the
trunks of the flooded trees. At the same moment the spar,
loosened no doubt by James's fall, cracked again, swung
in the current, then spun loose and away. The clutching
hands were torn from the stones, breaking Rob's grip,
and suddenly Rob was alone at the sluice, with the water
roaring past his feet, and the moon sailing out high and
white to light the waste of moving water where there had
once been a fair garden.

Ashley, 1835

He moved a hand. It met the familiar, soft
folds of a coverlet. He was lying, warm and
naked, in his bed in the pavilion. His limbs felt
heavy still, but with the aftermath of loving.
The linen under his cheek was wet with a forgotten grief.

Linen? It was silk, and smelled of lavender.
He opened his eyes. Her hair, soft and silky and
alive, was spread under his cheek on the pillow.
As he raised himself, suddenly light and wide
awake, she smiled up at him.

"What is it, love? What ails thee?"

He ran a lock of her hair through his fingers.
"I had such a dream, Nell. I dreamed I was
dead, lying out there in the grass, and my ghost
came drifting back to look for you, as they say
ghosts drift back to whatever anchors them to
earth. But you had gone, and all I could do was
wait here, lonely, while the years passed, and
were empty; only the other ghosts came and
went. And while I waited here, watching for you,
the trees grew, and the ways tangled, as if the
place still shut its doors against you, and I
thought you could never find your way to me
again."

"But I came."

His head went down to hers. His tears dried against her cheek. "You came. And they can never part us now, Nell, never again. This is ours, for ever, love. It was death that was the dream."

Twenty-One

JULIET: It is not yet near day:
    It was the nightingale, and not the lark ...
ROMEO: It was the lark, the herald of the morn,
    No nightingale ...
—*Romeo and Juliet*, III, v

So much I believe I saw, then there was nothing but the sheen of water and the moon out over it, and a rack of cloud blown away down a dying wind. The trees still roared. The water still poured past the pavilion. It had flooded the steps, and crept in under the door, and was meandering across the wooden floor. Pool joined pool and runnel, runnel. But before the shining skin had joined and flooded the boards, the water's impetus seemed spent. Movement ceased. The shallow pool lay, reaching from the threshold to the center of the floor, but going no farther, the last ripple of the flood that had drowned the garden, islanding the pavilion like a ship floating.

What brought me back to myself was the sound, distant yet unmistakable, of Emory's car starting. I stiffened, turning my head to listen, guessing the direction. Yes, it was his, and parked by the sound of it on the curved sweep outside the church gate, near the road. I heard the driver—James, surely?—gun the engine hard, twice, and then the wheels gained the surface of the road, and the sound faded rapidly westwards. My cousins—both presumably, for neither would have left the place alone—had gone. Let them go, let them go. Whatever the reckoning had to be, that was for tomorrow.

There is a gap after that, while I tried to reach Rob again, but shock, or exhaustion, or cold must have so numbed me that I simply sat there on the bed waiting for him to come. It didn't even occur to me that he had never known his way into the maze, and that I was penned here at the center, as inaccessible as any Sleeping Beauty.

I suppose I could have guided him through, if I had been able to hold my mind clear. Left and next right . . . straight . . . right and next left . . . straight . . . U-turn sharp left and repeat the lot in reverse . . . the first gate should now be beside you on your left-hand side . . .

But I didn't, and he never asked. I felt something move out of the dark like a caress, and knew he was sensing my exhaustion. I got it faintly, very faintly: *Hold up, love, I'm almost with you.*

I didn't know how. He was coming. I thought about nothing else. I waited.

Either he had found James's axe, or he had been up to the farm for another. I could hear the steady, hacking sounds, and the splashes, coming gradually nearer as he approached me through the maze. Slowly, but straight. He was cutting his way through. The hedges, overgrown and already sparse through neglect, had been further damaged by the weight of the flood and the debris it carried. I could hear the ancient stems parting, and the swish and splashing as he forced his way through. The yews that some long-dead Ashley had planted, and that had taken two hundred years or so to grow and thicken into those lovely head-high walls; and now Rob was slicing his way straight through, to me.

Rob Ashley. No one had a better right.

The crashing stopped. I heard the surging splash as he thrust through the last hedge, then he waded across the moonlit water of the clearing, and ran up the steps to the door.

Love?

Here. The south window, Rob.

The shutter went back with a slam, and his shadow blacked out the moonlight in the window. It wasn't James's axe he was holding, it was a heavy woodsman's axe from the farmyard; he had even thought to bring a dry blanket, which he wore wrapped like a burnous round his head and shoulders. He clambered through, and landed with a thud and a squelch on the flooded boards. Then he was beside me on the bed, holding me tightly and kissing me, and I was kissing him, and somehow, at some point, our soaked clothes came off and we were together under the warm rug, while the accumulated terrors and tensions of the night swelled and broke in a fierce explosion of love, and, with no more thought or reservation than two wild creatures mating in the woods, we took each other and then lay together, clasped and quiet, and outside, I swear it, the nightingale began to sing.

If anyone told me now that I could have slept like that, in all the damp and discomfort of the flooded pavilion, I would not have believed them. But, between love and exhaustion and deep happiness, sleep I did, and so did Rob, wrapped tightly together under the rug, and neither of us stirred until the early sun, reaching the window, threw such a dazzle of light from the water outside onto the ceiling mirror that it beat against our eyelids and woke us.

"It's still singing," I said sleepily.

"What is?"

"The nightingale. I told you—"

"That's a lark."

"Oh? So it is." I came awake then, to the blaze of sunlight and the morning birds and the warmth of Rob's body along mine. He was lying half on his back, eyes wide and wakeful, but with every muscle and line of his body relaxed, warm and still, into the morning's contentment. "Have you been awake long?"

"It doesn't seem like it. I suppose I woke at my usual time. Always do, even on holiday. First time I ever woke like this, though." His arm tightened, and I moved my cheek deeper into the hollow of his shoulder. "Bryony—"

"Mm?"

"What did they put the mirror on the ceiling for?"

I gave a little snort of laughter, deep into his shoulder. "I forgot all about that. It was supposed to be put up there by some loose-screw—your ancestor Wicked Nick gets the blame—so he could watch himself in bed with his lady friends. Good thing it was dark last night. Just think how off-putting if one suddenly saw oneself—"

"That's the point. One couldn't."

"But one can," I protested. "And very cozy we look, all bundled up like this."

"Aye. But then the bed isn't where it ought to be. You can see where that was by the moulding on the wall over there. The way that mirror's angled, if you were lying on the bed all you'd see was a piece of the floor hereabouts." He tilted his head back, examining it. "Is it meant to be like that, do you think? Or have the supports gone from one side? If so, maybe we should get out from under."

"It's always been like that. Well," I said, "poor Nick's been libelled about the mirror as he has about a few other things. Ellen Makepeace, for instance."

He misunderstood me. "Oh, it was true enough about her. Funny, isn't it, to think it all started here, him and her and the garden in the moonlight, and maybe even your nightingale . . . If he cared for her, that is."

"Oh, he did. He cared very much."

I heard the smile in his voice. "You might just be prejudiced."

"Maybe I am. But he did. I know he did."

I said no more. There would be time later to tell him

what I had found out about Nick and Ellen Ashley, and
what had happened in the cottage last night. Time to tell
him about my narrow escape from the trap under this
very floor. Time to find out what had happened to my
cousins, and where they had gone. Time for all the things
that the immediate future must hold; and after that, time
for the real future, ours. Rob Ashley's and mine. But
for the moment, let it go, let it go. Let us keep, while we
could, our own island world of joy. *It is not yet near day.
It was the nightingale, and not the lark.*

"What's the time, Rob?"

"Don't know. I forgot to wind my watch, I can't think
why. . . . Not much more'n half past five, I'd guess."

I gave a little sigh, and relaxed again. "Lots of time,
then, before anyone comes this way and sees the water
and starts looking for us . . . What is it, love?" This as
Rob sat up and began to unwind himself from me and
the blanket. It felt cold without him. "Where are you
going?"

"Nowhere. But I'm going to move this bed back to its
proper place."

"I told you, the mirror's quite safe."

"I dare say," he said, laying hold of the bed, and running it back with a powerful screech of wood against the
wall. "But I'd sooner be out of range."

"Why?"

"This is why," he said, getting back on the bed, and
pulling the blanket once more over the pair of us.

When I woke again Rob was not beside me, but as I
turned over I saw him, fully dressed and kneeling on the
floor near the foot of the bed.

The sun had moved appreciably higher, and now the
mirror's light fell, like a spotlight or a burning glass,
straight to the boards between the window and the foot
of the bed, where the trapdoor lay. Where the water had
washed over it last night was an irregular patch of damp,
already beginning to steam dry in the warmth. The flood

had scoured the dust of years from this section of the
floor, and now, quite distinct in the clean floorboards,
could be seen the sawn edges of the trap, with, midway
along one edge, what looked like a knothole in the wood.
In this Rob had inserted a finger. As I sat up to watch, he
gave a heave, and the trapdoor came up from its bed. He
carried it to the wall and propped it there. Then he
dropped to his knees at the trap's edge, peering downwards.

I opened my mouth to tell him about my experience of
last night, when something about his expression stopped
me. The light, reflected upwards from whatever water still
lay below the pavilion, lit him sharply, and showed his
eyes, narrowed against the dazzle, intent on something
below. Without looking up he made a beckoning gesture,
and nodded downwards. "Bryony. Look here."

His voice held discovery, and a kind of awe. I swallowed what I had been going to say, and instead twisted
round on the bed till I could lie prone, peering down over
the foot of it, into my prison.

The force of last night's flood had swept through and
then subsided, leaving the debris piled up against the walls
and supports where the whirlpool had flung it, and scour-
ing the center clean. Water still lay there, a sheet of clear
glass a few inches deep, lighted fiercely from above, where
the angled mirror threw the sunlight down.

It lit a picture, or rather, part of a larger picture; the
head of a leopard, snarling, with one paw upraised, the
claws out and ready. The eyes were huge and brilliant,
done in some lustrous shell-like stone which caught and
threw back the light; the teeth gleamed white and sharp,
and the yellow fur with the black spots, washed clean by
the rush of the flood, shone as brightly as on the day the
mosaic was laid and hammered down to make the floor of
some Roman's home.

We looked at it for some time in silence. A stray draft
of air moved the water, and the upraised paw stirred. The
eyes glared, and the yellow fur ruffled; a young leopard,

rousing, as vivid and alive as when, all those wild centuries ago, some Roman took and built over this quiet corner between river and hill, and brought his artisans from Italy to make this marvellous thing.

"That's mosaic work, isn't it?" asked Rob. "Looks like part of a floor or something; a big one, too. It must be pretty old to have been buried clear under the maze."

"I wouldn't really know, but I'd have said it was Roman."

"Roman? As old as that?"

"I think so. There were Romans here, a long time ago, and there was a tile kiln not far off."

"Yeah, I know. At Tiler's Hatch, where the flooded pits are. Do you suppose there's more of it?"

"I wouldn't be surprised. Perhaps when William Ashley cleared the ground for his pavilion he found this, and so—"

" 'The cat, it's the cat on the pavement,' " quoted Rob, very softly.

I sat back abruptly. I could feel my eyes dilated with the fierce, reflected light, as the last piece of the puzzle fell into place. "Of course! *Of course!*" I looked up at the wall above the bedhead, where the wildcat ramped in the center of the plaster maze. "That's it, isn't it? The old crest was the leopard, but through time people forgot why. Then poor doting William borrowed Julia's wildcat and her motto, and then, when he found this, he drew the maze round them for a coat of arms. But how do you suppose my father found out about the mosaic?"

"Well, you said he'd been studying the books. It was all in the poetry, wasn't it? I reckon," said Rob comfortably, "that if you'd taken enough time over them, you'd have found it out for yourself. 'What palace then was this?' Remember?"

"Of course," I said again. I drew a long breath. He was right, it had all been there, carefully riddled down in the little verses for anyone who knew; the spotted catamountain, the leopard from the sun, even the glass mirroring another flood: "But where the gentle waters, straying, move, See! Dionysus' creature here enskied. . . ." I lay down again, peering at the exposed mosaic. "No sign of Bacchus and the lesser godlings. They must have covered them up again, and just kept the Cat. No wonder the Survey never traced the Roman site. What d'you bet, Rob, that if we cleared the maze away, we'd find the rest of the villa?"

"You might say I made a start at it last night. I wasn't thinking about much, except getting through to you. But I doubt if the maze could ever have been put right again even if you wanted to." He added, slowly: "I suppose that you couldn't put a value on a thing like this?"

"Not really." I knew what he was thinking; that here was something which could save Ashley—the part of it that I loved—from the bulldozers of the contractors, and make it worth someone's while to clear the gardens and expose this magnificent find for people to see. There were societies and trusts and generous individuals who would join the local Archaeological Society to work on the site and preserve what was found there. Whatever the future might bring, it was certain that no builders would be allowed to touch this part of Ashley.

I bent again over the trap. The leopard flexed his claws, and his eyes glimmered. I had certainly been too close to him, last night, down there in his secret lair. It was easy to imagine that the scratches on my body were not just from the flotsam of the storm, but from those cruel claws. "Touch Me Who Dares." Yes, the Cat had been here before the Ashleys ever came, and he would outstay them.

Rob got to his feet, and pulled me into his arms, blanket and all. "Time we got out of here, I'm afraid. And time you put your things on. You're getting cold. Here they are, they're dry now." As I obeyed him, he carried the trapdoor over and began lowering it carefully into place. "Well, and so what do we do about it? Keep quiet, like William?"

I laughed, belting my housecoat round me. Neither it, nor the pretty nightdress from Funchal, would ever be the same again. "Old Scrooge that he was, he seems never to have told a soul. He doesn't even seem to have told Nick, just hugged it all to himself, and put it down in those little poems. No wonder he died of a heart seizure when he heard that Nick was using the place as a love nest."

"And then Nick got the blame for the mirror, too. Eh, well . . ." The trapdoor was firmly in place. He straightened. "Well, that's it. And now, the day's got to start. It won't be a good one, that's for sure, but at least we can face it together, and the mystery's almost over."

" 'Almost'?"

"I meant we've just about found out all your dad was trying to tell you. All but the last bit."

"I know that, too," I said.

"Well, then?" asked Rob.

I shook my head. "Not now. I'll tell you the whole thing later . . . after breakfast."

"Breakfast!" He stretched luxuriously, giving me that wide, warm smile of his. "You're dead right; that comes first! Your kitchen'll be flooded, but we might find some bacon and eggs in mine. Coming?"

We went out onto the pavilion steps. Now we could see how far the water had gone down; below us in the clearing it was not much more than seven or eight inches deep. In the windless morning air it lay still as glass, and under it, like a garden set in crystal, the grass and flowers stood straight, held by the lucid water as perfectly as if it were the air. Inside that gentle mirror the turf stood green and springy, with above it the buttercups floating, wide open to the sun, each petal supporting and supported by the weight of clear water. A shoal of heartsease stared up with violet faces, like underwater creatures watching the light. Even the pale speedwell was held in its frail perfection, not a petal torn. The lilies of the valley stood motionless, wax and ivory, flowers in a Clichy paperweight. A small rudd, lost from the moat, flicked by through the daisies with red fins winking.

We held hands and walked down the wooden steps into the lovely shallow glass of the maze. I led Rob through, and up past the wreck of the lower sluice, where the fishing cat, tumbled in the mud at the foot of the water stair, bore witness to the rashness of the men who had meddled there.

There was debris everywhere, but the moat was back in its borders, and the swans guddled happily in the Pool, with their grey flotilla alongside. The old house dreamed above its reflection, with nothing but a tidemark to show how high the water had risen last night. On the mud of the drive, under the lime trees, stood a rusty-looking Volkswagen. And on the main bridge, gazing around him, was my cousin Francis.

The other Ashley. Fair hair and grey eyes and elegant bones, and the same sweet line to his mouth that my father had had. My gentle cousin, the poet. He was surveying the wrecked garden, the mud lying on the bridge, the waterlogged avenue, with a contemplative expression that held no more than a suggestion of dismay.

He looked up and saw us approaching him. If he noticed anything strange about Rob's crumpled clothes, or my nightdress and bedraggled housecoat and bare feet, his expression gave no hint of it.

"Bryony!" he said, his face lighting. "Rob, nice to see you! What on earth's been going on here? It must have been some storm last night, to leave a mess like this. I would have thought the High Sluice would stand even a cloudburst."

"It would, if it hadn't been meddled with," said Rob, flatly. Then, as my cousin's eyes widened: "Aye, it's more of a mess than you think, Francis. We've a lot to tell you, and it's not good hearing, but I'm afraid it won't wait."

My cousin glanced from one to the other of us, and for the first time seemed to notice something odd about our appearance. "All right, then. Tell me."

Rob looked at me, and nodded. "It's your story, love. Go ahead."

So I told it, right from the beginning on that steep Bavarian road, leaving out nothing but the parts of it that were Rob's and my own. I said nothing, either, of the secret of William's Brooke; that was something I would have to tell Rob when we were alone. When I got to last night's scene in my cottage with Emory and James I hesitated, wondering how to gloss over Leslie Oker's telephone call, and the reason for Emory's sudden, murderous decision. But I need not have worried. Rob's growing anger at the scene I was describing was blinding him to everything but his own fury. To this day I am not sure whether his explosion of rage over Emory's attack on me was in words, or whether it burst straight from his mind into mine with the force of an armour-piercing shell. By the time he had got hold of himself, the tricky part was past, and the tale was told.

After I had finished there was silence. Rob sat down on the parapet of the bridge beside me, slid an arm round me, and drew me to him. I could still feel the ebbing shock wave of anger and protective love. Outside and beyond it, like something barely relevant, I was conscious of the tremor running through his arm. He kept silent.

The sun was really warm now, and the light skimmed glancing off the water below us. I half shut my eyes and leaned back against Rob's arm. Francis stood with his back to us. At some point in the story he had turned away to take a couple of paces across the bridge, and he stood there by the other parapet, looking down at the water.

We had been lucky, I thought, that the first herald, so to speak, of the daylight world had been the one man who could share its burdens with us. I knew that Rob, running parallel with my drifting thoughts, was, like me, thinking ahead, trying to come to terms with that world and what the night's work would mean, not only to Ashley and my family, but to our own future.

Some of it could be guessed at. Even if Emory eventually recovered (which, from Rob's account of his apparent injuries, seemed unlikely), the twins would never come back to Ashley, either to make a claim or to fight one. With Rob's claim hanging over it, the land was unsaleable, and therefore profitless to them. And any threat to Rob or to myself had been voided by last night's action; once Mr. Emerson and the police knew the whole story, Emory and James might count themselves lucky if they could keep clear of us. I would make sure of it, I thought. I would write down the story of the last few days, fact for fact, and lodge it, with photostats of the relevant papers, as surety for the future. Further than that, out of mercy for the twins' sick father, and for Francis himself, we surely need not go? Under English law, unless Rob and I chose to press charges, there were none that could be made. The hit-and-run accident in Bavaria was another matter; however relieved I was to know that it had indeed been an accident, I could not forgive Emory's subsequent act of brutal self-interest; but I was still not prepared to add to his father's troubles by giving information to the Bavarian police. I would telephone Herr Gothard as soon as I could, and ask him to send the photograph back for my files. As for the debts the twins had incurred, William's Brooke, as well as endowing the Court, would take care of those, and set their father's mind at rest. Then, presumably, the twins—or James, the survivor—would settle in whatever haven was left to them. South America? Mexico? Wherever it was, they would have to start again from nothing, and James, if left to his own devices, would fare no better than he deserved. . . . I could not find it in me to care, one way or the other, so long as I never saw them again. All I would ever grieve over would be, not the evil man and the weak man who had been here last night, but the two charming and wilful boys who had lived here with us, so long ago.

Francis turned and came back to us. He was grave, and rather pale, but otherwise gave no sign of emotion. It was like him that, when he began to speak, it was about my bereavement (which had been news to him), and my unexpected marriage, and not about last night's near-tragedy.

He was interrupted. Somewhere down the avenue, beyond the trees, a car door slammed. There was the sound of voices. Three men, two of them in police uniform, appeared round the bend of the avenue, and after them, hurrying to join them, the Vicar. They paused when they saw us on the bridge, and Mr. Bryanston raised a hand in a gesture conveying both relief and greeting. Even at that distance it had something about it, too, of a blessing.

". . . If we could just tell them the bare outline now, and let Emerson handle the rest?" It was Francis speaking again, rapidly, an eye on the approaching men. "He'll have to know it all, of course, then he can advise us. What I'm most immediately concerned with is what I'm to tell my father."

"It seems to me"—Rob, his anger gone, sounded his old calm, practical self—"that there'll be no need to add to your dad's troubles by telling him what your brothers were after last night. We'll think up some story for him, just as soon as we know where we stand with the law. The truth can wait till he's well enough to hear it . . . if he has to hear it at all."

He paused, glancing at me. I don't know what he read there, but he nodded as if answered, and spoke again, quickly, to Francis. "Something else I'd better say. I don't think, saving your presence, that your brothers will be in any hurry to come back, so it looks as if this lot's going to land on you. Now, we'd had plans, Bryony and me, to emigrate. That will have to wait a bit. We couldn't walk out and leave you in a mess like this, so if you want us to, we'll stay around, and help you get things straight. I don't know much about the sort of discovery we made this morning, but Bryony thinks that, given a push in the right direction, the place might even start to pay its way. So we'll help you push it, mate, and then it's all yours." He slanted another look down at me. "Eh, love?"

"Yes, Rob." I looked around me at the shining water,

at the grassy banks sloping straight into their own intense and clear reflections, at the tops of the orchard trees beyond, where the thrush's song, no doubt, still echoed in the blossoming bell tower of the pear tree. Then I looked again at the heir to all this, with all that it owed to the past, and the load of questions that was its future.

If he chose to stay here, to push the Court back onto the map in whatever guise—National Trust monument, market garden, farmstead, building site—I would help him do it. If he chose to claim it for himself, and stay here for the rest of our lives, I would do that, too. But if he chose in the end to leave the care of the place to Francis, who loved it . . .

Yes, that would be it. When I had told him everything, I knew that he would still say, with that tranquil expression, and the dark eyes fixed on his own, our own, far horizon:

"Francis Ashley, mate, it's all yours."